THRONE PRICE

LYNDA WILLIAMS
ALISON SINCLAIR

First Edition

Canadian Cataloguing in Publication Data

Williams, Lynda, 1958-
  Throne Price

ISBN: 1-894063-06-6

I, Sinclair, Alison, 1959- II. Title.

PS8595.i5622T57 2002   C813'.6   C2001-911176-2
PR9199.4.W544T57 2002

CREDITS

AUTHOR:	Lynda Williams and Alison Sinclair
COVER ILLUSTRATION:	Sandrine Gestin
TEXT DESIGN:	Gail Pocock
LAYOUT:	Daniel Blais
PUBLISHER:	Edge Science Fiction and Fantasy Publishing

FONTS

R Stempel Garamond Roman, Imprint MT Shadow, Arial

(5.0-20020612)

THRONE PRICE is a work of fiction

EDGE

Edge Science Fiction and Fantasy Publishing
P.O. Box 1714, Calgary, Alberta, Canada T2P 2L7
Printed in Canada

The authors dedicate *Throne Price* to all those who have encouraged its development through their interest over the years, with special thanks to David Lott, Lynda's husband, who slogged through heaps of proofing and printing in the line of duty, and Lynn Jennyc, our editor, who valued it enough to be critical.

List of Characters

White Hearth (Lor'Vrel, Ava's Residence)

Ameron Lor'Vrel – *Pureblood, Ava, Liege Lor'Vrel*
Amy D'Ander – *Royalblood, Ameron's daughter, Heir to the Purple Alliance*
Charous – *Commoner, Royal Gorarelpul*
Drasous – *Commoner, Gorarelpul*
Ranar – *Reetion, ambassador*

Green Hearth (Monitum, Vrellish, Ava's Oath)

Tessitatt Monitum – *Seniorlord, Regent Monitum*
Ditatt (Tatt) Monitum – *Royalblood, Tessitatt's younger son, Heir Monitum*
Branstatt Monitum – *Highlord, Tessitatt's elder son, Captain of Errants*
Di Mon – *Highlord, previous Liege Monitum, deceased*
Erien – *Highlord, ward*

Black Hearth (Nersal, Vrellish, Ava's Oath)

Horth Nersal – *Highlord, Liege Nersal, Ava's Champion*
Dorn Bryllit Nersal – *Highlord, Heir Nersal*

Lilac Hearth (Dem'Vrel, Avim's Residence)

Ev'rel Dem'Vrel – *Pureblood, Avim, Liege Dem'Vrel*
Amel Dem'Vrel – *Pureblood, Ev'rel's eldest son*
D'Therd Dem'Vrel – *Royalblood, Ev'rel's second son, Avim's Champion*
D'Lekker Dem'Vrel – *Royalblood, Ev'rel's youngest son*
Kandral – *Midlord, Captain of Errants*

Silver Hearth (H'Us, Demish, Ava's Oath)

Prince S'Reese H'Us – *Royalblood, Regent H'Us*
Princess Luthan Dem H'Us – *Royalblood, minor, Liege H'Us*

Red Hearth (Vrel, Vrellish, Avim's Oath)

Vretla Vrel – *Royalblood, Liege Vrel*

The two remaining hearths of Fountain Court are held in trust; Brown Hearth by Ameron for the absent house of Lorel and Golden Hearth by Ev'rel for the Golden Demish.

The Underdocks

Mira – *Commoner, physician*
Mona – *Commoner, Mira's daughter*

Killing Reach, Purple Alliance, Barmi (Non-aligned)

Perry D'Aur – *Midlord, Founder*
Ayrium D'Ander – *Highlord, Liege/Protector*

THRONE PRICE

CHAPTER I

SPACE SPRAWLED, IN ALL ITS VAST INDIFFERENCE, on the nervecloth display of the *rel*-ship's inner hull.

Erien sighed and rotated the cockpit. Images of stars swung past him, silver against black. He was damned to a slow rebirth if he knew what was wrong with this ship. Not, he thought ruefully, that the expression was anything more than an idiom to him. He was too Reetion to put faith in Gelack superstitions.

He notched up shimmer, notched down gap. The stars flickered. A transient thrust of acceleration was supplanted by the nagging sense of something missing, or just plain wrong. Under the reality skimming drive, which tapped the currents folded into unperceived dimensions of the universe, the spherical *rel*-ship flickered in and out of existence as it skipped across space, whining as it went.

The ship's ailment was a tedious, demanding puzzle, just the sort of job his superiors thought he deserved for his pro-Reetion sentiments. They were glad enough, all the same, to have a highborn working on Liege Nersal's ship since the problem with *DragonClaw* surfaced at displacements that only a higher Sevolite could tolerate.

The more Sevolite a pilot was, the harder he could drive a ship. That was what being highborn meant, in the fleet, being able to endure reality skimming well enough to terrorize less Sevolite space farers. But Erien preferred diagnostic work to the greater glory of keeping the Reetions confined to their outpost in Killing Reach.

Erien ground his teeth. He could feel the resonance in the little spaces between his molars. Once more he enumerated possible causes of the dysfunction. A misphasing of the drive: in a well-maintained ship the usual cause was space combat, but this ship had seen none since before the problem began. A hull flaw: some blemish in the space-cast hullsteel encircling him, but no hull flaw had appeared in dockside scans.

It occurred to him that if he did fix the *DragonClaw*, Nersal would fly it against Rire when the war began. Erien was Gelack enough not to contemplate sabotage; that would not be honorable. His three years in the fleet hadn't been easy ones, but they would have been impossible without Nersal. Undefeated in space or on the challenge floor, Horth, Liege of Nersal, didn't have to prove a thing to anybody but he had proven to Erien that there was such a thing as Gelack honor. Nersal was consistent to the core in his maddeningly Gelack values.

Gelion was an oligarchy, dominated by Sevolites, where status depended upon one's inheritance of the Sevolite genome. Rire was a compu-communist state where the burden of democracy was managed by artificial intelligence. In Gelack, you had to know someone's birth rank before you could structure a pronoun. Reetions weren't comfortable with Ranar's insistence he be named 'ambassador', because it sounded too much like a title. Reetions were confident about their social accomplishments, even to the point of being smug. In Reetion, to persuade was to conquer. The Gelack word for peace, which shared a common root with shame, implied death or dishonor.

A quiver disrupted Erien's diagnosis of *DragonClaw*. It was foreign —the displacement field of another *rel*-ship brushing his own. Adrenaline surged like a small flame in his gut. No one else was supposed to be out here.

Someone was.

He found the moving point on the nervecloth lining of the hull. It was a single *rel*-ship, probably as surprised to find him where he was, as Erien had been to be swiped by its wake as it passed. It was heading towards Liege Nersal's flag ship, the battlewheel called *DragonSword*, doing at least three skim'facs, on a course which would have brought it directly from the Reetion station, *SkyBlue*.

Except Reetion pilots did not fly at three skim'facs. Neither did nobleborn Sevolites, unless they were in a tearing rush.

The stranger executed a shimmer dance—a series of quick modulations—which identified him to the station before he got close enough to cause alarm.

Erien leaned into his harness, peering at the dancing point. He knew that pattern. It belonged to the man who had taken him to Rire when he was seven years old, and who had fetched him back again to serve under Liege Nersal. His appearance, here, now, wasn't comforting. Pureblood Sevolite Amel Dem'Vrel was a sore spot in Reetion/Gelack relations, and an ambiguous figure in the politics of Gelion's Fountain Court.

Whatever he was here for would not be trivial.

Erien docked on the heels of Amel's lozenge-shaped envoy craft.

Amel was talking to the dockmaster, a nobleborn named Nala, when Erien reached the staging platform.

"I'm here on the Ava's business," Amel was explaining, with his usual reluctance to enforce his right to speak down, "with a mail pouch for Liege Nersal." He broke off at the sound of Erien's footfalls, turned, and smiled. "Erien? Was that you out there just now?"

Erien had grown up since he first met Amel, but time had done nothing to dull the youthful glamor of the older man. Amel was a Sevolite Pureblood. Time, like the ravages of space travel, could gain no hold. He looked delighted to see Erien.

"That ship you're flying has a funny warble in its signature," Amel remarked. "Has someone rammed it through hard flying over the last couple of days, in this area? I've seen phase splicers with that history develop a sort of stutter—on engagement—almost as if they're still encountering an echo. Damnedest thing to diagnose. Unless you're skimming in the same ship within the echo's time and space perimeter, it's totally asymptomatic. Nice ship, though."

Erien merely nodded, a ubiquitous Nersallian gesture of acknowledgment. Envoys were normally looked down on—the task of ferrying dispatches reserved for the childless afraid to risk combat—but he was unburdened by such Gelack attitudes and Amel was a pilot of wide experience. He was also Pureblood to Erien's Highlord, a two-degree distinction in birth rank. Speaking in Gelack would oblige Erien to acknowledge that in his construction of pronouns, and he did not feel so inclined.

"Just a thought," Amel said, with a mild shrug, and shifted the mail pouch onto his right shoulder.

"Is it convenient for me to see Liege Nersal now?" Amel asked the Nersallian dockmaster, speaking undifferentiated *rel*-to-*pol*, which was a significant condescension for a Pureblood addressing a nobleborn.

"Convenient, Immortality?" Dockmaster Nala was normally a sober woman, but Amel's casual manner triggered Nala's Vrellish instinct to perceive him as a sexual banquet. Beautiful. Space-worthy. And Pureblood. Erien did not believe that Nala had anticipated such feelings, which made him annoyed with Amel on her behalf. If Amel behaved the way he should this wouldn't happen.

"I mean I could wait," Amel explained. "The dispatches are timely, but not urgent."

"Oh," said Dockmaster Nala. She resolved her problem with a deep breath and a wide smile reminiscent of the Vrellish of either gender looking for an opening in a duel. The change was not lost on Amel, whose expression shifted from patient amusement to something a little more guarded.

"Perhaps, then, you might like some company and refresh—" Nala began.

"I will escort you to Liege Nersal," Erien cut her off.

Amel looked at him with a well-judged, startled pleasure, which Erien greeted impassively. "Thank you," Amel said mildly.

"What about *DragonClaw*, Erien?" Nala reminded him, firmly, that although he might be her superior by birth, he was still her junior by fleet rank.

Erien said, "I will be back down to review Liege Nersal's logs and to follow up the Throne Envoy's suggestion."

Nala dismissed him with a grunt of irritation, letting the matter drop, and Erien became less convinced that he had rescued her from embarrassment. He hated to think he had rescued Amel, instead.

Amel fell neatly into step beside him, picking up the rhythm of Erien's stride. Erien had to remind himself it was not mockery. Amel had been trained as a sword dancer in his youth due to one of the intrigues festooned about him, from his own disappearance at the age of four months to the theft of his infant half-brother, known only as the Throne Price, which took place shortly after Amel himself was reclaimed as a Sevolite.

In between, Amel's good looks cast him as a commoner courtesan in the very court he should have been heir to.

Even Amel's reclamation had been a complete mess, muddying the waters of Gelack and Reetion relations for nearly two decades since. Reetions were appalled by the details of Amel's abusive experiences as a commoner, while Gelack prejudice seethed over the very fact that Reetion bioscience had successfully meddled with a highborn. Erien, who had lived on Rire, knew that Reetions had a hard time believing Amel's mistreatment was not typical of Sevolite behavior toward all commoners. He had also spent enough time among Gelacks to know that they in turn did not even try to acknolwedge that when the Reetions had used their psychiatric visitor probe on Amel, it had been to save his life.

They drew eyes and a couple of anonymous wolf-whistles as they crossed the bridge over the maintenance docks. Amel's past seemed to grant license which would be unthinkable if he had been raised Pureblood, or acted like he ought to be flying combat, wearing a sword, and properly speaking down. His commoner upbringing, Erien allowed, must have made for a hard start. But eighteen years should have been long enough to overcome any past, even if it did include formative years in the sex trade on Gelion.

Mercifully, they had the elevator to themselves. There was a fleeting moment of unsteadiness as the car began to move. Illuminated doors flashed past narrow windows. Erien held onto the rail, not for balance, but for resolution. He had only a few moments, and had no idea of how to ask what he wanted to know. Amel, as he knew from past meetings, was a master at evading inconvenient questions.

"Thanks for playing escort." Amel broke the silence with his liquid voice. "I thought you weren't speaking to me, after my gratuitous advice about a ship you know better than I do."

"I expect your explanation will prove to be correct," Erien said, annoyed at himself for letting his irritation show.

"That would make it worse," Amel remarked, "if you were really a Nersallian."

Erien shot him a sharp look. He did not need reminding that he was not 'really' a Nersallian. Not 'really' Monatese, either. And not 'really' a Reetion. Just a nameless youth who had to fit wherever he was put, whether that was pastoral Monitum, democratic Rire, or the Nersallian fleet. And possibly, just possibly, what he really was, was Amel's bastard, born to a besotted courtesan initiate while Amel was still, himself, a courtesan. There had been such a child, spirited away from court by Di Mon, Erien's Monatese guardian.

Erien put the thought away forcefully. In appearance, he could not help but resemble Amel—they were both descended from a limited gene pool, both black-haired and gray-eyed.

It meant nothing. Erien's face had a sharper, more Vrellish look than Amel's pretty Demish features.

"Ah." Amel's mouth toyed, very briefly, with a flicker of amusement. "I've offended. Sorry."

"You have nothing to be sorry for, Immortality," Erien said, stiffly.

"I thought we'd dealt with the Immortality stuff," Amel said, "the few times I visited you."

"I was a child then."

"Yes, you're—what? Seventeen. I expect you will be called to court soon, to swear to Heir Monitum after his investiture. If Tatt's mother, the regent, succeeds in investing him." Amel was playing with the possibility of being amused, again. He had no right to be. Not over a matter so serious.

Monitum was Erien's house, and Tatt—the heir to that ancient name—was the companion of Erien's happy childhood. Tatt was also the reason that Erien held out hope he was not Amel's bastard. It made sense that the late Di Mon would hide a highborn love child for the sake of protecting Tatt's right of succession. Tatt was Ameron's son, by outright gift, to his most devoted vassal house. In Gelack terms there was no greater reward one could bestow on a follower. Tatt's birth had also restored at least one Royalblood to the weakening Monatese bloodline, which was crucial if Monitum was to maintain its court status. No inconvenient by-blow could be allowed to threaten Tatt, even if he was the last liege's direct descendant. Erien would never have thought to do such a thing, of course. It would be enough just to be the natural son of the man who had been his teacher and protector for his first seven years, and whose death by suicide had been his young life's greatest tragedy.

"If Heir Monitum's mother succeeds in investing him?" Erien kept his tone neutral as he paraphrased Amel's glib remark. "Is there, then, some possibility that Heir Monitum will not become Liege Monitum?"

"No official possibility," Amel demurred. "I know Tatt, that's all. You've had an influence. He wants to introduce a sort of Reetion justice system that would make investigation of crimes against commoners a general Throne responsibility, in cases where the crimes are particularly deserving of attention. A sort of 'cruelty to commoners' society. Like your 'cruelty to house pets' organizations on Rire."

Erien would not hear Rire mocked. Or Tatt. "Is it," he asked, "that you think the effort unworthy of him? Or Tatt, himself, ineffectual?"

There was a stinging silence.

Some expression, which Erien could not read, flickered across Amel's face, then was smoothed away with exquisite courtesan control. Erien remembered then that Amel's experience of Rire had been quite different from his own.

"No," Amel said. "I didn't mean either."

The elevator slowed its descent, stopped, and shunted into a horizontal track, picking up speed. When at rest in real space, the battlewheel was a spinning torus, with the maintenance docks inside the inner ring and the main docks on the outer ring. The support staff areas were inboard of the maintenance docks, and the officer's areas outboard of the main docks, with the highest Sevolites preferring the strongest gravity. Sevolite cardiovascular systems, designed to sustain high g's, were not comfortable in low gravities. Erien had spent most of his time up in the maintenance bays lately. The increased gravity was welcome.

"I apologize, Pureblood Amel," Erien said as their car settled into its new, horizontal vector. "That remark was uncalled-for."

The apology was stiff and sounded insincere, but was deserved and necessary, for Erien to ask what he wanted to.

Amel looked relieved, which was irritating. Amel was a Pureblood. Erien was a Highlord: still a highborn but two birth ranks his inferior. They reinforced their relative status with every sentence they spoke—or that Erien spoke, anyway. Amel slipped in and out of grammatical peerage, uneasy with speaking down. But that was the trouble with Amel.

He occupied a place which he could not fill. Erien disliked having to depend on this man's goodwill. He disliked feeling he did not deserve it. And he most disliked feeling that, despite everything, he had it.

Erien said abruptly, "You came from Rire, didn't you?"

This time there was no fleeting consternation; Amel's face was polished and unrevealing. Erien continued, "Or at the least from *SkyBlue Station*." He could feel—although the elevator had not yet started to slow—that they were near their destination. His sense of space was exquisite.

Erien came to the point. "Have you taken the Reetion Ambassador back to Rire?"

"No," Amel assured him, "Ranar is still on Gelion."

Erien felt a short-lived relief. Ranar had not failed, but he was not safe. Rire's commoner ambassador could never be safe, negotiating with people among whom he and his kind would have been at best, servants, at worst, chattels.

Erien said, "Is Ranar well?" Some fleeting hesitation warned him of an evasion. He said, starkly, "I know the situation at court is tense. Tell me the truth. Or tell me nothing. I'd rather that than false reassurances." For it had been false reassurances Amel had tried to give ten years before on the homeworld of House Monitum. Erien had lost his Gelack guardian then. He would not lose his Reetion one now.

Amel swallowed. "Your foster father is fine," he said. "Ameron won't let anything happen to him. Ranar is too important."

The lift decelerated and stopped, and the doors opened, letting them step out onto the battlewheel's bridge, and away from each other. There could be no further discussion. They walked, again in step, around the perimeter of the bridge to Liege Nersal's office. The door guard—a man this time, to Erien's relief—saluted and then proceeded to ignore them. Through the wall of the office, which was currently transparent, Erien could see Horth Nersal standing in profile against a holographic star map. Was he preparing to move the blockade? Erien wondered. Or was he giving instructions to his subordinates, preparatory to leaving, himself, for Gelion? He would have to go soon, to attend the Ava's Swearing.

Erien glanced sideways at Amel, his hand fisting. He had squandered the time given him in useless feinting. The fundamental question had gone unasked. As Ameron's envoy between Gelion and Rire, Amel's attitudes and convictions must profoundly affect relations. And Erien did not know, had never known, what Amel felt about Rire. Amel might easily construe the visitor probe incident, eighteen years before, as cause to hate Rire. He had never shown it. But Amel, reared commoner, trained in powerlessness, graceful submission, and indirectness, never would. If Amel was Rire's enemy, he was a secret and most dangerous one.

Liege Nersal dismissed his subordinates. A nod acknowledged Amel and Erien. He was Vrellish tall, Vrellish lean, and Vrellish complexioned, with the same cast of face and black and gray coloring as Erien. Since he had attained full growth, Erien had a small measure of height on Liege Nersal and a larger measure of weight. Not that it usually did him much good in their sparring sessions. Not, at least, after Erien's initial demonstration of Reetion martial arts. Nersal had proved a quick study, reciprocating with fencing lessons.

House Nersal's liege and admiral was dressed in Nersallian black, with an embroidered dragon snarling in crimson on the silk shirt. As always, he wore his sword. As they entered, one of Nersal's hands settled on his sword belt near the hilt. That hand-to-hilt distance Erien knew as a sure gauge of Liege Nersal's comfort with the present company: one of them, at least, he did not trust.

"Pureblood Amel has just arrived with dispatches," Erien told his admiral, noting that, although Nersal was aware of Amel, he looked to Erien for explanation. "I encountered him between here and *SkyBlue Station*, while diagnosing *DragonClaw*'s warble." Erien hesitated before adding, stoically, "If you have recently flown *DragonClaw* hard in that stretch, I think Amel may have solved the mystery."

Nersal transferred his stare from Erien to Amel, who, Erien noted, looked nervous. Horth Nersal was quite possibly the most dangerous man in the Gelack reaches: Throne Champion, admiral of the best organized fleet in Sevildom, and a personal enigma due to his habitual reticence. He abjured the constant jousting for status within and between birth ranks. But then, Erien reflected, one need not bother to play when one is certain to win. Nersal ranked in the top two to five best swords in all Sevildom, in a class where only the death of one, on the blade of another, would settle the remaining ambiguity.

His task discharged, Erien awaited dismissal.

"I bring you messages, from Ameron," Amel opened, speaking peer to peer, either in deference to Nersal's reputation or out of his usual equivocation.

"Via the Reetion station?" Nersal's deep voice gave weight to his few words.

Erien held himself very still. He had not been dismissed. Was Liege Nersal accommodating his need to know what was happening? Or had he accepted Erien as an advisor on matters Reetion?

Amel's pulse jumped visibly in his throat. "I—visit there sometimes." Nersal waited.

"For reasons of my own," Amel floundered.

"Their admiral," Nersal said knowledgeably.

"Ann? She's a space service executive," Amel corrected. "One of *SkyBlue's* command triumvirate."

Good luck to you explaining that, thought Erien. He had made little headway himself in making Horth Nersal grasp how the Reetion command structure could accommodate cooperative decision making.

Amel continued groping through Nersal's silence. "Yes, I go there to see her. She's my . . . "

"Your *lyka*," supplied Nersal, as Amel hesitated. And that was another all-too-familiar problem for Erien. *Lyka* was technically the correct term for a Sevolite's commoner lover. And commoner pronouns were technically correct for Reetions. But Reetions were not Gelack commoners. They were a free people with enough determination and technological know-how to maintain a six-reach federation.

Amel actually sounded ill-tempered. "Does it matter whose station I take travel respite on? Or do you already consider yourself and Rire at war?"

"Rire has no lieges," Nersal explained, with just a little irritation, symptomatic of patience that was running out, "either to make contracts, or to make war."

"It has its own laws," Amel said.

"In computers?" Nersal asked.

"More or less."

"Like the computer they used to bend you to their will."

For an instant, Amel's sculpted face went blank. Erien gritted his teeth. How many years would it be before Gelacks ceased to interpret a necessary therapeutic intervention as a violation of a Sevolite Pureblood?

Amel gave himself a tiny shake and, with an elegant, very conscious flourish, handed Nersal the first of the dispatches. "This message is the most important. It is Ameron's formal request that you stand as his champion for the Swearing."

The dispatch was closed with a nervecloth seal, primed by a drop of Ameron's blood, and keyed to open when wet with the recipient's. Nersal passed up the seal's built in prick, preferring to draw his sword a few centimeters to nick the side of a finger. He wet the seal and flipped open the letter, one-handed, trapping the enclosure which threatened to slip free. Then he tossed the letter onto his desk, with what could easily be taken for dismissal. Erien was familiar with this quirk. The taciturn Highlord seemed to memorize a page without reading it. He needed long seconds, afterwards, to sort it out, with his head held slightly askance and down, as if it was easier to process images into words in that position. It was impossible to revive conversation during this period.

Erien could not help noticing that the enclosure, which Nersal still held, was closed with one of the iridescent decals used by the Ambassador of Rire, on Gelion.

Ranar? Writing to Liege Nersal?

"I will answer Ameron," Nersal said at last, when he'd digested the Ava's letter, "when I come to court."

That did not make Amel happy, Erien saw. It did not make him happy, either.

If Horth Nersal withdrew his support as Throne Champion, Ava Ameron would be in a precarious position. There was no one else in the Ava's Oath who was Nersal's equal on the challenge floor, to stand against the Avim's champion. Erien thought, once again, of the utter absurdity of having the destiny of planets decided at sword point. A heretical thought for a Gelack; a perfectly reasonable one for a Reetion. Except for Ambassador Ranar, who would have explained with scholarly patience, the advantage of having a mode of conflict resolution for an aggressive people which avoided risk to bystanders and space habitat.

Horth Nersal asked Amel, in his blunt fashion, "Your mother, Avim Ev'rel, favors war?"

"Even the Avim is sworn to the Ava," Amel answered with evasion. "Or there wouldn't be an empire. And this is empire business. So it's Ameron's opinion that matters."

The point was moot. That was the reason there was going to be a Swearing; to see who Fountain Court would support for its next Ava: Ameron, or Amel's mother.

"You know I am sworn to neither one," Amel answered Nersal's dissatisfied silence. He smothered a mirthless noise which might have been laughter. "I fly for Ameron. I live between Ev'rel's walls. Neither has asked for my oath. If you want to know what Ev'rel plans for Rire, you'll have to ask. But ask her, not D'Therd, and not Vretla." He named two of Ev'rel's most important vassals.

Nersal listened. He did not nod, or in any other way signal that he felt himself answered.

Amel plunged on. "Ameron's next dispatch explains his decision to include other houses in your blockade on the Reetions. There are enclosures for local powers, assuring them that the escalation is defensive. Ameron wants you to co-operate. Will you?"

Nersal's silk clothing whispered as he walked to his desk. He dropped the dispatch pouch and turned around.

"The Throne Price," Nersal said.

Amel faltered. "Y-yes?"

"Will Ameron produce him? This time?"

Amel inhaled. "I'm sure Ava Ameron wants to talk to you about that."

"Talk," Nersal said with disgust. He glanced at Erien, then back to Amel. "If Ameron does not produce the Throne Price, will you?"

Amel looked startled. Few people these days alluded to his role in the Throne Price affair. He had negotiated the contract between Ev'rel and Ameron which produced the child, and then stolen the four-month -old baby. Opinions were divided as to why; Amel had never said. Most people assumed that he, Ev'rel, or Ameron would produce the Throne Price at a moment opportune to his or her cause.

"I do not know what Ameron intends to do about the Throne Price," Amel got out at last.

Horth Nersal stepped forward to offer Erien the letter with Ranar's iridescent seal. Erien read his name in Ranar's smooth handwriting, and looked up in time to catch Nersal's small, dismissive head tilt. So, he had been allowed as far as he would be into the state secrets of Gelion.

"Liege Nersal," Erien excused himself with a nod, then, hardly looking at Amel, added, "Pureblood Amel," and withdrew, eagerly peeling back the vellum flap as he went, stopping just outside the office door to read his letter.

Ranar's handwriting was round and meticulous. It was not simply that Ranar had learned penmanship in adulthood, but that he had learned it in his role of ambassador to Gelion, in which every word had to be measured. It was the Reetion ambassador who was writing now, not the Reetion anthropologist or the foster father of a displaced Gelack ward. Erien could envision him, dark face quiet and intent over his work, holding the turquoise-inlaid pen, a gift from Di Mon.

"*Erien,*" Ranar wrote. "*You may have heard rumors of my detention, on Gelion, by Ameron.*"

So that was what Amel had avoided telling him!

"*This is true,*" Ranar continued. "*The custody is protective, but I do not feel, at this point, in danger. Certainly not from Ameron, in any case.*"

Except, Erien thought, *in so far as his faintheartedness puts you in danger. By this protective custody, he underlines the fact that you cannot defend your own case, as a Sevolite would, by the sword. Yet you have lasted longer as a swordless foreign commoner among Sevolites than he has been Ava; you even had a part in making Ameron the Ava.*

Protective custody did not seem a just reward.

"*Ameron has decided that he must renew his mandate, and has therefore called a Swearing, in six days,*" said the letter.

Erien glanced at the date; the Swearing was now only four days away.

"*He is under pressure to decide about Rire, and to produce the Throne Price.*"

Erien nodded, grimly, having just witnessed as much. It was still unnerving to know that Liege Nersal's attitudes were echoed elsewhere around Fountain Court, on Gelion.

"*You may be aware that Ameron has put off one or the other issue, at more than one previous Swearing, due to matters which seemed more immediately pressing. Perhaps they were, but I do not believe that either can be postponed again and do hope he realizes this. Regrettably, he has not spoken to me since protective custody was imposed.*

"*I do not fear for my personal safety should a clear majority swear allegiance to Ev'rel, instead of to Ameron,*" Ranar continued. "*Avim Ev'rel harbors some personal resentment about the visitor probe affair on Amel's behalf, but on the whole she is too intelligent to be incited by ludicrous hearsay about alleged Reetion atrocities. Her Dem'Vrellish sons are a separate matter. She appears to be losing control of both D'Lekker and D'Therd. I could be murdered on impulse, if a too-equal result at the Swearing escalates to general aggression.*"

Erien smiled grimly at the 'murdered'; it was so typically Ranar. When he spoke or wrote, even with such care, he was true to his Reetionness. When he could not be true to himself, he would be silent. But his calm—that was his greatest strength. It took a particular kind of fearlessness for a dark-skinned, commoner Reetion to tread the halls and corridors of the xenophobic, hierarchical court of Gelion.

"*More to the point, for both of us,*" said Ranar's letter, "*is that victory for Ev'rel would mean the end of current diplomatic progress. It is unclear to me whether she would actively encourage war. I believe she would base that on a careful cost-benefit analysis. Among other things, her grasp of our cultural disparity is as good as any Reetion diplomat's.*

"*Ev'rel's supporters do include, however, people who are openly in the conquest camp.*

"*At the very least she would drive SkyBlue Station out of Killing Reach and send me home.*"

Erien frowned slightly, thinking of Ev'rel, Ameron's rival, about whom he knew far too little. Just as fleet scuttlebutt paid less attention to Ameron than to his champion, Horth Nersal, Ev'rel was eclipsed by the reputation of her son and champion, D'Therd, one of the few swords who could hope to defeat Horth Nersal on the challenge floor.

"*My feeling is that such setbacks will not be accepted on the Reetion side,*" Ranar's letter continued. "*Attitudes have become volatile at home, due to doubts about Gelion's stability. People are more frightened than they acknowledge. I can see no other excuse for the recent debate about military intervention, should Ameron lose what is, by Gelack standards, an election."*

An election! Erien thought in unnerved exasperation. Gelack elections cost lives when their results were disputed and one of those lives could easily be that of the Reetion Ambassador. Erien could not feel academic about that. It was a bad analogy anyhow. Rire was a participatory, not a representative, democracy. Elections, when they happened, were for roles with well-defined duration and scope, not carte blanche power, and candidates had to be qualified.

Erien wrestled down his urge to argue, so he could read on.

"Most of my intelligence from Rire, of course, is brought via Amel whose position is increasingly untenable. I must convey my concerns about Amel, although I cannot produce a clear charge, much less evidence to substantiate it.

"Perhaps it is merely that he cannot be everything he seems to be."

That, Erien thought bitterly, *I knew when I was seven years old.*

"I do not doubt, having spent time in their company, that Amel is Ev'rel's lover. She is, of course, his mother. If it was only that, the relationship would actually make sense in Gelack terms, given the shortage of Pureblood Sevolites. Except there are no children. In fact he has produced no children since the single, accidental one, who—in infancy—was used by Di Mon to prove Amel's identity at court, through genotyping, while Amel himself was in Reetion hands."

Erien read the last sentence twice, but it contained neither more, nor less, information. It neither suggested nor denied he might be that misbegotten child, whisked away by Di Mon with the promise to see him raised respectably, as a Sevolite, free of the shame of his courtesan origins. He had always suspected Ranar shared Di Mon's knowledge of who he really was.

"At the same time," wrote Ranar, *"Amel is trusted by Ev'rel's rival, Ameron, to great lengths, which I have cause to believe is justified in at least some instances.*

"Amel is also close to influential Reetions. SkyBlue Station's Space Service Triumvir, Ann, is as near as Rire comes to a Gelack admiral, and is the principal advocate of the failed referendum in favor of military preparation in the Reetion Reach of Paradise. Could Amel have encouraged her in that?

"Gelack politics are personal. In that sense Amel's connections are not so atypical. He is Ev'rel's son, Ann's lover, and at times behaves as if he had given his oath of allegiance to Ameron.

"What disturbs me is that he manages to appear a mere errand boy when he surely must be pivotal. Amel knows more about Rire than any

other Gelack except yourself—not to mention his role in the visitor probe debacle, which is heating up again on Gelion with the recent surfacing of a disgusting new rash of derivative synthdramas.

Erien grimaced. Since Amel was a figure of some notoriety on both sides, there was illegal trade in prurient material based on memories extracted by the visitor probe during psychiatric treatment. Even Sevolites with no use for Amel were outraged by such exposure. But on Rire, information was, by definition, public.

"I fail to see how the latter could be a coincidence," wrote Ranar, *"when the misuse of data collected with the visitor probe is a flashpoint in the debate over whether or not Rire deserves to be recognized as sovereign.*

"Certainly these are interesting times," Ranar summed up the Amel issue.

"That's a curse, Ranar," Erien murmured, aloud.

"Your unique perspective may be more valuable now than ever," Erien read. *"I leave it to your capable judgment how it might best be exercised, provided that whatever you decide exhibits due regard for your personal safety."*

Erien paused, and reread the paragraph slowly, thinking, *What are you telling me, Ranar?*

"I know that you have always been exceptionally level-headed," wrote his Reetion guardian, *"but you are seventeen, and highborn. Di Mon considered it a vulnerable combination. It would sicken me to see such an excellent education squandered. Lurol would insist that I add, I love you."*

And Lurol would, Erien thought, with dry amusement and considerable affection for his Reetion co-guardian. She thought these things needed to be said, now and then. It was a concession to the counseling training which she had to take for fear of becoming too narrowly specialized, but Erien knew she meant it with all her heart where he was concerned. Her soul was in her research on the visitor probe, but her sense of family was vested in the Reetion child-rearing unit into which Ranar dragged her to assist him in raising Erien.

Amusement faded quickly as Erien read on.

"Don't send me any return message by Amel, no matter how you code it. The most innocent statements can be misinterpreted, and Amel defeats locks and ciphers with a casual genius which even he takes for granted and no one even seems to notice."

Not one of mine, Erien caught himself thinking. Was that Sevolite bravado? Perhaps. There were times he could envy Ranar his scholar's distance from it all.

"This letter is sent under Ameron's seal, as an inclusion in his communiqué to Horth Nersal, from whose hand I expect you received it. I am confident that Ameron informed no one of its existence, and

am personally grateful to him for respecting my desires in this matter, in the spirit of a courtesy extended to a guest in his household.

"In closing, I want you to know that the opportunity to observe and work with Ameron, these last few years, has been well worth any consequences which may result for me personally. He is human, with very human flaws, but if he fails to fit the larger-than-life expectations Di Mon's regard for him engendered, it is because he exceeds them, rather than the other way around. It's been fascinating."

No, Erien thought, *you will not apologize for Ameron, not in tones of summation and valediction.*

Erien looked up at the almost noiseless sliding open of the door, and saw Amel bowing himself out. Bowing, Erien thought, as though he was still a commoner obeisant to a Highlord and not two degrees Nersal's superior. Amel looked shaken, and pressed his fingers to his forehead, unaware that he was being watched by Erien. Then he visibly collected himself, glanced around, and met Erien's eyes.

I asked if Ranar was all right, Erien thought at him, *and you said, yes.*

Amel mustered a faint smile.

They held each other's eyes until the smile faded. *No,* Erien thought, *I have nothing more to ask you. I am going to learn for myself.* He stepped past Amel into the doorway of the office.

Liege Nersal nodded him in; the door closed behind him.

"Liege-Admiral," Erien said, "I would like to request leave."

There was a silence. Time spent introducing Liege Nersal to Reetion martial arts—and receiving reciprocal attentions to his own swordsmanship—had taught Erien how to interpret his admiral's silences. This was a waiting one, receptive to more words. "The ambassador of Rire has been placed in protective custody by Ameron because of the tensions surrounding the diplomatic recognition of Rire as a self-governing house, despite its lack of Sevolites," Erien elaborated. "Di Mon sent me to live with Ranar when he died. I believe he had a purpose in mind. I believe he wanted me to learn to understand Rire in a way only someone who had lived there would. Rire needs an ally who has some status among Sevolites. Whatever else is said of me, I am acknowledged to be Highlord. I think—I hope—that this is what Di Mon meant me for. To be a voice for Rire. I need—for him and for myself—to see this through. I don't know what I can do in four days, but, after the Swearing, whatever happens, I will come back."

Horth considered Erien as a totality, both words and man. Visibly, some decision was forming behind that austere face. "Go," Horth said. "Do not come back."

"I see," Erien said. It was a lie. He did not see. He felt unexpectedly bereft. He had not been a particularly good officer, true. There was no prize that the fleet had to offer him; indeed, he had endured it as merely an unhappy distraction from his true purposes. But he had expected it would end other than with, "Go. Do not come back."

Erien said, in a very level voice, "I'd like to ask one favor. A *rel*-ship. To take me to Gelion." He did not want to ask to travel with Amel. Not this time.

The Highlord nodded. "Take *DragonClaw*. Keep it."

This was a second shock. The ship mattered to Liege Nersal, and its unsubjective value was likewise considerable. It was followed by a third remark, in which Erien failed to grasp the Nersallian's logic, although he knew it would be there somewhere.

"Go after Amel leaves," Nersal said, "not before."

CHAPTER II

ERIEN DOCKED DRAGONCLAW at a Nersallian-owned berth on *Ava's Hand Station,* in orbit around Gelion. The excruciating whine had begun to fade before he reached the Killing Reach jump, and in the Reach of Gelion, the drive had been sweeter than a whisper, even above four skim'facs. He had surrendered the ship to the dock techs with real reluctance. But it was a *rel*-ship, designed for space. He rode down to Gelion in the co-pilot's seat of a Nersallian cargo shuttle, carrying planet-grown delicacies intended for the social events surrounding the Swearing. He was tempted to pilot it himself, but compounding his inexperience in planetary landings were the social rules which governed the use of the subterranean Gelack docks. It was wiser to let a veteran guide him. She was eager to do so, for the opportunity of delivering directly to the highborn docks, being, herself, only nobleborn.

Gelion's atmosphere was too thin, and the planet too far from its star to have evolved life on its own. The surface was host, however, to a panoply of lichens and simple mosses, the residue of some long ago terraforming experiment, and poets, desperate for something to approve about their homeworld, had extolled Gelion's painted mountains. As the shuttle swung into the final approach over the surface hangers and warehouses and the pilot switched from nervecloth to direct view, the setting sun lit upon the cracked peaks surrounding them and picked out dappled gray-green, gold, and russet. Then, with a roar and a jolt, they were down and speeding across a dust-swept runway, heading for the black mouths of chutes leading down to the buried city known as UnderGelion. The pilot decelerated like a Nersallian: hard and accurately. Erien, bracing himself, was glad he had decided not to try this landing. He hoped the pilot had some experience with the highborn docks. She told him so, but she might have lied to gain a highborn passenger. Using the highborn chutes would greatly simplify the delivery of her cargo, given the direct connection from the highborn docks—via the Palace Sector—to the plaza overlying Fountain Court. Erien was relieved when she proved she knew what she was doing.

Once docked, Erien obliged her by helping her claim a cargo cart, but then disappointed her by refusing to ride along with her out to the plaza. He needed to get his legs under him after flying in from the frontier. Besides, he had never seen Gelion, and he wanted to take a good look.

Unlike the green and prosperous heartland of Rire, Gelion's only merit was that it was situated at a nexus of jumps commanding the entrances to six reaches. The cargo—and the taxes—of an empire passed through Gelion's orbital stations and docks. Erien's first impression was of ordered chaos: an astounding swirl and bustle of people and electric-powered vehicles.

He spent the first few minutes skipping out of the way of cargo carts and private cars that seemed to observe no shared rules of right-of-way.

It was the behavior of the drivers of those cars that started to bring certain things into relief for him. They were remarkably patient with him—except for the driver of one car painted with an ornate crest depicting Demish Royalblood knots, who blared a horn at Erien and would have run him down. This served as a sharp reminder of the racial divisions between Demish and Vrellish blood-lines. The Demish driver was prepared to make him dodge for the sake of his Nersallian uniform because Nersal was a Vrellish house.

At least the driver had warned Erien with his horn. Commoners daydreamed at their peril. Erien felt his jaw tighten with anger as he watched one car with three black-haired Vrellish—one man and two women—scatter a group of working commoners. Commoner wits and Sevolite reflexes prevented casualties, but Erien fought an impulse to put himself in front of that car to make it slow down. He resisted it; this was Gelion, dangerous and rigidly hierarchical. He had no desire to find himself obliged to draw a sword within an hour of his arrival.

The docks sprawled, studded with small warehouses and private hangars, within a great, rectangular hullsteel box, high enough to accommodate a cargo shuttle and as big as a city district on Rire. At the west end, where Erien was headed, traffic converged either on the road leading down to the Palace Plain via the nobleborn docks, or a barrier pierced by eight gates. Beyond the gates was a wide street which led to a huge, hullsteel cylinder butted up against the back of the palace.

Erien and his pilot passed through the Nersallian gate together, empowered by Liege Nersal's signet of passage, and followed the plaza-bound foot traffic into the cylindrical structure which was known as the Palace Shell. Here, his pilot left him. As a nobleborn conducting a highborn's business, she was entitled to do no more than pass through onto the busy plaza, bustling with pre-Swearing activity. Erien could continue up, into the palace sector abutting the highborns docks.

Wide stairs led upwards to the first of four tiered balconies ringing the inside of the shell. The first tier was for arriving Highlords, like himself. His birth rank did not allow him to go higher. Royalbloods were entitled to use the second tier, Purebloods the third. There were so few Purebloods now that the third had been converted into an interior garden, complete with a small population of songbirds. Those did not respect blood rank: one fluttered onto the railing near Erien and rocked there, singing unheard over the human and mechanical racket. The highest tier was the Ava's, trodden only by Ava Ameron and his personal attendants, or, by Ava's privilege, the Ava's Envoy, Amel. The Palace shell was Sevildom's elitist society, made tangible.

But the architecture was quite beautiful, in an anachronistic way. Erien set his shoulder pack on a table near the edge of the Highlord tier and looked out and down. On all levels, silver-plated columns guarded the openings to the stairs. Here, on the Highlord tier, they were kept polished. Below, on the circular courtyard that pedestrians and cargo carts passed through to get to the plaza, they were tarnished black above head height and rubbed smooth by centuries of pressing bodies. The layered balconies ran three quarters of the way around the shell's circumference, the walls between them decorated in cast friezes of idyllic scenes: a seashore, a jungle, a desert, a forest; strange choices for subterranean Gelion. At the west end, across from where Erien was standing, grand doors connected the tiers with the palace, each one with a two-person exit guard. The Ava's door was the least ornate of all, blank but for the shields of Avas only a Monatese scholar would recognize. Above it all, through an anchored mesh supporting a myriad of glowing nuggets, Erien could glimpse a coffered ceiling that must, at some time in the past thousand years, have been glorious.

The net effect was magnificent and absurd, and quite appropriate as a first sight of Gelion—not merely the hub, but the heart of Sevildom.

Erien shouldered the wide band of his pack, a robust, black spacer's carryall in which he carried the sum of his worldly goods, and fell in behind a party of three men, all fair, one with the golden hair of the purest Demish. Engaged in animated conversation about a fencing tournament they were anticipating, the Demish Highlords did not notice Erien for some time. Then, as they approached the Highlord door, one glanced back, narrowed his eyes, and nudged the man beside him, hissing *kinf'stan*. The third man looked, and then all three closed ranks and slowed down.

Their assumption was doubly wrong. Erien was not Nersallian despite his uniform, and even if he had been, merely being Highlord was not sufficient to place him within the challenge right for the title of Liege Nersal, which was what was meant by *kinf'stan*. Perhaps the Demish Highlords knew that, but assumed the worst was possible. All *kinf'stan*—and they numbered in the hundreds—had lethal reputations on the challenge floor. The Demish Highlords appeared undecided about how to respond. One raised his voice sharply, but was rebuked before he got beyond his first syllable, and was urgently encouraged to admire a frieze. It took Erien a moment to realize that the Demish Highlords were pretending that they were in no hurry, rather than risk a conflict with him over which of them would pass first through the Highlord doors. He would have preferred to watch them go first, in case there was some quirk of protocol he was unaware of, but rather than risk being further misjudged, he went on alone.

Horth Nersal had issued Erien a signet of passage, which he now produced and showed to the guards.

The Highlord door was guarded by one Demish and one Vrellish retainer, which was a useful tradition because Demish Sevolites and Vrellish Sevolites were almost orthogonal to each other in talents and temperament. Demish were typically verbal, romantic, blond- and blue-eyed with long memories and good organizational skills. Vrellish were spatially gifted, quick-tempered and highly sexed, with gray eyes and black hair. It was said that the Demish never forgot a wrong, and the Vrellish never let a slight grow old enough to need remembering.

Most of the Fountain Court houses were hybrid in origin but still functioned, culturally, either as Demish or Vrellish. House Nersal, for instance, sustained a fiercely Vrellish identity, despite its origins as a Vrellish backcross to the dominantly Demish line.

House Nersal was still a new power, in Gelack terms.

Nersallians' upward mobility was one of Ranar's favorite examples in Gelack anthropology seminars, invoked to refute students who said the Gelack doctrine of sword law, known as *Okal Rel,* was an enforcer of political stagnation. *Okal Rel* defined the living universe as the stage of an eternal struggle between Sevolites for status. It imposed the rules for that struggle, but it allowed families to rise and fall within their scope, and hence—according to Ranar—was not stagnate. It had made more sense to Erien in Ranar's seminars than here on Gelion, face to face with customs and prejudices as old as Gelack civilization.

The Vrellish guard accepted Liege Monitum's signet at a glance and waved Erien through. The Demish one delayed him to test the card's clear section with a scan wand for proof of Liege Nersal's blood signature.

It was the same tool Gelacks used to authenticate honor chip currencies. Erien could, if he wanted to, turn his signet into Nersallian money. There were businesses Tatt had told him about in the UnderDocks that would do it for him gladly.

"Sorry," the Demish guard said, when his wand confirmed the blood sample as Horth Nersal's. "I've never seen one of those before, from him."

The Vrellish woman shook her head at this Demish obsession for talking about the obvious. "Carry on *kinf'stan*," she told Erien, leaping to the same incorrect conclusion as the Demish Highlords. "Ameron is expecting to hear from your liege-admiral," she added.

Erien decided not to explain that it was Amel who would be bringing the dispatches. If it would get him access to Ameron, it was an assumption that he would not challenge.

Beyond the doors, Erien found himself in a bright lobby facing a long stretch of white stairs. On the landing midway up the stairs, courtesan musicians performed a piano and woodwind concerto. A female dancer in a white body sheath and trailing veils performed on the stairs, gracefully sidling out of the way of passing Sevolites. The fifteen or twenty people in the room paid her no more attention than they did the other decorations. Everything was white and gold, and pillared in a style reminiscent of a Greek pavilion. Nervecloth vistas on the walls to either side completed the illusion of a Mediterranean beach or, rather, a Gelack impression of what one had looked like. The water moved and the wind shifted the leaves of the palms. The air was lightly perfumed with incense.

A Throne courtier in the long, full skirts worn by Demish ladies approached Erien. She raised a hand to her breast when he showed her his signet, but said, briskly, "One moment," and fetched a palace errant in Ameron's white livery. The errant was also Demish, a solidly built man with blue eyes and sandy hair. In addition to Nersal, which held Black Hearth, the Ava's Oath included steadfast Monitum, the oldest of the hybrid houses and holder of Green Hearth, and the Demish house of H'Us, which occupied Silver Hearth. This errant was obviously H'Usian, according to the braid pattterns on his jacket, even if he wore Ameron Lor'Vrel's colors.

"New to Court?" the H'Usian errant asked Erien as he, too, scanned the signet.

"Yes."

The errant handed back Horth's signet and smiled. "Why don't you take the Lorel Stairs? It's the shortest way up to the Ava's office. I assume you want to go there?"

"Thank you," Erien replied, speaking down one level as was expected. Both the errant's chest braid and his grammar declared him a Seniorlord.

The Demish courtiers withdrew, followed by a titter from the Highlord lady which the man gently admonished her for, although Erien caught him smiling as he did so.

He had more important things to worry about, like getting close enough to Ameron to get access to Ranar.

A woman, attached to another group, took note. Erien avoided eye contact. Her sword and costume identified her as Vrellish, despite her Demishly broad shoulders, and he didn't want to be bothered with any irritating overtures or invitations, or—even worse—attempts to draw his challenge out of sheer bravado. The Nersallians, because of their liberal inclusions in title challenge-rights, bred formidable fighters. And Erien was anything but, although he was a decent enough sportsman.

The Lorel Stairs had an unassuming aspect on approach. They seemed like backstairs for servants, except for their width. The staircase wound upwards around a solid core, bannisterless walls tiled in black, white, and gray in an abstract pattern. Erien took the shallow steps three at a time for the first turn, but as the pattern closed in around him, he stopped abruptly, acutely disorientated. There was something wrong with the walls. They moved. The surface became many surfaces, interwoven in strange, rippling abstractions which swirled into knots that made him feel he was phasing in on the brink of a Reach jump. Except he knew he was standing on Gelion, and the walls should be still and solid.

By an act of will he stayed calm. It must be Gelion's sluggish air, he told himself. The air, his concern for Ranar, and the after-effects of his flying. When he got to Green Hearth, after seeing Ameron, he'd ask for some *klinoman*. He rarely used the drug to relieve post-flight effects; he rarely needed to, no matter how hard he flew. And he didn't like its slackening properties.

He tried the next step and nearly fell.

"You'd better close your eyes," said a bold woman's voice from behind him.

It was the Vrellish woman from the Olympian room, downstairs. She stopped two steps below him, her hand braced on her thigh where she spanned a few stairs with one leg. "I am Zind D'Therd," she introduced herself in *rel*-peerage, which corresponded with her Highlord braid, "and a vassal of House Dem'Vrel, which is Vrellish enough that I would hate to see the Demish score on a Nersallian just because he was new to court." She grinned.

Erien squinted against the optical illusion induced by the Lorel Stairs, concentrating on the woman's broad shoulders and strong features.

"It's the tiles," he realized, "and the patterns in them."

"Just like the Flashing Floor," Zind said. "You'll have heard of that. Amel took a wound there, performing as a courtesan sword dancer, because the floor messed him up. It's in the visitor probe stuff of the Reetions." Her scowl did not apologize for having viewed those recordings, though she seemed to disapprove of them, or Amel, or maybe both. "This," she gestured to the walls without taking her eyes off Erien's, "is something that the Lorel Avas did to cow the Vrellish. The Flashing Floor and Lorel Stairs used to be the only approaches to the Ava's apartments. Ev'rel thinks they were intended as a sort of defense, because it did not in the least phase a Lorel. Ameron walks up and down here as cheerfully as a commoner."

Erien swallowed, nauseous.

"Personally," Zind opined, "I think it was just the Lorels' nasty sense of humor."

"I'll keep my eyes closed. Thanks," Erien told her.

"One hundred and nine steps to go, from where your right foot is." She betrayed a measure of Demish inheritance with her exactitude, and trotted back down again.

Erien decided to trust her information. She came across as refreshingly uncomplex for a court Highlord, even if she was, in all likelihood, Amel's niece. The ruling family of Dem'Vrel consisted of Ev'rel and her three sons. Only Amel, sired by Ev'rel's late half-brother, Ava Delm, was Pureblood. D'Therd and D'Lekker were Royalbloods, gifted to the Dem'Vrel by Ev'rel to help her secure her power. Erien knew from both Tatt and Ranar's correspondence that Ev'rel had given gift children to the Dem'Vrel through her Royalblood sons. By her name, Zind D'Therd Dem'Vrel was one of those children.

As he climbed with his eyes closed, Erien recalled to mind her jacket braid, subtracting the motifs that he recognized in order to isolate and memorize the components which were uniquely Dem'Vrellish. The Monatese herald who had instructed him in his early years had been a traditionalist, and Dem'Vrel was too much a come-lately to figure in his scheme of things. It seemed wise to correct the oversight, given the importance of House Dem'Vrel as the Avim's power base.

One hundred and nine steps later, Erien emerged in Ameron's inner office.

A plainly dressed man rose from behind a semi-circular desk, as surprised palace errants snapped to attention, then scaled down to mere curious interest when Erien showed them his signet. The quartet of errants was again a mix of H'Usians and Monatese, two men in silver and white, and a man and a woman in black and green. The man who had been seated behind the reception desk wore gray. He would be, Erien guessed, one of Ameron's conscience-bonded *gorarelpul*. Erien had known Di Mon's *gorarelpul*, of course, as a child, and others who served as techs in the Nersallian fleet. All of them conscience-bonded. This one was the first to make him feel anything akin to the superstitious chill that so many people reported when they fell under a *gorarelpul's* scrutiny.

"You came up the Lorel Stairs?" the *gorarelpul* asked, coming out from behind his desk. He addressed Erien commoner to Highlord, which confirmed Erien's suspicion. The only Sevolite who had ever been bonded—in ignorance—was Amel. The *gorarelpul* looked Erien over critically. "Would you like to sit down a moment, highborn?"

"I am fine," Erien assured him, politely. "After the first turn I kept my eyes closed."

"That's wise," said the *gorarelpul*. "Carrying something to focus on is another useful measure, if you ever need to do it again."

"Or march straight up them with your teeth gritted and your eyes open," offered the male Monatese, whose amusement suggested that Erien had not repressed all outward signs of his experience, "like your liege does, and damn the Lorels! Only time I've ever seen Liege Nersal stagger."

The errants laughed.

That would be very like Horth, Erien thought. He would try it himself some time, and see if he could habituate. Today he silently thanked Zind Dem'Vrel for her timely advice. He would not impress Ameron with his competence if he walked into the walls or fell over the furniture.

To the *gorarelpul* he said, "You are one of Ameron's people?"

He heard a slight smile, for his tact, in the man's answer. "I am *gorarelpul*. My name is Drasous, and yes, I am bonded to Ameron."

Erien knew, now, what was bothering him. It was not the *gorarelpul* himself. All those Erien had ever known were highly competent, judicious men and women who seemed quite at ease with the reality that their minds were no longer entirely their own. Conscience-bonding—brainwarping in slang—enforced obedience to a Sevolite master by autonomic hyper-reflexia associated with cognitive triggers. Disobedience could result in death. Sevildom demanded absolute loyalty of its most highly trained and independent-minded servants. Since his time on Rire, Erien found that the concept disturbed him profoundly—both that it was done, and that its victims seemed to accept it as necessary.

It was said, however, that Ameron's own chief *gorarelpul* was unbonded. The Court's conservative element discounted the story as a slur against Ameron. Unbonded *gorarelpul*, being commoner, could not be trusted to be both knowledgeable and honorable.

"If you have dispatches from Horth Nersal, you can leave them with me," Drasous told Erien.

"I do not," Erien was forced to admit. "Amel was to carry the dispatches from *DragonSword*. But I do need to see Ava Ameron."

"Oh?" Drasous was cool. The palace errants became alert, no longer dismissing him as a mere envoy who had not bothered to unpack his sword.

"I am Erien," Erien explained. "A ward of Monitum."

The Monatese errants visibly pricked up their ears. Drasous glanced at them. "Yours is not a name I am familiar with," said Drasous, politely enough. "You may wait in the anteroom, if you wish."

The Demish pair fell in on either side of him. "This way, Your Grace," said one of them.

If a signal had passed between Drasous and the errants it was subtly done. But it would make sense for the 'relpul to hold back the Monatese errants to ask them about Erien. Erien hesitated only long enough to decide he had nothing to gain by pressing his case. If the Monatese errants had heard of Di Mon's offworld ward, who had been sent to Rire, that would be useful. Whether they had or not, the *gorarelpul* would look beyond them for some confirmation of his identity—all of which would take time. Erien followed the two H'Usian errants through a large office occupied by at least twenty of Ameron's personal staff—commoner and Sevolite—and into what was clearly a waiting room beyond.

"How long will I—" Erien began to ask, turning back, but having delivered him, the errants had already lost interest. He gave up before they closed the doors in his face. Another pair of errants stood unblinking on this side of the door. They were both black-haired and liveried in Ameron's own beige-crested white. *What*, Erien thought, *did that mean?* He was beginning to weary of the effort of thinking like an anthropologist in what was supposed to be his own culture, trying to translate the cues of position, garb and status into allegiance and political stance.

Vent Amel down a long jump, anyway! Amel could have made an interview possible with a word! The thought prompted Erien to wonder whether Amel had, in fact, done the opposite. Amel should have been and gone by now, with Liege Nersal's dispatches. But that did not tally with the palace staff's expectation that Erien, himself, must be the courier.

Most of the occupants of the anteroom were standing, watchful, but poised to mingle if granted a desirable opportunity. They all wore overjackets in house colors, decorated with status braids. And swords. Erien's own sword was packed in his carryall. He should at least have thought to change into dress uniform, but the Nersallian fleet's stern, unceremonious discipline had completed the ruin that seven years on Rire had begun. His Monatese foster father Di Mon would not have approved the oversight. Erien backtracked over that last thought and put the ghost of the late Liege Monitum aside. He was on his own.

Along one wall of the anteroom, a chamber group of courtesans was playing. They were technically good, but lacked something in comparison to the orchestras Erien had heard on Rire. How strange, he thought, settling himself into a chair and stowing his carryall beneath it, that the passionate Gelack culture had given rise to such effete music, while orderly Rire produced music which had moved him to trembling silence when he first heard it, at only seven years of age. It had seemed the language of his heart. He wondered, idly, what the reaction would be if he pulled his flute from his carrier bag. Probably the errants would think it was some disreputable weapon and run him through. Gelack Sevolites were not musicians; music was a commoner trade. Nevertheless, he watched the musicians closely, absorbing the music. Since he had left Rire he had developed a superb musical memory, because he seldom had opportunity to hear new music played by trained musicians, just far more barracks ballads and Nersallians drinking songs than any man of his moderate habits should have to endure.

The woman in the trio of musicians, a striking redhead, gave him a quick survey and dismissed him with a slight but unmistakable tilt of her pretty nose. He had no idea of the criteria by which she judged, or what it meant. He did note, however, that the musicians seemed a little stressed.

The courtesans were obviously wearing their best, but the clothes didn't match, in quality, those of their audience. One of the tri-lyre's strings was unreliable. Stretched with age perhaps. The tri-lyrist played on regardless. They were a lower-class courtesan trio who had been advanced by a powerful patron, Erien decided, a powerful patron who was perhaps a little tone deaf. He was beginning to wonder what the etiquette might be for requesting that a musician retune—neither his early protocol lessons nor his study of Gelack culture under Ranar had covered such eventualities —when a slight ripple in the gathering made him look up at a newcomer.

The new arrival had just strolled in the door and now stood looking around the room with an air of possession. Equally unmistakably she was commoner, with an olive cast to her skin and fine lines beginning to show around her eyes and mouth. Her hair was a tawny frizz, held back from her face with a golden scarf. She wore a simple tunic patterned with autumn leaves of red, brown, and gold, outlined in gilt, over brown slacks. Her eyes met Erien's and both brows went up as she took in his slumped, travel-worn posture, his Nersallian clothes, and his carryall.

The waiting Sevolites drew back as she crossed the room. It was a subtle withdrawal, but although they were Sevolites and she was a commoner, they withdrew.

Erien got to his feet as she reached him.

This could be none other than Charous, Ameron's chief adjunct, the *gorarelpul* whom Ameron supposedly did not bond. She dipped her head in a sketch of a bow and waited for Erien to address her. It was polite for whoever had the higher birth rank to speak first, as the consequences of an error in grammatical differencing were greater the other way around.

"I am Erien, ward of Monitum," he proclaimed himself five birth ranks her superior with the inflection of his 'I' in Gelack. "I would like to speak to Ava Ameron."

She heard his pronouns and her brows rose again. She had an alert, slightly triangular face, like a cat's. "Charous. Royal *Gorarelpul*. Please state your business."

"My business concerns my guardian, the ambassador of Rire."

And? said her eyebrows.

"When do you think it would be possible to see Ava Ameron?"

"You are the ward of Monitum, not of Rire," she reminded him of his first declaration.

"I am the ward of Monitum and of Rire."

She glanced down at his Nersallian leathers. He said, "I have been serving with the Nersallian fleet for the past three years."

"Monitum, Rire, and the Nersallian fleet," the *gorarelpul* said. "You have indeed had a varied career, Highlord Erien." As Ameron's chief *gorarelpul*, she was responsible for the Ava's intelligence service and for dealing with covert threats to the throne. He had the sense that he was not in her files, and that the omission irked—if not worried—her.

"I think," Erien said, "that was what Di Mon—the late Liege Monitum—intended. I believe he prepared me for this crisis."

"Did he?" said Charous thoughtfully. "Please wait here."

Erien watched her autumnal back as she crossed to the doors. The errants standing guard received her with a nod. She said something quietly to one, and he glanced towards Erien. The other one opened the door for her, and she disappeared.

She returned with alacrity. Her mild interest was replaced by an intensity of focus Erien found unnerving. "You're to come with me," she said crisply. "He wants to see you now."

The 'he', so differenced, could only mean Ameron.

All eyes were upon them as they went through the double doors, through the outer administrative offices, and into the reception area where Erien had been before.

Three people were just emerging from an adjoining hall. They made an interesting group—and illustrious, Erien realized, decoding the braid decorating their collars, cuffs and waistcoats: a Nersallian Highlord and two Demish Royalbloods, a man and a woman. The man's costume identified him as the admiral, and regent, of H'Us. Admiral H'Us was a sandy-haired man with the youthful face and the aged eyes of an Old Sword. He had been admiral all through the ninety-year-reign of his late mother. The Nersallian Highlord was a woman, straight-backed, gray-eyed and austere, in trousers, jacket and braids which proclaimed her not only *kinf'stan* but of Horth's blood. The Demish woman wore no braid at all. She was a golden-haired girl in the full skirts, high collared bodice, and pearled cap of an unmarried Demish princess. Noticing Erien, she gazed at him with wide-eyed innocence. Her eyes were sky blue and very young. He did not know whether protocol would allow him to smile or not. He wanted to. Then Charous swept him past them, and down a short hall, lined with doors. On the very threshold of what had to be the Ava's personal office, the famous Blackwood Room, Charous suddenly turned and held out her hand. "I'll take that," she told Erien, nodding toward his carryall.

Within the room, a man's voice called, "Charous!"

The voice sent a shock down Erien's spine. It was unmistakably a voice of command.

"Give me your bag," the *gorarelpul* said narrowly.

Erien handed it over, and walked past her into the Blackwood Room.

Ameron Lor'Vrel had come halfway across the bare floor. He halted now, staring at Erien. As Erien entered, the door swung closed behind him with a heavy sound. Erien hardly noticed.

Ameron was a tall man, even for a Sevolite. He was dressed in a white shirt and gray trousers, the shirt embroidered with the fern motif of Lor'Vrel. He had the deceptively thin Vrellish build, and abundant Vrellish vigor, but his untidy shock of hair was brown, not black. Even though he stood still, the air around him was expectant of action. His gray eyes were iridescent with energy.

No single detail of Ameron's appearance explained why his presence awed and overwhelmed people—even Erien, who was not educated to be awed. Perhaps it was his history. This was Ameron, last survivor of the hybrid house of Lor'Vrel. He had lived two lives, one which had ended two hundred years ago, and one which began nineteen years ago. He had come to power for the first time in the midst of the Killing War between Gelion and Rire, imposed a solution, and sealed the frontier between Gelion and Rire. Eleven years later, he'd been lost making a jump and was mourned. It was rare for ships to return after days of time-slips, let alone years.

It was Di Mon and Ranar, attempting the same jump nearly two hundred years later, who had freed him. That Ameron had emerged sane was a testament to his strength of character. That he had gone on to reclaim the throne from Ev'rel without bloodshed was testament to his charisma. Statesmanship had held that throne, this time, for eighteen years. Now he faced his old dilemma, Rire. That was, at least, how Erien interpreted the Ava's stare. But living legend or not, this time Rire was going to wrest a fresh solution from him: the beginning of a relationship between equals.

"I understood you were in the Nersallian fleet," the Ava said, giving no quarter or sign of recognition apart from what might be extracted from the bare words.

They had met, once, when Erien was six years old. Erien had been reared on the legends of Ameron's wisdom. He had seen compassion and generosity demonstrated, then, towards the ailing Di Mon. He had presumed that he might feel it himself in some measure, now. Certainly he had not expected to receive such a cold welcome. He took a moment to find his balance.

"I asked to be released," said Erien. "I thought Ranar might need me."

"Need you for what?" Ameron spoke as he was entitled, Pureblood to Highlord.

"I am highborn," Erien said. "I thought that might help Ranar."

A silence greeted that. Then the Ava said, "They say you do not fight."

"No," Erien said, and struggled with his better judgment for a moment before adding, "They say the same thing of you, Ava."

Ameron snorted a breath through his long, thin nose. It might have been amusement. It was hard to tell. Whatever it was played out in an instant and was gone. "What kind of help have you in mind?"

"I will know better after I have seen Ambassador Ranar. I understand you are holding him in protective custody."

"If that is a request," Ameron said, his tone stinging, "it is denied."

"Then I will wait," said Erien, "until we can discuss it further."

"Wait where?"

Erien wanted to say, "Here, until you are tired of the sight of me!" But the atmosphere in the room was too tense. "Green Hearth, if they will take me in."

"They will. See that they do not regret it."

Erien nodded. "I will, Ava Ameron. But will you consider my request to see Ambassador Ranar? I would not like to act without his guidance."

"Young man," Ameron said, with sudden tart humor, "I trust you will see fit not to act at all."

"Why?" said Erien. "Ranar is restricted by his commoner status, and by the rumors spread about him. Which, by the way, are untrue."

"Amel says otherwise."

Erien felt his face harden slightly. "Amel is hardly in a position to know or judge. I lived with Ranar for seven years. He is neither a rapist nor a child abuser, which is what Gelacks are saying when they say he is homosexual."

"I believe," Ameron said, "Amel understands the distinction. Gelion, however," he conceded, "does not."

"Then Gelion needs education, not coddling of its prejudices."

Ameron's eyes were sparkling dangerously. Erien took a firm grip on himself, speaking quickly but levelly. "I appreciate that you are in a difficult situation politically and cannot commit to a course which will undermine your standing, but Rire will not wait indefinitely. The situation in Killing Reach is tense. The Nersallians have mounted a blockade, and I was barely able to prevent them mounting so close a blockade as to risk Reetion pilots' lives. Reetion pilots do not have either the stamina or the ships that Gelacks do. It is only a matter of time before someone on one side or the other does something provocative. You of all people know this, Ava. We have too few people on either side with an understanding of the other, but I've lived in both cultures. If you won't let me see Ranar and you don't want me acting on my own, then use me as a resource!"

Ameron raised both eyebrows. "You claim to be a Gelack. Would any Gelack address his Ava thus?"

"I've read the Monatese biography of you," Erien said, unsure, exactly, what he meant to explain by that.

"Gods," murmured Ameron. Perhaps the reminder of his own rebellious youth restored a modicum of good nature. He forbore to remind Erien that he had been Heir Gelion, not a houseless ward, when he argued against his Vrellish mother's handling of the Killing Wars.

"You will go," Ameron said, "to Green Hearth. Young Ditatt will doubtless be pleased to see you, and you may listen to him rail against my other iniquities. Leave Ranar to me. Leave Rire to me. And for the time being, leave Gelion to me." The last was spoken with real force, and accompanied by a sweep of the arm towards the door. Where Horth dismissed with a bare nod, Ameron dismissed with united will and body. Neither were to be gainsaid. Erien bowed slightly, and left.

Behind him, he heard the Ava's gusty, "Charous! Where is Amel?"

Chapter III

AMEL NEARLY CHANGED HIS MIND ABOUT VISITING MIRA as he reached the top of the stairs that led down to the UnderDocks. As he hesitated, other pedestrians brushed past, jostling him. It did not offend him. He was not prince enough for that, despite his Pureblood birth rank. The crowd contact was a comfort to him, as if—as he had believed in his youth—he really was a commoner, going about his business with his head down, muffled in a traveling cloak against the chill of Gelion's open spaces and the unwelcome attention of those with the power to do him harm. His commoner's instincts let him blend in with the crowd.

All his anxiety was inward.

He had the dispatch from Liege Nersal in his pack and an undischarged report of Rire for Ameron. It would be better to turn back to see Ameron first, and then slip off. Except he knew he wouldn't be able to manage that.

His anxiety peaked, and was pushed down. This was just another homecoming, like a hundred others he'd made in the eighteen years since Ameron took the throne. Of course there were political tensions; of course he could not be caught; but there was no greater reason than usual for anyone to be watching for him to slip up. If they were—either Ev'rel's spies or Ameron's *gorarelpul*—he had taken the usual precautions. He had stashed his envoy craft on the surface, passed through the docks as a nondescript nobleborn, and left them disguised as a commoner. After he'd made his visit he would do it all again in reverse, take off, turn around and land again as Pureblood Amel Dem'Vrel, Royal Envoy.

It was his most reliable method of stealing time to visit Mira.

Mira operated a medical clinic in the UnderDocks. He was not related to her by blood, but he never thought of her as anything but his smarter, older sister; and of her mother as his mother, although Mira's mother had died when he was only six years old. His birth-mother, Ev'rel, who took him—broken—into House Dem'Vrel as a young adult, was something entirely different to him.

Amel and Mira were raised in secret quarters by the dean of the *gorarelpul* college. Mira's father never told Amel his origins, so he grew up believing that he had been adopted for his exceptionally strong pilot's aptitude, which was unusual for a commoner. Mira's father wanted her to perpetuate his dry and bitter life of secret research into the nature of Sevolites, but Mira fiercely desired to train as a medtech on *TouchGate Hospital Station.* Fatally confident, at ten years of age, Amel had borrowed a ship to fulfill her dream. He thought he knew his worth and could repay the ship's owner, H'Reth, by flying for him. Instead he was sold as a child whore when he refused H'Reth's sexual demands. That was only the beginning of all that lay between Amel and Mira, with guilt enough on either side to give pain; but even more importantly, Mira was all that Amel retained of the child who had believed that he was good, brave, and magically invulnerable.

He wanted to see her. Now. Before he saw Ev'rel or Ameron. Besides, he had contraband for her that he'd imported through his lover, Ann of Rire. He couldn't take that home to Fountain Court. It might be medical supplies and literature to Reetions, but it was *okal'a'ni* bio-science to Sevildom.

A large man gave Amel a particularly hard bump. "Hey! Move or get out of the way."

Amel caught his floppy hood before it fell back, and said, "Sorry."

The rough tradesman was already gone, a belt of tools clunking beneath his cloak. Most travelers wore cloaks in UnderGelion. What was not seen was less apt to be stolen. Cross with himself for drawing even this much notice, Amel slipped down the stairs with the crowd.

The stairs leading down to the UnderDocks were wide and shallow, as if they had once been something grand. Now, bare hullsteel showed through worn carpet on the inside track, which was favored by foot traffic regardless of whether it was going up or down.

At their base, the stairs opened out on the buried city known as UnderGelion. There was good light this close to the Citadel, which was the seat of power.

Amel turned away from the light and sound.

He went faster now, struggling with his eagerness. It would not do to stand out too much among slower moving pedestrians. His chosen route passed store fronts and entrances to courtesan dens of modest respectability, all well lit and policed by local toughs.

Off the commercial strip, the UnderDocks quickly broke down into a labyrinth, maintained and fought over by the commoners who survived by selling what could not be obtained elsewhere. The lighting here was poorly maintained. Amel wove his way through the safer lanes, turning here and hurrying there, until he stopped at a medtech station with a battered white cross above its heavily dented door.

The clinic was closed. If it wasn't, a paid tough would be stationed to keep watch. The district might be dangerous, but Mira's clinic was an asset to all sides of most disputes.

Amel stroked a middle finger down the door's familiar dents, with mixed emotions for this evidence of old assaults. It was frightening to think of Mira's drugs and valuables inspiring attempts to break the door down. At the same time, this proof of its resilience made him proud. No UnderDocks vandals broke into what he sealed up, or harmed what he loved.

There was a buzzer for emergencies. Amel didn't use it. He only pretended to. Then he let himself in with a series of quick taps on a nervecloth panel, which worked despite the scars of flame and acid.

Amel entered a waiting room with a bench and a couple of sleeping pallets. The lights came up. He waved to where he had mounted a well-disguised monitor, then secured the door behind him and went through a similar lock on the far side. The waiting room was bare and smelled of antiseptic.

He was in a small consulting room flanked by an operating theater and dispensary, both locked. Straight ahead were living quarters. These were spartan without being implausible. There were two beds, a table, and shelves filled with personal items.

Amel picked up a portable Reetion holostage and stuck it in his pack, frowning. He shed his commoner cloak, leaving it on the otherwise bare table.

The medtech's real home was through another, hidden, door. Amel knew where to look for the disguised touch panel. The door slid open quietly. He went through.

The woman working at the laboratory bench looked up with a slight, abstracted frown as the door closed. She was, like him, in her mid-thirties; but unlike him, she looked it. Mira was commoner-born and commoner-used. The use life had made of Amel hadn't marred his well-integrated physical beauty or stiffened his dancer-trained movements. There had been times when he'd despised his stamina, but on the whole he embraced his highborn regenerative powers for the gift that he knew them to be. He loved his body's supple strength and his beauty's license to elicit trust whether, he admitted, it was always deserved or not.

Mira transferred a droplet of liquid from one vial to another, carefully discarding the spent vial and pipette into a cleaning solution.

"I'll be with you in a moment," she murmured, but flashed him a quick, distracted smile.

He sat down on a couch to watch her finish what she was doing. She came round to him, bent, and gave him a sisterly kiss on the cheek. She smelled of solvents and cultures; it clung to her dark blonde hair. "I hope you've brought me something nice," she said, but her heart was not in the childishness.

"Where's Mona?" He asked after his best fan, Mira's eight-year-old daughter from a relationship with a fellow medic who had died when the child was two.

"Upstairs working on the computer," said Mira. She grinned. "When are you going to smuggle me in one of those Reetion arbiters?"

"Don't even ask," Amel said, with a touch of foreboding, which he shook off. "The Reetions are very touchy about their artificial intelligence devices."

"If anyone could steal one, you could."

Ordinarily, he would have enjoyed that compliment, but the foreboding spoiled the pleasure. He heaved up his pack and brandished the portable holostage at her. "Mona left this out where your patients might see it, in the public living quarters."

"You bring her too many toys," Mira said defensively, then turned her palms outwards instead. "I know, I know, I have to pay attention too. I'll talk to her."

He started to rise. "I'll go find her. You're busy."

"Don't go. Not just yet." She slung his pack onto the bench and fidgeted with the clasp. "Does anything in this need to be stored?"

"It's all packed according to instructions."

"Good," she said, with sudden decision. "It can wait."

She sat down beside him. "I need to talk to you. I've been listening to what people say about that trash that's going around about you. And I've heard an ugly rumor: there's a kill-show playing. I've let it be known I'm interested in hearing more—"

"Mira—"

"—but so far, nothing. You might tell your courtesan friends to be wary of customers who pay them the complement of suggesting that they look like you. It's not a healthy thing, right now."

"Are you done now?" he asked tartly.

"More or less," she said, reserving her options with a frown. He knew that frown well. She was an inspired researcher, capable of making contributions to Reetion understanding of Sevolites through the collaboration of his connection with Rire. He understood that she lived for that research. But she would insist that she knew more than he did about coping with the world at large, and his own special problems in particular.

"How could you," he demanded, "be so stupid as to actually tell someone you are interested in something to do with me! Maybe I'm missing something, but haven't we been studiously avoiding that? You are supposed to be Asher. Not Mira."

Asher had been the name of Mona's dead father.

"It's perfectly natural for me to take an interest in a possible source of customers," replied Mira.

"Dead customers?" Amel challenged.

"Then you've heard the same rumors?"

"No!" He was on his feet now, pacing. He stopped.

"There are always ugly rumors," he insisted. "People start them for half a dozen reasons, from idiot titillation to sheer bungling. If you've heard—what? that someone's killing courtesans who look like me?—That's probably just people confusing some synthdrama they've heard about with reality."

He cast her a smile that would have nuked most frowns. "Remember the rumor that I'd been slashed to death on Ava's Square by some death-of-a-thousand-knives?"

Mira's frown merely shifted toward indignation. "I never really believed that."

"You hadn't heard from Rire, about the reception of your 'Highborn Phenotype Complex' paper," he teased. "You were panic-stricken."

"I was *worried* about *you*."

"Uh-huh."

"Amel, will you ever be serious?"

"I told you not to ask about kill-show rumors. That was serious. And I've told you, forever, to pay more attention to Mona. What if she takes a Reetion holostage into your clinic and turns on a 'Kid's Connection' episode? I don't know." He looked around him, proud of the luxuries that he had provided but seeing an unhealthy microcosm also. "Maybe it's not right for her to grow up here."

"Amel." Mira's tone was a dunking in cold water. "We lived in less space, with fewer amenities, until you were ten and I was twelve. In fact, Mona interacts with more people than I did, because of the clinic. Now stop playing games."

"What games?" He was hurt by that remark. His concern was genuine. It made his insides gel to think of anything happening to either of them. Particularly Mona. Mona had only been two when Amel found her again. He had watched her change from a sick and dejected child to a delightful dreamer, and able companion to Mira.

"I have a child who left out a few toys," Mira explained her accusation. "Fine. That is a problem. You are featured in a nasty proliferation of pornographic synthdramas, which may have escalated to live kill-shows. Think about it a minute," Mira ordered. "Whose problems should we be working on?"

She paused, thin arms folded over her thin chest. The weight of the docks, above, and all the censure of Sevildom, could not humble Mira. She was invincible, as long as she had her work. He admired, and occasionally envied her for it.

Conceding defeat, he collapsed onto the couch. "All right. I'll pay attention."

"You won't," she predicted. "You'll ignore it as much as you're able to."

He laughed. "I beg your pardon, but I wade through more innuendo in a day than—"

"I don't mean superficially. I know you can be glib as hell."

He scowled. "You've been reading Reetion psychiatric literature again, haven't you? I'm not rejecting, or subliming, or withdrawing, or any of those other post-traumatic stress syndrome things they talk about. I'm just living in the present."

"If you're so sane," Mira said, "explain why you continue to dress like a courtesan when you ought to be trying to be a Pureblood."

"I do not dress like a courtesan."

"Oh, Amel!"

"I dress the way I want."

"Provocatively."

"Listen, I could dress in shuttle tarps and be accused of that. But if I look and act highborn, it only provokes worse things, like challenges! I'm damned if I do, and I'm damned if I don't."

"So you please yourself, and to the void with the consequences!"

He snapped to his feet. "Don't worry! Your precious connection to Reetion research forums isn't going to get snuffed in a kill-show!"

That hit hard. He immediately regretted it. It frightened him to know that he could wound Mira.

He closed his eyes and tipped his head back, trying to think clearly. A great, disturbed, and complex mass of feeling fought the effort, like the rumblings of monstrous indigestion. That's all it was, too, he thought, shit that had not worked its way out. There was nothing in the darkness that he wanted to retrieve, and nothing that he wished to know that could be learned from it.

"I didn't mean that, Mira," he said softly. "I'm sorry."

Her tone had a new, brittle chill. "I never asked you to take any risks for me."

"Don't—"

"Or make any sacrifices."

"What I do, I do willingly."

There was a silence, pregnant with unresolved tension. He had felt it there before, between them. There were things that they dared not discuss.

This was not what he'd come here for.

She turned at the sound of her daughter's arrival.

Mona had short, black hair and her mother's light build, but the resemblance ended there; or perhaps, Mira's intensity was merely focused differently in her daughter. Mona throve on a feast of mankind's stories, retrieved from Reetion storage crystals. No matter how much Amel brought for her, there was always some new request: for a reference that wasn't included in the last recordings, or more of a current series she was following. He even carried intermittent correspondence between her and a few Reetion pen pals; Mona wrote under cover of the persona of a miner's daughter on a remote Reetion outpost.

"How long has he been here!" Mona cried, as she flung herself at Amel, with a sharp look at her mother. "Oh, you're both horrible."

With the child in his arms, Amel laughed, cured of all lurking terrors. Her hug was sweet delight, as innocent as spring water.

"Where have you been? You've been gone for so long," Mona said when he set her down. She didn't let go of his hand. He sank on one knee to stay close to her.

"Eight days? Is that such an eternity?"

"Eight days in space maybe. You haven't been to see us for seventeen. Isn't that right, mother?"

"You count. I don't," said Mira.

"Seventeen days!" he said. "No wonder you look taller."

"Have you brought me anything new?" she asked.

"I've made you something," he said, getting up to fetch it from his pack, "in addition, of course, to the usual shopping list of data crystals and books and mail and candy. Those are in the pack I gave to your mother. Plus a pirate's vest from Killing Reach. Perry D'Aur gave it to me. You'll like it; it's embroidered and sewn with beads that are all made of jewels. A real pirate used to wear it, so it may be too big for you yet."

"Can I see it?"

"Of course, when I'm gone. I can't stay long."

Her face fell.

"Not today, anyway. But I should be at Court for a while now. I'll make it down again. Now, pay attention."

He dangled a bauble from his palm with a flourish. It swung at the end of a gold chain.

Mona looked puzzled.

"Yes, I know, it doesn't look impressive," Amel said, "but it has secrets to tell when you wear it."

"What do you mean?" Mona caught the bauble in her hand. It was large for a child's neck, and shaped like a plump lozenge.

Amel handed Mira a wrist band that was equally dull to look at.

"The pendant," he said, "broadcasts life signs. Nothing fine tuned enough for diagnosis, but you could tell if the person wearing it is awake and active, for example, or sleeping."

Mira looked up from the wrist band control unit. She might cannibalize it and the pendant if he stopped explaining. She knew many of the tiny components used were common to all Reetion crystronics.

"You know how tracking devices are less than useless in UnderGelion, because of all the hullsteel?" he said. "Well, I think I've solved it. That pendant and receiver use a location solving algorithm that works with hullsteel echoes and resonances. It's not perfect. But as a rough cut, if you had the wrist unit and were looking for the pendant, it would head you in the right direction. The fewer hullsteel walls between, the better the resolution."

"Mona hardly ever leaves the clinic," Mira reminded him.

"I know," he said. "What I really want is something you could signal me with all the way from here to Fountain Court, but this is as far as I've got. It came to me while I was—" he reconsidered confessing the details, "—working on something for Ann. It's only a start on the problem, but I thought I might as well give you the prototype. It wouldn't hurt for Mona to wear it, would it?"

"You're paranoid, you know that, don't you?" Mira told him. "I'm not going to let Mona wander off alone because I'm hunched over a test tube and ignoring her."

"Actually, I thought she might use it to track you, if you take too long making a house call."

Mona giggled.

"If it does work," said Mira, playing by rules as old as childhood rivalry, "you could probably publish the algorithm."

"It'll work," he bragged, sufficiently rewarded by her tacit admission that he'd impressed her intellectually, "but if other people knew how, it might be less useful to me. Now I really do have to leave. Ameron is waiting for a report."

"You only just got here!" complained Mona.

"I know," he said, "but I'll come back again, soon, now that I am home. Walk me to the clinic door, Mona?"

"Sure!"

Amel took his dispatch from the pack, left the rest, and took Mona's hand. "Bye, Mira!"

"Remember what I said about the kill-shows!" she called after him as the secret door closed. Amel put the dispatch pouch into an inner pocket of his flight jacket.

"What's a kill-show?" Mona asked him in the outer living quarters.

He retrieved his traveling cloak off the table. "Nothing I want you to worry about, except that, just perhaps, people around here might not feel too kindly towards Reetions. Now, tell me why you left your holostage lying around where somebody like that might see it?"

The child made excuses, swore to reform, and chattered to him about things she'd studied on the hand-held holostage while he was gone. She was curious about references to the psychiatric probing performed by the Reetions.

"Where did you come across that?" Amel demanded.

"In a citizen's discussion archive."

She spoke Reetion. He switched them both firmly back to Gelack, although he spoke to her in commoner peerage, which was, strictly speaking, absolutely wrong. "I thought I excised all references to me and the visitor probe from what I brought you."

"Most of them," Mona said with a pout. "It leaves blanks."

Amel frowned. "You are getting to be altogether too Reetion, if you've so little tolerance for that."

The child laid her hands on his forearm, looking up to him with a heart-rending, open look. "Tell me the truth, please, Amel? I like the Reetions. But mother said that the bad things people know about you come from Reetions." Mona wrestled with a very personal morality and ended looking fiercely Gelack. "I won't like them anymore if they hurt you. I'll hate them!"

"Oh no, Mona! No." The threat of hatred, toward anyone, from Mona, frightened Amel. He went down on one knee, his commoner's cloak draped over the sleeve of his Sevolite flight leathers, and held the child by her shoulders. She felt more potent, in his hands, than the abyss that lay in ambush in his past; and yet he still feared its power, as if she, too, could fall in, just by standing too close. He despised himself a little because of that.

"Don't hate the Reetions," he said to her. "What happened to me then, was—" he stopped because he felt suddenly nauseous. White-noise was building up behind his eyes, threatening disorientation.

He denied it with a shallow gasp, and said, "It was a misunderstanding. Yes. Something like that." He smiled, feeling better now that the threat of disorientation had passed. "I had a knack of putting myself in the way of things like that. But not anymore. It wasn't, exactly, the Reetions' fault."

Mona was still troubled. "So they did hurt you."

He rose, resting his hand on her shoulder. "Let me tell you about Reetions. All the children learn the way you do, but there are teachers to help; and they all go together to see for themselves what it is that they are learning about. They have rules about how many children people can have which seem very harsh to us, but every child on Rire is loved, and there are choices," he rolled his eyes. "So-o-o many choices! You have to *be* a computer to understand Reetion laws, so it is just as well that their computers keep track."

"They are called arbiters, silly, not computers," Mona cheered up, once again speaking in Reetion. "Computers are the ordinary dumb ones."

"Only eight years old," he complained, "and I've nothing left to teach you."

"Oh no, I couldn't have built that pendant you gave us. How did you get the idea?"

Amel stroked the side of his face starting from behind an ear as if the gesture had its origins in a stiffness to be worked out. "Doing something that I shouldn't have been doing with an arbiter."

"That isn't possible," Mira said with Reetion confidence.

"You know," said Amel, "I'm relieved to hear that."

He stayed talking with her for too long.

This was what he'd come for. But the warm glow began to fade as soon as he left the medic's station.

Nervousness grew as he made his way out of the UnderDocks. The dingy passages were too familiar. He had lived here for six terrible months, as a child of ten. The eyes that marked his passage seemed too knowledgeable, as if they envied his elevation, ridiculously high above their station. He loved the luxuries he took for granted now, on Fountain Court. At the same time, he wanted to belong to the common-born in a way he could never belong to the Sevolites of Gelion. He had been a commoner, once. To Sevolites, he would always be an indigestible morsel, which they could neither swallow, nor spit out. He was Pureblood, yet he had been dominated and humiliated by other Sevolites, and by the dark-faced, masterless commoners of Rire.

His sense of being watched made his skin prickle, so that he became acutely conscious of the sweaty lining of his flight suit. He forgot not to hurry. He almost ran.

Amel emerged from the UnderDocks onto the hullsteel Palace Plain, and stopped. The underground city before him cast a spell with the memories it invoked, and with the grandeur of its slow decay, busy with life. The view took his breath away.

It was a panorama of darkness and scattered light, most densely populated in the environs of the docks and the Citadel. Where there was settlement, there was light; elsewhere the palace plain was dark. If the entire hollow semi-sphere had been illuminated once it was not during living memory, and for highborns that could span centuries.

To Amel's left was a shipping yard, where cargo from the docks was loaded onto trains, powered by charge packs, which traveled the plain's circumference to Southtown. There had once been a northern loop, now abandoned to the subterranean dark.

Wandering vendors milled about outside the UnderDocks amid the Sevolites and drivers who used the road called Ava's Way to reach the artisan district of West Alcove. Amel had been driven along that road to assignations with Demish ladies, after he'd risen from the UnderDocks to the position of high-class courtesan.

The brightest spot in sight was the Apron District, skirting the foot of the Citadel. Occupied by Demish nobleborns, it was an orderly, well-appointed town of low villas surrounded by walls. Each house had its own lighting, which waxed and waned with the artificial day, and extended to the streets and parks. Amel had visited the Apron District's brightly colored gardens, pools, and patios to entertain, flirt with maids, and chat up any kitchen staff who could be conned into appeasing his rapacious teenage appetite for Sevolite delicacies. Here, also, had lived the man who taught Amel to hate.

Liege H'Reth was one of the contacts used by Mira's father to smuggle in contraband drugs and bioscience supplies from *TouchGate Hospital*, to help him in his forbidden research on the nature of Sevolites. When Amel decided to take Mira offworld, H'Reth loaned him a ship, saying that Amel could pay him later.

Amel did pay, in the end, but not the first time that H'Reth demanded it.

At ten, Amel—who believed himself the cleverest and boldest of children—lacked the experience to know that it was stupid to resist the inevitable.

After six months in the UnderDocks, Amel was prepared to beg for the patronage that he had rejected. He would have died anyhow, of sheer misery, if H'Reth had not hit upon a scheme to have him trained as a regular courtesan in the hope that Amel could better bear his unwelcome attentions. Before H'Reth dared to do that, however, he blackmailed Mira's father into secretly bonding Amel to him as if he was H'Reth's *gorarelpul*. To begin with, the intent was only to ensure that Amel could not betray H'Reth's homosexuality. It was after Amel became popular with powerful women that H'Reth learned to use him for political purposes.

An intrigue which left Amel in Reetion hands during an attempted invasion was the last of H'Reth's follies.

The visitor probe saved Amel's life when he finally rebelled against the conscience-bond imposed upon him.

But the Reetions did not stop there.

His bright and detailed memories spilled out, a legacy of his unsuspected Golden Demish heritage, and the Reetions were frightened by what they learned. They improvised, and used the visitor probe to exploit his sympathies, inducing him to lead H'Reth and the invaders to their deaths.

Amel survived.

He was good at that. But it had taken a year to recover from the probe experience; a year before the vivid flashbacks, which the Reetion psychiatrist, Lurol, called 'clear dreams', ceased to disable him.

A whole year of being arbitrarily flung into the deepest cesspools of his past was hardly a promising start to his debut as a Pureblood, in his mother's house; but Ev'rel accepted him. She accepted it all, even valued him for what he'd suffered. What she asked in return had not seemed much, compared to where he'd come from, and the unwholesomeness of her own past helped to forge a bond between them.

Then Ameron came to court.

Amel's stare lifted, nervously, toward the Palace, set on top of the Citadel.

The Citadel loomed between the Apron and the docks, like a truncated cone, driven into the hullsteel floor of the plain which it dominated. The higher your residence in the Citadel, the more powerful your place in Sevildom: from Spiral Hall at the bottom, to the Ava's Palace at the top, with the highborn residences of Fountain Court sandwiched between them.

Impenetrable hullsteel separated Spiral Hall and its Palace Plain entrances from the highborn territory above, which was accessed only by a status-layered set of bridges from the docks. This meant Amel could not cross the plain to the Citadel and ascend up through Spiral Hall, but had to retrace his steps. The arrangement had a certain logic in Sevildom's status-bound world view, but Gelion's wiser heads—including Ev'rel's and some Monatese scholars'—found it curious.

The original purpose of the Citadel was one of many puzzles bequeathed to modern Gelacks by the extinct house of Lorel. In foul humors, people said the whole of UnderGelion was a spoiled cast for a new sort of Lorel space station, crashed into the crust of Gelion, and only later colonized.

Personally, Amel did not believe that lodging the docks in stable planetary bedrock could have been accidental.

But whatever the origins of the architecture, to get to the top of the Citadel you couldn't enter through the bottom.

Amel made a conscious effort to stop wool gathering. He felt dangerously untethered, like a weather balloon at the mercy of the elements. He needed his wits about him as he retraced his steps back to his sequestered spacecraft, so that he could arrive again as Pureblood Amel Dem'Vrel.

"Sweet bun? Take one for an Ava's token?"

Amel started at the unexpected solicitation from a food vendor.

It was a perfectly ordinary approach, the seller avoiding all pronouns to evade the problem of not knowing his customer's birth rank.

Amel peered at the commoner out of the recesses of his hood. The man was past middle age and bent, making the lithe Amel twinge in empathy at the evidence of arthritis. All the same, Amel knew he should move on. His face was entirely too well known, and Amel did not want to be recognized down here—by anyone.

The food vendor took a step closer, making Amel's heart rate speed up. "A sticky bun for you, master?" He had decided Amel was a better-off commoner, a safe bet in this vicinity for someone going swordless beneath a cheap, synthetic traveling cloak. To be polite he spoke up a rank as if to a Fractional Sevolite.

Amel thought of buying the unappetizing bun, but hadn't any currency small enough. He began to demur, but while he dithered the old man moved closer to press his case. He had bad teeth, which was ordinary enough among houseless commoners; the smell set off a tiny, bright memory flare of foul mouths. Amel reacted as if stung. His hood fell back.

The old vendor gasped.

The vendor would have dropped his wares if Amel hadn't caught the tray and helped him set it back into its carrier.

"Didn't mean no harm," the vendor pleaded, shaking. "Gotta eat. Didn't mean no harm."

The commoner's panic swept other considerations from Amel's mind. He freed his cloak and swept it around the bowed shoulders, wanting to contain the shaking somehow.

"I won't hurt you," Amel promised, speaking as simply as possible in unranked *rel*-to-*pol* address.

The vendor tried to tear away, stumbled, and spilled his tray of buns, candy sticks, and cards.

Amel stooped to pick them up. And froze.

The cards were pictures of himself, brightly colored and cleverly drawn. They weren't pictures he wanted to look at.

He continued putting the buns and candy sticks back on the tray, as a lump formed in his throat.

On his knees, the old man was making a whining, terrorized sound.

"I'll just—get rid of these, okay?" Amel said, at a loss, the cards clutched in one hand. "You keep the cloak." Somehow, he did not want it back. It ought to cover the lost revenue the prints represented, too.

He backed away from the old man, skipped a step, like a skittish Monatese stallion, spun around and began to run.

The cards were fire in his hand. He ditched them in the first public refuse bin and continued to run flat out, not caring what anyone thought. It was diverting to weave around slower traffic, if nothing more, and his body rewarded him with the release of tension. He opened his flight jacket, confirming by touch that Liege Nersal's dispatch was safe inside. If he ran fast enough, he fancied he could leave behind the looks he attracted, like a *rel*-ship out-racing light.

When he reached the back stairs of the Highborn Docks, where other eyes couldn't follow, he stopped. There he put his head down, hands on thighs, and waited until he could breathe normally once more. There were a lot of stairs between here and the Palace Plain. Now that he wasn't creating a breeze, he was hot. He shed the flight jacket. The shirt beneath offended his nose with fresh and stale body odor. It stuck to him, wet with perspiration. He slung the jacket over a shoulder and walked on.

The two palace errants who stood with crossed swords, statue-like, at the highest level of entry to the Palace Sector, let him through without a second glance. One day he was going to tickle one of them to see if the errant really was human. He might have, by now, if it wasn't so impossible to get to know them well enough to guess how they would react. They belonged to an honor guard, established during the Demish Golden Age, which took its duties ridiculously seriously.

The doors opened directly onto the Flashing Floor.

"Shit," muttered Amel, and did what he always did: closed his eyes and navigated by memory.

Halfway across the floor, something else happened. First he thought it was just a post-flight memory flutter, tossing up those stupid cards.

It began with a flash of color. But it wasn't the cards. This memory was two decades old. In it, his dance partner's body sheath spun past his eyes, interrupting his shock at a floor which had sprung to life and ceased to be merely flat. He knew the move, and knew his sword would not be in position to block. Her blade slashed flesh; the wrongness registering, at the same time, in her face, and his body.

Amel found himself down on one knee, hand spread on a small patch of the Flashing Floor. His fingers gave him something to look at. The watching guards had seen highborns do worse than collapse on the floor before.

That had to be all it was.

Flying too much, and the Flashing Floor.

He took a deep breath and got up.

A Pettylord Demish guard hovered. "Do you need help, Prince Amel?"

"No—yes! Why not?" he screened his eyes with one hand, waving vaguely for the dropped jacket with the other. "I need that."

The Pettylord picked it up and got him across the Flashing Floor without further incident.

Amel said, "Thanks."

"No problem, Immortality," said the Pettylord, slapping him on the back with the ready familiarity which Amel sometimes liked in social inferiors, and sometimes resented as a cheap shot. He wasn't sure which to feel in this instance. He didn't know the man. It wasn't worth following up every inappropriate liberty; in fact it made him feel safer, somehow. If Sevolites did not take him seriously, he might just survive longer.

The Flashing Floor opened onto a gallery of reception halls. Ameron's offices began at the nearer end. At the far end, the Palace Sector stepped down through a succession of connecting rooms to the Plaza on the roof of the Citadel. That was the scenic route to Ameron, from Fountain Court.

The architecture's clean largeness made Amel feel like something that ought to be cleaned up off the marble floor.

He shook it off.

Ameron's anteroom was sprinkled with nobleborn petitioners, hoping the Ava would give them an impromptu interview.

"Pureblood Amel," one whispered, nudging a companion.

"The courtesan?" the other said, and turned to stare, undeterred by Amel making eye contact.

If only, Amel thought sourly, he frightened the people he wanted to, not just pathetic old men selling pornography to fill their stomachs. To command any Sevolite's true respect, though, he would have to wear a sword. He abandoned the staring match as soon as the nobleborn had the decency to at least look somewhat embarrassed.

Three courtesan musicians played, a little listlessly, in a corner. Amel recognized the woman. Her UnderDocks establishment was a favorite of the young Heir Monitum's—Ameron's gift-child to his First Sworn house—whom Amel knew, fondly, as Tatt.

Amel took one of Ev'rel's honor chips from a pocket of his flight jacket and dropped it in the courtesan's flute case.

"Your right hand B string is flat," he told the youngest male musician, who was playing Amel's favorite instrument: the somewhat folksy Gelack tri-lyre, which sounded like a cross between a Reetion guitar and a harp, with a synthesized rhythm line produced by a nervecloth-covered swelling between the stringed wings of the instrument.

"The string is getting tired," said the young man, speaking up. "I would have stopped to tune it, if I thought anyone would notice." He returned Amel's smile with the warmth of hero worship.

The flautist moved deftly between them. "Thank you, Pureblood Amel," she said, the pale purple chip of translucent plastic containing cells of Ev'rel's blood, held up between forefinger and thumb. "Your generosity redeems this visit."

Her name was Vish. She was red-haired, green-eyed, and too well endowed to sword dance. She knew how to dress to look both tasteful and sexual. Amel admired that. He worried, though, about her attachment to Tatt. She came from a den in the UnderDocks.

Vish bowed.

Amel appreciated the sway of her breasts in her moderately loose toga, but only because he instinctively noticed details about women. He took his leave at once and passed unchallenged into Ameron's outer offices.

Busy officials—some lesser Sevolites, some commoner—looked up to smile, or hope for a kind word, or a present. He had his special friends among their ranks, but was careful not to openly acknowledge them. It would only expose them to Charous. The enmity of Ameron's *gorarelpul* was a mounting anxiety, but when he thought of Charous, he pictured, involuntarily, the quick, economical stride with which she walked, with an irritating fixation on the backs of her thighs and trim hips. He wished he could turn that off. He didn't even like Charous!

One of her fellow *gorarelpul* appropriated him now. "Ameron wants to see you at once," he told him.

Ameron confirmed that in person, by appearing on the far side of the office area. Everyone who had been seated rose in a great, gentle murmur of bodies.

The Ava was simply dressed, in white, with the fern crest of Lor'Vrel on his left breast. He looked stormy. It had to be urgent if he couldn't wait for a *gorarelpul* to fetch Amel.

"You are late!" Ameron accused.

The Throne staff sat down again, leaving the two Purebloods facing one another.

"I—" Amel began to answer, confused. Late for what? he wondered.

"Come," the Ava ordered, and disappeared back the way he'd come.

Amel followed, passing between two rows of desks manned by curious civil servants.

Charous was waiting in the inner reception room. Ameron waved her away. Amel avoided eye contact with Charous. Their distrust was mutual, yet she always managed to make him feel as if whatever charge she harbored against him couldn't be wholly refuted, even if he wasn't clear about its nature. If he could imagine her capable of simple, honest emotion, he'd swear she was jealous of the time he spent alone with Ameron.

He was going to pay, somehow, for her being excluded from this interview.

The Ava's famous Blackwood Room was plainly furnished, apart from the ancient mahogany desk it was named for. Ameron kept the desk bare, either to avoid distraction, or to drive himself out of the office often enough to remain balanced. The Ava loved women, horses, and wide open planetary vistas of sweeping power. The latter two he went to the Monatese homeworld to indulge in. The first had contracted to a single focus since he met Ayrium, of the Purple Alliance. Ameron did not use the term—except when it suited him—but Amel considered Ayrium and Ameron to be genuine *cher'stan*: lovers even death could not part, who were destined to find each other again and again in each reincarnation.

Amel took Liege Nersal's dispatch from his flight jacket.

"Erien is at Court," said Ameron.

Amel lowered the hand holding the dispatch.

"What does he know?" demanded Ameron.

"No more than he ever has, unless—"

"Yes?"

"He seems to be have made an impression on Liege Nersal," Amel admitted.

Ameron pounced on that. "How so?"

Amel summarized Erien's success in getting Liege Nersal not to let his patrols exceed Reetion proximity tolerances, ending with, "They work out together, duelling lessons in exchange for learning Erien's Reetion martial arts. That's how Erien got close enough to have an influence."

Ameron sat, brooding, but much calmer. "Erien did make a comment about preventing the Nersallians mounting too close a blockage on Rire." He shifted, frowning. "But duelling lessons? Is Erien good enough to interest Nersal as a fencer?"

"No," Amel reassured the Ava, "but he has an unusual repertoire of moves. Reetions fence, too. For sport."

"Sport!" Ameron snapped, and scowled. "What has Nersal told Erien? Why send him to me without warning, now?"

"Maybe he didn't," Amel realized with a pang, and produced the dispatch once more.

Ameron pricked his finger on the seal to disarm the blood cipher. Charous wouldn't have let him do that if she'd been around. She preferred to use a blood extract, particularly in private where proof of trust was not a factor. She said she feared poison. Amel thought she just liked to win arguments with Ameron.

"Erien comes before me. Discharged," Ameron read Liege Nersal's message aloud, and thwacked the vellum letter down. Leather was always preferred over paper or volatile data stores, because it was once living, and animal.

"At least," said Ameron, "I was meant to be warned."

"I left before Erien," Amel confirmed. "Nersal held him back." The confession was difficult. Ameron was touchier than he had been at their last encounter. His tension showed.

"Why, then, did Erien reach me before you?" Ameron probed. "Did you report to Ev'rel first?"

Amel couldn't falsely implicate Ev'rel in his lateness. Such cover would be too politically charged. He mumbled, "No."

Ameron sighed. "Amel, I am convinced that you would walk through fire for me. But never by the route I choose."

"Liege Nersal wants the Throne Price acknowledged this Swearing," Amel warned, sensing imminent dismissal, and suddenly aware he had not said half of what he must.

"I know that!" the Ava snapped.

"Then why not immediately? Before something else goes wrong!"

Ameron paced. He couldn't seem to think without doing that. Amel decided thinking was a good sign, and kept his mouth shut.

"Nersal wants the Throne Price acknowledged," Ameron repeated, long hands clasped behind his back. "Fine. But he does not want me to acknowledge Rire." He turned back. "Does he know Erien has proclaimed himself Rire's champion?"

"Did he?"

"Most definitely, right here, a little over an hour ago," Ameron frowned.

"What message did Ranar send Erien?"

"I don't know."

"If anyone could tease open a blood cipher and put it back together, you could."

"I didn't think you wanted it read."

"I didn't!" Ameron flared. "Then!" He tossed his head back, rediscovering his honor somewhere overhead. "Ah, Gods, Amel. I don't regret that you respected my seal, in your keeping. But tell me then, simply as opinion since you know them both, did Ranar summon Erien to court?"

"I don't think so."

"Why not?"

"Ranar is a Reetion. He thinks of Erien as a son. By Reetion standards, Erien's too young and coming here is too dangerous."

Ameron accepted the insight like nourishment. It frightened Amel. He was only guessing! Experience had taught him that Ameron would get impatient if he stressed that.

"Not summoned," said Ameron. "So, why did Erien come?"

"He's young, and he's got Vrellish blood," Amel said. He felt that made it obvious. "And he does care about Ranar."

"You are sure about that?"

"As sure as I am about anything to do with Erien. He doesn't like me so he will not open up, but my failure to impress him favorably shouldn't cast long shadows." He pleaded with Ameron's wavering judgment. "There's good cause for a young man, unsure of his parentage, to be ambivalent about me showing up in his life at critical junctures."

"If he despises you for what you've suffered, he is no loss to my court," said Ameron.

"I didn't say he despises me—for that," faltered Amel, both grateful and alarmed.

Ameron had already moved on. "At least I now understand Nersal letting him come. He would respect Erien's wish to champion Ranar's cause, even if the cause is one he will, himself, oppose. He is the soul of *Okal Rel*, is Horth Nersal. So, I must acknowledge the Throne Price. But as my heir? Or a political adversary over the Reetion issue? It can hardly be both. And the wrong choice may cost me my champion."

"You're not going to recognize Rire?" Amel cried. "But you must! I haven't told you what you sent me to *SkyBlue Station* to find out. Ranar is right—I don't think Rire will accept more postponement."

"Accept?" Ameron was acerbic. His brow lifted and his mouth turned down.

Amel struggled with a nebulous cloud-mass of things he understood and couldn't package in a way that made them palatable.

The Ava's 'offended Sevolite' expression dissolved in his usual energetic froth. He tapped the knuckles of one hand in the other palm, stroked his Pureblood-smooth chin with a thumb, and straightened suddenly with a decisive inhalation.

"Rire is not my principal problem right now."

"You won't recognize Rire," Amel guessed, anxiety sinking through his viscera like a stone.

"At the moment it does not look favorable," said Ameron. "H'Us might still be won, if we play the 'equality' language down, but not without his niece's wedding, which hinges—again—on Liege Nersal. Even House Monitum is getting leery. It is unclear that I have done enough to soften the economic blow which the already creeping trade in crystronics and medicines would deal Tessitatt. But Monitum will do what it is told. Vretla Vrel will not. The Vrellish prefer D'Therd's response to the Killing Reach legacy and visitor probe insult: teach them their place and have done with it. Dwelling on the bad logic of that only reinforces every inflammatory slur against Rire, since it is, unfortunately, true that Reetions have no honor in war. If Nersal sides with the Vrellish this Swearing, I'll go down. I am surprised, in fact, that Ev'rel hasn't openly declared her support for the Vrellish point of view. Her own champion is in the Vrellish camp on the Reetion matter, and Liege Vrel is a key vassal of the Avim's Oath."

"I think Ev'rel has a fair idea that actually fighting Rire would not be what Vretla Vrel expects it would be." Amel tried to keep his annoyance to a minimum. Not even Ameron gave Ev'rel due credit for intelligence or the power to keep her vassals under control.

Ameron sensed he was bordering on forbidden terrain, and reverted to his preoccupation with his champion, Liege Nersal. "Does Nersal know Ranar is boy-*sla*?"

Amel's gut squirmed to hear it put like that.

Ranar was under house arrest because Amel had confirmed, to Ameron, the rumor that Ranar was homosexual. This was common knowledge and unextraordinary on Rire. Ameron had not spoken to the Reetion since.

"The Nersallians know homosexuality is a Reetion practice." Amel reshaped Ameron's question, using the Reetion word for homosexual instead of the Gelack slang boy-*sla*. "So Liege Nersal knows that."

"It is one thing knowing it's a 'practice'," Ameron put Amel's euphemism in mincing quotes, "and another to know that you are talking to one."

"Ranar isn't—*sla*," Amel argued, but in Gelack this was tough logic. The *rel* form of *sla—slaka'st*—covered rapists, child abusers, flesh probers, and those who used sex drugs on unwilling partners. The *pol* form, *slaka*, meant victim. These were the only terms applied to homosexual practices. In Gelack there were no words to say, "Ranar is a homosexual, but not a pervert."

Ameron sighed in exasperation. "I will grant that in his own way, that Reetion is as impossible as Horth Nersal. I could not convince him to loudly deny the charge." He paused, recalling something more, and frowned. "You ought to know Ranar's likeness features in the contraband Tatt was investigating, that portrays you as a *slaka* to Reetions."

"Ranar!" Amel's insides chilled. He shook his head, freshly disconcerted. The chill was driven off by anger. "The only thing Ranar ever lusted after was an explanation of fertility manners, or the proper definition of *mekan'stan*! He's a—a cultural anthropologist! Not a *slaka'st*!"

Ameron was seated behind his desk again. He leaned forward. "What is a 'cultural anthropologist' Amel? I mean in terms we understand. He's told me himself of course." He frowned. "Often."

Amel drew a deep breath, let it out, and shrugged. "He likes to study us the way some people admire really complicated Demish poems."

"Mm," said Ameron, "I thought as much." He smiled. "He's a Lorel."

Amel didn't like the joke. House Lorel had been slaughtered on Gelion, the year before Ameron was born. Amel liked Ranar. The Reetion was so ruthlessly decent, and unflappable.

"*Ack*," said Ameron, going to the door to signal the conclusion of the interview. "Erien will just have to stay bottled up with Tatt in Green Hearth until I sort it out."

Amel realized he'd failed to make his principal report. "Don't you want to hear about Rire? You asked me to find out what the Reetions thought."

"And?" said Ameron.

"They think that if you postpone acknowledging them again, you are not serious, and they aren't sure your reasons are—well, honorable."

"Really?" Ameron took this in with delight, then he laughed. "Perhaps we are teaching them something, after all, if they put it like that."

"They didn't exactly, I did—but—"

"Amel, I will take it under advisement, but I have more to worry about now than I did when I asked you to find out what Rire thought. So long as Rire is not a threat they'll have to wait, and so will Ranar.

Still, I may yet present him to the Ava's Oath this Swearing, as Liege of Rire, or whatever he likes that means the same which we can agree upon and the court will grasp."

"But if Liege Nersal did ally himself with Vretla—"

"Then I would no longer be Ava." The possibility clearly left a bad taste in Ameron's mouth. "Use your influence in other quarters if you are concerned by that."

Amel shut up. Ameron held open the door. "I should expect you to use your influence, in fact," Ameron added gruffly, "if Ranar's personal safety is at issue following a Swearing which leaves me Avim, and Ev'rel Ava. Boy-*sla* or not, I like the cursed Reetion."

Ameron clearly didn't want to dwell on anything to do with Ranar. Neither did Amel, suddenly. He went out.

Blessedly, Charous was not around. Amel paid no attention to any of the other staff on the way out of Ameron's offices.

The courtesans were still playing in the anteroom. He avoided eye contact, but green-eyed Vish appeared at his elbow, claiming his attention.

"I fear our patron, Royalblood Ditatt, Heir Monitum, has neglected to collect us," she told him, in spotlessly respectful grammar. "No doubt more pressing business has come up."

"Tatt?" Amel smiled, thinking of the effervescent young Royalblood who had all of his sire, Ameron's, energy. "You mean he forgot." He spoke to her casually, *rel*-to-*pol*, without adding the weight of the seven-degree suffix he was entitled to, nor the one-degree indicated for pronouns which referred to Tatt.

"Just so," she said. "You know him well enough, I see, to understand." She allowed herself enough of a comradely air to respect the spirit of his grammatical choice without presuming a breath farther with her own pronouns. A wise strategy, he thought, imagining the situation from her point of view. Being familiar without trespass was a courtesan art. The green eyes, red hair, and well-filled toga didn't hurt either. His sympathy was engaged as neatly as if he'd been less well-versed in trade secrets. She knew it, too.

"Would Your Immortality, perhaps, be so kind as to stand in as escort to Green Hearth?" she asked. "Once there, I am sure we can cope."

It was a bold request, but expedient for her. If Tatt really had forgotten a promised pick-up, Vish's group was stuck. Amel wondered if Erien's arrival had something to do with Tatt's absence.

"Of course, if Your Immortality is not going our way—" Vish feared she had made a misstep now. Amel couldn't bear that.

"No, no," he said. "I'd be glad to help you out."

She bobbed a bow in his direction. "You are very kind."

Her ensemble fell in by her side and one step back. The older male, who was maybe twenty-one, kept his eager junior partner under wraps. Amel was grateful, although he ordinarily enjoyed feeling like something of a patron saint to courtesans.

"Have you been flying hard?" Vish made polite small talk as Amel pulled his flight jacket back on, conscious of his sweaty smell—all the more so because of the floral-vanilla perfume of his Golden Demish body odor. He considered that particular trait more appropriate for princesses.

"Here and there," he admitted.

"Lilac Hearth will be grateful to have you safely back."

A tingle flushed his skin at this innocent remark. Just how long had he been away from Lilac Hearth? Over a month. The last time he'd came back, he'd seen only Mira and Ameron. He was angry with himself, now, for not also spending time in Lilac Hearth. He had sojourned with the Purple Alliance instead, before going on to *SkyBlue* on Ameron's business. On the other hand, the business he'd been discharging before that had been Ev'rel's. Still, he should not have limited his reporting on it to a dispatch.

"We aren't taking you out of your way, I hope?" Vish asked, again.

"What?" Darting feelings of anxiety pinged in Amel's stomach. "Oh no, not at all. I can't avoid Fountain Court."

That was a peculiar way to put it, he realized, but the awkward silence was mercifully short. Vish filled the social space between them with talk of the pre-Swearing calendar. Amel offered whatever insider knowledge he could. Most of it was too out of date to be any use. She pretended to be grateful anyhow.

I am afraid, Amel finally grasped. That explained the feelings which had been ambushing him since he left Ann on *SkyBlue* Station, to start home.

Eighteen years ago, he had mediated the contract which bloodlessly transferred the title of Ava from Ev'rel to Ameron, in exchange for one child sired by Ameron on Ev'rel. The Throne Price. It was at times like this, when the balance between them was precarious, that he felt most vulnerable.

Both wanted his loyalty. But neither Ameron or Ev'rel wanted him formally sworn.

In Ev'rel's Oath, D'Therd was simply and utterly opposed to Amel. Whether the Golden Demish would accept Amel, or not, was hard to judge. He was a scandal. At the same time, he was more Golden Demish, by virtue of his paternal grandmother, than anyone else at Court except young Princess Luthan, whom the H'Usians made so much of. Politically, Amel suspected Ev'rel wanted him smoothing over the ruffled feathers of the Golden Demish from Demora in backrooms, not up front where he would be too visible. Vretla Vrel, the third pillar of the Avim's Oath, wanted him sworn; but her interest was much, much too personal. She'd been one of his best clients before they found out that he ranked her in blood. Her acceptance, now, would hinge on him child-gifting to her. Once, he'd dared to imagine he could do that safely; but overall the prospect terrified him, exactly because it could seem so seductively reasonable. At the very least it might lead to Vretla and D'Therd crossing swords.

The Ava's Oath commanded, in principle, five of Fountain Court's eight hearths. In practice, Ameron's power base rested on three, just like Ev'rel's, since Lorel and Lor'Vrel were mere vestiges, voting with Monitum. The other two were Demish H'Us, and Vrellish Nersal, and neither of them were ready to share a table at meetings of the Ava's Oath, with Amel. He wasn't even sure the Monatese regent, Tessitatt, would accept him. Her son, Tatt, at least, was a friend.

Amel did better with the younger generation of Fountain Court.

They, however, did not hold much power.

The more Amel brooded on these issues, the less he wanted to be at court at all. Except, there was so much on Gelion that he loved, beginning with Ev'rel and Ameron. The problem was to keep them from doing each other harm.

He could do that. He always had. The ache of tension, developing across his face and the back of his head, was the problem. He had to stop panicking and relax.

Vish was heroically sustaining a one-sided conversation.

Amel brought his mind to focus on her. "I'm sorry. You were saying?"

"It doesn't matter," Vish told him. "We're there now."

The conversation had carried them down from the Ava's offices and across the plaza, which was busily being prepared for the influx of highborns who would conduct copious amounts of business during the Swearing ceremonies.

At its east end, the plaza was cupped by the base of the Palace. To the west, it jutted over the Palace Plain in a huge slab. This was known as the Balcony. It was famous—albeit most often in legend—for highborns who had plummeted from it to the roofs and gardens of the Apron District below. Immediately beneath the plaza lay the eight pie-shaped wedges of Fountain Court, and under Fountain Court the highborn arena known as the Octagon, which was similarly divided. Spiral stairs intersected the wedges, with entrances that led to the plaza.

The tops of the stairs were considered hearth territory. Each hearth guarded and decorated theirs in their own fashion.

Amel and the courtesans stopped before the pavilion over the entrance to Green Hearth, which belonged to House Monitum. Monatese errants in dark green livery acknowledged Amel's presence with their stares, curiosity dominant over professionalism.

The silence was awkward.

"Unless Your Immortality would rather take us down through Lilac Hearth?" Vish ventured, afraid she had erred in guiding their steps straight to her goal.

Amel was disgusted with himself. He was the Sevolite, she was the courtesan. What was he waiting for? Vish to introduce herself to the errants?

"No, no," he assured Vish and focused on the Monatese watch-captain. "I, uh," he double-checked the man's braid to be sure he had the correct declension of pronoun, "I think Tatt—Heir Monitum—is expecting these courtesans."

"That is possible," the Monatese watch-captain allowed, a bit stiffly, Amel thought, as if subversive corruption was equally plausible. Or perhaps, to be fair, he was simply embarrassed. Even people who had acclimatized to Amel's past were freshly challenged by the porn outbreak stirred up by the Reetion question.

Amel began to disengage, telegraphing it with his body language.

"Perhaps if you would come in, to explain it yourself," the errant said quickly, forestalling him, "in case His Highness isn't expecting them?"

Ah, Amel interpreted the watch-captain's demeanor, *or in case Tatt's mother, the regent, doesn't want Tatt to be expecting them.* The insight cleared his irritation. He wasn't the issue. It was Vish and her companions. They were from the UnderDocks. Fountain Court rarely looked beyond West Alcove for its entertainment.

Amel smiled readily, and was gratified to see his diagnosis confirmed in the errant's face. "If you like. Certainly."

CHAPTER IV

THE MONATESE WATCH-CAPTAIN POSTED TO THE PLAZA entrance into Green Hearth looked unimpressed by Erien's appearance, his Nersallian signet, or his claim to be a Monatese ward. The captain was an austere-looking man, with the lined face and graying temples of an old nobleborn. Quite possibly, he had served the household since his early teens, and had known Di Mon, who had been the present regent's uncle.

"Regent Tessitatt is absent from Green Hearth."

"And Heir Monitum?"

The watch-captain merely nodded, as if in requited expectation, and said, "Heir Monitum is on the Octagon." Erien could almost hear him think: here is yet another ill-chosen companion. Erien was equally certain that sober, drunk, or on his deathbed, the watch-captain could never be brought to admit that Tatt's choice of companions might be anything less than exemplary. Tatt was, after all, Monitum's first Royalblood since Di Mon's predecessor.

The watch-captain let Erien pass. He also summoned a second green-liveried man to supervise him on his way down the narrow staircase into the public reception hall of Green Hearth. Here, the very air felt different—not merely because Monatese air filtration technology was superior to most. He smelled—Monitum. Wood, wood oil, leather, earth, age. The antiquity of Earth-bound tradition. The floor was parquet, hardwood worn with a thousand years of feet. On the walls were images of pastoral Earth, or of Monitum painted as pastoral Earth—Erien recognized a view from the great house on Monitum itself. But in the painting the landscape was green, all green, whereas most views of Monitum were marred—to Gelack eyes—by the dusky turquoise of the tenacious native vegetation. Erien had never been to Green Hearth before, yet so familiar were his surroundings that he had the sense that he need merely turn to look out over the bizarrely piebald landscape of Monitum. He need merely turn again to find Di Mon standing in the doorway leading to the family rooms, watching him with that grave, intense regard which was so unsettling and so embracing. The smell was a key which opened a locked door in Erien's mind, the door he had slammed closed shortly after leaving Monitum ten years ago. Behind that door was his last sight of Di Mon, Liege of Monitum, dead on the floor of his study, with his sword lying beside him. Erien had thought that door would never be opened again. It was flying, he told himself. Flying not only left the nerves raw, but the mind. Reetion studies of Amel's visitor probe records suggested that Sevolite memory was not passive. It actively renewed itself after reality skimming. This place, these smells, evoked that memory, which he did not want renewed.

Erien shook himself and continued down the spiral staircase to the Octagon.

The Octagon was the playground of the eight hearths. Sectioned, as was Fountain Court, into eight slices with a central area common to all, it was used for dances, for drama and for other diversions, depending on the inclinations of each house. But one feature common to every hearth's wedge of the Octagon was the practice floor. The Sevolite doctrine of *Okal Rel*, the honorable path through perpetual conflict and struggle, was a doctrine of individual risk and individual gain. Dueling was a means of settling everything from minor insults to house titles. Ranar was of the opinion that it was an elegantly engineered solution to the expression of aggression among Sevolites. Unlike power or projectile weapons, swords threatened no one but the participants. And they had powerful symbolic value, Ranar added, for a people who still retained something of a primitive's belief in symbols.

But for all its deadly intent and symbolic power—or because of it—sword fighting was the sport and living art of Sevildom. When a hearth's liege or champion sparred, their vassals and retainers watched, and not merely because their hearth's profits and well-being depended upon the skill displayed. Good Swords were a pleasure to watch; even Reetion-influenced Erien had learned to see that. And the two sparring on Green Hearth's floor were very good indeed.

One was Tatt, Heir of Monitum, gifted by Ava Ameron to his faithful vassal house through Tessitatt, a Seniorlord Sevolite, and niece of the late Liege, Di Mon. Tatt was Erien's age; they had spent their earliest years in the same nursery. He had become, Erien thought, everything he promised to be: quicksilver with step and blade, with an uncanny ability to recover from over boldness and small carelessnesses, and an almost fearless persistence. The strengths and weaknesses of the little boy with his first sword were still those of the young champion, though the strengths had been refined and the weaknesses much diminished.

But though diminished, the weaknesses were still there. His sparring partner was Dorn Nersal, Horth Nersal's firstborn and acknowledged heir. There might be better duelists in the empire—although Dorn Nersal was still young—but there was no better technician. If ever there were a man able to exploit over-boldness and small carelessnesses, it was Dorn Nersal. As Erien watched, Dorn feinted, exposing himself just slightly; Ditatt attacked; there was a brief flash of blades and Dorn landed a crisp head cut to Ditatt's brown unruly hair. Even with an edgeless practice sword, that would have hurt. But Ditatt's howl was one of outrage. He fairly danced with frustration, pounding his ungloved hand on his thigh. "I fell for that. I can't believe I fell for that."

The Nersallian clapped him on the shoulder. "If it's any comfort to you," he said, his manner affectionate but his grammar properly differenced, Highlord to Royalblood, "you're harder to sucker than you used to be. I'm having to get subtle."

Ditatt landed an ungentle punch on the center of his opponent's protective jacket. "I'll get you for that," he vowed.

But Dorn, who had noticed Erien, raised his bare hand. "A moment," he said, and came towards Erien. "Do you wish to speak to me?" he said, in the inflections of fleet dialect which presumed, despite birth-peerage, that Erien would answer as a junior officer .

Erien realized that his fleet uniform had caused Heir Nersal to misconstrue his purpose. He regretted that, while sparring with Ditatt, Dorn had looked as near to carefree as Erien had ever seen him. Being heir to Horth Nersal would have been a burden to any man, without the certainty that, should his father fall, he would face the challenges of any of the *kinf'stan* who thought themselves his match. Dorn Nersal was not yet thirty, but his eyes were the eyes of an Old Sword.

Erien said, "I have no message. I am not here in any official capacity whatsoever. I am the ward of Monitum, returning to request privilege of abode of the regent or heir of Monitum." He was saved from finishing with, "The liege-admiral has discharged me," by Ditatt's delighted, "Erien!" and an enthusiastic, sweaty embrace which almost dumped them both at the base of the spiral stairs. The errant who had accompanied him down padded back up the stairs, plainly regarding his escort duty as discharged.

"Erien," said the heir of Monitum to the foster brother he had not seen for ten years. "You haven't changed a bit!"

Erien worked some breath back into his lungs. Tatt had a very royal hug. Over Tatt's shoulder he caught Dorn Nersal's slight smile, which did not entirely fade after he met Erien's eyes.

Tatt set Erien at arms' length, without showing any sign of wanting to let him go. "You've come to court to see me sworn?" he said. "Or to swear yourself?"

"To be honest, Tatt, I'm here on Ranar's account. I thought he might need some help."

Dorn's face grew reserved. He was, in addition to being his father's heir, the son of Liege Brylitt of Killing Reach. Liege Brylitt was as conservative as Nersallians came and an advocate of honorable conquest of Rire, although Dorn, by Tatt's account, was more an advocate of live-and-let-live, preferably with two jumps and a reach between. Dorn began to ease away. Tatt let Erien go and looked him up and down. "How strong are you?"

The word he used had only one connotation in Gelack: how strong are you on the duelling floor?

"Do you think it might come to that?" asked Erien.

"Heir Monitum?" An errant was beckoning them from the far side of the spiral staircase, towards the public end of Green Wedge. The view out onto the Octagon floor—the public area—was blocked by a movable screen. Tatt had written Erien lamenting Dorn's insistence on sparring in a closed gym. Tatt was a dedicated sportsman and tournament entrant, shamelessly proud of his skills. But he was Monatese, not Nersallian. He did not have twenty eyes studying him for exploitable weaknesses, most belonging to his own kin.

The errant met Tatt midway and whispered in his ear. Tatt's face lit with excitement. "Lilac Hearth's screen is down. It's D'Therd and D'Lekker. Come on!"

An expression of concern crossed Dorn's face. Ditatt said airily, "There's no harm in looking, is there? And with you and Erien with me, what harm can I possibly come to?" He slid by the movable screen and disappeared. The Monatese errants followed him smartly.

Erien said, "What is it?"

Dorn hesitated a moment, then said, "There's antagonism between Tatt and D'Lekker Dem'Vrel." Another hesitation. "My father says you have a level head. Tatt will need that behind him. D'Lekker is dangerous."

"You're not sparring with him for your sake," Erien realized. "You're practicing for his."

Dorn merely nodded, and pushed aside the screen. Erien, behind him, saw his shoulders tense as he exposed himself when he would have preferred to remain unnoticed. Tatt had a good friend in this man. And why, he wondered peripherally, might it have occurred to Horth Nersal to discuss him, a junior Nersallian officer, with Dorn?

"It isn't that I have doubts about Tatt's ability," Dorn said quietly, as they started across the floor. "He is as good as D'Lekker—in fact, better. But he is too generous an opponent. He would go to meet D'Lekker where D'Lekker is strongest, and not bring D'Lekker to meet him where he, himself, is strongest."

Before them lay the Octagon floor, where duels amongst the highborn were contested, where honor was defended, titles won and lost, and where brave men and women died. Even a wound that was not immediately mortal—and most wounds were not—could prove so, through hemorrhage, sepsis or regeneration gone wrong. Di Mon had been suffering from regenerative cancer when he took his own life.

Though Dorn led quickly, he, like everyone else, walked around the central area of the floor, which was octagon shaped, rough underfoot, and by tradition, earth brown. That was the duelling floor itself. The surrounding area was tiled white, and clear of furniture.

They joined Tatt and were absorbed by a cluster of half a dozen Monatese errants who had managed to combine guarding their charge in possibly hostile territory with spectating. Beyond the spiral staircase, identical in design to the one in Green Hearth, and between twin potted lilac trees, the Dem'Vrel champion, D'Therd, and his younger half-brother, D'Lekker, were sparring. The contrast between that pairing and the one Erien had just been watching was immediate. Dorn's word, generosity, had been an unlikely word, but was a good one, Erien realized. He had seen generosity on Green Wedge. He saw its lack now. D'Lekker seemed to hurl himself against D'Therd, bombardment by blade, muscle, and will. He was, as Dorn said, dangerous, not because of his technique, but because of that will. But D'Therd stood like a fortress, unyielding. He was, after all, lead contender in that elite class of Swords who might beat Liege Nersal, the Ava's Champion. The Throne Champion's son watched him with a quiet intentness, his brow slightly furrowed, as D'Therd retreated quickly before his brother's attack, snapping off parries and ripostes with a fine precision and cracking his tip hard down on D'Lekker's shoulder. D'Lekker did not react, but he turned his back to walk back to his place and D'Therd brought his tip down in a perfectly judged stroke between D'Lekker's shoulder blades.

D'Lekker spun, his body coiling with energy. For a moment, he and his brother looked at each other, D'Lekker's face black with anger, D'Therd's firm, and then D'Therd made the slightest of motions towards their audience, efficiently reminding D'Lekker of their presence.

Erien found that he had a certain sympathy with D'Lekker. He, too, had had a tutor who would not compromise his standards, even in public. D'Lekker looked at them with angry eyes, saw Tatt, held Tatt's eyes a moment with hostility and defiance, and turned back on his brother with savagery. D'Therd met each attack, precisely and with no more violence or energy than it required. He was, Erien thought, the most economical sword he had ever watched. He watched with increasing fascination and an eerie sense that this man, maybe, would understand the principles of the Reetion martial art Erien had made his own, where force was not met with force but yielding and redirection. Horth Nersal had never quite grasped the essence of it. There was no yielding in D'Therd's movements, but as D'Lekker's attacks grew more forceful, D'Therd became calmer, almost detached. Erien understood, now, what Dorn had been saying: Tatt, fighting D'Lekker, would try to meet his speed, force and fury. And Tatt would lose. He remembered the look D'Lekker had given Tatt, and he understood Dorn's worry. There was a grudge there, and Tatt—high-hearted, strong-principled Tatt—was vulnerable. He touched his foster brother lightly on the arm.

"Tatt," he murmured, "let's be gone before they're done."

Tatt frowned, but Dorn, at his side, nodded agreement. Tatt shrugged, and led off briskly, his step not as light as before. Outclassed as D'Lekker had been, it had still been an impressive display.

Erien asked Tatt, "Does Lilac Hearth usually have its screens open?"

Tatt understood the implications of the question; he looked at Erien with respect. "No. It must be because of the Swearing." Ev'rel's champion was flaunting his prowess.

"What is Ev'rel's attitude towards Rire?" Erien asked.

"She has Vretla and Spiral Hall sworn to her," Dorn said.

Vretla was Liege Vrel; Spiral Hall, a mix of highborn and nobleborn Vrellish, many landless. And the nearest unclaimed habitable land were the six Reetion reaches. That the Reetions called them their homes was irrelevant; to acquisitive Sevolites, Reetions were masterless commoners, and commoners were not entitled to land. Their subjugation would be endorsed by *Okal Rel*. In a few words, Dorn had encapsulated Di Mon's, and Ranar's nightmare.

"Spiral Hall couldn't stage an orgy in a courtesan den," Ditatt opined. "Vretla doesn't know what she wants, and even if she did, half of the Red Vrellish would swing one way and the other half the other, on principle."

Dorn smiled slightly, and said to Erien, "He's right, to a point. Vretla's Vrellish are not unlike the *kinf'stan*. Which means," with a certain warning air, "that given the right leadership, and the right inducement, they would be a formidable force. Vretla may not have the political skill, but Ev'rel—consider what Ev'rel has made of the

Knotted Strings. When she was exiled there, they had no economic or military presence beyond their own territory, and were barely able to eke out a subsistence living, with a smattering of nobleborns for flyers. In thirty-five years, she has built up the Dem'Vrel enough to make her Avim, second only to Ameron in the oaths she holds."

"Getting Demora from the Golden Demish was a large part of that," Tatt pointed out as they shouldered through Green Hearth's screens.

"It was a rightful title challenge," Dorn said mildly.

"I never said it wasn't," said Tatt.

Dorn gave him a sideways glance. Tatt harrumphed, and jumped up to catch a step of the spiral staircase from beneath. He looked down at them and said, "But Luthan tells it differently. Princess Luthan Dem H'Us," he added, to Erien. "She's half Demoran." He began to climb the twining steps, hand over hand, body dangling, legs swinging. They watched him around the first turn. Then Dorn turned back to Erien.

"Ev'rel could organize Red Vrel politically," Dorn said. "Whether she could make an effective fighting force of them remains to be seen. And I suspect any such force would disintegrate into a squabble over the division of the spoils. But that would be in the aftermath." A slight pause let Erien appreciate that. "But as to whether she would," said Dorn, "I think that, like Ameron—perhaps even more than Ameron—Ev'rel has taken the trouble to study the Reetions. She does not underestimate them as adversaries. She is a very careful woman, and a meticulous planner. She will not declare herself either way until she is ready."

There was a thud overhead. The stairs vibrated and Tatt's untidy brown head appeared over the edge. Like most structures built by highborns, the stairs lacked banisters. "Are you coming up or am I coming down?" Tatt flaunted a foot over the edge.

Dorn chose to return across the floor to his own hearth, departing with a final, mild, "Try to keep him out of trouble."

Tatt leaned perilously from the stairs to call after him, "Tomorrow! At Luthan's."

Dorn waved in reply, without turning around. The errants straggled back to their own practice, exchanging sportsman's commentary on the bouts they had watched.

Erien started up the stairs. He was halfway up when he heard a sudden, "Oh, no!" and heard Tatt start upwards at a run. The errants escorting them looked up. Erien hastened his step and emerged to see Tatt greeting a red-haired courtesan with outstretched hands, a kiss and a chagrined, "I have horsehair for brains! I forgot all about you, Vish!"

"I know, Heir Monitum," she said, with sweet impertinence, "but Pureblood Amel was kind enough to act as our escort."

He kissed her again, quickly, and turned to Amel, who was standing halfway up the spiral stairs. "Amel, thank you, again, for salvaging my neglected duties." Amel raised a hand in acknowledgment, smiled, and started lightly up the stairs.

As Amel disappeared out of sight, Ditatt murmured to Vish, "You didn't tell Amel anything about our arrangement?"

"Of course not," said the courtesan.

"Good," said Tatt. "Mother's due back any minute—I'll take any responsibility that needs to be taken for you not being set up."

Vish smiled, withholding any comment on the impossibility of a courtesan blaming a highborn for anything.

"You'll be playing before dinner, for Mother and anyone else she brings home, and myself, and Erien. This is my foster brother, Erien," he gestured enthusiastically towards Erien. "Vish and her group are here to play for us." Erien could see Vish reassessing first impressions. Her bow was a little deeper than need be; perhaps she thought, as Tatt's foster brother, he would share Tatt's expansiveness. The other courtesans' faces were bland and polite. Neither Erien, nor they, mentioned having seen each other in the Ava's anteroom.

Tatt swept them towards the family receiving room, exchanging bright banter with Vish, and holding her hand. The male courtesans followed, taking in their surroundings with wary glances. Tatt saw them in, bustled around as they got settled, and left as they began to tune up. He leaned against the door with a "Phew", saw Erien looking at him and said, "It's exhausting, being me."

Not that the fatigue showed. Tatt sprang away from the door immediately and caught Erien by the arm, saying conspiratorially, "Amel and Mother think it's an infatuation. I mean me and Vish. I can't have them thinking it's too much of an infatuation, because then they might decide to interfere, but I can't have them thinking that it's anything else."

He took Erien out the end of the Throat into Green Hearth's Family Hall, opened a door and pulled Erien into a study. Ditatt's own study, by the modest dimensions and utter disorder. A Monatese-style computer with a Reetion crystronics-reader was perched in the middle of the desk, almost concealed by the stacks of disks, chips, documents, bound volumes, maps, discarded shirts, broken blades and other sporting paraphernalia that covered the desk and spilled onto the floor. The bookshelves that lined the room on two sides were similarly cluttered. The third wall was largely occupied by a framed genealogical chart of the Monatese dynasty. Tatt saw Erien looking at it and winced.

"Mother wants to keep my mind on my place in the greater scheme of things." He tucked back some of the debris with a hand, and sat on the edge of the desk. Erien recognized, amongst the chaos, parcels of the hand-written notes he had sent Tatt over the years, concerning the legal system of Rire. Somehow, out of a decidedly unscholarly scion of Monitum, there had arisen a legal reformer, determined that commoners would have the protections that *Okal Rel* allowed them: a legal system which transcended hearth boundaries, and allowed those who could not fight or speak for themselves representation. It was a bold ambition for a young man barely of age, and Tatt pursued it with all his formidable energy.

"Tatt," Erien could not help but say, "how can you work in this shamble?"

Ditatt looked around. "I know where everything is," he said, "and more to the point, nobody else does." He bounced upright, and a small avalanche of odds and ends slid from his desk onto the floor. "Gods, it's good to see you, Erien!"

"So if it's not an infatuation," Erien said, "what is it?"

"Justice ministry business," Ditatt said promptly. "Vish is one of my informants. She keeps me up on what is happening in the UnderDocks. That's why I've arranged these auditions. If she's up here, we'll be able to meet quite legitimately, which'll reduce the risk for her. Not to mention this being my way of thanks. She's great in bed, too, if you're interested."

"Thank you, Tatt, but no." Erien smiled, a little dryly. "I wouldn't like to make you jealous."

"I hadn't thought of that," Ditatt said, cheerfully. "I don't want to overplay it. It's just to keep everyone off track. I've got Amel nicely worried. He doesn't think it's suitable, you see. An UnderDocks courtesan and me. But as long as he thinks it's personal he'll go out of his way not to mention it to Ameron, and if he gets too worried he'll come and sit me down for a talk before he does anything." With one of his mercurial shifts of mood, he slumped suddenly into a disconsolate heap on the floor. "I only wish it weren't necessary." He looked up, plaintively. "Even a couple of months ago, Ameron was supporting me. He let me have Throne errants when I needed them, had his *gorarelpul* giving me information, got me access to the Demish libraries, kept me supplied with Throne honor chips so I could pay my informers, and suddenly *chhh!*" He drew a finger sharply across his throat and let it drop into his lap. "Or not quite *chhh!*, but as good as. Suddenly he decides it's a good idea to slow down, not to push the idea of rights of appeal for commoners and a non-partisan court system this year. Suddenly his errants are busy, the money's dried up, Charous won't talk to me, and Mother and the protocol officers want four hours of my day every day to rehearse for the Swearing. I mean, how difficult is it to give an oath? You just have to remember your name and his name—it's not as though we've used the long form of the Oath of Service for about three hundred years. How confused can I get? There's Ameron," left hand held out, the left being dominant in most Vrellish, "and Ev'rel," right hand out. "And the Throne Price, I suppose, if he's still alive." Tatt sat up slightly. "Now, there's an idea. He's no older than I am. He might be open to new ideas." He slumped again. "It's no use. Ameron needs my oath. Di Mon was his First Sworn, and this Swearing is going to be as close as Swearings can be. So I'm going to lay my head on my block," and did, slumping sideways with outstretched neck, "and swear in as Liege of Monitum. But Monitum doesn't need me. Not me: Tatt. My mother's a much better liege. She even wants to do it. But she's not even Highlord, and I'm Royalblood, and so she's supposedly been marking time all these years. There's support she hasn't been able to give Ameron because she was only a regent. So I'm supposed to stand up and swear and make everything right. All Monitum wants is an android that can say, 'The Council of Privilege recognizes Liege So-and-so', and 'We will take your information under advisement', and about six other appropriate things at appropriate times. Oh, and bleed the blood and fulfill child contracts. Monitum's so locked into tradition that it runs like some kind of machine. And Ameron likes us that way. They're my house," he said moodily, sitting up, "and I'll never let them down. But when I swear as Liege Monitum that machinery will just run me over and crush me. I've got no choice," he said, in a small voice. "Ameron needs me to swear—second sworn after Liege Nersal with not a breath of reluctance or dissent. And the thing I care about—the thing I really care about—will never happen. Erien," he bolted to his feet, and caught Erien's hands, "tell me you'll help me. Please. Tell me you'll make it happen. I could bear it, just about, if I knew someone like you would take over the Justice Ministry. Someone who believes in it as much as I do, but who didn't have any house alliances to claim him."

"I may not have a house alliance," Erien said, gently, after a moment, "but I have loyalties. To Di Mon and Ranar. If Ranar is unacceptable, someone must replace him as liaison between Gelion and Rire, and I am the logical person. I have experience of both cultures, and I am acknowledged as highborn." Tatt drew breath. Erien said, "I think this is what Di Mon intended me for, when he asked Ranar to take me to Rire."

Tatt dropped his hands, clapped Erien's shoulders, and said, "You realize you'll have my support."

Erien smiled at the dignity and the generosity, and at the slight pomposity of Tatt's endorsement. "I do realize, Heir Monitum. And you will have mine."

There was a hard knock at the door. "Heir Monitum?"

"In here."

A tall man in a plain, unbraided brown jacket pushed open the door, and swiftly closed it behind him. He said in a low voice, "There's been a killing down in the UnderDocks, in a courtesan den called Rose Court. It looks like it could be one for us."

The intruder wore nothing to indicate either status or allegiance, but by his green eyes and familiar address to the Monatese heir, Erien knew that he must be Ditatt's half-brother, Branstatt. Branstatt was Tessitatt Monitum's son by Horth Nersal's dead brother, Branst. He was Highlord, but a love child—an accident—born outside Demish marriage or Vrellish contract. His green eyes came from Branst's Nesak mother. Horth Nersal had retroactively gifted him to Monitum, honoring his brother's wishes over the objections of the *kinf'stan*, and Branstatt had remained contentedly at Green Hearth as Tatt's close friend and the captain of his personal guard.

Tatt introduced him to Erien, and Branstatt sketched a travesty of a Nersallian salute by way of greeting. "Good to see you've finally escaped the rigors of the frontiers for the fleshpots of Gelion," Branstatt greeted Erien. Sobering, he added, "We could do with another sword, going down to the UnderDocks."

"Has Mother borrowed my errants again?" Tatt said, in the manner of an offended small boy. He and Branstatt used peerage with each other, which was testament to a close friendship since Tatt ranked his brother one level in blood.

"I've got Marrit and Deyne left, that's all," said Branstatt. "I believe," he added, "that Mother thinks depriving you of errants might keep you out of trouble." By all appearances, he personally relished the thought of trouble. Branstatt was *kinf'stan*, Erien thought, even if he bore a Monatese name.

"Maybe," Ditatt said grimly, "but she's wrong."

"Tatt—" Erien said, worried. The UnderDocks on Gelion had a reputation as a grim and unsavory place.

Tatt turned to him. "Erien, when we go down into the UnderDocks, it's dangerous, yes. But we can leave and the people who live there can't. If we get hurt, we heal. We can fight off infections that kill commoners. And when someone does us wrong, we have swords. When it's commoner against commoner, it's bad enough, but there are Sevolites who go down to the UnderDocks and use commoners—in ways that should have them flayed on Ava's Square." All trace of the merry young swordsman was gone. "*Okal Rel* carries obligations as well as privileges, and I will remind Sevolites of that, if it costs me my life. That is my purpose, as Rire is yours. I offered to help you. Are you going to help me, or not?"

CHAPTER V

AMEL WAS GLAD TO GET OUT OF GREEN HEARTH, until he reached the plaza.

Kandral, Ev'rel's captain of errants, was waiting for him.

The errant captain stood, two lunges deep, into the open space inside the ring of eight pavilions. He was worn to a tough residue of lean muscle and leathery countenance by Ev'rel's wars, but there was no weakness about him. He had lost a tooth, and not being highborn retained his more impressive scars from Dem'Vrellish clan duels. Ev'rel valued Kandral for his absolute loyalty. Amel knew Kandral was cruel, and as much his personal enemy within Lilac Hearth, as Charous was at the Palace.

"Welcome home, Immortality," said Kandral.

"Thank you, captain," Amel replied formally. He always talked down to Kandral, who was Midlord. He enjoyed it.

"Procuring courtesans for Green Hearth?" Kandral smiled, using his grim appearance for effect as much as Amel used his beauty. "Or were you breaking the boys in for Heir Monitum?"

Amel refused to understand the double slur, touching both himself and an old scandal in the history of Green Hearth's liege house. There was no point arguing while they were without an audience to check Kandral's venom. It was pointless, and Kandral knew things which Amel would not want to debate with him, even in private.

Instead, Amel simply side-stepped.

Kandral snatched at his arm. The contact held Amel frozen, like a cold slap of ice water.

"I'd be careful, if I were you," Kandral hissed, resentful. "The Avim did not appreciate a month's desertion, and even you can become a bore. She may yet come to her senses and let D'Therd use you for sword practice. Or throw you out an airlock, like the Nesaks do to worthless commoners."

Kandral's hand touching Amel's upper arm made his ears roar. Adrenaline demanded some reaction, but Amel was afraid of playing into Kandral's hands. Were it simply a contest of agility or strength, he could easily overpower the Midlord. But he wasn't as vicious. Giving Kandral an excuse to defend himself might be a big error. He still wanted, very badly, to break something—preferably the Midlord's face with its fixed, nasty leer.

He was rescued by an unambiguously highborn entrance.

A bolt of dark energy sprang from the top of the Lilac Hearth stairs, scattering Kandral's errants. Kandral faded away like a bad odor.

"There you are, at last!" cried D'Lekker Dem'Vrel, sweeping up his eldest brother in a bear hug.

Amel winced as the hilt of D'Lekker's sword pressed into his back. Ev'rel's younger Dem'Vrellish son was fresh from exercise, still carrying his sheathless sword, and wearing gloves.

"I missed you, Heir Dem'Vrel!" D'Lekker declared, with passion.

"Lek! Beware the Gods!" Amel protested over D'Lekker's shoulder, reluctant to hug back. "Don't give them ideas it might amuse them to play out!"

"Well you *are* Heir Dem'Vrel. Or you should be. You are the Pureblood. And you are older than D'Therd by twenty-seven months!"

"I'd be dead too, if D'Therd believed for twenty seconds that anyone but you could possibly be serious about that. Back off!" Amel wrestled the younger man to an arm's length grip. "What's with you? You'd think I'd time-slipped a century or something. It's only been a month."

"D'Therd," D'Lekker muttered, stepping back. "D'Therd can do no wrong so long as Mother thinks he might beat Horth Nersal." D'Lekker's full mouth flirted with a sneer but could not overcome a fundamentally haunted look. "It was a bad month to be gone."

Amel felt a guilty pang. "I'm sorry. But I'm back now."

D'Lekker weighed the inadequate apology against the pleasure of Amel's presence, a pout thickening on his mouth. He looked right with a sword held carelessly in one hand. It was who he was. If he lacked D'Therd's invincible genius with the weapon, he was still a brilliant swordsman in his own fashion, exuding a creative violence which fascinated, even as it appalled, with its potential for wanton destruction. The carelessness was equally distinctive. D'Lekker lacked tact. In conversation he was too enamored of the sort of cleverness which, Amel guiltily acknowledged, he himself had modeled. Lek blew hot and cold. His exuberance won him hearts today, which petty spite cost him tomorrow. His good looks were untidy and brooding; he was larger than Amel, and bigger boned, without the excessive prettiness of Amel's paternal inheritance.

D'Lekker's scowl slowly dissolved under Amel's concerned attention.

"I've so much to tell you," D'Lekker said, deciding to forgive him suddenly, as he threw an arm around Amel's shoulders. "Come, walk."

"I really ought to—"

"Later! Once you go to Mother, I know she won't let you out again until breakfast. My turn first."

"Is she waiting?" Amel inquired, anxiously. "Does she know that I'm home?"

"Later!" Lek turned back to shout an order to Kandral. "Take the guard below."

"Highness!" Kandral objected. "What if the pavilion should be attacked?"

"I'm armed," D'Lekker scoffed, waving his sword in a grip just beneath the hilt. "Go on."

Kandral obeyed with a requisite hand-to-sword bow.

"As if it ever happens," D'Lekker muttered with a texture of boyish disappointment. "Once in a hundred years perhaps! Those errants hang around up here to keep out hawkers and vagabonds." He turned to other matters before Amel found his emotional balance. "Who were the courtesans?"

"Courte—" Amel's temper flared up. "Who told you that? Hasn't anyone anything better to think about?"

D'Lekker grinned. "Sure, when you're not around. Have you been sleeping with the red-haired woman?"

"If I had," Amel was tart, "it would be none of your business."

"Mother can tell who you've been sleeping with," D'Lekker wrinkled his nose, enjoying Amel's discomfiture, "by smell." He lifted a hand in the precise direction of Gelion Reach's jump, as instinctively well-oriented as any superior pilot. "Through jumps, across reaches—"

Amel was quietly furious. There was nothing to gain and everything to lose by showing it, so he didn't. He acted bored. "Very funny."

"Did you see your tough little Killing Reach nobleborn? Or Ann, the Reetion warrior? I was wondering when they would start missing you. You kept close to home an unusually long stretch, until a month ago. You had a fight with Mother then, didn't you?"

"No. Not particularly."

"Then why were you gone so long? New lover?"

"Actually, I got bored of my regular haunts, so I worked my way through the Nersallian fleet jumping everything that moved until I wore them out, and went to learn some new techniques on Rire. Will that do for excitement? Now if you want to talk, talk. But cut the crap out."

"Are you mad at me?" D'Lekker asked, frowning. He looked nearer to five than twenty-five when he pulled a sulk.

Amel sighed. "I'm not mad at anyone. I'm just—tired."

D'Lekker lifted his chin in the direction of the Balcony, jutting out over the plain below. "Let's go sit on the edge, like we used to do."

Amel inhaled, and held it. He'd found D'Lekker sitting there once, as a child, and had joined him to get his attention. D'Lekker had been thinking about jumping off. They'd had some of their best talks there in the years that followed. It seemed to calm D'Lekker to sit with his feet dangling over the glow of the Apron District, a fatal distance below, or to walk the Balcony's edge with a Sevolite's utter confidence. Like most places you could fall off, there were no safety nets or banisters.

"I'd rather not. Sorry, Lek," Amel demurred, quickly following up with an honest explanation before his sensitive brother could feel slighted. "I've been having a few—dizzy spells."

"Are you sick?" D'Lekker's concern was touching and quite genuine.

Amel shook his head and surprised himself by being honest. "I've felt something like this before. Now and then. Heavily, in the first year after the Reetions went tramping through my head. It'll clear up when I've rested, I'm sure."

"Clear dreams?" D'Lekker sounded awed. "The total recall attacks the Reetions said you'd have?"

"Nothing that definite," said Amel. "I haven't had a clear dream for years. Why would they come back so suddenly? No. It's some post-flight consequence of being over thirty and still flying."

"Amel," D'Lekker gently reminded him, "you're Pureblood."

Amel scowled at him. He was right of course. Amel could not blame commoner aging for his difficulties. It was a sloppy little bit of subconscious denial. The scowl transferred, eerily, to D'Lekker's features, where it looked sinister. "When we go to war with Rire," D'Lekker promised, "whether you want revenge or not—I'll take it. For the visitor probe."

Amel's throat constricted. "Don't say that, D'Lekker. Don't ever kill people for me."

D'Lekker's jaw locked. "It's too late for that."

"Not Tatt!" For the second time in five minutes, Amel's heart reacted with highborn force to a rush of unnecessary adrenaline. He nearly blacked out. D'Lekker pulled him down to sit on a decorative bench, beside him.

"I thought you'd react like that." D'Lekker sat beside Amel, very close.

It couldn't be Tatt, Amel thought. Unless it had happened just now. D'Lekker had come up, off the Octagon, and Tatt had been dressed for fencing when he'd left him, moments earlier—surely there had not been time enough!

"It wasn't Heir Monitum," said D'Lekker. "Not yet, anyhow. Ameron has called him off, so he hasn't been interfering with me quite so much."

"Who—?"

"Liege Tast of Spiral Hall. Killed her in our second close. Her *mekan'st* challenged. I killed him, too. Mother wasn't happy about it. I wasn't happy with Mother!" D'Lekker scowled. "Mother ruled that it wasn't a title challenge, so Tast's heir inherited. She did it to please Liege Vrel, that's all. And to stop me winning anything for my clan! I think I should have had that title. Why not? Spiral Hall's within our sphere of challenge, or could have been, if I'd been clever enough to make it so before I drew. I mean, I understand nobleborns not being allowed to challenge for titles above themselves, but if a Royalblood—"

"You killed Seril Tast? And—" Amel groped unsuccessfully for the name of the Vrellish nobleborn's *mekan'st* and gave up. It was Seril Tast whom he had known. She had been one of his Vrellish clients. That was why D'Lekker took an interest in her, and that was what she had died for.

The visitor probe recordings of Amel's reconstructed memories covered only six hours and twelve minutes of his most traumatic moments. Seril hadn't qualified for inclusion, but D'Lekker had found out on his own. He made a hobby of collecting such details, to razz Amel and irk D'Therd, who was sick to death of what he disparagingly called Amel's 'whoring', as if it was an on-going practice. Perhaps it was. Amel had to admit, he could not seem to get past the experiences of his youth to a future that wasn't defined by them.

Liege Tast didn't appreciate D'Lekker snooping around, but bedding Amel as a courtesan was something Vrellish women were more likely to brag about than flinch over. It was Demish ex-clients who suffered embarrassment.

D'Lekker could not strike sparks off Tast until the Killing Reach smut began penetrating court, about eighteen months ago, when the question of recognizing Rire warmed up. Liege Tast distanced herself from it by calling Amel down for being weak enough to be broken by the Reetions. D'Lekker took exception to that.

Liege Tast's jeering had hurt Amel. She was right, after a fashion, for all that she knew nothing about the visitor probe. Amel could no more have resisted what happened than flesh could deny a sword once it made contact. But he had let it come to that. He could not imagine Seril Tast letting herself be closed up in the probe's white-lined case by concerned-looking Reetions in medical uniforms. She would have died first. It was nonsense, all the same, to claim that she would not have given them her memories, no matter what. It was not a choice he had made. She had no idea what she was talking about.

He did not want her dead for it.

He remembered the way she rolled clear, after making love, and fell asleep all at once.

"Why?" he implored D'Lekker, the thickness which preceded tears beginning, deep down.

"I don't make a fuss about the smut," D'Lekker told him, proudly. "It doesn't bother me anymore. It is flattering, if you think about it properly. People lust for you. Even when they're saying how awful you are, they are thinking about it. Aren't they? If they collect the pictures to burn them, they look at them first."

Amel didn't like this explanation. Had he encouraged Lek to find smut 'flattering' by preaching restraint? The Gods of Rebirth must enjoy watching him try—they made him work it out so often—but no matter how he did, he couldn't seem to stop deserving the worst he could imagine.

"But this wasn't about sex," D'Lekker glowered. "She called you *pol*: a weakling and a coward."

Amel swallowed. His mouth had gone dry.

"You are not *pol*," D'Lekker roared, propelled up by the force of his conviction. "I know you're not!"

I am going to cry, Amel realized, dismally. D'Lekker stood over him, raining down his frightening affection and towering righteousness. Amel blinked in a vain attempt to hold the tears back. Who did he think he was crying for? Not Liege Tast. If she was watching from the limbo of waiting souls, she would tell him to be *rel*, and spit on him.

D'Lekker's face softened. It took on the 'drinking you in' look, which Amel recognized in lovers, and others he could move with the equally important arts of poetry, music, dance or just being there when he was needed. It was a spell that he knew he could cast. When D'Lekker was a child, he'd been content to see it in his eyes as he told him stories, sitting on his bed, or when he lay beside him to dispel the nightmares which Lek would not talk about. It disturbed him now; the milk of a little brother's love curdled by the acid of his own, dark impulse to violence, as the child's body became a man's.

He thought bleakly, *I am so foul.*

"If they knew what I know, about how much you can endure . . ." D'Lekker's large, powerful body sighed down before Amel, a hand braced on the bench beside Amel's thigh. "If they'd seen what I have," D'Lekker's voice fell very low and soft, "with their own eyes."

"What?" Amel coughed the word and swallowed it back. Squirrel-frantic demons of panic scurried in his gut and dove back again into his spine. "What—do you mean by that?"

D'Lekker shot up again, brusque. "I've seen the visitor probe record."

Amel said, "Oh."

D'Lekker planted a foot on the seat beside Amel, jabbing his sword tip with ill temper into the wood of the bench's back. "What does Seril Tast know about Reetion mind probes? Or *sla*-dens? She'd have died from a tenth of what you've suffered. I told her so. I said—"

Amel stood up, to physically move D'Lekker back. He laid a hand on the younger man's shoulder and squeezed, once. It was all the comfort he could bear to offer.

Blessedly, even D'Lekker wasn't too thick to sense that Amel was overwhelmed, and let him walk away.

Amel took the stairs down into Lilac Hearth.

Ev'rel was chatting with Kandral at the base of the stairs.

Seeing her struck a visceral blow. She looked so poised and beautiful. He even caught Ev'rel's distinctive scent, from her favorite toddy of cloves and honey stirred into a heated glass of the Monatese whisky called Turquoise. The toxic grass used to dye and flavor the expensive whiskey imparted a slight olive shade to her skin from heavy, long-term use.

Her long black hair was thick. She wore it bound at the nape of her neck in a golden clasp. At her waist she wore an elegant stiletto. He had never seen her use a sword. Her dress was slit to just above the knee, for ease of movement and, though a dress, owed nothing more to Demish tradition than the stiletto did to Vrellish mores. The dress was glossy, and plain black.

It was a dress she knew he liked.

Electric contact spread through his fingers as he brushed her arm, moving past. "I'll be right back. Give me five minutes."

She cocked an immaculate eyebrow at him. "I may still be available."

He didn't like that. When she acted as if she didn't care what he did, he knew he was in trouble. But he couldn't cope with her right now. Not until the threat of another panic attack subsided.

Kandral materialized at his elbow before he disappeared through a servant's door, into a gallery that led to the hearth's kitchens.

"Leave me alone," Amel threatened.

"Avim Ev'rel is concerned about you," said the errant captain, as if Amel's unprovoked snarling proved that reasonable.

"Touch me again and I'll break your hand," Amel said hotly.

Kandral seemed unimpressed, but let him escape into the commoner back rooms of Lilac Hearth.

It took only a cup of warm herb tea in unthreatening surroundings to calm Amel down, although he did wish Ev'rel kept more women among the staff. He had never been able to befriend the male cooks and waiters of Lilac Hearth, as he did the fat, motherly women in Silver Hearth's kitchens—some of whom had known him as a courtesan sword dancer, begging leftovers, when he was fourteen years old. That reminded him that he had brought home six colored scarves for Princess Luthan's servants, forgotten in the pack he'd left with Mira. It was trivial, except he did not forget even trivial matters. Especially not those he looked forward to, however small and self-indulgent the attendant pleasure.

When Amel emerged from the kitchen, Ev'rel was no longer in the reception hall. A servant told him she had left no message, but had gone to the family rooms at the back of the hearth.

Amel headed there, through the Throat. Identical in structure in every hearth, the Throat was a series of connected chambers stretching from the entrance off Fountain Court, through the reception hall, all the way to the back of the hearth. Family Hall ran perpendicular across the back, reflecting the curve of the back wall unless—as in some hearths—it was squared up with a false wall. He disturbed no one except servants as he passed.

D'Therd and D'Lekker's voices warned him that the last room, called the family lounge, was occupied.

"We settled that on the Octagon," said D'Therd. His voice was deep and hard as rock. "I am coming with you to keep you out of trouble. I don't want you murdered in the Underdocks in some disgusting fashion we can never live down."

"Your concern is touching, as always, Brother," D'Lekker's voice was mercurial. "However it is I, not you, who's doing something to defend House honor."

"Amel's honor!" It was D'Therd's favorite contradiction of terms.

"My honor requires no defending in the UnderDocks," Amel announced himself with rebellious bravado. "I did six months, live, there, when I was ten, and I'm still a living legend."

D'Therd would have hit him, but Amel dodged. The swordsman became livid.

"You! You make jokes! You should be dead of shame, or cleaned in the blood of your denigrators."

"D'Therd," Amel pointed out, "blood is a lousy detergent."

D'Therd grabbed him. He shouldn't have been able to. Amel was disappointed in his reflexes. He tried to break his half-brother's grip, and found himself wrestling. This, he knew from experience, was an error. As a Pureblood, he might have had superior stamina, but both of them were highborn. That wiped out most of the unfair advantage he would have enjoyed over a nobleborn like Kandral. D'Therd was not only larger, but stronger in his arms. He worked out so heavily there was a noticeable lopsidedness in the muscles of his sword arm. A sudden twist sent a wrench of pain shooting up Amel's arm from his elbow.

D'Lekker piled in before they found out how much damage D'Therd wanted to do to Amel. Rather than wrestle with both of them, D'Therd left with a dire warning to D'Lekker not to go to the UnderDocks without him.

D'Lekker helped Amel up. "Are you all right?"

"Yes!" Amel warded off D'Lekker's attentions. He could make a fist. The elbow wasn't happy about moving, but it would.

"Sit down," D'Lekker urged him.

"No; I've got to find Ev'rel."

His half-brother hesitated. "You're mad at me, aren't you? About Seril Tast. I can't do anything that pleases you." He sounded unhappy.

Amel floundered. "I'm very pleased you rescued me just now," he said. D'Lekker was like a child, still. Very physical. Amel tried to dispel the gathering clouds with a light touch.

The touch broke an invisible barrier. D'Lekker hugged him back with an abandon that forced Amel to quell panic. He hated to be pinned, enveloped, held down—

D'Lekker let him go as he tensed up. "You are hurt!"

"No, no—just—it doesn't matter. It's nice to be home," Amel smiled. It was true, despite the elbow. Fortunately, it was his right one. In this regard his Vrellish heritage won out, and he was dominant in his left hand.

"Where are you going with D'Therd, anyhow?" Amel asked.

"On patrol. There've been some run-ins, with Heir Monitum's people, over you."

"Me?"

"Your synthdramas. There are UnderDocks dens catering to the taste with live enactment. Heir Monitum makes a fuss over the courtesans. I confiscate the contraband. It's stepped up while you've been gone. Some of the new animations project you into scenes which were seen only through your eyes, in visitor probe originals. You should see it, it's clever."

Amel swept silky hair off his forehead. "I did it once," he declined. "That was adequate."

"Better, then, that I take care of it," D'Lekker agreed, and took his leave.

Amel suffered a guilty pang. "Lek!"

D'Lekker turned back at the door.

"Be careful?"

The twenty-five-year-old child grinned, and bobbed a bow. Then he was gone.

D'Therd did not deserve his honorable reputation, Amel thought sourly, as he tested his elbow. If Amel was supposedly so beneath contempt, why bother to bully him? Spite quickly palled, though. He couldn't help appreciating that D'Therd must be tense, with Liege Nersal due back at court for the Swearing. All Scvildom seemed convinced that the two champions would face each other. Amel could summarize his last eighteen years as a campaign to prevent just that. There was nothing particularly nasty about D'Therd. He just wanted what all Sevildom wanted. And he had no use for cripples. Particularly ones who messed up Dem'Vrel's brand new respectability, and who had influence with Ev'rel despite that.

Amel flexed the elbow again, and let the spite go.

D'Therd was just D'Therd. He had to find Ev'rel. Now.

He tried the luxurious, walk-in bath, and found a servant putting out towels. That made Amel suspect he would find Ev'rel in his own bedroom, waiting for him to change into his bathrobe.

The door to his room was locked, but that didn't mean she could not be inside, waiting for him. Ev'rel had the access code. It was everyone else he locked out, self-conscious of the musical instruments, half-constructed poems, unmade bed, and dancing togs tossed in a salad of unfinished projects around the edges of a bare, cleared dance floor. It was here that he danced for Ev'rel.

She made him feel proud of his body as an instrument of his art, watching with a critic's appreciation, and goading him as ruthlessly as any courtesan dance master. Here, she valued what he valued in himself, that which would not fit the Sevolite mold—with one exception: they never made love in his bedroom.

Ev'rel was a complex client.

The room had been tidied. It was something she did when he was gone for too long. All that was out of place was a piece of writing paper, crumpled, and unfolded again, and left lying on top of his mattress.

Amel picked the abused bit of paper up.

It was a poem which had intoxicated him, over a year ago, with the notion he was going to write something immortal. Poetry was a courtesan art which he had once believed he had as great a talent for as dance, but he knew now he was only a technician in the heroic forms, solving language puzzles the way he solved algorithms. Where he succeeded best was with humor. The unfinished poem was as close as he had ever come to challenging the greats of the Demish Golden Age, rather than mocking or copying them. It was written in a technically formidable style, dating from a time when poetry was respectable for Demish princes and princesses. Patterns of inflection and sound repetition invoked a second poem, from stressed words, in counterpoint to the first's meaning. On the page, it was a grueling description of a soul-consuming flight, redeemed by brutal details from a tendency to melodrama. Spoken aloud, space and time became a lover—cold and empty, infinitely deep. The poem spanned seven interlocking stanzas. The form required eight. Amel couldn't finish it.

The paper, crushed and smoothed out again with care, left him with no doubt that Ev'rel had put it there on purpose, as proof of her displeasure.

I should never have written the thing down, Amel decided. That was the error. He had it in his head, still. He would never get rid of it! He suspected, now, that he had written it down exactly because he knew she just might find it one day, combing through his things when she was missing him. That was stupid, and a little cruel of him, wasn't it? He gnawed his lower lip as he thought.

He crumpled the page up again, impatient with their childishness. She hadn't cleaned his room today. If he had left it for her to find, she had likewise left the evidence of her reaction on his bed, for him to discover.

He threw the crumpled page away and went to seek her in her private office.

"Ev'rel?" he inquired of the dark as he stepped inside.

There was no answer.

He turned the lights on.

Nothing here was out of order. Recent envoy reports were filed, by priority, in an uncluttered in-basket. Contracts and inventories were out of sight in archives, their content scanned into Reetion crystronic storage, which he had integrated for her with the nervecloth technology of Monitum: her preferred interface medium, learned in childhood. Her desk reminded him, in fact, of the late liege of Monitum, whom she had called Di Mon, like a member of his family. She had learned statesmanship from Di Mon. Her father's household taught her other lessons, petting and spoiling her in small things, while her father violated her childhood bed, and her adult half-brother, Delm, played every nasty, envious trick he knew how.

When Ev'rel let Amel into her childhood world, he saw his own. He, too, had lived a dual life, comfortable enough in West Alcove, but vulnerable to a summons from the Apron District. He, too, had known pride, and the struggle to justify how every support for it could be pulled out from under you behind closed doors. He had even passed through a numb phase, like the coldness Ev'rel wore like armor. That was why H'Reth had sent him to West Alcove. He owed his reconstructed life to the philosophy of high class courtesans.

Ev'rel had built hers subduing the Dem'Vrellish Reaches. It made her cruel.

After she had achieved power, Di Mon's statecraft came to the fore. She appointed governors for competence, whenever possible, and hammered like a patient blacksmith on the resisting metal of poor soil, ignorance, and long stretches of space that had to be traversed between habitable lands. In all this, she was hampered by the low blood of her subject Sevolites.

The houses which became Dem'Vrel were, at best, nobleborn. It took highborns to knit together the far flung Knotted Strings, and establish court alliances. Ev'rel did not want more children. Having helped her through the Throne Price's gestation, Amel knew that she experienced pregnancy as a parasitic trespass. She demanded the Throne Price of Ameron, in spite of that.

She had to. Amel would not child-gift for her.

In the beginning, it was for the sake of his friends, Perry D'Aur and Ayrium, of the Purple Alliance. There was rivalry between them and the Dem'Vrel: competition for a place in the economics of the empire and for possession of Golden Demish Demora, taken from Ayrium's father, Prince D'Ander, by D'Therd's sword. Amel had been in the thick of that, still probe-stunned, and barely able to grasp that Prince D'Ander meant to make him Ava. D'Ander did it for his own reasons, of course, in which Amel's mental incompetence did not factor. He might have won, too. The event was D'Therd's first major duel; D'Ander had a twenty-five-year-old daughter and a *rel* reputation. But D'Ander died and lost Demora. It was a blow to his allies in the Purple Alliance; and it was hard not to have liked D'Ander, despite his ambitions. Amel felt vaguely responsible. When Ev'rel demanded him, he went willingly, but promised that he would not child-gift for Ev'rel.

The clear dreams were very bad, then. It got worse when Amel found Mira working for Ev'rel, as her medic. Things got very confused. Dark. And personal.

Then there was Ameron. If Amel child-gifted for Ev'rel, he would force Ameron into a breeding war to buy allies. Amel believed in Ameron's *cher'stan* bond to Ayrium. He also understood Ameron's political reluctance, due to the complex challenge rights and prejudices of the houses which supported him. Chief among those prejudices was Ameron's distrust of his own Lorel blood, turned loose in quarters where a child's ambition might recoil on him. The Dem'Vrel would have taken the gift of Amel's blood, to sire them highborns, and damn the fuss about his past, or whether his blood was more Vrellish, Demish or Lorel. They were already, proudly, mongrel. And they needed highborns. The Vrellish were a little fussier, but Vretla Vrel, herself, was ready to accept Amel despite his Demish blood, and would probably share him with Spiral Hall when she was sated.

Child-gifting would have made Ev'rel secure.

He did not do it.

Not then, and not now.

He was afraid to.

At times like this, his help from the sidelines, his flying, his information systems, even his love, felt very little to give in compensation.

He needed to see Ev'rel now, instead of dreading it. He needed to know that what he could give was still enough.

Ev'rel's bedroom was his next stop. The walls were hung with red and gold draperies, worked with patterns which suggested swimming bodies. Her wardrobe, vanity, and four-post bed were ancient rosewood. His tri-lyre sat where he'd left it a month ago.

He checked the adjoining bathroom. No.

That left her workshop.

The workshop was a self-contained slice off the boudoir. It had a sleek, padded floor; a bar stocked with Turquoise whiskey, honey and cloves; and a console for programming the nervecloth that lined its ceiling and walls. The mimicry of a pilot's cockpit was unmistakable, but Ev'rel's preference was for art, not navigation.

She had done a wallpaper piece on the forests of Monitum which Amel could lie and watch for hours. Unlike the real thing, it lacked stinging insects and it never rained on you. They would look at it, staring up from the workshop's comfortable floor, and talk about the day's experiences: she with a heartless insight which made him laugh despite his more generous impulses.

It was not that he disagreed with her about people. He just wanted to believe their excuses, rather than judge them by their behavior. The Reetions had overcome their supposedly paramount morals to save themselves by using him against H'Reth, but they regretted the necessity—or so they said. His Purple Alliance friends had been forced to surrender him to Ev'rel—so he volunteered. It made a better story like that. The less he asked of people, the better the odds that they would not show him truths he couldn't bear.

It reassured him to be useful to Ev'rel. Ameron used him, too, in his own fashion, but Amel wasn't indispensable there. He was not even important. Ameron was a bright, clean sky, to which he could turn his face, but could never climb up and touch.

The workshop was Ev'rel's inner sanctum. It was also where they made love.

He was disturbed by the addition of a drop-down bar lock on the outside of the workshop door. That the room was lockable from the inside, he knew, because he'd made it so. It was soundproofed also. She liked to edit clips of him performing erotic dances, set to loud music. They both considered his dancing private. He did not see why a bar on the outside should be necessary. It gave him a queasy feeling.

The door was ajar. He could see just enough to know that the walls were active.

Amel frowned.

He had to challenge Ev'rel about the outside bar. Maybe she had a reasonable explanation. He would do it now.

What he saw on the walls when he slipped through the door made him forget the bar.

It was Mira. Captured in the display wall.

Ev'rel rose from her console, picking up a drink. It smelled of cloves. Her sleeve fell away from her smooth, olive forearm.

"What took you so long?" she said.

Her scent went straight to his groin to invoke a telltale flush, but his eyes stayed on the display wall.

"What is—that?" he accused, with a stabbing arm.

She turned around, her hair loose and swept over one shoulder. She had taken out the gold clasp. "Mira," she answered him, blandly, "when she was twelve years old."

Amel swallowed around a hot, thick lump. The images were based on his visitor probe record. His memories, however, did not include seeing himself from a third person perspective. On the wall, he and Mira stood in the lobby of *TouchGate Hospital Station,* on the brink of her career in medicine.

"Remarkable, isn't it?" said Ev'rel. "I am trying to determine how it was done."

On the wall, Mira was a bird-fragile child, quick and sharp. She was talking to a worship-struck, beautiful, ten-year-old boy, cocky as all get out, and not about to be shown up.

"Are you sure you can find the next payment?" the child Mira asked. "You can't go back to Father, you know that!"

"Even commoner pilots are valuable, Mira. I'll make enough. We can be together between jobs."

She frowned. "Medic training is very intensive. I don't know how much time I'll have."

"Well," he shrugged, studiously nonchalant, "when we're both free, of course."

Amel shoved past Ev'rel to turn the pictures off.

"Who put me in the picture?" he demanded.

"I don't know," she said. "Reetions? Or some Killing Reach enterprise?"

He set the heels of both hands to his face above his eyebrows, pressing hard. His elbow twinged.

"It is remarkable artistry," said Ev'rel. "They had nothing to go on but pictures of your sixteen-year-old self, your sense of body in space and tactile data, tone of voice, and glimpses you saw of your own hands, feet, and other body parts from an owner's perspective but—"

"I don't care how it was done!" he cried, and threw out his arms.

Ev'rel watched with an air which made him feel he was throwing a tantrum. When that penetrated and he calmed down, she quietly turned the show back on.

"Are you sure you are going to be all right?" Mira asked, with just a touch of concern marring her smooth brow.

Oh, please, Amel thought, *not this*. His ten-year-old self was about to launch into an incredibly stupid string of boasts about having it all under control. He was really headed for that six months in the UnderDocks which cured him of his idiot self-confidence.

The images winked off. Amel's body was clenched. He had to will his muscles to relax.

Ev'rel touched his leather-clad arm. "It's seeing Mira," she said. "You took her death very hard."

Amel succeeded in loosening his hands and jaw. He summoned dancer's body lore to gentle his long muscles. The flutters in his stomach died down.

Ev'rel dropped her hand. "I regretted telling you about her death," she sighed. "I thought I'd never get you out of the UnderDocks, hunting her life down, as if you could bring her back by finishing everything she had left undone. I had nothing to do with her accident," she concluded, emphatic, and paused. "You do believe that?"

He nodded.

"Good," said Ev'rel, relieved, and smiled. "This would be an unfortunate time for you to doubt I have kept my side of our bargain. Mira left us. I did not pursue her afterward."

He looked toward the ceiling. Ev'rel had it casting a warm summer's day. He experienced it in a sensory gulp, but remained conscious of her as she folded her arms and leaned back against her console.

"So," she moved on, "let's discuss your trip. What was it this time that kept you away so long? Ameron's business? Or one of your women? Perry D'Aur I hope. At least she is Gelack. You cannot appreciate how awkward it is for me to explain that the Reetion station commander is your *lyka*, let alone admitting that you are more nearly the *lyka* and she the *lyka'st*. The only sense Liege Vrel sees in it is if I am using you as a spy. And she is not sure that would be honorable. But with a month to reflect on it, I find I am forced to D'Therd's conclusion. You are more likely to be the spy in my household, for Ameron."

He broke eye contact with the ceiling.

"Done?" he asked, curtly.

"For now." She was cool again.

"I think," he said, "I'll take a bath. Thanks for having the servants set it up."

He stayed angry all the way back to the walk-in bath, but it wore off as he stripped out of his flight leathers.

Of course Ev'rel was tense. This was the Swearing that could make her Ava. Vretla Vrel was pressuring her to retaliate against what she considered Rire's offenses, and D'Therd was openly eager to acquire Rire for Dem'Vrel. Nersallians liked to acquire land themselves, and the H'Usian Demish wanted to sustain isolation. So there were cracks, over Rire, in Ameron's supporters. It was conceivable that Ameron would end up with nothing but Monitum. Ev'rel smelled blood. It both frightened and excited her. She had never intended to be, forever, Avim. It was simply safer, eighteen years ago, to put off her ambition to be Ava.

Amel relaxed as he gave his body up to the bath's attentions. The hot, swirling water was wonderful. It sucked away the ache of D'Therd's job on his elbow. He took shampoo from the servant, scrubbed, and dunked to clean the soap out, rearing out of the water with a blissful 'ah' of satisfaction. There were some awfully nice things about being highborn.

"Is there anything else I can get you, Immortality?" the bath attendant asked.

"No, thanks," said Amel.

The attendant was male, of course. Ev'rel dismissed female staff who paid attention to him, whether it was a pretty young maid or an aging cook. He went out of his way to find them new positions, and ignored them henceforth, for fear of Ev'rel taking notice. The whole thing was one of their sillier wrangles, and he was almost glad it had exhausted itself, after eighteen years, by denuding Lilac Hearth of female servants.

"Please go?" Amel suggested to the servant, reluctant to get out, naked. Just feeling self-conscious stirred a petty, pointless violence in him. Sometimes he dreamed of beating up a hovering male servant, which horrified him. When reduced to bloody pulp, his victim would sometimes have H'Reth's face—but sometimes he became one of the children, less enduring than himself, who had died as he watched in the UnderDocks, during that terrible six months.

Amel closed his eyes and lay, submerged, on a shallow ledge. The hot water sloshed in his ears. His dark hair spread out. He could still hear well enough to know that the door opened, and closed. He thought it was the servant going out.

When he heard something clank, he sat up.

Ev'rel was in the steamy room. The clank was her stiletto dropping on a bath-side table. She was taking her shoes off.

He waded over as she hitched up her dress to sit on the top step.

She stretched out a foot as he approached. He took it, and began massaging it.

"No courtesan," she said, "can ever have a Pureblood's strength in his hands."

He smiled to himself. She could hardly know. She never used courtesans. But he liked the work. Her foot and ankle were fine things all on their own, quite worthy of all his attention. He moved his self-awareness into the shape and texture beneath his hands, ignoring little grumbles of complaint from his right elbow. The reward her flesh gave back drew his hands up her calf by recklessly unregulated inclination.

She said bleakly, "I have missed you."

He felt whimsical. "Come into the water."

"In my clothes?"

"It's only water."

She hesitated. He held her uncertain stare. At last she laughed. "You're mad, you know," she said, and joined him.

He put his hands on her, guiding her down though it was wholly unnecessary. His body wanted hers with its own animal logic, struggling through a backlog of confused associations.

She tensed as his hands moved strongly over her breasts and thighs in the swirling embrace of the bath. That was a warning, but he felt drunk. He nuzzled her soft hair and mouthed her throat.

Pain really shouldn't have surprised him.

She didn't release his scrotum at once, but continued to handle him, just hard enough to douse his ardor.

He spoke through his teeth, roughly. "Don't."

She released him with a reproachful look, and waded out of the bath to sit, numb and wet, with her feet once more in shallow water, staring across the room at a wall of false marble.

He came to sit with his back to her, one step lower.

Neither spoke.

After forty seconds she said, slowly, "Why did you do that?"

He sighed. "I don't know. I'm not thinking very well today. I just react."

Ev'rel turned around. He shivered slightly as she touched his back. He stirred the water with a foot, in silence, for three seconds, then he volunteered, "Lek told me about Seril Trast."

"Ah, that." She felt down his spine, her range slowly spreading out to trace the definition of his muscles. He kept as still as he could, his nerves brittle. "It caused a ruckus in Spiral Court," she remarked. "I cannot have that. I need Vretla Vrel's support."

"And D'Therd's?" he asked.

"Of course," she said, and shifted, settling back to back against him.

"I think," said Amel, feeling her skin against his, her warmth and their wetness. At the same time his extremities began to dry and cool off. He repressed a shiver. "I think," he began again, "D'Lekker may be worried that he and the Lekker clan aren't as important to you. That you are wondering whether you need them."

She said, blandly, "It's possible."

Amel pivoted around. "Then you don't?" he accused.

She smiled. "D'Lekker worries, Amel. It's in his nature. He's obsessive. Do you know, I've had to lock him out of my workroom? He's supposed to be removing your synthdramas from circulation but I caught him trying to add my dance clips to his own collection."

Amel was relieved about the explanation for the lock. He said, unhappily, "I wish he wouldn't."

"If he got them, he'd use them to get at D'Therd somehow. I can't have that, particularly not now. I've warned him to stop being childish. That, and a padlocked bar, ought to be enough. But now that you're back, maybe you can set up something better."

He turned toward her. "Ev'rel?"

She was caught by his disturbed expression. "What is it?"

"I don't spy on you. I don't spy on anyone. At least, I don't want to. I just—am. I can't be what I'm not. For you. For Ameron. For anyone. I don't care what D'Therd believes, but you can't believe it's more than that. You know it's not."

She stroked his face, cupping his jaw with her hand, and leaned deliberately into a deep kiss to which, he knew, he was not supposed to respond.

"I read your poem," she said.

"I didn't finish it because it was wrong," he insisted.

"No," she said. "You did not like the ending."

"It doesn't have one."

She got up, collected her things, and said, in parting, "We have to talk."

He sat in the steamy room for ten long minutes after she was gone. Then he sprang up and pulled on a dressing gown.

When he caught up with Ev'rel she was standing in Family Hall, fully dressed, reading a message delivered by a servant.

The servant cast an uncomfortable glance at Amel.

"For Your Immortality," the servant said, sounding strained, "from the Princess Luthan Dem H'Us. It just arrived." Amel smiled to let the young man know he had done nothing he would suffer for by yielding it to Ev'rel. The servant was new. This was an old quarrel. Ev'rel opened everything addressed to him which didn't have a blood seal on it. She would have opened those, too, if she could.

"Princess Luthan Dem H'Us invites you to 'the special event we've discussed often'," Ev'rel read aloud, and looked up. "What is that?"

"Nothing." Amel felt protective toward Luthan, and cross with Ev'rel—who had so much more personal freedom—for prying into what the Demish girl considered private. "It's just Luthan calling in a promise. I told her I'd play for a little gathering she planned for Dorn Nersal, if I was at court when she held it, of course."

"You should go." Ev'rel extended the invitation to him. "I have decided that I approve of Admiral H'Us's little, infatuated grand-niece. If, that is, you could charm the Admiral a tenth as much as you do the ladies of Silver Hearth."

He put the invitation in a pocket of his dressing gown. "I don't think I should go. The way I've been acting, I'd only put my foot in it, even with Luthan."

Ev'rel smiled. "I've often wondered what you find to talk about with a Demish virgin."

"There are other topics."

"I wonder," mused Ev'rel. "Perhaps I should one-up Ameron's offer to H'Us, of Heir Nersal?"

"One-up?"

"You are Pureblood. And Princess Luthan is fond of you, is she not?"

He felt absurd: flattered, shocked, embarrassed on both his own and Luthan's account. But marriage? Demish marriage. Luthan had very high standards concerning that, aside from the politics. "I couldn't do that to her!" Amel blurted.

"Don't panic." Ev'rel was cool. "H'Us wouldn't have you in the family."

Ev'rel headed for her office, down Family Hall. Amel followed. It wasn't until they were inside, and she turned to look at him with a raised eyebrow, that he realized he was still wearing nothing but his dressing gown.

"You've hurt your elbow," she observed, in a sleek tone.

His composure shattered. He raised his left hand to the stiffening joint as his heart rate climbed swiftly.

"You've been carrying it awkwardly," she explained, "for you, that is. It's barely noticeable. Except to me."

He lowered his left hand to his side, a sculpture in ambiguous emotion.

"Let me have a look." She came forward.

The smell of cloves and Turquoise resin penetrated to his spine with sexual messages. "It's trivial," he murmured.

When her fingers touched his arm, he pulled back. "Don't."

She withdrew with a sudden frown. "Despite what you might like to think, the most attractive thing about you, at the moment, is your encyclopedic grasp of Demoran protocols and Dem'Vrellish tax accounts. You are a vain creature," she concluded, "in your own fashion." She plucked a filed dispatch from its rack. "I've been keeping this aside for you. You negotiated the terms, and as usual did not record all that was talked about."

She slapped the document into his raised hand.

"I am certain they are cheating us," she told him. "Write the response that proves you know, and why it is ill-advised, or I will send Kandral instead, with a hand of fighter pilots."

Amel nodded.

"Then you can brief the chief herald on Demoran protocol, and introduce him to Princess Chandra, whom we have here to swear the Demoran oath. When and if I insult her, it should not be out of ignorance."

"I can do that," he promised.

"See me again when you are done. We do need to talk. Oh," she nodded to indicate his dressing gown, "before you see Princess Chandra, do put on some clothes."

The door opened behind him as he inhaled to respond. He spun. It was only the herald. The dignified older man bowed. He was carrying a suit of dark blue silk. Silk was a Vrellish product. Ev'rel bought a lot. It would do for the work at hand.

Amel took the suit.

"I will wait outside, Immortality," the servant excused himself. Amel was grateful for the small mercy.

Ev'rel got on with her work. Amel hesitated long enough to feel foolish, then donned the clothes, picked up the dispatch he'd put down, and left to do his chores.

Princess Chandra was insufferably superior. The tax accounts were, indeed, altered. By the time he was finished with both, and half a dozen little matters which inevitably arose after a month's absence, the household was winding down for Lights Out.

He found Ev'rel at her vanity in her bedroom, having her hair brushed. She dismissed the servant when Amel turned up. The servant bowed himself swiftly out.

Amel crossed the floor to her, feeling luxuriously tired. There were a few little things he wanted to share with Ev'rel about the tax problem and Princess Chandra. He was looking forward to bed after that, with clean sheets, on clean skin, in a warm room.

Ev'rel wore an embroidered silk dressing gown, rendered in Monatese greens on black. She looked stunning.

"Sit down," she said, taking the letter he'd written concerning the Dem'Vrellish tax fraud.

Amel moved his tri-lyre off its stool. Doing so, he discovered a card. It was a picture card, like those he had taken from the bun vendor.

Ev'rel finished the letter, and put it on her vanity. "Very good," she said, "I'll sign that. Tomorrow is early enough for dispatch."

The card spoiled Amel's mood.

"That's the latest manifestation," said Ev'rel. "You should take a look."

"I've seen them," he said, all the delicious relaxation gone. He did not sit down.

Ev'rel said, "Come and braid my hair."

He slid into position behind her and picked up the brush. He liked doing this. Her hair was thick. It left a herbal smell on his hands from the shampoo she favored.

"The pictures on the cards feature Rire," said Ev'rel, watching his face in her mirror. "Torture. Rape. Yes, I know," she read his expression in her mirror, "you don't want to think about it."

"I can cope with it," he told her, selecting hanks to braid.

"Yes," she said, "but can Ameron?"

Amel's hands stopped. She turned, took his hands down from her hair, and guided him to the upholstered stool. He perched on one end to avoid the card. Ev'rel moved it to the top of her vanity, letting him glimpse himself tied into a whipping frame bedecked with exotic paraphernalia.

"Where did you get it?" he asked Ev'rel.

"D'Lekker confiscates them in the UnderDocks."

"You should not encourage him!" Amel erupted in ill-humor, standing up. "You know he will run into Tatt!" He paused, wrestling with suspicions he could not hold back. "You want them to fight, don't you? It would polarize opinion as effectively as D'Therd going up against Liege Nersal, but it's cheaper. You don't have to risk your champion."

"Ameron has called young Heir Monitum off," Ev'rel pointed out.

"That won't keep Tatt out of the UnderDocks!" Amel was angry. It was utterly useless to be angry, but it was better than revealing the fear he felt building up inside.

Ev'rel rose also, leaving her hair loose.

"I cannot control D'Lekker," she answered his wild speculations. "I cannot control D'Therd. Not entirely. No more, I suppose, than Ameron can control Heir Monitum. But—" She paused, considering him like a puzzle with a missing piece.

"What?"

She debated strategy with herself. He recognized the symptoms of impatience in her. As she made up her mind, her mouth became hard. "There is something that I want you to think about."

He nodded, wary.

She paused to weigh her words before she continued. He waited.

At last she said, "Attacking Rire will be a disaster. You know that?"

He nodded.

"We would conquer in space," Ev'rel went on, "but Reetions are not Gelack commoners. They will quickly do things that offend *Okal Rel*, to resist us."

"Reetions are self-governing people," Amel spoke for Ann, who was not there. "They don't believe in *Okal Rel*." His face labored with his puzzlement. "They don't seem to believe in anything."

"Why should they believe in *Okal Rel*?" Ev'rel scoffed. "Do you? I certainly do not believe I will come back stronger if I consent to stake all on the outcome of a duel. Swords!" she complained with disgust. "They would be worthless if fleets did not back them up."

"If it was just about fleets," said Amel, "we'd be fighting in space all the time, threatening the precious things we fought over. The Monatese say we have done just that, when *Okal Rel* has broken down in the past. They say that's how Earth was lost. Isn't that too awful to imagine? I know you resent needing to act through a champion. I know Ann doesn't understand Gelack honor. But *Okal Rel* isn't all bad. It's about—limits. About valuing something more than winning. I can admire that."

"But Ann does not understand," Ev'rel echoed his own words back.

Amel frowned. He had had this argument already. With Ann. From another perspective. He had lost that one.

Ev'rel took his silence as her answer.

"So, if the Avim's Oath must have its war," Ev'rel cut to the root of the matter, "I suppose I must hope that the Sevildom which emerges from *Okal Rel's* collapse will be more willing to be led by me, than by Ameron. I think the odds are good."

Fear shot free up Amel's spine.

"The Reetions will, of course," Ev'rel continued, "unite all Sevildom against them as no Ava ever could. What do you suppose Rire will do? Take highborn prisoners to turn against the rest of us? We know that can be done."

Amel made no sound as he lost control. He just buckled. This time, he actually glimpsed the visitor probe's interior. It was there and gone. White-lined and alien.

He came to himself, collapsed in Ev'rel's arms, and clung, shaking.

"Are you hurt?" She was worried. "What is it?"

"Post-flight . . . " he muttered.

"How hard did he fly you?" Ev'rel said in anger, speaking of Ameron. Amel shook his head, denying exploitation.

Ev'rel led him to the bed and helped him lie down. She stayed beside him to loosen the waist sash of his dark blue lounging costume, and helped him out of his slip-on, leather shoes. "Better?"

He smiled. "Yes, thanks."

"What I want you to think about," she said, "is child-gifting. To Red Hearth and the Dem'Vrel. On my behalf."

Amel would have sat up, but her arm penned him. "Hear me out," she said.

He relaxed again, carefully, trying not to let her closeness distract him. He could smell her skin and feel her warmth. The words were chilling in their cold cloak of reason.

"I could weaken D'Therd's influence on Dem'Vrel, and give Vretla Vrel a reason to stay home, if you would only be sensible. Vretla does not want to die the last Vrellish Royalblood. She would like to have you in her bed, too. She remembers you from when you were a courtesan. The Dem'Vrel are thirsty for high blood. They'd want you if you were fresh from the UnderDocks, still black and blue and starting at raised hands. You can hardly claim it would be a chore. You mind your manners at court, I know, but I am well aware that you don't confine yourself even to your *mekan'stan* when you are away from court. All you would have to do is stop using your cursed Luverthanian drugs, and start taking your fun closer to home. Is that so much to ask?"

The more she talked the harsher she was. Amel became very still, attending with his every sense not only to her words, but each nuance of her manner. At last she noticed this and stopped.

"You think I would be jealous!" she accused his silence.

He did not know a safe response to that. Muscles clenched in his abdomen.

"Don't be idiotic," she told him. "I would have warred on Rire and your Purple Alliance friends by now if I were that simple. Children are politics on Gelion. This would be a political solution, Amel." Her voice dropped its stridency all at once. She stroked his hair from his face, painfully tender. "I might be able to prevent a war. You want that, don't you?"

"Yes," he said, faintly.

"Think about it," Ev'rel said, rising. "That's all."

She walked away from him then, to the workshop door, where she turned back to smile at him over a shoulder draped in black tresses. "Coming?" she invited.

He got up very slowly, and followed her.

Inside, she set images running on the walls: their private record of him dancing. The door locked as he closed it. He let himself down on the padded floor. It was cool, but quite comfortable. She knelt beside him with a white silk scarf in one hand, avoiding eye contact. The room was dim. Eerie light came from the dancing figure on the wall. He joined his wrists above his head. She tied them, loosely, to remind him that he was not to be present, except as a sort of prop, like the recorded dancer. She turned on music with a visceral pounding roll, poured herself a drink, and fed him Turquoise from her fingers, drop by drop, then slowly traced it over him, until the room's effects combined to stir her need for more. Then she made him erect with her hands, straddled him, and before the music stopped, was able to steal her own satisfaction from the jealous hurts of the past, ending in a wrenching sob.

He freed his hands with a simple tug and took her in his arms, feeling profoundly sad.

"Thank you," she whispered to his neck, below the music's rhythm.

She hated to thank anyone.

He held her. "I've done worse," he murmured back, "with less pleasure."

She detached herself. He let her go. She busied herself at the console turning the music off and the lights up. The dancer was subtracted, leaving the walls blank.

"You could betray me," she said with her back to him, and drank from her tall glass. "You might tomorrow. Yet I keep you close."

"You know I won't," he answered her. "Not for what's private between us." He came up behind her and touched her lightly on one shoulder. "Consider it a whore's honor."

"Oh no," she said, turning to face him, their bodies close, her voice gone soft with love, "a courtesan's."

He smiled. He knew it was wrong, but that pleased him. She grew serious as she stared at him. "How," she asked, "can you do it?"

He shrugged. He could smell her. It felt not the least wrong to be naked for her, and he liked to be naked, for the sheer freedom of the sensation. He wanted to bury his face in her loose, tangled hair, but he knew she would resent that. Instead he took a strand, rubbed it gently between his fingers, and let it go, watching how it fell against her shoulder. "My abusers were men," he answered, "and my teachers were women. It's harder for you. Your abusers were men also, and I am a man. I even look like my father."

"Oh no," she denied, "you don't look like Delm. Beauty—" she cupped his face, slipping a thumb gently between his teeth, then pressing hard, "—is how you wear it."

Amel turned his head aside, not liking the pressure in his mouth. Her thumb traced his saliva down his chin and throat.

She moaned softly. "Why must I need you?"

"I'm told," he said, "that I shouldn't want you, either."

She was alert at once. "By whom?"

"No one in particular," he said, and began dressing. "People."

Ev'rel frowned. "You're not healed, Amel. You're as broken as I am. You just pretend better. I know every crack. That's why I trust you."

"I don't know if you know them, or you make them," Amel said lightly, and straightened. He had his pants on. He carried the rest of his costume over an arm, bare chested.

She smiled. "I wonder what your friends would think of you being my *slaka*. Would they wonder, like D'Therd, how you can bear to go on living?"

"Probably," Amel tossed off. But it hurt. She knew he detested her defining their relationship as abuser and victim: *slaka'st* and *slaka*. She was always cruelest when she had yielded to her inclinations, as if she must take revenge on him for being the stimulus.

He began to leave.

"Amel!" Her voice was breathless, almost frightened.

He was recaptured by his pity.

"I put you before politics," she reminded him, "before wisdom. Only I do that. Only I need you, just you, that much."

He nodded slowly, pity dissolving to shared disillusionment. It made irrefutable sense to him that other people could not really care about him. He was careful not to show them more than they might want. Only Ev'rel wanted all of him. Valued the worst of it, in fact. He had tested the depth of her need and believed it was real. Mira would be disgusted by the depth of his own need to feel certain that he mattered, that much, to anyone.

He broke eye contact.

"Remember it," she said, "when the friends that you put before me suggest that I am not good for you."

"I'm sorry," he mumbled, unsure, exactly, about what.

She stiffened where she stood, her arms rigid by her sides. "I am afraid of the power you have over me," she confessed, "afraid of what you know. I wake at nights, when you are off somewhere on others' errands, afraid that you have destroyed me, and afraid that you won't come home, without knowing which hell I fear more."

He swallowed, feeling liquid inside. "I will always come home."

"It is only you I trust," she told him. "You. Only."

The diamond hardness of her 'only' provoked a vivid memory of Mira, standing, talking with him on *TouchGate Hospital Station,* saying goodbye as if she did not care whether they ever saw each other again.

He swallowed.

Ev'rel made a deliberate effort to laugh, with some success. "Only you are mad enough."

"Mad, and at the moment, tired," he took up the lightness with relief. "See you tomorrow."

"Amel!"

He left his hand on the door, looking back over one shoulder. She seemed distant from him, majestic even in her dressing gown.

She said, "Think about co-operating. The sooner the better, if I am to buy Rire's safety. That is what you want, isn't it? Ann has shown you pictures of children in their mothers' laps, and lovers strolling in some Reetion park."

She said too much. She seemed to realize it.

Amel answered with flawless self-control. "I do appreciate the timing issue."

Chapter VI

"HE WAS HARDER ON YOU THAN HE SHOULD HAVE BEEN," Branstatt told Erien, quietly. Tatt strode ahead of them, flanked by two errants, a man and a woman. Erien merely nodded in answer to Branstatt's comment; nobody need explain Tatt to him.

They had entered the docks from the Palace Sector via the Highlord door, since that way saw the most Vrellish traffic in the Highborn Docks and Tatt—who was entitled to use the Royalblood level—did not want his excursion remarked upon. From the floor of the Highborn Docks, they descended to the Nobleborn Docks and took the stairs down to the UnderDocks.

As they did so, Branstatt undertook to brief Erien. "The UnderDocks —most of it—isn't so dangerous, if you use common sense. You'll notice that we're not wearing House braids or colors. There's always a risk of running across some grudge down here, but if they don't know who you are, they don't have anything against you. And they think they'd better not touch you, just in case. The sword's enough to identify you as Sevolite. That and the walk. Most highborns couldn't pass as commoner if their lives depended on it. Look at him," he said affectionately, of Tatt, striding ahead in unconscious presumption and immovable expectation that the crowds would part before him. "The rest of it is watching what you have on you, watching what you say about your business, and watching your back. We've been down here a few dozen times now—only lost one man, back near the beginning."

Between rigorously upkept store fronts the walls were splashed with murals: the district's equivalent of a newsletter, since most of the population was illiterate. New editions were painted over the old. The productions ranged from high realism through abstraction to crude graffiti. Often, they took forms only locals understood. But Erien could not mistake the dark faces of Reetions depicted here and there. He would have liked to stop and study the murals, but Tatt led them purposefully on.

Clothing, though not always clean, was far from drab. The locals' brightly dyed, vat-drawn synthetics ranged in style from imitations of court garb to simple tabards and trousers. Natural fabrics were worn as ornaments, tufts of fur, ropes of woven leather, medallions of leather or fur or stretched silk on metal chains. Natural fetishes were for good luck, or for a better rebirth if luck ran out. There was a thriving trade in natural products for various charms, as well as Earth-authentic relics and Ameron icons, Branstatt told Erien, and laughed at his expression, promising to bring him shopping some day soon.

They were a surprisingly mongrel people, these UnderDocks inhabitants. Once or twice Erien caught sight of a swarthy face which might have belonged to a Reetion, and here and there he saw dark eyes with an epicanthic fold, or a broad nose. Here, too, were people with unmistakable Sevolite traits, whether or not they wore swords.

The most difficult part of it, Erien found, was the smell. Ventilation was poor compared to Fountain Court; the air felt thick, and since water was a purchasable commodity, it was used for drinking, not washing. Overlying the inevitable human odors was a great olfactory squabble of spices and perfumes, all no doubt pleasant enough when contemplated alone.

"This is the store front strip," Branstatt remarked. "It's kept up. The proprietors pay hired fists to patrol, even a few hired swords, though you won't find more than Fractionals and maybe a few Pettylords living in the UnderDocks. If we have to go off the beaten path you'll see something else again." He shook his head. "We cleaned out three of the local gangs in succession, each one worse than the last. There's something in the air that makes souls fester. But even the better locals don't like us throwing our weight around.

"So, since they've called us down here," Branstatt continued, as they emerged into a crowded marketplace, "something's happened that people down here don't want to try handling on their own." He lengthened his stride to catch them up with Tatt, who had just turned into an alleyway.

The narrow little street was tiled in a delicately colored, worn frieze of roses beside a stream, which suggested the establishment it led into had once enjoyed better days. Halfway down to an apparent dead end, Tatt and his escort stood talking to a nervous-looking youth wearing a remarkable draggle of leather and fur jewelry. Something passed between Tatt's hand and his, and the youth bolted towards the supposedly blind end of the alley and slithered through an opening in the wall. Branstatt's mouth quirked. "I hope you paid him only what he was worth."

Tatt looked fleetingly guilty, and vividly excited, his color high. "He says that nobody's in there except the body and some medtech from outside the district. The staff left."

"Fled, more likely," said Branstatt. "Someone will be back. They can't all have somewhere else to go."

The doors beside them were also painted with twining roses, though a much inferior depiction to the frieze underfoot. Above them was a single red lantern, a sign common to West Alcove courtesan den and UnderDocks whorehouse alike—anywhere sex was among the entertainments bought and sold.

"Let's go," Ditatt said. Branstatt slipped ahead of him. Holding the door, he scanned the unseen room, then eased back. "Marrit, go and check where that boy went," he told one of their errants. "See if we could use it ourselves to get out. Then go down to the other end and keep watch on the market plaza. Deyne," this to the woman errant, "guard the door. Any sign of trouble, get in here and warn us." The errants nodded to each other, and then Branstatt led Tatt and Erien into the den.

It was a large room with a single cream-painted wall; the remaining three were draped in faded rose, concealing doors to the private rooms. The carpet underfoot was worn, with well-washed stains. There were a number of chairs and small tables, arranged in an arc around a low, wide bed in the center of the room. Lamps of scented oil imparted a heavy, artificial fragrance to the air. Three of the chairs had been overturned. A carafe lay on its side, its contents spilled.

There was only one woman in the room and a draped form on the bed. The sheets seemed very white, and the blood on them—and on the woman's gloved hands—as brilliant as ground gems.

She was of average height, with a thin, bony face set in unforgiving lines. Her hair was a dark blonde, severely cut and showing gray. She looked as though she had not had enough to eat for a long time, and did not care. The left shoulder of her shirt had been replaced by mesh, showing the tattoo worked into the skin beneath. The tattoo was black and silver. Only medics trained by the Luverthanians themselves were allowed the insignia.

Tatt identified himself. She stooped, a stiff movement, and jerked back the sheet. The corpse was that of a boy in his mid-teens. His face was flushed, contorted, teeth bared and lips drawn back. She had not attempted to close his eyes, one of which was a distinctive iridescent gray, and the other brown. The pupil in the gray eye was normal, that in the brown drawn to a point. A curve of gray showed beneath the upper eyelid, the contact lens dislodged by his struggles. She flicked back a strand of black hair to show the smudges of hair dye on his temples. Erien heard Tatt swallow beside him, thickly.

The woman pulled the sheet back further, showing a thick pad saturated with congealing blood covering the boy's abdomen. She worked it away from a long, torn wound, and hooked her gloved hand between the lips of the wound she exposed, lifting skin away from underlying membranes. Satiny fibers glistened in red. Erien concentrated as her fingers explored the wound, demonstrating where the layers of tissue had been torn apart by probing fingers. She said, her first words, "I tested for semen, deposited in the wound. The tests were positive."

Tatt gagged, and bolted for the door. Branstatt went after him. Erien met the woman's eyes, and merely nodded understanding. Blood and semen, the sacred substances of Gelion. Bodily integrity and bodily secretions were powerfully defended. And in Gelion's perversions, brutally mocked, gratuitously mixed.

There was no point, he knew, to emotion, even as he almost envied Tatt his reaction. It would not serve the dead man or the cause of justice if he were to feel. Some other night his dues would be paid in nightmares.

For now he asked, "Was that the cause of death?" The passive, he thought, sounded cold. This was—had been—a man, a very young man. "Did that cause his death?" he said.

The woman's expression eased slightly, understanding the rephrasing. "He died of Rush intoxication. I suspect the terminal event might have been a brainstem bleed, but I would need to do an autopsy to tell you more."

"You are?"

"Asher." She turned to show him the tattoo on her shoulder.

"How did you come to be here? Were you called when he—"

She made a harsh, wordless sound of mockery. "You think the people who did this would call a medtech? I've been hearing about these things. I've been expecting this. It was only a matter of time before they'd kill. You realize, I trust, this is supposed to be Pureblood Amel."

"Amel?"

There was very little resemblance, in death. There had been probably only a tenuous similarity in life. But the black hair dye, the gray contact lenses, the fineness of feature; still Erien had to ask, "Are you sure?"

She snorted, bitterly.

Erien said, "How much genetic analysis do you know?"

She stiffened; a white rim appeared around her pupil.

Erien said, "If there is semen, there is genetic material. If there is genetic material, then these assailants can be genotyped. We can identify them. If you know the techniques."

"Who are you?" she said, in a stifled voice.

"My name is Erien, a ward of Monitum. I have lived on Rire."

"Ah," she said, a shallow gasp.

He heard a sound behind him, Tatt's voice, drained of its usual energy, saying, "I'm all right."

Erien took the sheet that the medtech had drawn back. "Please—just for a moment." He covered the boy's body and face. Tatt came up beside him. His face was parchment-colored and his eyes were watery and a little bloodshot. His voice was rough with nausea and emotion. "Who did this?" Tatt demanded.

The woman was not entirely pitiless. With a wary glance at Erien she eased Tatt away from the bedside and towards one of the chairs against the far wall. Branstatt went with them. There were glasses and a half-filled carafe there; she sniffed at them, found a clean one, filled it, and offered it to Tatt, who vehemently pushed it away, either still nauseated, or repelled by the thought of drinking from the same bottle as any who had been in the audience.

Erien drew down the sheet again, placing his body between Tatt's eyes and what he uncovered. He did not know exactly what he was looking for. But he had to be able to ask questions of his own, and not merely rely upon the medtech's answers. Carefully he studied the minutiae of the corpse, etching them as a series of frames in memory. Tatt and Ranar would be relying upon his eyes. Even if he did not understand all that had happened here, someone else would.

Amel, perhaps.

He eased upright, looking at the boy's face. Only people who did not know Amel very well at all could think it a strong resemblance. *Dear Gods*, Erien thought, with a sudden rush of emotion and bile. He did not like Amel—indeed, he detested the man for what he had done ten years ago on Monitum—but to be the object of this kind of . . . of what, exactly? Given his own exposure to the visitor probe records, and the complexities of Ranar's position, he was well-versed in Reetion understanding of psychopathology. But the textbook terms did not encompass this. A young man had been tortured to death in a re-enactment of the imagined torments of another. Extreme objectification, said the textbooks. Sickness, said Erien's gut instinct. A profound sickness of individuals, or of the society. And Amel was the medium and the target of that sickness. How must it feel to live like that?

Or were Sevolites themselves the targets of that sickness? Was this a torture perpetrated on a commoner by Sevolites, or on the effigy of a Sevolite by commoners? Human history was replete with the bloody overthrow of oppressors by the oppressed, and hatred worked itself out in many small and ugly ways before the revolution.

He could not, he said harshly to himself, allow himself to feel.

The boy's wrists had been bound. He followed the ridging of the bedclothes to the head of the bed, and found a fragment of the straps caught in the frame. Someone had been determined to remove evidence but had been in too much haste to be thorough. Underneath the bed, he caught sight of a torn and crumpled wad of paper, daubed with color. He pulled it out, and kneeling, carefully spread it out. His breath went out of him as though he had been punched.

It was a poster, well-drawn—hideously well-drawn. It showed Amel, suspended by the wrists in a bizarre adaptation of a Gelack flogging frame. His head was wreathed in wires, there was agony on his face, and around him stood—no, lounged—four dark-skinned men, all wearing Reetion medical blues, open to show their naked loins.

The one behind Amel, naked, erect, swaggering, was drawn with Ranar's face.

There was a woman, too, fully clothed, standing at a control panel and surveying the scene with a satisfied smile. It was Lurol, the psychiatrist who had used the probe on Amel. Under Reetion law, parenting required two or more adults to commit to the child, and the family unit, regardless of whether the adults concerned were blood relations, friends or lovers. Lurol had made Ranar's adoption of Erien possible by agreeing to be his Reetion mother.

Someone came up beside Erien. Tatt's voice said, "Erien are you—?" Tatt stopped and looked down at the poster. His clear, vivid features showed dismay and revulsion, but no surprise.

Erien said, in a sick voice, "Are there more like this?"

Tatt crouched beside him, with an uneasy glance at the bed. "Oh, Erien, I thought you knew. I thought you knew that . . . that was the way things were. Of course none of us who know Ranar believe this for a moment, but—"

"Too many people do not know Ranar, and some of them want to believe it."

"They won't win," Tatt said, stoutly. "Asher's got names of the people who run this den and descriptions of the people who were here when she got here. She didn't see—much—by the time she arrived, but there are people out there who saw everything. We'll run them down." His eyes moved to the covered corpse on the bed. "And then it'll be to the death." He tucked a hand under Erien's elbow. "C'mon, Erien. I'd offer you some wine but the stuff in this place is foul. And anyway, it's not strong enough. Monatese Turquoise is the thing. Lots of it. Think how much luckier you are than I am." Two-step differenced pronouns made his point for him. "You don't have to work so hard to get drunk."

"Heir Monitum," the medtech said suddenly, with an authority that made even Tatt look at her. "Don't," she said firmly, "be ashamed of the way you reacted." Tatt flushed, caught in blustering bravado, and unsure how to respond to such a challenge from such a source. She continued before he could collect himself. "I have a friend who says you are one of the good ones. His standards for goodness seem to me overly lax, but about you, I have to agree." An eyeflicker in Erien's direction said that she was not so sure about him.

Ditatt didn't know what to say. Branstatt, standing behind him, caught the medtech's eye and gave her a single nod which conveyed 'You did the right thing this time, but watch it'.

Erien folded the poster with hands which shook slightly, and said, "If you are finished, then I have a few medical questions." She had not told him whether or not she could do a genetic analysis. It might be that she needed a promise of immunity from Tatt, since that kind of science could be so readily labeled *okal'a'ni*, which was worse than merely criminal, meaning, literally the negation of *Okal Rel*. That was punishable by death.

The errant, Marritt, burst into the room. "D'Therd and D'Lekker Dem'Vrel! And a six-guard," he cried.

The medtech went ashen. "I have to go," she said.

"We won't let them—" Ditatt started.

"You can go out the back," Branstatt interrupted him.

She caught up her bag and half ran for the draperies surrounding the back door, into the private rooms. Branstatt followed, a stride behind. Plain as his discourtesy to Tatt was his urge to protect his House's only Royalblood from himself. He wanted no reason for the Dem'Vrel to pick a fight. Tatt was left standing with his mouth open.

The draperies thrashed closed over the medtech and Branstatt as the front door flew open. Two Dem'Vrel errants herded the Monatese guard, Deyne, inside, who must have delayed them at least long enough for Marritt to give warning. Deyne's eyes sought Tatt's, angry and imploring his approval of her decision not to fight. D'Therd Dem'Vrel followed, filling the doorway, and almost obscuring D'Lekker. Erien caught the vicious look D'Lekker sent at his half-brother's back, which vanished completely as he caught sight of Tatt.

"Why, Heir Monitum. What an unexpected pleasure!" He flicked a sparkling eye over the two Monatese errants and Erien. "Is this all your bodyguard? I heard Ameron had jerked on the purse strings, but I didn't know what to believe. I suppose it must be true."

D'Therd had turned his cold eyes to the still moving draperies. He tilted his head as though listening. "Who else was here?"

Tatt tossed his head. "Nobody. The place was empty when we arrived."

D'Therd started towards the drape, hand on hilt. Branstatt pushed the drapes aside at the last safe moment, and stood in D'Therd's way, making it look entirely inadvertent. Tatt's voice was a little shrill. "Empty, Branstatt?"

"As we thought, Your Highness."

"I heard a door close," D'Therd said.

"That was me," Branstatt said, "taking a quick look outside." He stepped aside then, sweeping the drapery with him, his very manner conveying, 'But if you're not satisfied, go ahead; I won't take offense'.

D'Lekker whipped the sheet away from the corpse. He blinked once, in shock, and a fleeting expression of nausea crossed his face. Then he looked up with a pleased smile. "So which one of you upchucked?" he said amiably, looking at Tatt. "How are you ever going to deal with this dirt if you can't keep your breakfast down?"

Ditatt said, "I am investigating this, D'Lekker."

"You don't have the Throne's backing. You don't have anyone's backing, except this rag-tag oddity here." He flipped a hand at Erien.

Ditatt bared his teeth. "You have no idea what I have."

D'Lekker dropped the sheet. D'Therd was prowling the room; Erien saw him note where something had been torn off the walls.

"Face it, Monitum, you haven't been able to convince anyone that you're any use at all. Why don't you just go home and sire babies like a good gift-child? You'd avoid a great deal of humiliation that way, and you'd no doubt live longer." He jerked a head at Tatt's errants. "Get them out of here. They're just in the way."

Instead, the Monatese errants closed around Tatt. D'Lekker laughed. "So that's what they think of your ability to fend for yourself!" He caught sight of the paper in Erien's hand. "What's that?" D'Lekker snatched it from him. "I thought so." He reacted to the picture of Amel on it. "This is my jurisdiction."

D'Therd glanced over his shoulder and grunted distaste. D'Lekker jerked the poster away, as though fearing it would be taken from him.

"That," Erien said levelly, "is unfounded fabrication. The visitor probe apparatus does not look like an instrument of torture, and Amel was not, and never would have been, sexually assaulted by Reetions. Reetions find non-consensual or coercive sexual congress as repugnant as the Gelacks find homosexuality."

D'Therd gave him a look of utter disgust. He was one of the most physically intimidating men Erien had ever met, with Vrellish height and darkness, Demish breadth and bulk. Contrary to Court fashion, he wore a sleeveless shirt beneath his braided vest, no doubt for complete freedom of movement, but also to display the powerful muscles of his dominant right arm. Erien had no doubt that D'Therd was aware of the impression he made. Beside him, Horth Nersal would have seemed slight. Erien felt breakable.

"Oh, really," D'Lekker said. "What are you? A white Reetion? Tell us more."

"He is Erien, ward of Monitum," Tatt said. "He's with me. You don't care about Rire, or justice. You just care about your precious family name."

"Reetions are revealed by the filth they spread." D'Therd's pronoun was the lowest he could use, reserved for *okal'a'ni* polluters of honorable conduct and people without souls—the one being cause or effect of the other, depending on which interpretation of *Okal Rel* one subscribed to in this regard.

"The majority of the material that is presently disseminated," Erien said, "is Gelack in origin, and loosely, if at all, derived from the original visitor probe records, which account for a bare six hours and twelve minutes of recalled experience." He snapped a hand at the poster. "There are a dozen errors in that, from the fact that the visitor probe looks nothing like that to the fact that Reetions circumcise male children in infancy and Gelacks do not."

D'Lekker and D'Therd both glanced involuntarily at the poster. Tatt looked greatly startled. The errants, tense, and stony faced. Erien seized advantage of their collective shock. "If there is a problem, it is within Gelion. And I can assure you, all this prurient interest—on both sides—will only obstruct our being able to inhabit the same universe."

D'Therd's flat and deadly stare said that he had no intention of cohabiting.

With a thoughtful expression, Tatt lifted one of the oil lamps from the table and balanced it on his fingers, rocking the oil back and forth. D'Lekker promptly stepped forwards to take it from him—and Tatt pounced, snatched the poster from D'Lekker's hand, slammed it flat on the floor and smashed the glass lamp down upon it. The glass burst, oil flew and ignited. D'Lekker yelled in fury and grabbed at the poster, trying to jerk it from beneath its mantle of yellow flame. The motion merely fanned the fire; the others moved back as he flapped it, cursing, until the flames licked at his fingers, then he dropped the fragmenting poster and stamped furiously on it. Tatt, face lit with unholy enthusiasm, grabbed the wine carafe he had earlier disdained and sluiced it over the burning poster and D'Lekker's feet.

D'Lekker stopped stamping. "You did that deliberately."

Tatt straightened. "Any part in particular?" he asked sweetly.

D'Lekker drew his sword. Tatt jumped back, his sword clearing his scabbard. D'Lekker stepped carefully clear of the spilled oil and wine and small isolated flamelets, scuffing his feet to clean them.

The Monatese errants looked horrified, the Dem'Vrellish expectant.

Erien put force into his voice. "Stop it, both of you!"

All eyes turned towards him, except for the duelists who continued to stare each other down. Erien said, striving for the right pitch of emotion, "Think what would be said if either of you were killed or even injured, fighting down here, over this."

"You've been asking for this," D'Lekker told Tatt in a low voice.

"And you're going to give it to me?" Tatt said, with a quick, taunting feint of his blade.

There was a searing rasp of blade from scabbard. Tatt half turned to face D'Therd; D'Therd brought his blade whipping down the length of Tatt's, and Tatt's blade seemed to peel back out of his unfolding hand. D'Therd turned, keeping his body between his brother and his brother's opponent, and his blade flashed around D'Lekker's and snapped it free from his grip. D'Lekker's sword was still in flight when Tatt's thudded to the stained floor. D'Lekker stayed where he was, face to face with his brother. Tatt, reflexively, started to stoop, and without turning, D'Therd swept his sword back, blocking Tatt's reach with steel. The tableau held.

D'Therd said, "The ward of Monitum is right. I want no more disgrace."

D'Lekker jumped back, slipping on the mulch of the poster and righting himself, and stalked to his fallen sword. His face was a study in sullen fury as he slammed his sword into its scabbard. "You, and your precious honor," he said in bitter hatred, to his unyielding brother.

D'Therd did not deign to respond. He stepped away from Tatt's sword and watched as the younger swordsman bent and collected it and returned it to his scabbard. Tatt straightened and faced D'Therd, eye to eye: he had the height to match Ev'rel's Sword Champion, though he was by far the slighter man. "I don't need to thank you," he said.

D'Therd nodded, unmoved by either churlishness or defiance. "You will go now, Heir Monitum."

D'Lekker said, "They ought to be searched."

"If they are persons of honor, they will not take anything that does not belong to them," D'Therd said. "Now, do what you have to do, so that we can leave this foul place."

"Bastards," Tatt said savagely, as his errants herded him outside. "Arrogant, interfering, bigoted bastards. All that they care about is their sacred name, as if they had any history or honor worth defending."

"I am very glad," Branstatt said in a measured voice, "that you did not fight D'Lekker."

Ditatt stopped in the middle of the hall, his eyes suspiciously bright. "You think I couldn't take him on? You think I couldn't beat him?"

There was a beat's silence, and then Branstatt said, "Ditatt—Your Highness—if you had Liege Nersal's own left hand, it would still stop our hearts to see you risk yourself against D'Lekker Dem'Vrel. There is no certainty in the outcome of a duel, and you are too precious to us. Forgive us."

Ditatt stared at him. "You haven't answered." Then his eyes suddenly overflowed and he swiped at them, ducking his head. "Damn you! Damn you all. I wish I were a friendless bastard even my brother didn't like." He took a clumsy clout at his half-brother, and Branstatt moved smoothly in to receive it. Ditatt caught his shoulder and hugged him sideways. "And you!" he said, lifting a bright and tear-streaked face to Erien. "When you told us to stop it, I damn near dropped my sword. I'd have sworn it was Ameron. Don't do that again!" His face lit, contemplating possibilities. "Unless I tell you to!"

"I won't," Erien said, slightly unnerved. "And Tatt," Tatt looked at him enquiringly, "thank you. For what you did with the poster."

"Oh, it was nothing." Tatt snickered. "Actually, it was fun. Watching him trying to put it out, getting to throw that wine. All they've got is a body, and it won't speak to them. Branstatt, did Asher tell you where she was going?"

"No, Highness, and I would have followed her, but—"

"But for the Dem'Vrel." Ditatt spat. "Vent them. I need some good Monatese Turquoise to get the taste out of my mouth. Then we can conspire to find our Cinderella." To Erien, "Have you heard the story? Ridiculous old Earth thing about a servant girl and a shoe and a dance, but Luthan—you'll meet Luthan tomorrow—tells it like it means something. Anyway the girl rushes off and the prince—it's a Demish story—has to find her. Which is what I have to do, though I don't think I'll offer to marry her. Even if she can't do anything more to help on this one, we could do with a good medtech to advise us. And you— can you really see the mistakes in these posters and such?"

"I've seen the visitor probe," Erien said, quietly, to undercut Ditatt's hectic energy. "I've lived on Rire."

"And you don't scare easily! You lectured D'Therd Dem'Vrel, with him hulking over you like a battlewheel. That was worth seeing."

Erien smiled slightly. "So my efforts were not wholly in vain."

Then the brilliance in Ditatt's face wavered and went out like a lamp. "Oh Gods," he said, and began to shiver. Branstatt caught Erien's eye, and shook his head slightly, reassuringly. It was not a reassurance Erien needed: Ditatt had always been high strung, even in the nursery, but he was also robust enough that simple solutions were all that were required.

Branstatt said, "Come on, Your Highness. Let's go home."

The woman errant, Deyne, fell into step beside Erien, trying too hard to make it look casual. Erien waited for the question. It came as they made their way out of the UnderDocks.

"You've seen the visitor probe?" she asked.

"I lived with the woman who designed it," Erien said. "Lurol is not a monster, merely a somewhat self-absorbed scientist."

Deyne did not seem to understand.

Erien went on, aware of other ears as well. "When Lurol put Amel into the probe, at *SkyBlue*, he was suffering from the effects of a conscience-bond, and Lurol was trying to save his life. Lurol went on to try and save herself—" there was no avoiding that pronoun, and his efforts not to speak of Reetions as commoners sounded artificial to his own ears, "—and everyone else on the station, by finding out as much as she could about the people who were besieging them, by examining Amel's memories. The man besieging them was Liege H'Reth, who had been sexually abusing Amel, and who had conscience-bonded him."

"But why . . . flaunt it?" Deyne said. "Why make it all available?"

"An unavoidable consequence of the Reetion political and judicial system," said Erien. "There was an inquiry regarding Lurol's actions—because she acted without due process in many instances—and Amel's visitor probe testimony was part of it. The Reetion system is founded upon completely free access to information, especially information used in policy decisions, and there are large areas of life which Gelacks would consider private that Reetions consider to be of public concern. Once Amel's testimony was admitted to the public domain, it remained so. Unfortunately, the material from Amel was so outside ordinary Reetion experience that it received extremely wide exposure. Most material on public record is never seen by a human eye. There is simply too much of it." He paused. "There was no malice. They are simply a different culture, with different standards."

She looked unconvinced. "They're commoners."

"Actually," Erien said, "they're not. You'll have met Ambassador Ranar. Where would you place him? Reetions are not Sevolites. But they're not commoners. They," this time he used the Reetion collective pronoun, "are Reetion. To think otherwise is a fallacy."

From the front, Tatt remarked, "Do you suppose D'Therd could be impaled on a sharp point of logic?"

All of them, except Erien, thought that was hilarious.

Chapter VII

Amel dreamed of torture.

He came to with a snatch of breath, sitting up on his floor mattress.

The room was faintly lit by a nervecloth panel on one wall. He did not recognize it as his own room due to Ev'rel's cleaning. That passed. He felt better once he'd recognized it.

He bowed over raised knees until the physical side effects of his dream settled. Although it was early, it was after Lights Up for the household. Amel pushed back his bed clothes and got up, disinclined to catch at the nightmare's coattails. Sleep which could not be kind, he would gladly abandon. He did regret leaving the warm sheets, but he was not in a frame of mind to enjoy dozing.

He wanted his favorite knee-length tunic, filched from the bedroom of his Purple Alliance *mekan'st*, Perry D'Aur, as a keepsake. It was a sloppy thing, cozy over bare skin, and he could use the reminder of a world beyond the Gelack court. But he could not find it.

He searched his wardrobe and trunks. He looked even in unlikely places. Doing so, he discovered that Ev'rel had left nothing but formal wear and dancer's togs in his wardrobe.

A boy came in with a package while Amel stood in his underwear, trying to decide what to put on. The boy set the package on the floor with a quick, "From the Avim," and fled without looking at Amel.

Amel opened the present. Silk caressed his hands. It was an off-white tunic, with tiny wild flowers delicately strung down the left breast. The embroidery was definitely West Alcove, with days of meticulous artistry in every playful tendril and blossom. The tunic came with black tights, a wide belt, and a white leather tri-lyre strap tooled in the same tiny wild flowers.

The strap reminded Amel that he'd offered to play for Luthan. So did the note from Ev'rel.

He dressed, pausing only to admire the metalwork of the belt which, though wider than he usually liked, was perfectly fitted. The prominent clasp reunited, in its halves, the sun and ship of the Dem'Vrel crest.

Dressed, Amel sped with stealth to the kitchens without encountering his brothers.

Years of practice had taught him how to raid the pantry without upsetting the inventory, by signing out food to himself, as himself. Unfortunately, a dish washer noticed him and fetched the cook.

"Just some breakfast," Amel told the gray-haired, steely-eyed man who greeted the intrusion into his domain with displeasure.

"Certainly, Immortality," the cook said, "in the breakfast room."

"Lek and D'Therd . . . ?" Amel asked.

"Heir Dem'Vrel is out for morning exercise," said the cook, "and his Highness D'Lekker is not up." He commandeered a young waiter, who came in carrying Ev'rel's breakfast dishes. "See to Pureblood Amel's needs, in the breakfast room."

"Yes, sir," said the waiter, stowing his dishes with military efficiency to take on the new assignment. As soon as the cook was gone, the waiter relaxed. "D'Lekker was out late," he told Amel, with a gossip's enthusiasm, "doing more poking around in the UnderDocks. Are people really making kill-shows of you?"

"I do not know," Amel said, and kicked himself mentally for accepting the waiter's undifferenced address by reciprocating in equally simplified grammar. He mended it as best he could by belatedly adding the seven-step suffix to his *rel*-case 'I'. "Make it a double breakfast," he told the waiter. "I can't remember when I last ate."

He could, in fact. But he didn't count Nersallian rations.

At least sticking to fully-differenced pronouns discouraged more familiarity.

Amel was savoring his second plate of baked beef strips and colorful nut and vegetable mince when he heard his brothers' voices.

". . . and a place for a cool head," D'Therd was lecturing.

"Your honor is nothing more than being nodded at by old blood at receptions," D'Lekker scoffed, "or did you back down to Heir Monitum for fear of his sword?"

"*You* ought to be afraid of that," D'Therd insisted, speaking down, *rel*-to-*pol*, although both of them were Royalblood.

"Was there a fight?" Amel found himself on his feet.

D'Therd had already noticed him and ignored his presence.

"Ah!" D'Lekker beamed at Amel, mercurially abandoning his anger. "Wonderful! I told Mother that cut would hang well on you."

It took a heartbeat for Amel to grasp that D'Lekker meant Amel's new clothes.

D'Therd made a disgusted sound. "I will eat later."

"There would have been a fight," D'Lekker bragged, blocking D'Therd's retreat, "if D'Therd hadn't made me back down."

"One day," D'Therd told him, dangerously, "you are going to go too far. And you," he turned on Amel with a snarl, speaking down as if Amel was common-born, "should have been the corpse in the UnderDocks."

"What corpse!" Amel ignored the grammatical insult. "What's happened?"

D'Lekker let D'Therd pass. "I'll tell you all about it," the younger brother cheerfully offered.

Amel put D'Lekker aside, feeling him stiffen as he realized the intent behind Amel's touch. Amel would have to mend that later. He needed this straight, and fast.

He overtook D'Therd in Family Hall, running backwards in front of him to make him stop. When D'Therd made to swat him aside, Amel blocked, usurping the larger man's momentum to lunge them both painfully into a table against the wall. Mindful of yesterday's twisted arm, Amel didn't let D'Therd get a grip on him, but sprang back.

"What happened?" Amel demanded, in anger.

D'Therd shook himself clear of a broken vase with a scowl. "Ask Heir Monitum, since he's taken it on. Now get out of my way, or I'll draw my sword."

That was a sobering thought.

Amel fled ahead of D'Therd, down Family Hall, and through Lilac Hearth's Throat to the entrance hall. He barely remembered to snatch a cloak and did no more than pull it on, leaving it hanging off his shoulders.

Green Hearth was just across Fountain Court. Its stiffly brocaded porter raised an eyebrow when she saw who had come to call.

"Pureblood Amel Dem'Vrel, son of Avim Ev'rel and the late Ava Delm." She acknowledged his identity, which was unique enough to manage without any of the usual clothing clues.

"I want to see Tatt—Heir Monitum," Amel announced.

She let him in. The woodland smell of the planter-lined entrance hall, was, as always, pleasurable. "If you'd wait in the guest lounge, Immortality?" She gestured for him to carry on.

"No, I'll, uh, wait here, if that's all right? I know Tatt's on his way to visit Princess Luthan, as I am, and I thought we'd go together."

She offered no comment, but left him to wait in the moist air. He remembered he had left behind his tri-lyre and its brand new strap. One of Luthan's servants would have to fetch them, later.

He fingered a waxy leaf, listened to the trickling water sounds, and paced, twice, the length of the entrance hall, watched with interest by two house errants stationed near the inner doors to Green Hearth's Throat. After the first trip he shed the cloak and draped it over his arm; then he tossed it over a stained-wood bench and sat down, feeling leaves at his back.

"Amel?" The inner doors opened on Tatt, who immediately dismissed both house guards.

Amel rose.

Tatt was half-dressed for Luthan's, green velvet vest unlaced over a white shirt and green waistband, sheath empty of its sword. He met Amel's eyes with his direct stare, emotion flowing as freely as fresh air. "You've heard? I should have notified you personally. I confess, I was counting on seeing you at Luthan's in half an hour."

Amel took Tatt, gently but firmly, by both forearms, reassured to feel him whole. "What happened? Growls are all I can get out of D'Therd. D'Lekker implied that you nearly crossed swords!"

"Never mind that," Tatt gestured for Amel to precede him into the guest lounge, but Amel hung back.

"I do mind, Tatt! D'Lekker wants to kill you! You're important. It will make a big impression at Court. My 'honor' is just an excuse and there's not a damn thing I can do about it! If there's a body, and it's something to do with that, can't you leave this one alone?"

"The body was a teenage prostitute, overdosed on Rush, who'd been raped and flesh probed in a staged enactment of some mythical Reetion abuse of you!" Tatt hit back.

Whiteness closed on Amel. He stared at it, paralyzed. Nothing but white, inside and out. Then, like an ax blow the whiteness fell, and was gone.

Tatt guided him to a bench in Green Hearth's entrance hall.

Amel separated himself from the help, adverse to touch. "I'm all right." He seated himself. "Sorry."

"No," Tatt insisted, upset but respecting his wishes, "I am. I shouldn't have told you like that. I should have explained that it isn't about you. Not this. Not now. Both for Erien's Rire, and that boy, this is something I have to do. You understand?"

Amel nodded. The attack had wiped him like a slate. "Can you get me a drink?" he asked.

"Sure!"

Amel just sat, feeling his way back into body and soul, methodically, finger by finger, and thought by thought.

Ditatt reappeared with a tumbler of Monatese Turquoise whiskey.

Amel gave him a crooked frown. "I meant water."

"You need this more. You're white as a background star."

Amel accepted the advice, and the glass. The potent liquor thrilled his palate with the first swallow, burning with slow heat down his throat. The smell aroused whispers of Ev'rel. He nursed the glass.

"So," Amel murmured to the drink in his hands, "I really am playing in kill-shows." He couldn't find any expression to put on.

"You knew such things were happening?"

Amel shook his head. "Only rumors."

"Where did you hear them?"

He looked up, into Tatt's earnest face, and lied. "Nowhere in particular. Here and there. The docks. You think the cause of death was Rush?"

"We're sure. The body probing wasn't fatal, though, I confess, it was the hardest to stomach."

A corner of Amel's mouth tugged taut. "You might not think so, if you'd tried both."

Tatt blinked, shocked.

Guess that wasn't funny, Amel told himself. He had to fight the urge to draw his arms in about himself and huddle, smaller and smaller, in a curled ball. "Sorry," was all he managed for Tatt, and not in a pleasant tone. The Monatese heir's sympathy irked more than D'Therd's callousness, because Amel was truly sorry, to have fetched it out, by showing himself to be so vulnerable.

The opportunity to turn Tatt's sympathy to his advantage occurred to him in unison with the realization of what he needed to know, but could not ask. He spoke before he'd quite completed either thought.

"Could the medic say whether he died quickly, or if they'd increased the dosage in controlled amounts?" Amel asked.

"No," said Tatt, "just that it was some sort of brain hemorrhage. She said we'd need an autopsy to determine more, and we don't have the body now."

"That's too bad."

"Why?" a new voice asked.

"Erien!" Tatt relinquished Amel's side to stand, looking flustered from reading emotional mine fields. "I've told Amel. Tactlessly, I'm afraid."

Erien's keen attention was fixed on Amel. "I want to know," Erien said, very reasonably, "your reason for asking about the Rush dosage."

"To know how long the boy suffered, surely," Tatt volunteered in Amel's defense. Amel blessed him for the spontaneousness of it, even if Ditatt didn't realize, as Amel did, that Erien was on the offensive here.

"That, too, of course," said Amel, to thank Tatt. He held Erien's stare, aware that successful dissembling was more a matter of body language than words. His body was a good actor, and this was an easy role, because it was half sincere. He merely had to focus on that half. The 'Mira half' was none of Erien's business, which kept his conscience safely off the stage.

"I asked," Amel told Erien, "because a steady build-up is the hallmark of a planned event, while a sudden jolt, causing death, suggests something more impromptu and unplanned."

"You know that?" Erien double-checked.

"Yes. Kill-shows aren't entirely new. Just spreading out of their usual bounds. Not everything I learned in the UnderDocks got recorded by the visitor probe."

"You resent Rire for that experience," Erien deduced, coldly. "It is hardly surprising that you would. What was done was wrong, and yet, it has been studied to the point of madness without reaching a planetary consensus of what could have been done that was better. Gelion hasn't even the common sense to start with the correct facts. You were mind probed without consent, and induced to act against a Gelack invader on behalf of a vulnerable space station. The only thinkable alternative for the station was to self-destruct, which would have killed you, too. How does any of that translate to the degrading fantasies stuck on the walls of that room where we found the murdered boy?"

"Erien!" Tatt was, as always, ready to defend the underdog.

Amel didn't want the role. He rose, cloak retrieved with flawless grace and laid over one arm. "It's all right," he said to Tatt, "it's just the way Reetions talk. As if space stations make decisions, and rights get hurt, not people. He's right about the facts, of course. He's good at facts." He smiled, to prove he could. It surprised him by dispelling some of the coldness he had purposefully reflected back at Erien.

"If I can do anything to help with your investigation, let me know," Amel told Tatt. "In the meantime, could you make my excuses to Luthan? I don't feel up to playing for her party right now. Perhaps Erien could stand in as musician? I understand he isn't hopeless on the flute. Transpose the right wing melody line of her tri-lyre music up an octave; that ought to take care of it. You can integrate some of the left wing counter-point in ornamentation, if you're good."

Walking away from them both, Amel knew that he had to evacuate Mira. Figuring out how spared him further dunkings in emotional backlash. It was a puzzle to be solved. He was good at that.

For a moment he nearly turned back to ask Tatt for passage through Green Hearth. If he hadn't been so busy bristling at Erien he would have thought of that at the time, when it might have passed for natural. Lilac Hearth was not a good second choice. Ev'rel could be getting the story from D'Therd or D'Lekker even now. Once that happened, Amel could not expect to pass unhindered. Ev'rel especially enjoyed knowing he was wrestling for his composure when, for the less observant, he maintained a serviceably cool facade.

Amel went, instead, to Silver Hearth. Ev'rel expected him to be there. And he might need Luthan's help. If Erien found that suspicious, let him. There were plenty of excuses he could cook up, like needing to check the score he'd told him that he could adapt.

Princess Luthan, to the shock and chagrin of her chief maid, agreed to see him in her dressing room. She was well and thoroughly dressed, in full skirt, bodice and petticoats. A lady-in-waiting was fixing Luthan's torn hem. Everything else about Luthan was pressed, washed and curled to perfection.

She looked so pretty Amel couldn't help but smile.

"Oh, Amel," she said, "I'm such a child. I've gone and torn my dress at the last minute."

"By means of what offense?" he replied, in his best parlor manner. "Running in the halls? Frisking? Climbing on a chair?"

She wrinkled her nose at him. "A person has to move about."

"That's what Demish dresses are carefully designed to stifle. So," he passed judgment, "it deserved the tear."

She giggled, ending unexpectedly with, "You look lovely!"

Amel spread his arms to show off his tunic. "It's from Ev'rel. She cleaned out everything else in my closet that I could reasonably wear."

"Don't complain," she accused him. "You like it."

"I do confess," he said, "it's beautiful. Listen, Luthan, will you be long? I badly need to talk with you, alone."

The lady-in-waiting looked up, needle in hand, with a look of quiet dismay.

Luthan only frowned. "The hem will do," she said.

"But your uncle, Admiral H'Us—" protested the lady-in-waiting.

"I'll see Prince Amel in the visiting parlor, not here," said Luthan, "but keep everyone out for ten minutes, will you, please?"

The lady-in-waiting looked straight at Amel, to assess the threat. He smiled. She paled, and plucked at Princess Luthan's sleeve without taking her eyes off the dangerous male presence. "Your Highness, I don't think you should. Not Prince Amel."

"Oh, honestly!" Luthan exclaimed. "What do you think he's going to do? Seduce me? In ten minutes?"

"But with your marriage to Heir Nersal so close—"

"Psh," Luthan flaunted her worldly wisdom. "Dorn Nersal would be relieved if Amel did seduce me. The Vrellish think virginity is something to be pitied, you know. But don't be afraid for me, Rissa," Luthan assured her friend, patting the back of Rissa's hand. "He'll never manage it. You see, I know I could never get back into all these clothes fast enough to receive my guests."

The lady-in-waiting's expression suffered this series of kittenish shocks with progressive alarm that was just too priceless. Amel laughed.

"Luthan," he admonished, "you're horrible. She doesn't mean a word," he told the lady-in-waiting. To Luthan he added, "I'll meet you there," and made his own way to the visiting parlor. As he left, he heard Luthan following up with clucking reassurances.

Luthan's visiting parlor was cozy. It was brightly lit and well padded with drapery and cushions, but less cluttered than when it was ruled by Luthan's predecessor. Amel had known it well, then, when he visited the late Liege H'Us. He had played his tri-lyre, read poetry and listened to her recount her long, and largely uneventful life, while she died of regenerative cancer. The modern parlor's puffy upholstery was done in pastel floral patterns of yellow, green, and blue, on a base of white. It smelled of peppermint tea. A maid, setting up the tea things, fled, looking back at the door for a 'too good to be true' double-take. This effect of Amel's good looks was more superficial than the 'drinking you in' stare, but equally prone to hit either sex. It had nothing to do with attraction. People did it, Amel had decided, to confirm that he was real; or perhaps to confirm that he was not. Beauty could create great distance even when it drew a second look. He shook the feeling off, angry with himself for being spooked over trivia.

Luthan rustled in and sat them both down on a couch, taking his hand. "Now," she said, looking at him soberly, "what's up?"

Her heart-shaped face, framed by golden curls, affected Amel's own sense of the gloriously beautiful, and in fact she was more Golden Demish even than he was. With a look, she could melt his heart, though her body felt oddly remote. She lived for him in her face and those wide blue eyes. Perhaps it was her youth which kept his usual sexuality out of the question—she had only recently bloomed into womanhood—or all of the petticoats, or the sturdy sense of friendship which he valued so much more. Right now, he relied on it.

"Luthan," he pressed the soft, creamy fingers holding his hand, "I need to ask a favor, a serious favor, of you."

"I understand."

He inhaled to impress on her the nature of 'serious', and found that the words turned to air in his mouth. She did understand. Beneath the golden, curling tresses, and the petticoats, Luthan was her own special sort of bedrock.

Instead, he let his worry show. "There's a friend. Someone who doesn't deserve the hate that might be unleashed on her if—well, if things to do with me don't work out."

"Who?"

"I can't tell you that. Not yet, anyhow. She is a commoner. She has a little girl," watching Luthan's expression turn knowledgeable he immediately added, "not mine. The child is also commoner. But these people are precious to me. More precious than I can sometimes bear to think about. I may need a safe place for them, for a little while, if I can't immediately get them both away from Court."

"Amel," she drew his hands closer, "what's this about?"

He shook his head, undone by her concern, and looked away from her into the soft pastels of the couch. Its floral pattern was Sevolite-friendly, without repetition which would jump out at a talented navigator like a visual assault. The colors soothed. But her gentle touch threatened to drain his soul, melting down his compartmentalized roles into one man. That would betray too much. Gently, he claimed his own hand back.

"You are owed an answer but I can't give one," he said. "It is personal. At least, it concerns something that I feel I have the right to take my own risks over for my own reasons. These people though, they deserve better than that."

He'd said too much. He saw an echo of the depth he spoke from settle into her expression, as if he'd conveyed emotion without other meaningful context. Just raw fear and raw love.

Fear lay on the surface of his skin, fresh and palpable. He couldn't afford to dwell on it. He'd freeze up. Not to mention the pressure building up that warned of another clear dream attack.

He rose quickly but in good order. "I have to go now."

She stood with every bit as much vigor. "You aren't coming then? To play for us?"

It was touching that she seemed crushed.

He pressed a palm to her shoulder with affection. "Ah, but I've arranged a substitute. Pr—" He'd been about to say 'prince'—appropriate enough in Demish circles, however Vrellish the man involved—but Gods! He really was coming apart. He covered the error with a plausible cough. "Erien, ward of Monitum, is on Tatt's hands at court."

"Erien?" Luthan touched her throat in a typically female gesture, for a Demish woman. She knew the name. Amel knew that Tatt had shared Erien's letters with her. "But Erien is with the Nersallian Fleet, in Killing Reach."

"No, he's freshly discharged by Liege Nersal himself," Amel told her, "not, apparently, suitable. And he's worried about Ranar, his Reetion guardian. Erien plays the flute. I thought it would do him good to get his mind off politics for an hour."

"He plays the flute?" Luthan batted long, golden lashes.

"I thought you might be curious," Amel smiled back. "You've heard so much about him, through Tatt."

"And he's here? At court? And coming? Today? Now?"

Amel was delighted by her betrayal of a girlish crush, for all he wasn't sure that it was a safe one. Erien was much too cold. He just hoped she figured that out, fast. For now he kissed her forehead. "Yes, gift-wrapped."

"Oh Amel!" she gave him a parting swat. "I didn't mean it like that. I've read bits of his letters, that's all. About Rire. Letters that he sent to Tatt. He's got a wonderful mind for analysis."

"Luthan," Amel ignored her protests, "about my other business. I need to know if I can count on you."

"To harbor precious commoners for you?"

He smiled. She summed it up succinctly, but in earnest, not with sarcasm.

"And they're innocent?" she asked. "I mean, of anything awful?"

"Yes," he insisted, "I promise that."

"I promise too, then," she told him.

"Thank you Luthan. Thank you—more than I can ever let you know!" He gave her a swift, heartfelt hug, and quickly begged the more immediate favor.

"Can I pass through Silver Hearth? I want to get up to the docks."

"Certainly," she said.

"Give my best to Amy, and to Dorn Nersal," he said politely in parting, quite sure the Nersallian would not care one way or the other. He tried to like Dorn Nersal for Amy's sake. She was Ayrium's daughter, by Ameron, and Perry D'Aur's granddaughter.

"I will. Be careful!" Luthan finished on a rising note.

Three traveling cloaks were hung up near the base of Silver Hearth's ascent to the plaza. Amel took two, rolling the deep-blue velvet lady's garment inside the plainer black escort's one.

Around the cloaks he formed a plan, determined to be free of the haunting fear of being followed, even if it cost him precious time. At the top of the stairs, he made small talk with the H'Usian watch-captain until he had successfully conveyed the impressions he desired, should the man be openly questioned by Lilac Hearth, or more cleverly tapped by some minion of Charous'. He let the watch-captain know he was seeking a distraction from the news of the kill-show, which had understandably unsettled him, but that he was afraid to go very far afield, alone.

The H'Usian watch-captain recommended an establishment on the plaza. It proved a nice place. Nothing fancy. Dancers performed on a central mat, outside a pavilion, surrounded by tables. Amel ordered wine and food.

His presence awed the two young sword dancers on stage. As Pureblood Amel he could not perform for Sevolites, but he'd become legendary in courtesan circles by showing up to work out with them behind closed doors. The dancers eagerly showed off. When they had finished, he smiled, got up, and slipped his shoes off to join them on the mat, fully aware that he'd thereby become the main attraction.

"You've put a lot of work into your stop-action poses." He acknowledged the male dancer's greatest gift, which was his precision of execution. "It works well against your partner's fluidity."

"I can't get the knack of a pose, Immortality," the girl confessed. "My stop action just looks jerky."

"Then be fluid."

"You mean—just don't pose?"

"No," he said, "I mean, when you stop, stop like water. Water doesn't come to rest all at once, but when it does, it is tranquil. Be tranquil." Amel took the boy's realistic-looking plastic sword and led the girl back on stage.

By now, they had attracted a fresh audience. The bundled cloaks sat on his chair, inviting any wary watchers attuned to his habits to assume that he was sufficiently diverted by his passion for dance to get careless.

Memorizing the pair's routine had been unconscious and effortless. He drew on that knowledge now, cueing the girl dancer with a few moves.

They worked through a passage. He stopped them, showed her what he meant, and repeated the section five times, in isolation, before putting it back into sustained action. It was wonderful to feel her working with him and picking the idea up.

The audience accepted this trivial display of his forbidden art with silence, not sure of the right way to react.

"Let's go inside," he told his partner, hand around her waist still, relaxing from the pose they'd halted at.

On the way, he handed the male dancer's sword back, saying, "Thanks." The straight armed gesture and finality of tone, achieved its goal. The girl's partner hung back.

"Oh," Amel tipped his head toward the cloaks he'd left behind, "could you bring those?"

The boy obeyed and turned back to fetch the cloaks.

Amel let the girl assume he wanted a private room. She passed seamlessly from artist to prostitute, like any good courtesan.

"I want your help," Amel told her, as soon as they'd sat down together on a serviceably wide couch.

Her eyes widened. She gave a slight start at her partner's knock.

He came in. "Your cloaks, Immortality." He addressed Amel with proper differencing.

"What's your name?" Amel forestalled his departure.

"Wade." The boy put on a wary sulk.

"What's the cloak worth, Wade?" Amel asked, tipping his eyes toward the velvet one.

Wade shrugged. "Enough," he said, and hedged his bets. "Perhaps."

Amel found his suspicions offensive and turned to the girl, instead.

"I'm Vale," she told him.

He nodded his thanks for the offered name. "Vale, I want you to wait here, with Wade, while I leave in his dancer's drape. You have one?" The boy nodded. He was about fifteen, Amel estimated. The girl was maybe a year older. The boy was relaxing, the girl was tensing up.

"After twenty minutes," Amel went on, "I want both of you to let yourselves out, in these cloaks, which you may keep afterwards as payment."

"What do we do?" Wade asked, excited and willing now.

"Walk toward the UnderDocks, keeping your faces covered."

Wade nodded.

"Will it be dangerous?" Vale asked.

"If you're questioned," Amel told her, "tell whoever asks, quite truthfully, that I paid you to play decoy. They might reclaim the cloaks. I don't believe there is more risk than that. I won't claim that there is none; on the other hand, I do not know for certain that I'm being followed at all right now. It may be simply a matter of giving people something misleading to report after the fact." He paused to let them think about that. They trusted him implicitly, he could see that. It gave him pause, but he was certain that what he had told them was the truth. "When you get to the UnderDocks, take off the cloaks and come back again in something of your own."

"We'd be impersonating Sevolites." The boy pointed out the deal's biggest drawback.

"Which only matters," said Amel, "if you get stopped. But here," he unclasped the leather belt that had been holding his tunic in stylish folds at his waist. The leather was worth more than the jeweled ship-and-sun buckle, but the latter proclaimed House Dem'Vrel allegiance. "If any lesser Sevolite interferes with you, show this, and explain that you are acting at my request. If you are taken to Avim Ev'rel, she'll ask you questions but she won't do you harm. You have probably heard that she and I are *mekan'stan*. We are."

Both courtesans nodded, gravely.

"Let's get started then," Amel said, and rose.

Wade fetched him a courtesan dancer's drape, which was slinkier than a Sevolite traveling cloak and made of synthetic fibers.

Amel put it on, flipping up the hood, and left through the back of the pavilion, slipping around a worker delivering food. He made his way quickly through similar, mundane scenes, in the alley between pavilions on the plaza, looking for an opportunity to get passage to the UnderDocks. It came in the shape of an electric-powered garbage car. The driver accepted his claim to be an UnderDocks courtesan brought to the plaza by a Vrellish woman, deserted, and in need of passage home. Amel was careful not to offer more than the wages such a person could afford. The cab was clean. Amel kept his hood up, screening his features from all except a direct, face-to-face inspection. The driver was male and not interested in Amel. He made off-color jokes and fished for stories about Vrellish women. Amel was used to that from when he'd really been a courtesan.

He did not, however, want to actually transverse the UnderDocks in a courtesan's dancer drape. Instead he bought himself an electrician's overall, and tied the dancer's drape around his waist, inside, to change his shape a little. The problem of his infamous face he solved by bandaging half of it in a torn shirt, soaked in his own blood from a shallow cut he made in his scalp. A small knife which came with the electrician's tools served for that. Amel's Sevolite blood pressure took care of making an obliging mess before the bleeding stopped. The net result looked bad enough to explain him walking into Mira's clinic. His new clothes smelled of oil, and the bandage of dust and blood, but at least they masked Ev'rel's shampoo.

Mira was open for business.

Amel let himself in as any patient would.

Three other walk-ins, seated or lying on mats just inside the door, sized him up as competition for the medtech's attention. Ability to pay was the usual parameter. In Mira's clinic, severity of need could tip the balance, which paid too, in goodwill that dissuaded vandalism.

Amel kept his head down, and masked his face with a stiff-fingered, trembling hand. He didn't stop by the mats, which brought a seated patient to his feet, saying, "Hey!"

"Wash, gotta wash," Amel muttered, trying to convey the impression that he had suffered a chemical burn. He could do UnderDocks dialects flawlessly.

"You have to wait, like everyone else," said the disgruntled patient, and started for him as Amel made for the examination room.

Mira came out, armed with a skin-press hypo.

"This guy—" complained the self-deputized patient.

"It's all right," she said firmly. "I'll see him."

The patient looked annoyed. "Is it going to be long?"

"Come at Lights Up tomorrow, if your problem can wait but you can't," said Mira. "I do things in my own order."

With a glum look, the patient accepted that and stalked out.

Mira, of course, had recognized Amel. She always could.

"He keeps getting the Itch." Mira cited the vernacular for a common sexually transmitted fungal infection which had flared up in the UnderDocks three years before. She, and other clinics, were stocked with the cure for public health reasons. It was free the first time, with escalating fines thereafter, and a stiff penalty for failure to report. Control relied on it being administered, in person, by each medtech, with records kept by patient genotype, taken from blood samples. Mira approved of the system. Amel never told her that Ev'rel was its architect. He wished he could have, but Ev'rel was a subject they avoided.

"Are you injured?" Mira asked him, dubiously. He was standing straight, now.

He pulled the bloody bandage off. "We have to talk. Now. Where's Mona?"

"Here, of course." She inspected the source of blood, in his scalp, with practiced callousness. "Huh. Even Mona can fix that."

"Mira—"

"I have patients to get rid of. Go wait with Mona and get cleaned up."

Helpless before her logic, he agreed with a nod.

"And have her seam that cut," Mira called. "It's good practice for her, and even you can catch infections. Nasty ones, if another highborn was the incubating host."

"Yes, Mira," Amel said, vexed by the needless fuss.

Mona was delighted to play doctor and to have him to herself while he cleaned up in the little bathroom on their secret apartment's second floor.

"It's so soft!" Mona fondled his dancer's drape, which she held in her lap.

"But synthetic. Feel this," he stroked the front of Ev'rel's gift tunic, which he'd just pulled on. Mira buried her face in it, tickling him as she rubbed her nose back and forth, then turning the gesture into a hug with her cheek pressed against him, hard.

She said, "Mmm. It's silk."

Amel stroked the back of her dark head. The skin of her neck felt baby-new, fine hairs lining up to point down her back beneath a childish, round collar. He remembered, when she was two, wanting to hug her as hard as he could, as long as he could, and to entomb her forever in some vault to which no harm could come. But entombment was its own harm.

"Mona." He moved her back and dropped to his knees, his freshly washed hair still damp. The bathroom he'd built for them was small. They filled the whole space between the sink and the shower.

"Yes?" she said. He held her by the elbows. Her small, clever hands lay on his arms, toying with the silk sleeves.

"I see you're wearing my pendant," he noticed.

Mona lifted a hand to the bauble around her neck.

"Mona," he began anew, "don't you think you'd like to live where people made things like the pendant?"

"On Rire?"

"Yes."

"With you?"

"Sometimes."

She was growing wary. "Would you come more often than you do now?"

He could not lie to her outright, so he said nothing.

"Less often?" She sounded afraid, and small.

Amel hugged her. "Oh Mona, poor Mona, it's hard to explain now, but one day it won't hurt. You'll be happy. You'll have so much more."

He could feel her begin to quake in his arms and was ashamed. He could lie better. Why hadn't he?

"Mona." He took her by the shoulders and demanded her attention with a grave, parental look. "It is getting very dangerous for you to stay here. You and Mira. Dangerous for us all. I need your help to work something better out. Do you understand?"

She blinked, and answered with a sad, mindful nod.

He wiped tears from her cheek with a thumb. "When I've worked the problems out, you know I will come, as often as I can."

"I thought," she said, in a small voice, "that Rire was a long way. I thought it wasn't safe, when I was little, to take me so far."

"Well, you're not so little as you were."

Mira was standing in the jam of the door, feelings showing only in the bloodless tensions about her mouth and eyes.

"Come on," Amel stood, and lifted Mona to sit on his left arm. "I'll take you to your room. I have to talk to your mother."

"I wish you were my daddy," Mona murmured, on his shoulder.

"Don't," he soothed. "You had a good daddy." *A real daddy, who Mira should talk to Mona about more often, in fact.* It was an old complaint, comfortable, although now, perhaps, was not the right time to remind the child about protectors who had died and abandoned her.

He left Mona with instructions to pack whatever things she wanted him to send after her, without adding that it might not be possible. For now, she was to take nothing at all.

Mira was waiting in her lab.

She looked old.

She was not old, he reminded himself fiercely. She was just commoner. The lines on her face showed, that was all.

Expecting a barrage of questions, he waited.

When it was clear she would not start, he cleared his throat. "You were right. About the kill-shows."

"I know."

"I am going to take you and Mona to Ann, at *SkyBlue Station*, right now. She'll look after you. She owes me a favor."

"Things are getting that precarious for you," Mira diagnosed.

"No, for you," Amel tried to impress on her. She inhaled, but he was suddenly angry, and vented at her. "A medtech attended the victim, with Tatt. A smart medtech. You're helping him, aren't you? You're poking around, although I told you not to."

She stood up with such dignity it silenced him.

"And I've found, not one madman, or profiteer, but a ground swell of fascination with you in pain, coupled with a growing violence toward Rire. A sprawling fascination, lewd, aggressive, even worshipful. Out of control, Amel!" The spike in her tone pierced him.

Shades of unsettled horror toyed with his courage like some obscene foreplay. He caught his breath.

"I can take care of myself," he said with slow deliberation.

Mira sat down. "No, you can't."

"Really?" He traded fear for anger, grateful for any exchange for a commodity he did not want. "And you can? That's why you were so self-sufficient—when I found you again—that you were letting Mona starve!"

"I've seen you brought lower," she struck back.

Amel raised a fisted hand to his mouth, tapping it on his lips to hold words and anger back. Whiteness threatened. *Not now!* he begged the demons stalking him. *Not now.* Visceral memories scrambled his stomach and made nerve endings prickle as if he stood naked and vulnerable before a foe. But there was no flash of disorientation. He dropped his fisted hand.

"That's true," he said, faintly, and sat down on his couch.

From behind her desk, Mira leaned forward. She said, "Come with us."

"I can't."

"You can't afford to take us, in the middle of all this, and come waltzing back!"

"I'll explain it."

"Amel, tensions are high, all around. Come with us."

"I can't leave, now, Mira."

"Why?"

He inhaled against profound hopelessness, mumbling, "You won't understand."

"It's Ev'rel." She said it with hatred so black that it curdled the blood in Amel's heart. "I know her, better than you do. I worked for her. I did that because she's worth working for. Any argument you could give me to excuse her I could once have given you. The Throne Price changed that. Forever. Gods, Amel! Surely it must have for you as well."

"I don't want to talk about Ev'rel!"

"What?"

"It's not just—Mira, he's here. Erien. At court. And Ameron's Swearing is coming up."

Mira shook her head, denying these secondary distractions. "You trust her," she realized, with cold contempt. "You trust her damn promise."

"She did let you go," he insisted.

"To run. To hide from her the rest of my life, in fear. To leave her clear to do what she likes with—"

He could not bear what else she might say, and cut her off, crying, in mortal shame, "Mira, I've done the best I could!"

Weakness overcame any resistance to tears left by crippled pride. He turned his head aside, rubbing fingertips over the skin above his eyebrows.

Mira said, with damning sadness, "I know you have."

Pity was a terrible blow.

"Let me get you out of here," he begged.

She was implacable. "If you don't go, I won't go."

It was her ultimate weapon, but she asked the impossible.

He swallowed. "Then at least—let me take Mona. Princess Luthan has agreed to harbor innocents for me. Commoners. No questions asked. Let me take her there until I visit Ann."

He was glad then, of everything he'd told her about Luthan. Her mouth firmed. He knew she loved her daughter every bit as much as he did. She gave him a sober nod.

CHAPTER VIII

"WHY DON'T YOU JUST SAY IT and get it over with!" Tatt swung from the wardrobe door, with a brilliantly embroidered shirt in his hand.

Erien said calmly, "Tatt, I don't think that would suit me."

Tatt glanced at the shirt and dropped it, pointedly eliminating it as a subject of conversation. "You've had the same judgmental expression ever since we spoke to Amel. Just tell me what I've done wrong."

Erien sighed, "I'm not sure you have done anything wrong."

"But! I can hear a but!"

"Tatt, do you realize that Amel probably did not know anything about Asher until you told him?"

"He asked me if the medtech had been able to tell whether it was an accidental overdose."

"Neither you nor I have much medical background. Since we knew what had caused the death, he had to infer we had a source of information."

Ditatt stepped over the heap of discarded clothing to confront Erien. "What's wrong with Amel knowing?"

"There may be nothing wrong," Erien said, "but he manipulated you into disclosure instead of asking you outright. He used your compassion for his distress to put you off guard. Why would he do that?"

Tatt flushed, vividly and sullenly, and stalked past Erien and out the door. After a moment's indecision, Erien bent and began to gather up the discarded clothing, returning each piece to its hanger. Tatt was dreadfully untidy; he would not have lasted a day in the fleet. Untidy, impulsive, trusting, thoughtless in small ways, and deeply committed to the greater justice. *I should not have said anything,* Erien thought. *I should not have upset Tatt simply because Amel had upset me.*

Tatt walked back in as abruptly as he had left, Erien's flute case in his hand. "Here," he said tersely.

"Tatt, I don't have time—"

"You have time to come and be pleasant to the future Liege H'Us, who is a very nice girl and potentially a powerful ally, if that is all that matters to you."

"I'm not an entertainer," Erien said, choosing the politest of terms— but there was no evading the sexual meaning underlying any word for musician or performer. The only professional musicians on Gelion were courtesans.

"You can say that again." Tatt went to the wardrobe. "Let me put it this way," he said over his shoulder. "If you disappoint Luthan, I'll take it out of your hide. On the Octagon. With a sharpened point." He leaned into the wardrobe and hauled out a jacket in charcoal and slate gray. "Here. Is this drab enough for you?"

Erien, who had adopted nondescript dress along with imperturbability as a protective measure—so long ago it had been more instinct than rational decision—felt as uneasy seeing distinctive clothing on himself as he admired it on others. He was wearing, quite comfortably, his black fleet uniform, stripped of all insignia. "Yes," he said, drawing on the jacket.

"It's tight across the shoulders," Tatt said critically. "You must have some Demish in you." He made an exasperated noise. "Didn't it even occur to you that if you came to court you might need something other than a dress uniform and fatigues?" He sounded very like a tutor they had both had, years ago, on Monitum.

"No," said Erien, quite truthfully.

"The Reetions have ruined you," Tatt said. "You'll have to go in Monatese livery for this afternoon. Everything formal I have is braided."

Erien drew breath to ask what was supposed to be happening this afternoon, but Tatt said abruptly, "Why shouldn't Amel know about Asher?"

Erien was silent. In all honesty, he did not himself know. All he felt was a profound and instinctive mistrust of a man so careful, so unwilling to let himself be known by others. A man, he admitted, rather too much like himself. Only the camouflage was different. Amel's was by far the more successful. His exhibitions of affection, attention and indulgence quite disguised how little he was prepared to give in other coin. *I, at least,* Erien thought, *do not hide what I am.* But that was cold comfort, after the recognition of likeness.

"You don't know, do you?" Tatt said triumphantly. "You just don't like him. Well, I know him, and the worst he'll do is tell Ameron to find something for us to do to keep us out of trouble. And Erien," Tatt added conspiratorially, "it's never worked before." Tatt caught up his cloak and sword, the cloak black with turquoise-lined flares and a brilliant blue lining, and the sword a dress version, the hilt inlaid with turquoise and abalone. He swung the cloak around his shoulders with a flourish. "Come on. Try not to look like the specter of doom. Today's important to Luthan." He frowned at the flute case. "Are you really able to play that, or should I send a runner for a real musician? Vish might be free, though it's a trifle early for her," he added, with a certain air of self-congratulation. "She's becoming quite popular."

"I can play it. But what is the event?"

"Shh. You'll find out when you get there."

"And this afternoon?" Erien said patiently.

"Didn't I tell you? The betrothal. Dorn's and Luthan's. The Lion-Dragon accord. The marriage alliance between Nersal and H'Us. However you want to think of it. Ameron's decided to make it formal before the Swearing." Ditatt frowned. "It shows how worried he is. The promise of the betrothal prevented H'Us from giving his Oath to Ev'rel. He's always wanted a Nersallian alliance, so it was too good to pass up when Ameron persuaded Liege Nersal to accept a Demish marriage and to gift the children, in Vrellish terms, which exempts them from sharing the *kinf'stan* challenge right—nobody in their right mind should sleep with a Nersallian without that clause in the contract," he added with feeling. His mother's only youthful folly had given her a Nersallian son, Branstatt, who was disenfranchised of his *kinf'stan* status by a similar agreement. "H'Us jumped at it, quite uncommonly friskily. And as long as Nersal swears to Ameron, then H'Us will follow. But he's been wavering again. He really doesn't like Rire. H'Us is an old-style treaty isolationist, can't fathom why Ameron's changed his mind. He wouldn't, not over a mere two centuries." Ditatt pulled a solemn face. "Still you'll like Luthan," he said, with another swift change of mood. "She's interested in everything and has a very original mind. She's a sweet girl, too. Very pretty, in a Demish sort of way, but she'll be beautiful in about twenty years," predicted Ditatt, sagely. "And in a year she'll come of age, and officially become Liege H'Us. That's if her uncles will ever let her do anything, which I doubt. At least not without a fight." He looked as though he rather relished the prospect. "So if you come with me, and are nice to her, you never know, it may help Ranar. Though," Tatt added, looking Erien up and down, "what she'll make of you, I don't know."

When Erien's attire had passed Tatt's critique, they took their cloaks—although Tatt wore his over his arm—and crossed Fountain Court, unaccompanied by an escort, to enter Silver Hearth.

"We just go ahead and show ourselves in, when we're expected," Tatt said proudly, with a nod for the H'Usian errant standing guard.

"Luthan decided it was hypocritical to have servants waiting on us while we discuss the rights of commoners. She serves the refreshments herself, too, in her sitting room."

Erien withheld comment.

They branched off the entrance hall before the Throat, passing quickly through tidy errant barracks, through a children's playroom, emptied of children, though not of the relics of children. They were ornate and pristine, these relics: a trio of rocking horses in pastels and gold, a small table with an ornamental tea set neatly arrayed, a wardrobe hung with fancy dress clothes. The centerpiece—taking up a quarter of the room—was an entire miniature village, spread on emerald green hills along a flowing stream. Each of the tiny people was set in place in carefully composed groups of pastoral labor, not one isolated, misplaced or tipped over. Erien would have stopped to study it—he had never seen such a thing, and it spoke to him of a childhood quite unlike either of the ones he had enjoyed, on Monitum and on Rire—but Tatt whisked him on, through a white-tiled vestibule, to a pair of white doors painted in trellis-weave.

"These are the ladies' rooms," Ditatt explained to Erien. "In Green Hearth the same space is full of old books and empty guest rooms, in Red Hearth the guest rooms are occupied and Vretla throws parties. You'll have to tell me what Liege Nersal has in the 'cheeks' of Black Hearth, one day."

The doors opened on happy sounds of conversation. The room had an open, airy look, despite the white drapery covering the walls and the floral-patterned sofas. There were small tables beside the sofas and two prominent easy chairs, but no big table obstructing the middle of the room. Tea things sat off to one side on a serving sideboard. White and blue carnations stood in ancient china vases on the floor near the doors.

Serving peppermint tea to Dorn Nersal and a Vrellishly-attired woman was a short girl with a cascade of golden hair who wore a white dress with long sleeves, a high collar and full skirts that swished briskly as she moved. From the back she looked like one of the miniature milkmaids, full grown and come to life.

"Luthan!" Tatt skipped formalities with abandon.

The girl with the tea pot turned around. She was the same young woman that Erien had seen in Ameron's receiving room. Her hair framed an equally doll-like face, but the flush on her creamy cheeks made her look only half tame, although she was thoroughly at home in the padded, domestic atmosphere of the room.

Her eyes held Erien's with bold engagement, lacking device or apology.

"May I introduce the Princess Luthan H'Us," Tatt said, and bowed with a flourish, "both Heir H'Us, and ranking Royalblood around here at ninety-two percent Sevolite." He had, Erien noticed, slipped effortlessly into the gendered nouns and pronouns favored by the Demish court, with its strict distinction of male and female domains.

Luthan continued to stare straight at Erien.

"And this—" Tatt gestured with an open hand, "—is Erien."

The name meant something to her. The blue eyes widened. Steam from the tea pot wrapped her in the smell of peppermint.

"Oh," she said, coming abruptly to herself, and quickly put down her pot of tea, "oh, I'm so pleased you came."

She rushed forward, catching Erien by the hands, "I've heard so much about Rire. It must be lovely—but do you really need a computer's permission to have children?"

Her hands were warm, dry and soft, unhardened by swordwork.

"Luthan!" laughed the other woman, who was wearing pants. "What a question to greet the man with!" She was beige and fawn against Luthan's white, her black hair caught in a plain clasp at the back of her neck.

"But, Amy, he's lived there," protested the Demish Princess. "And I want to know." She did release Erien's hands, blushing mildly at her forwardness.

Erien could still feel the touch. "The short answer is yes," he managed, "with the addendum that permission is seldom denied outright, though partners can be asked to wait, for a reasonable interval, or move somewhere appropriate. The arbiters are responsible for monitoring and predicting population demographics, and ensuring that the population does not exceed optimal density. Optimal being what the environment and what the social structure can stand."

Tatt whispered, audibly, in her ear, "If that's the short answer, do you really want to hear the long version?"

Her golden eyebrows drew together slightly. Tatt seized the moment. "Amel sends his regrets. He's . . . something's happened," he added with airy avuncularity. "Nothing to worry about."

"Yes, Amel came to tell me so," said Luthan. "But it did seem, to me, it must have been something serious," she narrowed her eyes slightly at Tatt, but decided to appeal to Erien instead.

"Do you know what it was?" she asked.

"There was a killing in the UnderDocks last night," said Erien, "a young courtesan who had been made up to look like Amel."

Luthan's eyes widened with a little gasp. "Made up?" She looked from Erien to Ditatt and back with determined innocence. "Why would—oh, it's something to do with—" Vague as they must have been, the implications sunk in with a loss of color as she raised a hand to her throat.

Tatt gave Erien an angry look. "Erien's going to deputize for Amel," he strove to salvage the situation. "He's quite competent with that thing," Tatt rapped the flute case with his knuckles, "supposedly."

Luthan was tempted to a shy but dubious glance at Erien's flute. When she looked up and found his eyes on her, she smiled her thanks. "Whatever you can manage will be very much appreciated," she said, as an afterthought. Then she briskly resumed her role as hostess. "Erien, have you met Dorn? And Amy?" The young woman in fawn and beige inclined her head without rising. Royalblood Amy was the elder of Ameron's two love children by Ayrium. Unlike most love children, who were by definition unplanned for in the political scheme of things, Amy had an inheritance: she was heir to her mother's Purple Alliance in Killing Reach. Her father also treated her as de facto master of White Hearth, his own official Fountain Court residence, which for the obvious reason that Ameron was the last Lor'Vrel on Gelion, was seldom used. Although just seventeen, Amy looked years older than the less worldly Demish princess. She wore trousers and a sword with a worn pearl handle.

"Highlord Erien," Amy said, and then smiled with sudden mischief. "My mother remembers hauling you out of a tree on Monitum under the impression that you were a *gorarelpul* assassin after Father."

Erien was sure that Ayrium did. He wished that he, himself, did not.

"I remember that," Tatt said. "I think it was the only time that Ameron visited while you lived on Monitum. He took you to ride with him." That spoken with a trace of old envy. "You never did tell me what you talked to him about."

Luthan rescued Erien with a brisk, and slightly quelling, "Would you like some peppermint tea, Prince Ditatt? Or I have lemon, or orange flower, or blackberry or . . . I've always wanted to try some of that Reetion hot chocolate," she added to Erien, "but I understand it's not good for Sevolites."

"I like hot chocolate," Erien said, mildly, "though whichever of my Reetion guardians gave in to me, when I asked, was never very popular with the other two. It contains a stimulant, called caffeine, which Sevolites are sensitive to. It tended to make me a more active and impulsive child than usual. Rather like Tatt, in fact."

Tatt made a face at him. Amy said, "The Gods forfend."

Luthan served peppermint tea. Tatt perched on the edge of the sofa to drink it, his sheathed sword resting against his ankle, giving the impression of being ready to leap up and move at the least excuse. Amy and Dorn were more relaxed. Erien eased away from the group, having noticed the stack of music beside the tea tray on the sideboard. He put down his cup and saucer—he did not particularly like peppermint tea—

and slid the top sheets from the stack. They were a mixture of plastic and parchment, the parchment covered in antique musical notation, the plastic a modern transcription in Amel's hand. The transcriptions were scored for tri-lyre. The most challenging, and the most deceptively simple, was a three part setting with a single melody passed back and forth between the three parts. He laid it aside regretfully. He could have extracted the melody but it would have eviscerated the piece, for it was the harmony that made it. None of it was flute music, he thought, with unreasonable resentment. None of it was written to display his instrument's true voice.

He became abruptly aware of Luthan at his shoulder, studying his face. He said, "Princess, forgive me, it's been a long time since I saw new music."

"Oh," she said, "I thought you were just shy."

He blinked.

Tatt was absorbed in telling Dorn and Amy a long and highly embellished version of Erien's childhood encounter with Ameron. Luthan glanced towards him, with affection, and then turned those blue, blue eyes back to Erien. "What were you and Tatt arguing about before you came in?"

Erien looked at her, wordless.

"You were arguing about something. It was written all over both of you." Her confident assessment gave way to anxiety. "I hope it wasn't about playing for my party. You don't have to. I mean, I know it is an imposition to ask . . . you." The pronoun, downward differenced as it was, nevertheless stood for everything she did not need to say. One did not expect a Sevolite to play entertainer. Erien, though he had resisted, knew he had done so out of annoyance at Tatt and Amel.

"No," Erien assured her, "it was not about this. I am very pleased to play for you. And this," his fingers brushed the music, "is like a feast to a very hungry man. All I've heard for the last three years have been barracks songs and the occasional Nesak religious chant. But could you tell me what I'm playing for?"

"Didn't Tatt tell you? Oh, I could hit him sometimes."

"He was being mysterious. Only that it was something important to you."

A flush came up on her fair skin. "You know the marriage contract is to be announced this afternoon, for me and Dorn? It's important. To my house, and to Ameron. And it's all right. I've always known I wouldn't get to choose. But Amy and Dorn are in love. I believe in love. I wanted them to have a celebration of their own, first. To let them know it's all right. I mean, if Dorn treats marriage like a Vrellish child contract."

She said it with such a stubborn expectation of dismissal that he did not know how to respond. He had little experience with Demish ideas of love, and he was sure neither Reetion nor Vrellish interpretations of human sexuality belonged here. He felt very awkwardly male. He said, at last, lamely, "That's . . . generous of you, Princess."

"No, it's not," she said, a little fiercely. "It's right."

Erien looked back at the music. "Is there anything here you think particularly suitable? That you like?" he amended, trying to unstiffen.

She gazed at him. "You are shy, aren't you? Your letters aren't." Then she blushed and burrowed into the music. "I like this one," she said, "and this one." She laid both down before him and turned away, still flustered. Tatt caught his eye, scowled, and gestured threateningly with a fingertip. Luthan glanced from one to the other, startled, then decided to set it aside, and went to the door to call in her ladies-in-waiting.

There were eight of them, all fair-haired though none as golden as Luthan, blue-eyed, dressed in skirts and young-looking. The youth, Erien knew, was deceiving—highborns could be any age, from Luthan's sixteen to over a century. But as with Old Swords, it was the eyes that told. The truly young were maidens, as innocent as Luthan. The others were matrons: veterans of at least one marriage, child-bearing, and perhaps widowhood, not high enough in status and influence to secure their independence, and so destined either to remarry or serve as attendants to a superior.

He thought suddenly, oddly, of the tropical aviary on the Reetion world of Mega, home to the most extraordinary collection of species, native, adapted native, imported and re-engineered, found in Reetion space. He remembered sitting cross-legged on one of the high platforms while the birds pranced and preened and flitted all around him. Flashes of yellow eyes, or white-rimmed blue, or long-slitted bronze. Tails like lace, or blood-tipped spears, or barred fans, or a spray of flowers. Their voices ran quicker and higher than any instrument; all around him, they were a tiny, living symphony. For the first time, here, he wondered whether the birds had felt their space too small after the skies, or whether they had truly grown accustomed to his intrusion. He felt awkward and drab and dark, amongst all this avian, exotic splendor.

In the midst of her ladies, Luthan caused an outbreak of "oohs" and "aahs" liberally peppered with faint exclamations of "a Monitum?"—intrigued—and "not Amel then, at all?"—with disappointment.

Luthan appealed to him, with a glance, for confirmation, over an anonymous whisper, "Can he play though?"

Erien shrugged out of the jacket with its too-tight shoulders, and arranged his music on the stand, then occupied himself with fitting together his flute.

Luthan briefed everyone once more, and the ceremony began.

It proved tender, sentimental and a little absurd, cobbled together as it was from poetry and lushly romantic old drama. It was a ceremony with a single priestess, a handful of acolytes, and a cluster of benign agnostics. The priestess was Luthan, flushed and earnest in her consecration of her groom's love for her friend, and her acolytes were her younger ladies, maidens like herself. The agnostics were Tatt, Dorn, who endured with dignity and affection, and Amy, in whom Erien perceived a determination to have whatever she could, on whatever terms. The elder ladies were spirited players, but players were all they were: there was a stage, and they stepped onstage and off, and from offstage watched with variously indulgent, knowing, and sad eyes.

Someone had taught Luthan how to use her voice. Amel? Erien thought briefly—a thought he found easy to forget. She read the old poetry well and movingly, with a musicality that Erien found easy to take his lead from, using his instrument as accompaniment and commentary. He found, as the timbre of her voice and the rhythms of the poetry made themselves familiar, and persuasive, that he was improvising more than reading the music, collecting the melodies that he heard from and around her, simplifying them to a single, sweet song; a pure sentiment, freed from its burden of cloying poetry. Stopping, letting it go, was sudden and almost bewildering; the way it always was when he played with other instrumentalists and the session was suddenly over, with people insisting on food and sleep and other tasks. He looked at Luthan with a blank wonderment that she should have wanted to stop.

She was gazing at him with deep, poetical appreciation. Caught in admiration, she flushed brightly and turned away to fuss over her guests' departure.

"Thank you so much for indulging me," she stood on her toes to kiss first Dorn, and then Amy, chattering in a voice which had lost the discipline of poetry and become a young girl's again.

Erien was so preoccupied in watching Luthan that the fresh outbreak of petticoated excitement across the room escaped him, until he heard Amel's voice.

The courtesan-prince stood near the door, cloaked in Luthan's ladies paying court. They were making a fuss about him, and someone or something that he had by his side, completely masked by the full skirts of Demish fashion. Amel basked in the attention, letting them feel the material of his rather questionable shirt and even arrange his hair, bantering lightly the whole while, and returning their intimacies in calculated measure. Erien found he could predict that if touched, Amel would touch back, with the boldness about half discounted. Even the ratio of his voice to the female babble felt managed, though the flow was irreproachably natural.

Luthan caught sight of Amel and abandoned leave-takings to greet him, watched by everyone in the room.

Amel drew her aside, brushing her ladies gently away with just enough finality to make a little space without eliminating their value as human screens. The most determined hovered, still hoping for another turn. Erien could see, now, that Amel had a little girl with him. She was dressed in simple, commoner clothes that were as neat as her short, brushed hair. The child studied the room with wary eyes, from her place lodged against Amel's side, beneath his arm. Amel spoke with Luthan in a low voice, answering her questions with a sincere gravity which suggested to Erien that Luthan was not hearing the truth, or hearing only as much truth as Amel thought seemly or in his best interest.

When Amel started to leave, the little girl caught Amel's hand in her own and dragged him back with all her small weight, with near panic and complete determination.

"I don't want to stay here! I want to be with you!" She raised her voice above the levels Amel had set, tacitly, addressing him in commoner-peerage. The ladies rustled.

"Oh dear," said Luthan, clearly, in a freak silence.

Amel settled on his haunches before the child, soothing her. She shook her head again, but there was resignation in it. She knew she must stay, and the best she could hope for was to register her objections, to provoke irritation and anger which would justify the tears that 'for your own good' denied her. Erien well knew how she felt, picked up and moved and left for the convenience of adults. Much good that would do either of them.

Her protests faded, embalmed by Amel's coaxing. But when Amel started to rise, she clutched at him again with one hand, and with the other pulled at a chain on her neck. On the chain hung a fat, gray locket, too large for a child. She pressed it on him. He protested. "But I gave it to you, Mona."

"To make me safe. You said I'm safe here. You said it isn't safe with you. So I'm safe and you're not. You should keep it."

She was defying him, Erien knew, to show Amel that his assurances were lies. Defeated, Amel bowed his head and let her slip the locket over his head and into his shirt.

"Now give me the other part," the child said.

Amel began to answer, "I don't have that. You know who wears—"

Luthan mustered cover by calling her ladies together and discussing the ceremony loudly and vacuously for a few exchanges.

Erien decided to get closer. Luthan intercepted him.

"Thank you so, so very much, for playing." She laid both hands on his arm, then snatched them back, feeling his coolness. Her eyes followed his and she said, quickly, "Amel, now and then, brings me orphans. Or children in need, temporarily, of shelter."

"Very charitable," said Erien.

Amel was saying a final goodbye now, standing with the child plastered against his chest. He stroked her head, the expression on his face as unguarded as Erien had ever seen him. Then he composed himself and eased her away. Over her head, Amel met and held Erien's eyes with a wary look.

Luthan caught the child's hand, placing herself subtly but definitely between the child and Erien. Amel leaned forward into a quick peck for Luthan and left, with a final parting stroke for the child beside her. The little girl watched him go with all the tearless dignity of a seven- or eight-year-old.

Luthan had the wit not to offer empty comfort. "Mona," she said, tugging the child gently around to face their audience. "I'd like you to meet my friends," she used the simplest of nursery grammars, which nonetheless pegged the friends as Sevolite and Mona as a commoner. "This is Princess Amy, and this is His Grace, Dorn, the heir of Nersal. This is Prince Ditatt, Heir Monitum . . ." Tatt bowed. The little girl frowned at him. "And this is His Grace, Erien, a Highlord."

"Erien?" Mona echoed, faintly but with evidence of a thinly repressed boldness of nature. She looked Erien up and down with her hazel eyes, then pursed her small mouth with a 'wild-horses-wouldn't' expression. But she kept looking at Erien as if he were important, somehow.

Erien had so little experience with children he suspected that it was his imagination.

"Would you like to see where you'll be staying?" Luthan asked the child, and quickly passed her off to a servant who had dutifully materialized.

"She seemed better kept than some of the urchins he's brought before," remarked Tatt.

"Oh, yes," Luthan brushed it off, "the mother is an artisan of some sort. Temporarily indisposed. Thank you again, so much," she told Erien, looking regretful about something unfathomable, and rushed off to the next guest before he could respond.

"There, you see," said Tatt, referring to the departed child, "there's no way Amel would ever harm a commoner."

Erien just frowned. Nothing rang true in the exchange he'd just witnessed, except the child's devotion to Amel and the demonstration of Amel's power to charm Demish women.

"I must say," Tatt remarked as they crossed Fountain Court, "you are not as unfit for polite society as I thought."

Tatt, Erien reflected, could be insufferable when he tried.

Tatt continued, "But if you're going to come to the betrothal this afternoon, we will have to do something about your dress. You cannot wear fleet formals and a borrowed jacket. Why won't you let Mother's *gorarelpul* genotype you, and be done with all this dithering. It wouldn't help for tonight, but it would mean that in the future you could go around dressed as who you really are."

"Because," Erien said, tensely, "I am content to wait for Di Mon's plans to unfold. He promised me I would know when it was time, and I see no point in presuming—"

Ditatt snorted. "'No point in presuming'—Erien, that's rich. You told Horth Nersal how to fly his blockade. You tried to tell Ameron what to do about Rire. If that's not presuming I don't know what is. What's so sacred about Di Mon's plans? Don't you want to know who you are?"

"No," Erien said. "I don't. I have freedom of action, now, even if it is limited. Once I have a house, I will be bound to that house's interests. As you well know."

Tatt's subdued silence rewarded him. Erien felt cruel, and raw. He was not ready to confide to Tatt that knowledge of who he was would end all hope of his being who he wanted to be. And probably confirm him in an identity, and a relationship, he dreaded.

Once you are officially Liege Monitum, he thought, looking at Tatt, *there will be no more reason for the Monatese to hide the identity of Di Mon's love child. You are the heir Di Mon wanted for Monitum, and your claim will be established and declared by then. I will ask the regent, Tessitatt, in secret. And then, even if my father is not Di Mon, but Amel—I can bear knowing, for myself. It is merely the public claim. I do not think I would dislike the man so much if it were not that our futures will be shackled together in the eyes of Gelion.*

"Well, Erien," Tatt said at last, with a twisted smile which sat ill on his face, "best of luck in defying your destiny." They were spared the ensuing silence by Branstatt, who was waiting for their return in Green Hearth's entrance hall.

Branstatt looked strained and mutely triumphant. "I've got you a witness," he told Tatt, in a low voice, "from the den."

Tatt shrugged on the cloak he had carried both ways across Fountain Court. "Come on."

Branstatt lead them quickly across the plaza and down through the docks to a clean, bare room that he had rented, near the Rose Garden in the UnderDocks.

The witness was sitting on a chair, guarded by the woman errant, Deyne. He tossed a fallen lock of black hair from his forehead, making no move to stop it sliding back, and looked up at them from beneath its shadow. Along his hairline, brown makeup was still worked into the roots, like mud. There were heavy shadows under his eyes, and the beginnings of the lines that would wear deeper in years to come. He wore a plain white shirt and shapeless drawstring trousers, both too large. He had fine, well-kept hands, Erien noticed, but the cuticles of both thumbs had been picked until they bled.

"Stand up," Deyne ordered. The witness gave her a blank, dumb-animal look, and stood, picking himself bone by bone out of the chair, making it a graceless, clumsy, effortful display, but willing and wordless, so that no reasonable man could object. Tatt's thoughts were all too readable on his face. He would ask the young man to sit down again, and have his courtesy made absurd. The errant pre-empted Tatt, with a hand on the courtesan's shoulder, dumping him promptly and efficiently back into the chair. Tatt said, "Thank you, Deyne." Then he sat briskly down himself and said, "I'm Ditatt Monitum." He needed to give no title; the pronoun carried the full weight of Royalblood-to-commoner address. There was only one Monatese Royalblood. "I understand you were down at the Rose Garden yesterday when a courtesan was murdered."

"Murdered," the youth said, a little mockingly. Murder was not a term often used to describe the killing of a commoner by a Sevolite.

"Murdered," Ditatt said, with an edge to his voice. "I am going to find the people who were responsible. I am going to deal with them as they deserve. You can help me."

"Have I got a choice? I mean, Highness, I didn't get that impression from your errant here."

Tatt looked up at Branstatt. Branstatt said, "I was watching the Rose Garden. I knew the people who worked there would be back—they'd nowhere to go. I knew you'd want to talk to them." He spoke with a degree of belligerence, defying Tatt to indulge himself in the niceties of offering a choice to their reluctant witness.

"I don't," Erien answered the courtesan quietly, "think you have a choice. And I think you know it."

The youth looked at him with a tired effort at superciliousness. "Erien, Ward of Monitum," Erien introduced himself. "I can foresee several possible scenarios. We inquire, and our inquiries make someone afraid of the possibility of witnesses and evidence, who therefore returns to the Rose Garden to eliminate both. Or we inquire, and fail to obtain evidence, and someone becomes confident that they can escape retribution, and returns to the Rose Garden. Or, someone else hears that the Rose Garden is a fine place for such entertainments. None of those options sound desirable to you, do they? Therefore you are best served by seeing we succeed in our inquiries."

The youth swallowed. "I've got another place," he said. "I was just going back to collect my things."

Tatt's expressive face showed pity as transparent as the lie; the courtesan looked away. "I don't know why you want me. I wasn't there."

Erien stepped forwards, licked his thumb, and, spread his fingers on the unwashed hair to brace the courtesan's head and swept his thumb hard along the stained hairline. He held his thumb in front of the youth's eyes long enough for him to appreciate the brown smear on it, and then stepped back to his place. Not a word had been spoken. A closing, a touch, a flinch and a silent display of evidence. But what had passed between them had been as decisive as any crossing of blades.

"They said they were friends of one of our regular clients." The courtesan changed his tune. "They knew some of the things two of our women let him do. They wanted us to close the den for a special event, invitation only. A dramatic presentation. They had pictures of what they wanted."

"We saw," Tatt said quietly.

"They said we didn't have to do it for real, just make it look real. Courtesans know how to do that," he said, with a flare of malice towards Tatt.

"What was the name of the young man who died?" Erien said.

The youth looked at him, his mouth slightly open. His teeth were small and widely spaced enough to be noticeable. Not a West Alcove courtesan. "What do you care?" he said, flatly.

"I care," Erien said, precisely. "I want to know it." And he wanted to remind the other of it. He was discovering that he was capable of precious little mercy to those who would walk away from evil, pleading self-protection or powerlessness. Tatt glanced up at him, troubled doubt in his eyes over these tactics.

"His name," the youth swallowed. "His real name was Tellen. He went by Star."

"Will you tell us yours?" Tatt asked.

"Shaun. Just Shaun. It's old Earth," he added, laying claim to perhaps the only distinction he had.

"What happened?" Tatt said, quite gently.

"They got excited." The courtesan used a word Erien had seen only in one of Ranar's treatises. It was courtesan slang and it conveyed an entirely courtesan meaning. Erien wondered, hearing it now, how Ranar had come to learn it. Probably from Amel, somehow.

Tatt, he saw, did not know the word. "They'd brought along *sish*, and Rush, and some other drugs. Took too much themselves, I guess. And they began to yell at us—the men, and some Vrellish women—telling us to do it for real, telling us that we were filthy Reetions—*sla* and *okal'a'ni*—soulless offenses to unbodied souls—like they were Nesaks or something. Crazy. They began to tell us what they would do to us, that the men would sodomise us until our guts ruptured, that you can kill commoners with Rush—" The cruelty of shocking his betters left him suddenly. "They threw things at us, glasses and chairs and knives, then they came at us. And we ran. But Tellen couldn't run. He was tied up," he finished in a mutter.

Tatt drew another thin, strained breath, and stood up. Erien thought he was going to be sick again. There was no color in his face. Imagination and empathy made even so sparce and evasive a telling overwhelming for him. But after a moment, Tatt sat down and gestured to the courtesan to continue.

"The rest of us got away," said Shaun. "Some of us were hurt because of what they'd been throwing at us. We know a medtech who trades treatment for information. She looked after us. We told her what happened." He swallowed. "That's all I know about it."

"The medtech was not there, herself, when it happened?" asked Tatt. Shaun shook his head.

Tatt said formally, "I'd like descriptions of the Sevolites who were there."

"What happens to me, after?" Shaun asked him, hesitantly.

Tatt leaned forwards and spoke with an uncommon, grim deliberateness. "We are going to find the people who did this and we are going to kill them." He promoted Erien, for the purposes of inclusion, to Royalblood. "You will be able to return to your den without fear of retaliation."

"I'm twenty-four," Shaun pointed out. "I'm tired of pretending to be a kid, worrying about the lines and the muscles."

"What is it you want?" Tatt asked, a little off guard.

"Off Gelion. I want passage to *BlindEye Station,* in Killing Reach. And chips to live on for a month. I want—"

"Branstatt," said Erien, "I think you can take him outside and let him go."

Tatt looked ready to protest, but held back to see where this was leading to. Branstatt, understanding, set a hand on the courtesan's shoulder.

"Wait!" Shaun said to Tatt. "It was you I came to see, Your Highness, not the errant."

"You did not come to see either of them," Erien said, precisely.

The courtesan looked from one to the other, bitterly angry at the ease with which his desperation could be exposed. "You'll never do it," he said, starkly, to Tatt. "Sevs don't kill Sevs over commoners."

"That's what a lot of people think," Branstatt said. "That's where a lot of people are wrong." He looked at Erien. "What do you think? Throw him back?"

Tatt said, suddenly, "No. We can get you to Killing Reach, if that's where you want to go. A job serving Monitum might be safer though."

"Stacking freight, or plowing?" The courtesan shook his head. "I'll take my chances with the Purple Alliance and Killing Reach pirates."

Ditatt said, "Very well. Is one month's worth of money enough for you?"

Branstatt rolled his eyes. The sheltered, aristocratic Tatt had trouble with the boundary between naivete and compassion. Branstatt plainly did not, which was probably just as well for Tatt's lean budget.

"I'll see to the details," Branstatt promised, "though it will have to be after the Swearing. It would be hard to scrounge a pilot to fly anyone somewhere, slowly, before then."

Shaun inhaled, but glanced at Erien and decided against trying for more.

The rest of the interview was tediously mechanical. Shaun proved a fair observer of the Rose Garden's clients. None of the Sevolites took notes. Branstatt looked as if he would have liked to, more than once, but Tatt simply drank details in and asked good questions.

"Well, brother," Branstatt remarked, as the door closed on Deyne and her charge, "you have probably made an enemy of every *gorarelpul* in UnderGelion."

The remark made a slumping Tatt look up.

Branstatt elucidated. "You've just ruined the market on informers. They'll all be expecting free passage to Killing Reach and a handful of honor chips in the bargain."

"I didn't expect him to ask for Killing."

"Nor I," said Branstatt, and added, to Erien, "You've been in Killing: think he'll last?"

"He has a fair chance of connecting with the Purple Alliance on *BlindEye Station*," Erien said. "What he'll become, I don't know. But he's entitled to try, I think."

Branstatt grinned at him. "For all you hide it well, you're as much of an idealist as our prize Royalblood, here." He clapped Tatt on the shoulder, and let his hand rest there, tightening. "You recognized one of those descriptions, didn't you, Tatt?"

Tatt looked at him with barely subdued anguish. "The slash on the face that Shaun described, almost healed—that's Roel Airst of Spiral Hall. I was there when he got that slash, fighting Sanna Bryllit of the *kinf'stan*."

"It was pretty much inevitable," Branstatt said gently, "that at some point it would be someone you know."

"Yes, but I've sparred with him," Tatt said. "I've been den crawling with him." He shook his head as they walked. Integrity would not let Tatt reject what the courtesan had said in favor of his own prejudices, but Erien could see that he was desperately tempted. Tatt caught his breath with an audible snatch as he stopped, before turning toward the stair that went up to the docks. Straight ahead was the way to the Palace Plain, and across that, the entrance to the base of the Citadel, and Spiral Hall.

"I'm going to Spiral Hall," announced Tatt. "I'm going to ask him." He headed off. Branstatt fell in. Tatt turned a grim, pale face towards him. "I have to go alone. I'm the one who knows him. I don't know what I'm going to say to him, or what he's going to say to me." He swallowed. "But if he was part of this, then I have to know why. I thought . . . he was a decent person." He looked at them a moment longer, as though they might offer him exemption from his self-imposed obligations. His hand settled on the hilt of his dress sword. "A healing slash," he said, to himself. "In a few days nobody would have known it was there."

Then he went on.

Erien said quietly, to the errant, "Go with him."

Branstatt was going to go anyway. "He'll put up with me," he said, quickly. "I don't entirely count as not alone. You would. You go make sure he isn't missed upstairs."

CHAPTER IX

"HAS THE AVA LEFT YET for the betrothal reception?" Amel asked, stopping a Throne secretary. Amel had just stepped from between two marble pillars off one wing of the colonnade which bisected Ameron's offices, but his manner put the man at ease despite the suddenness of his appearance.

"Yes, he has." The secretary returned Amel's smile. "Is there something I can help you with, Immortality?"

"No." Amel paused as if thinking his problem through. "Is the Royal *Gorarelpul* available?"

"Charous went with the Ava's entourage," said the secretary, "although, of course, she won't be allowed into the actual reception." He looked like he approved of that. "I can't blame you for not wanting to be in the public eye yourself," he added, discomfort creeping up on him, hand-in-hand with an inquisitive sympathy. "We heard, of course, about the business in the UnderDocks." He hesitated. "Was it really anything like that?"

"Rape? Or the visitor probe?" Amel snapped.

The Demish man's eyes widened, briefly, then his eyes dropped.

Amel felt a pang for the sarcasm. He forgot, sometimes, that he could intimidate his lessers. "It's all right," he said.

The secretary shook his head without looking up. "No, Immortality, I should not have said anything."

"Consider it a service." Amel was breezy once more. "I need practice answering that question. So, no, what the Reetions did to me was nothing like that."

"It wasn't that bad, then?"

Paralysis stunned Amel. It was white all around. Like a tomb. His face blanked. He reanimated himself with a conscious effort. "No," he said, "not bad."

"I'll wait in the living quarters for Ameron to get back," Amel told the secretary. "If Charous isn't available, don't bother informing her staff."

"As you wish, Immortality."

Amel attracted nothing worse than a pitying look from another acquaintance as he passed through the colonnaded hall. Most of Ameron's staff avoided eye contact. That was fine with him.

He slipped down an intersecting corridor into a hall where he knew Ranar of Rire was held under house arrest.

A palace errant turned to meet him, hand floating instinctively toward her sword. She brightened when she realized who it was.

"Hello, Ketatt," Amel greeted her. "Who's on duty for Charous?"

"Drasous." She named Charous' second in command. Her eyes slid from his face, over his questionable costume, and back.

Damn my clothes! Amel thought. *It would be Ketatt on guard!* She was Monatese, with a particularly Vrellish disposition. She had propositioned him more than once, and on less provocation than being decked out in quasi-courtesan clothes. He turned her on. The feeling was mutual. But he'd decided not to do anything about it.

"I have heard," she said, with sympathy and anger, "about the murder in the UnderDocks. Heir Monitum will bring them to the sword."

Her defense of him slashed his composure and reciprocated lust welled up. Sex was all-absorbing, and with someone like Ketatt, simple—at least to start. His body was for it with a will which signaled her back. She advanced. His body never asked his permission to respond. Amel side-stepped around a planter, backing up, and called to mind starscapes which looked nothing at all like anything female, as a sort of antidote.

"I am not afraid of the Avim," Ketatt said in a low voice, picking up where they'd left off in a previous conversation, months before.

"Unfortunately," Amel confessed, "I am." He could not help remembering Seril Tast. One way or another, he was poisonous. "Besides," he cast about for inspiration and realized his clothes could be put to use, "I need to borrow a dressing room. Lilac Hearth purged my wardrobe again while I was off planet, and I don't want to attend Princess Luthan's reception in this costume."

Ketatt drilled him with a stare which rearranged all his constellations into breasts and thighs. His earlobes warmed.

"You should let me give you those fencing lessons," she reminded him of an earlier bid for his attention. "Then you could defend yourself better."

But not from you, Amel thought, feeling hot.

He said, "I'll think about it," and organized a cooling smile, which paid off.

"I will let Drasous know you are around," she said, stepping back.

"Don't bother," he instructed. "I'll check in with him on my way out."

Or, he thought to himself, *maybe not.* He wished that he had not run into Ketatt. He liked her, and all the staff who had let him pass would answer to Charous. He was uncomfortable with that.

At least he had no qualms about the two large, Demish nobleborns with stony eyes and square jaws who stood guard at Ranar's door. He didn't recognize them, and they showed no sign of warming up. He stopped and considered them the way he might a tough lock.

"Rire is at issue, at the betrothal reception," Amel improvised, "so Ameron has sent me to see Ranar. I need to speak with him at once."

It would have helped if his clothing backed up the suggestion that he'd come from the reception, but this wouldn't be the first time he had turned out to a formal occasion less than traditionally attired. They let him pass.

Ranar sat, reading, in a comfortable chair. He did no more than look up when Amel came in. The caramel tone of Ranar's skin was still a shock, in Gelack surroundings, although Amel was used to seeing Reetions when he visited Ann. Ranar had 'gone native' to the extent that he wore Monatese lounging wear. It was, Amel thought, a bit brazen, since these particular clothes must have been a gift from the late Liege of Monitum, Di Mon. The braid and signets of rank were actually Di Mon's. Not many people knew why Di Mon, whose public character was beyond reproach, might give something so personal to his Reetion ally. Unfortunately, Amel did. It was one of his least comfortable secrets, to know that Di Mon and Ranar had been lovers. But since Ranar did not know that Amel knew, it was impossible to tell him off for flaunting a private proof of Di Mon's good regard. Amel just felt extremely uncomfortable.

Ranar closed his book as Amel closed the door, making a one beat harmony of sounds.

"Amel?" The middle-aged Reetion was imperturbable, although he had to realize that this was no social visit. Amel was shaking. It came upon him suddenly, much to his disgust and irritation. "Is something wrong?" Ranar asked.

At that moment Amel hated Ranar. Yet he was risking Ameron's trust by being here at all. He sorted through a blizzard of emotions with angry dispatch.

"I'm here," Amel said curtly, "to take you home." He spoke in Reetion. Ranar answered him, also, in Reetion. "Ameron has ordered that?"

"No."

In his mid-forties, Ranar was just beginning to show the typical commoner signs of wear. He was soft-bodied compared to a Sevolite, and slightly round-shouldered, but insufficiently interested in food to have put on weight like many commoners. He had a way of deploying his body comfortably and just forgetting it. To Amel, who felt himself in body contact with the very air, it was a peculiarly disturbing habit.

The Reetion scholar laid an arm across the back of his couch, his book forgotten in his lap. "You must have some compelling reason."

Amel gritted his teeth. He could smell the anthropologist taking notes behind the somber diplomatic agenda. He would not be studied by a Reetion!

"The feeling at court is turning ugly toward Rire," he told Ranar. "There's been a killing."

"I heard."

"Really?" Amel crossed to the implacable man as if to seize him and shake him, but stopped short. "But do you understand? I don't mean sitting there, as if you were reading it in a book. I mean here," he pulled his fisted right hand to his stomach. The small but violent gesture produced a stab in his strained elbow. "Try to feel yourself mobbed, stripped, dragged somewhere, handed over to a crowd as apt to re-enact your supposed crimes as to beat you to death mercifully. Have you ever, personally, dealt with something like that? You may be prepared to die for what you want—but not like that. I promise you! There are worse fates than death."

"I believe you," Ranar said, with profound respect.

Amel had not wanted that. He smelled fear; the smoke from tarry black *ignis* cigarettes; bad gin; stale urine; the smells rode waves of hoots and laughter; the sound penned a child, on a stage, with a naked man. Amel exploded in omnipotent fury as the man reached for the child, but the hand he struck with was too small. The sounds and smells fled, leaving the room once more Ranar's, but his raised left hand remained a boy's. He snatched air through his nose. With a blink, his hand resolved into a man's. Slowly, he forced it down, doing his best to make the gesture natural.

It took a whole second for Amel to recall where he was in his conversation with Ranar. "If you believe me," Amel said, "then you'll come away. Now."

"I cannot."

"Ranar!" Amel felt the refusal as pain. "Don't do this. What would it solve? Whatever else you are, I know you're not what they'd kill you for. It's wrong. Like—burning books, or making babies fight with swords. It's not your *rel*," he resorted to a Gelack word. The one Ranar had written volumes on.

"I appreciate the warning," said Ranar. "And I do understand that court sentiment concerning the visitor probe is not something that you can control."

"Look at it this way." Amel tried reason, though he knew Ranar was better armed on that front. "What good will it do getting killed by a mob? It will only get their blood up for more slaughter. It's wasteful. You understand Gelacks. There aren't many Reetions who do. Not even Ann. If there's a chance to stop the fighting early, you're the one who could."

"There cannot be any fighting." Ranar was firm. "Rire is not armed. Ann's station in Killing Reach is there to constrain the exchange of information and those goods, which I have agreed with Ameron are conducive to ill-feeling on either side. It is well understood that 'commoner' tactics, such as destroying battlewheels, would be provocative, while our pilots cannot match your *rel*-fighters. Rire will not war in Killing Reach ever again."

"But if Ann was attacked—" Amel insisted.

"She would surrender *SkyBlue Station*."

Amel frowned. "You don't know her very well."

"Those are her orders. To surrender, and negotiate."

"But if she didn't. If there were enough Reetions who thought—"

"It isn't her decision to make," Ranar explained with patience. "Her defense proposal was defeated. Reetions do not work in secret, and the only tactics possible would have invited a repeat of the Killing Wars. If attacked, we will surrender and negotiate. That's what was agreed upon."

"Agreed on by the Reetion Net," said Amel, "which Rire dominates, and Rire itself is a comfortable distance from the consequences of *SkyBlue's* elimination. The worlds of Paradise Reach are acutely aware that Killing Reach itself used to be Reetion territory."

"Not, precisely, Reetion," said Ranar. "The Old Regime, which Ameron's mother encountered—"

"They were brown, masterless, commoners!" Amel shouted.

Ranar only blinked to show his surprise at such excessive volume.

Amel ran a hand through his sleek black hair, trying to calm down. "Ranar, the distinction doesn't matter to us. Old Regime or Reetion Administration, you're liege less commoners. Don't you see Ann won't accept that?"

"Nor do I," said Ranar. "But Ann's orders are to surrender. It is not possible for her, as *SkyBlue's* Space Service Executive, one of three station triumvirs, to have plans which deviate from the Reetion Net consensus."

"Imagine, for a moment, that it was."

"It's unthinkable. Rire functions on the basis of complete freedom of information. Everything is arbiter conveyed, inventoried, and administered. Unsanctioned plans would be flagged through routine net-synching operations, which would raise an alarm even if someone had managed to gain the co-operation of a single arbiter, during temporary isolation."

"Please, Ranar." Amel was out of strategies. "Go home. And look after your own house. Take Erien with you."

Ranar sat up, dragging his draped arm off the back of the couch. "Erien's here? At court?"

"To support you," Amel told him, "with a sword, if necessary."

"You brought him here?" Ranar accused, alarmed.

"He came on his own! But it isn't a safe time. You must understand—I can't keep them apart anymore. Ev'rel and Ameron. Or Rire and Gelion."

Both started at the sound of the door.

If nothing else, Amel thought, he had finally unsettled Ranar. He should have mentioned Erien sooner! Ranar's weakness was his parental feeling for his young charge.

Amel felt sick to his stomach when he saw Charous.

Hoping to brazen it out, he abandoned Ranar to stride quickly past her, into the hall. Drasous waited there. Just Drasous. Charous had dismissed the Sevolite guard, probably because Drasous was armed with a needle gun. The needle gun was only barely tolerated as a quasi-weapon with a medical excuse for existing. It had a short range, was spring loaded, and launched a slim needle meant to deliver a drug payload to a possibly uncooperative patient. Whatever Charous had in this one would probably knock Amel cold. Dodging would be more dangerous than getting shot, since the needle could be fatal if it struck a vital spot.

"What were you doing in there?" Charous asked.

Amel turned his back on Drasous, deliberately, to face her. "I wanted to clear up some questions regarding Reetion government."

"At Ameron's request? When you were not at the reception?"

"I never said that, exactly."

"You did, in fact," said Charous. "I think you had better wait until Ameron can help us clarify the matter."

She gestured for him to walk ahead, back to the business offices.

He scowled. Charous would be only too happy to have an excuse to drug him into oblivion. The thought made his spine crawl. He hated being drugged! Being helpless!

Amel caught his breath. A giant leered into his face. The heat of a naked body held him from behind. He hurt. There was blood in his mouth. He was being held, shoulders aching, by both arms. The giant pressed a needle gun into one side of his groin. "This'll stiffen something more appealing to the clients than your spine." The sex drug. Rush. This was the first time he'd been shot up. As a child in the UnderDocks.

He was clear dreaming.

There really wasn't any room for doubt, or denial.

He was ashamed to feel his knees buckle, until he realized that he hadn't fainted. He must have moved suddenly. Lunged against phantom restraint. The sting in his upper arm informed him that he'd been shot by Drasous. He recognized the effects of *klinoman*. The dose was moderate; he didn't black out, just lost muscle tone. Laboriously, he began to get up off the floor. Charous helped him.

"You've been making a lot of mistakes lately, Amel," she remarked. "Taking advantage of Ameron's trust to see Ranar. Being seen leaving the UnderDocks."

She had been incautious, to get so close. He lashed out. There was a satisfying *whap* as his arm struck her rib cage. Charous staggered. He could not hurt her. *Gorarelpul* were deadened to pain. But he still wished he'd been able to do it harder.

Drasous took charge of his arms.

If he had succeeded in embarrassing Charous by catching her off guard, she refused to show it. "We'll take you somewhere you can rest, while it wears off," she told him. She had a knack for meticulously differencing her pronouns without showing the least bit of respect. "By then Ameron will be back. He'll find out what you were really up to."

Chapter X

TATT TURNED UP WHILE ERIEN WAS WAITING for the Monatese party to assemble at the foot of the stairs in Green Hearth's reception hall. Erien was glad to see him. He'd been wondering how he would explain Tatt and Branstatt's absence to their mother, Tessitatt. His usually effervescent foster brother swept past him, face locked in grim lines. Erien followed. He caught up with Tatt a room further down Green Hearth's Throat.

"Tatt!"

The heir of Monitum turned. He was not wounded nor spattered with another's blood. But grimness, in Tatt, was almost as ugly as a wound.

Tatt saw him, but spoke to a servant. "Send my valet to my room."

Erien stopped. They could not talk openly in front of a valet. Was that Tatt's objective? Tatt carried on down the Throat to Family Hall. Erien turned back to meet Branstatt as he arrived.

"He made me wait outside," the errant said briefly, and denied further conversation by putting the stairs between them, trailing a hand on the open steps. It had not been an easy admission for Branstatt. He was part of the family as well as being Tatt's captain of errants, but he made a point of stressing the *pol*-form of the Gelack for 'he', which he owed to Tatt's Royalblood rank, even adding the one-step differencing suffix. Normally he addressed his half-brother in *rel*-case peerage, except in formal circumstances.

Tessitatt's arrival snapped Branstatt back to attention.

"You aren't dressed," she remarked to her eldest son.

"Tatt did not leave me time," Branstatt told her, in *rel*-peerage: a courtesy on his part, since he was Highlord by birth rank, and Tessitatt was only Seniorlord. "Will I do as I am?"

She frowned. "At least put on a formal jacket. I want your Nersallian braid showing."

"I'll wait for Tatt," offered Erien.

Tessitatt inspected his costume with a critical eye. When she reached his face she shook her head. "No," Di Mon's niece told Erien, "you come with us."

"I'll catch up with you," promised Branstatt.

The Monatese party climbed the spiral stair in silence. There was a full hand of Green Hearth errants, including Deyne, and three other Sevolites who were hearth guests from prominent families of Monitum, each with two or three errants of their own.

Tessitatt sought out Erien as they reassembled on the plaza in the Green Hearth pavilion. "What did Tatt keep Branstatt tied up with until the last moment?" she asked.

"I—did not get a chance to ask," Erien compromised.

Di Mon's niece had his frown. When she used it, it was just as minimal and just as definite.

They continued in silence, across the plaza, into the Palace, and up a long stately avenue of white marble rooms connected with shallow flights of stairs and flanked in colonnades with intersecting halls which stretched in both directions. In some places tall velvet drapes screened off whole sections, or the avenue belled out on the sides into courtyards with second and third stories. Fountains, statues, and verdant plants were common themes in the understated elegance of the decor.

"Avim Demlara's Walk," Tessitatt remarked as they approached the end of the glorious architecture.

Erien, who had been watching the pedestrian traffic thicken around them, only grasped that she was giving a name to their surroundings when the reference penetrated his preoccupation. Demlara Dem had been Sevildom's second-most powerful Pureblood during the height of the Demish Golden Age, when being Avim meant being the Ava's Queen. Her Ava died duelling, after which she reigned forty years through the agency of sword champions, chosen by competition from among her male relatives. Di Mon, who had enjoyed history, had once told Erien that Demlara's reign was marked by moderate administrative competence, and unparalleled devotion to the arts.

Tessitatt stopped, letting the foot traffic on either side move past. She was not cloaked. Her hand rested on the hilt of her sword as she looked around. She was taller than Luthan, long legs emphasized by close fitted trousers and a short, tight jacket crusted in Monatese heritage. "Everywhere you turn," she said, "there is history, pressing down and settling upon history. It isn't hard to believe, living in UnderGelion, that we are all cycling through the same habitat eternally in new flesh."

She expected no answer. Erien realized, momentarily, that she'd stopped because she recognized Branstatt's quick steps, behind, catching up to them. He had done no more than add a formal, braided vest, but it did show off his paternal Nersallian heritage, which was an inalienable right of birth. Membership in the *kinf'stan*, from which Branstatt was excluded, meant being entitled to challenge for the title of Liege Nersal, as a consequence of any *kinf'stan* highborn being entitled to challenge any other for whatever title he or she possessed. Definitely a two-edged sword, that, since the *kinf'stan* were over a thousand strong, and included some of Sevildom's best duelists. Erien could understand why Tessitatt had denied Branstatt's existence, until Liege Nersal had agreed to declare him the gift-child of his brother, Branst, and personally stand against any objections. Even so, it was considered too dangerous for Branstatt to hold any Monatese title, even if Tessitatt was not at all shy to have him proclaim his Nersallian blood ties with pride.

"You're aware of the nature of the Flashing Floor?" Tessitatt asked Erien, before they went in.

"Yes," Erien said.

The Flashing Floor was where the reception was being held. It was, of course, the other visually booby trapped approach to the Ava's offices besides the Lorel stairs. Erien also knew of it from the visitor probe record of Amel's accident there—as did the Dem'Vrellish woman who had helped him up the Lorel Stairs. Unlike her, Erien had not studied the visual rendering. He had read the arbiter-generated transcript instead. Reetions at Ranar's educational level considered text superior to imagery for the study and debate of serious political or judicial affairs. Skillful multimedia productions could give irrelevant factors too powerful an influence.

Viewing the Flashing Floor from Amel's perspective, instead of reading about it, might have better prepared Erien for meeting it, all the same.

It was worse than even the Lorel Stairs.

One look was enough to disorientate Erien. Branstatt caught one elbow and Tessitatt the other.

Branstatt hissed, "Don't look down. Close your eyes if you have to, but don't look down." Erien nodded—which should have been a mistake, but the motion seemed to restore his sense of his body, and his body's proper place in space. The peculiar vertigo receded. "It's like going through a jump," he muttered.

"Or two, or three, at once," Branstatt agreed with him.

"The floor is a creation of the Lorel Avas," said Tessitatt. "It was laid during a period when Vrellish power, in particular, threatened them. Ameron uses it for potentially contentious gatherings where both Demish and Vrellish must attend. Demish highborns won't often fight spontaneously among themselves. Duels tend to be well planned and the consequences elaborated by contract. But the Vrellish, as Di Mon always said, are tinder awaiting a spark. Di Mon considered the Flashing Floor a damper on that," she smiled. "Of course he couldn't stomach it himself, he just liked to pretend that he could." Tessitatt changed gears, and said to Branstatt, "I must go congratulate Admiral H'Us. Take care of Erien."

Erien thought, with what he knew was Reetion logic, not Gelack, that it would have been simpler to confiscate the swords. But everyone here was formally dressed, which meant armed.

The impressive gathering distracted Erien from the lure of the floor. The guests clustered in wedges and phalanxes of liveried errants and more variably garbed Highlords and Royalbloods: Monatese in black and green; Dem'Vrellish in red and blue; a smattering of Demorans in white and gold; Vrellish in red, with some red and black; Ameron's errants in beige and white; H'Usians in silver and blue; and Nersallians in their plain, martial black. They all wore the full braids allowed their blood status, genetics and titles, as trim on collar and cuffs and as lacing between panels of leather, velvet, silk or satin vests. The Demish princes' vests were the most densely woven and elaborate, a whole ancestry carried on their chests embellished with the old Demoran art of 'narrative knots'. The highborn Demish women were in skirts, a rare lesser Sevolite woman appearing in their errantry here and there.

Erien, nameless and houseless, wore plain Monatese livery, without braids. He would have felt conspicuous, had he not been so thoroughly overlooked in such illustrious and status-aware company.

Tatt showed up, at a trot, his hand on his sword to stop it swaying as he ran.

He wasn't out of breath. He joined Erien and Branstatt with a flourish to show off his clothes, or perhaps how fast he had managed to get into them.

He wore a formal shirt, overjacket, and cloak, as befitted a Monatese highborn. All were new, plainer cut than his wont, but no less brilliant: brown, green and turquoise, in solid panels. His braids claimed Lor'Vrel, Monitum, and Vrel ancestry in their knots and colors. Despite the flourish, he was, for Tatt, subdued.

Branstatt leaned over to whisper to Tatt, "Only time I ever feel sorry for my uncle."

Highlord Horth, Liege of Nersal, actually looked nauseated. It was in the tension of his lips and the slight flicker of his eyelids when he happened to glance down. He hung back, towards the boundary of the floor, amid a formation of his less-affected nobleborns—whom he allowed closer to him than usual, presumably to block the sight of the floor—making occasional sallies through the company to put in an appearance. Erien watched him collect a wine horn and fruit cup on one such trip, stand listening a while to Admiral H'Us who was chaperoning Luthan and Dorn, then pass both wine and delicacy to a servant untouched before retreating to his safe haven.

The floor didn't bother Ameron at all: he was no more a navigator than he was a swordsman. Nor, seemingly, did it affect Ev'rel, although Erien noticed that she kept her head up. The Avim was a lovely woman, with an understated richness about her which made it clear that she could have been devastating if she had chosen to dress for that. Instead, she had chosen a stately manner and look, in contrast to Ameron's extroverted charm.

Both knew that they were the center of attention. Their styles of receiving it differed sharply. Ev'rel held court. People presented themselves to her, and were received with civilities appropriate to their stations and allegiances. In this, she seemed Demish. Ameron mingled. The H'Usian and Nersallian nobleborns loosely attached to him as an unofficial honor guard had difficulty keeping pace with their charge without too obviously rushing. Clearly, Ameron was enjoying himself. He touched people readily, with a hand on a shoulder or arm or back, and laughed often, leaving an awed look on two out of three faces, particularly those who least expected to be so honored.

Dorn Nersal paid his respects to both Ava and Avim early. Liege Nersal didn't. The Throne Champion appeared indifferent to the social expectation that he be seen with Ameron, though he watched the Ava circulating from a distance for as long as he could withstand the temptation of letting his eyes drop floorward. He showed no sign of paying court to Ev'rel either, nor of the attention he commanded in his own right for not yet having done either.

At Ev'rel's side, her own champion, D'Therd, looked straight ahead, jaw firm, indifferent to temptation. D'Lekker wove through the Vrellish ranks, wine horn in hand, overstimulated excitement in his face and movements.

Vretla Vrel lost her composure just after the Monatese arrived, left Ev'rel's side, and swept past Ameron, hand white on her hilt, cursing, "Gap grind you Lorels!" Ameron's honor guard tried to pretend that they hadn't tensed up as she kept going.

"One down," muttered Branstatt. Tatt seemed not to have heard; he was gazing unhappily across the floor towards the Vrellish contingent, who were resorting themselves in the wake of Vretla's departure. Erien realized suddenly that Tatt's distressed expression had attracted attention—Dem'Vrellish attention. D'Lekker was watching him with narrowed eyes. Erien stepped smoothly into D'Lekker's line of sight, turning casually away as though to address Tatt, and then deliberately looked down at the Flashing Floor. It curled beneath his feet with unexpected suddenness, and even though he thought himself prepared, he staggered, responding to the false cues of eyes and brain. Tatt and Branstatt escorted him to the edge of the floor, and set him staring at the fine latticework which formed a false wall on this side of the hall. The false wall was broken by a series of archways which led into small semi-private bays. The alcoves dated from the era of the Blue Demish Avas, the house which Ev'rel's had absorbed when she turned Blue Hearth into Lilac, following the death of her half-brother, Ava Delm.

"You have to stop looking down," Tatt chided Erien.

Branstatt said nothing, merely gave Erien a sidelong glance which told him that the errant had been perfectly aware of why he'd induced the minor crisis. Branstatt said, "Tatt, will you tell us what happened down at Spiral Hall?"

Tatt blinked, staring at the latticework, and shook his head tightly. But almost immediately, he spoke. "He cried. He wanted me to kill him. To stop the nightmares." He breathed with the slight catch in his throat that Erien remembered from the nursery, when small Ditatt was trying to be self-controlled and Monatese. Branstatt moved from Erien's side to Tatt's and put a hand on his half-brother's shoulder. Tatt said, "It was worse than he,"—the 'he' denoted a commoner—"told it. Hearing it from someone who had done it."

"So your friend was involved," Branstatt said, with ready sympathy for Tatt.

"He said it was like a madness came over them all. He went because he was curious. It seemed daring. A way to be involved in all the speculation going around. Then there were drugs—he didn't claim that he was innocent!" Ditatt insisted, as if this was a point of honor, and subsided again, a hand swept through his hair in vexation. "He threw things. Shouted. He said he didn't actually—" he balked at this juncture. "He just—ran. When he could, he ran. I don't know what to do. I promised that courtesan—"

"You may not have to do anything. His shame will do it for you," Branstatt said, a quietly ruthless summation. "Did he give names?"

For answer, Ditatt pulled a scrap of paper from his pocket and thrust it at the errant. He said in a suffused voice, "I feel sick. I don't know what I'm doing here, posturing and pretending that nothing else is as important as political alliances. I should be downstairs."

There was a scuff of shoe behind them, a deliberate scuff. Tatt swung round, with Sevolite swiftness, hand halfway to hilt before he that saw it was Deyne. Branstatt laid a gentling hand on his arm. Deyne held her ground, though with some trepidation.

"Regent Tessitatt would like you to pay your respects to Ava Ameron," she told Tatt.

The summons, Erien thought, could not have been more ill-timed. Tatt, breathing hard, flashed a look across the floor to Ameron and Tessitatt that belonged to neither dutiful son nor loyal servant.

Branstatt said firmly, "Your Highness, you are here because it is part of your duties as Heir Monitum, and part of the loyalty you owe your father and his Throne. If either he, or you, ceased to hold the power you do, you would no longer be able to administer the justice you aspire to. This is for the Justice Ministry as much as it is for anything or anyone else."

Tatt gave him a single dark glance, then schooled his face—poorly as ever—and started across the floor. Erien checked Branstatt as he made to follow. "Captain. Is anyone here on that list?"

Branstatt shook his head, and Erien felt fleeting relief . . . until Branstatt said, "But two of the families are represented," and he had to trot after the quick-moving Tatt.

Ameron plainly knew Tatt's mercurial moods. Deftly, with one arm, he drew Tatt around and away from the Dem'Vrel. Ameron did not let his son speak, this not being the place for an outburst, but he walked Tatt slowly across the floor, until Tatt's composure was firmer.

Watching them, Erien was unaware of Luthan's approach until she appeared, disconcertingly, at his side. She was dressed in what he presumed must be the height of Demish ladies' fashion: full, indeed stuffed, white skirt of some lustrous material, with panels embroidered in white and silver thread, and blue and white matching overdress with the same embroidery. The sleeves were full to the elbow, with tight forearms and frilly cuffs. The collar was high, and frilled. Her blonde curls were partially tamed by a tight mesh cap of silver and white lace.

"The ceremony will start soon," she said, taking his arm in a sisterly fashion, her skirt brushing his ankles, "and I've only just managed to escape Uncle H'Us. Please, will you escort me to Ev'rel's party?"

His immediate thought was to decline, having no clear idea how it might be interpreted, or of her motive. But he looked into her heart-shaped face with its rose flush and wide blue eyes tilted up to his, and he heard himself saying, "Yes, of course."

She slipped her arm through his, for strength. Now that they were so close, he could feel her trembling in her layers of rich clothes, and he deduced they were about to do something which Admiral H'Us would not approve of. It was, however, too late to come to his senses.

"Is Prince Ditatt all right?" she said, quite audibly, though her lips barely moved.

Erien glanced around. Ameron had moved on, but he still had Tatt with him, and was steering him with touch and glance. The sight reminded Erien that Ameron was considered a master horseman. Ameron had control. And as long as Ameron had control, Tatt would come to no harm.

"He's finding," Erien said, "that separating the guilty and the innocent is more difficult in practice than in principle."

They were too close to Ev'rel for Luthan to answer. Seeing them approach, Ev'rel herself cleared the way with a gesture.

"Princess Luthan of H'Us," Ev'rel greeted her.

"Avim," Luthan curtsied, but it was not Ev'rel herself for whom she'd come.

Luthan owed her Golden Demish appearance to her Demoran mother. The Demoran Princess Chandra, who sat on an upholstered stool beside Ev'rel, was that mother's aunt. Something, however—spirit, or simple health—gave Luthan's china doll features more life than those of the pale Demoran Princess.

Chandra wore a high-necked tunic under a flowing, blue gown in which every line of white marbling told some story. Fine blue veins showed palely through skin so fair it was almost translucent in the upper layers. Her large, blue eyes were the color of Luthan's. Her limp gold hair hung shining to her buttocks. On her face was clear proof of bruising from recent space travel.

"Princess Chandra." Luthan curtsied in an unusual fashion, one leg straight out, lowering her head toward her knee far enough to dip a third of her height before straightening, skirt held out in a fan. "Your presence at my betrothal does me honor, mother's kin."

The tall, pale woman smiled. It was a subtle thing, but made all the more distinct for her otherwise lifeless mask of aristocracy. "You seem pleased with the match, child." Her grammar spoke down to Luthan in an archaic fashion, employing additional inflections to those in current usage. Ranar had studied Demoran art culture but, all the same, Erien found himself lost.

Luthan was a touch surprised, and slighted, by whatever subtext was conveyed in the grammar duel. "I do my duty," she responded.

"As did your mother." Chandra reached up to brush Luthan's curls with the tips of long, tapered fingers. "Her spirit's blessing on you."

"I haven't any doubt of that," replied Luthan, not unkindly.

"Then you were a comfort to her. I have heard pleasant things of you."

"Oh?" Ev'rel took notice. "Ah, yes, Princess Chandra talks to Amel, of course. Prince Amel is a frequent guest at Luthan's parlor meetings."

"Parlor meetings?" Chandra raised a thin, exquisite eyebrow, ignoring Ev'rel in favor of Luthan. "Do you hold court?"

"Not exactly," Luthan looked like a tomboy caught tree climbing in petticoats. "It's more . . . "

"A forum for discussing matters concerning mistreatment of commoners," Ev'rel rescued Luthan from her own embarrassment. "Luthan's knowledge of recorded Demish cases often proves invaluable. But speaking of your meetings, Princess, didn't Amel attend today?"

"Yes!" Luthan stepped, firmly, on Erien's foot beneath her ample skirt. "He left early. I thought he'd be here before us."

"Princess Luthan?" An anxious lady of Silver Hearth swept her skirts back in the courtly, Demish fashion, bowing first to Luthan, then more deeply to Ev'rel. "Please forgive me this intrusion, but your uncle—"

"Objects to her speaking to Princess Chandra," Ev'rel cut through any excuse which might be forthcoming. "Come, I'll escort Luthan back and claim culpability on Chandra's behalf, shall I?"

Chandra met this with a frosty look. "I beg no leave to speak with hybrids."

Ev'rel ignored her, patting Luthan's hand. "Never mind. At least you stand higher in her regard than barbarian conquerors. Who is your silent friend?" It was the first sign that she'd been aware, at all, of Erien. She was already bearing Luthan away through the parting swirls of sword-bearing Vrellish nobleborns.

Luthan colored. "Erien, Ward of Monitum. He grew up with Prince Ditatt."

"Ah, yes," Ev'rel cast a quick look back over one shoulder, looking for Amel in him, Erien could not help feeling. There was a distinctive sharpness about Ev'rel when Amel was at issue.

"Serious fellow," was Ev'rel's comment.

Luthan answered with restored reserve, having already reclaimed her hand from Ev'rel. "You are gracious, Avim, but I am Liege H'Us, or shall be. I do not require excuses to explain myself to my guardian."

"Really?" Ev'rel seemed genuinely pleased by this show of spirit. "Demish regard for female wisdom has improved, then."

Luthan opened her mouth and closed it again, unsure how to react. Ev'rel resumed control.

Erien could not hear any more. He considered following, but he had no real excuse and was not sure who to assist in the matter.

Besides, people were forming up to hear the contract performed aloud to all the gathering by a H'Usian and a Nersallian herald.

Tatt appeared by his side, as the Vrellish broke up to drift into the forming circle. He seemed much more his usual self. He leaned over to whisper in Erien's ear, "We can escape when the Demish start on about their great-greats."

"Should we? Won't it be impolite?"

"It's all very well for them—blondes don't suffer from the floor. Although," his natural impulse toward justice rose up immediately to confront the prejudice, "I once saw Amy's mother, Ayrium D'Ander D'Aur, all but faint on Ameron's arm when she crossed it, so I suppose some must." He glanced at Erien. "How are you doing?"

"I'm managing."

"I see Luthan was managing also—to lead you astray," Tatt began, wickedly, but caught Ameron's look of censure for the whispering, and fell quiet.

The contract reading itself was soon over. "Nersallian influence," noted Tatt. "Demish contracts would go on until tomorrow." As he predicted, the Vrellish began to melt away in small groups as the more elaborate, Demish ceremony started. This involved genealogical recitals by all of Luthan's relatives, decorated by autobiographical details of particularly colorful dead ancestors, often delivered as direct quotes. Precedent for aspects of the contract were also on the agenda.

None of it seemed to have anything to do with the golden-haired girl who stood respectfully listening, her hands folded on the beautiful embroidery of her overdress, her head poised. Her expression was missing something: not blank—beautifully composed and pleasant— but still, he had the sense of absence. That lively, innocent mind was elsewhere. No one but Erien seemed to notice it.

Tatt fidgeted pointedly at his side. Erien leaned towards him, "I'm waiting to hear her."

"Luthan? She doesn't get to speak."

"Why not?"

"Erien!" said Tatt in mock exasperation, more loudly than he should. The speaker gave him a haughty look. Luthan emerged from her reverie and sent a tiny smile in their direction. Tatt jerked his thumb towards Erien, and shook his head minutely. Luthan's smile widened briefly, and then she turned her head forwards and withdrew again.

Tatt waited a moment, then tilted his head towards Erien. "She's female, that's why. Or hadn't you noticed?"

"Then it would be even more appropriate," Erien whispered back. "The women have the greater investment in the progeny. Patrilineal descent is an artificial construct, made possible only by social constraint or technologic assistance. Most early human societies were matrilineal."

Somebody nudged him firmly in the back. "Regent Tessitatt's complements," murmured Branstatt. "Hush!"

They hushed, except when, sometime later, Tatt tilted his head toward Erien and whispered, "See what I mean about interminable."

"Mm."

Even Demish eyes had begun to glaze before the recitation wound down. Tatt raised his eyes to the ceiling and murmured, "Thank the ancestors," which earned him a frown from Ameron—who, if he could not hear the murmur, could certainty perceive the sentiment. The Demish dispersed, in an ordered, formal saraband of stances and bows. Luthan, as the underage Liege, was last to be allowed to move. Erien watched her surreptitiously work aching feet in dainty slippers, all the time smiling charmingly at her well-wishers and supplicants. The remaining Vrellish and the Demish princes withdrew, after Ameron and Ev'rel. Some younger highborns, Demish men, and Vrellish of either gender gathered around Dorn, unthinkingly excluding Luthan. Dorn would have resisted on her behalf, but she signaled her compliance with a small head-shake, and eased away. Limping just a little, she headed for one of the latticed alcoves. Tatt bounded forwards, heading enthusiastically into the heart of the people surrounding his friend, Dorn. Erien followed. Or thought he did. He realized suddenly that his path was taking him after Luthan, and stopped. Venting floor! He couldn't even trust himself to walk a straight line.

She had not seen him. As she passed behind a potted shrub, her dress winking pearly white through the lattice framework, he decided that she wanted her privacy. But just as he moved off, he heard the movement of other bodies inside. He checked, his hearing sharpened despite himself.

"Oh, I'm sorry," Luthan's voice was soft but crisp with embarrassment.

"Just getting off that damn floor," said a rough, female voice. "Don't flinch girl, we're Dem'Vrel, not one of Vretla's Spiral Hall she-wolves. I wore a skirt myself, before Ev'rel's time. I'm Bal Kranst, this is Zind D'Therd Kranst, my gift child for services rendered." Her pronouns pegged her as Seniorlord and Zind as Highlord. For the Dem'Vrellish, that was the top drawer. Her dialect suggested wind and rock, and words that could be shouted across the moors of FarHome.

"The Princess makes a beautiful bride!" Zind's voice was familiar. She was the Dem'Vrellish woman who had helped Erien up the Lorel Stairs. "Princess Luthan Dem H'Us," she added in mock grandeur. "Do you think you can cope with a Nersal?"

"Lay off. She's a friend of Amel's," said Bal.

"Oh well then, there's nothing we can tell her!" Zind laughed.

"Not that sort of friend!" Luthan said, alarmed.

"Maybe you do need help, after all," Zind teased with mock gravity, "if you've passed up that opportunity."

Through the leafy lattice, Erien saw Zind move to cut off Luthan's retreat. "Nersallians do not like new ships," Zind stage whispered, "or virgins."

"Dorn doesn't strike me as hard work." Bal paused to spit chewed leaves into an oiled cloth. Chewing *ignis* leaves was a common alternative, among spacers, to smoking them. It was considered uncouth at court. "Now the father, Liege Nersal—"

"I don't want to discuss men like they are some sort of—some sort of perfume, or food, or I don't know what!" Luthan flared up. "Let me out!"

"Perfume?" Zind had the air of an adult cat hissed at by a feisty kitten. "I'd hardly call Dorn, or Horth Nersal, that."

There was a second's silence, then both Dem'Vrellish women laughed.

Erien stepped into the doorway of the alcove, taking care to scuff his footsole lightly. Zind swiveled, sword half drawn, but froze instead, surprised. "First *kinf'stan*, now Monatese . . . errant?" She remarked on his livery.

Luthan went from the brink of frustrated tears to wide-eyed interest.

"I never thanked you, on the Lorel Stairs, earlier," Erien greeted Zind. "I regret if it was help offered under false pretenses. I am not Nersallian, though I traveled under Liege Nersal's signet. I am a ward of Monitum."

"A Highlord ward?" Bal chewed, picking up his rank, of course, from his grammar. "Must be some bastard of the late Liege Ditatt Monitum, maybe by a Nersallian. A love child the Nersallians kept, in exchange for Tessitatt's Branstatt." She wadded up her spit rag and stuffed it into a vest pocket.

"No." Zind slammed home her sword and looked Erien over with new interest. "He's Amel's. The late Liege of Monitum, Di Mon, kidnapped the courtesan's baby that he used to prove who Amel was while the Reetions still had him. Look at the family—"

"Leave us alone!" Luthan lost her temper, and immediately blushed scarlet. "I—I mean me. Get out!" She pointed imperiously.

"Or—you'll call your uncles and man-cousins?" Zind was equally amused and nonplused.

"She will not need to," Erien said quietly, passing his hand lightly over his hilt.

Bal gave him a measuring look, and touched her daughter's sword arm. "Come on. The Avim won't put up with needless trouble."

Zind made up her mind and shouldered out. Bal followed.

Luthan let out the breath she'd been holding. "Thank you! Why is it those most recently out of skirts themselves are the ones who have got to be the meanest?"

Erien thought about his own experiences, with young, untried Nersallians. "They are proving something to themselves. Shall I leave you now?"

"No! I mean—" She sat on the bench Bal had vacated, checking first for any nasty reminder of Bal's chewing habit. "I'd like your company. If you'll give it. I've always found Monatese the most civilized of the Vrellish."

Erien smiled faintly at her very Demish prejudice. "If I am Monatese."

"You certainly act like one. Oh, you mean what she said about—" she broke off, reading him, he felt with discomfort, like an open book.

"I do not begrudge Amel victimization in which he had no fault," Erien insisted. It irked him that she might think his reservations were simple, adolescent ones bound up in wanting to avoid embarrassment. He was not unfair. It was who Amel was that offended him, not what had happened to Amel in the past.

Luthan dropped the subject like a thorny rose. "Oh, my feet!" she said, working off one sparkling white slipper, then the other, and spreading her toes. "Yes, Demish princesses do have feet," she said, a little snappishly, "and mine hurt. I hate these silly shoes that are supposed to make my feet look smaller. Mine are not that big," she said, and appealed to him a little plaintively. "Are they?"

"No," Erien said, and stopped, at something of a loss.

She looked at him, and then quickly swept shoes and feet out of sight underneath her wide skirts, sitting primly upright. "Thank you for taking me to see Chandra, earlier," she said. "I don't think Ev'rel cares. I should have warned you, though, that it wouldn't make you popular with Uncle H'Us."

He smiled reassurance at her.

She patted the bench beside her. He hesitated briefly, then sat down beside her.

Luthan sighed. "It makes me sad to think of beautiful, gracious Demora ruled by people like Zind and Bal. But it makes me sad, too, when my mother's kin won't accept me because I'm impure of blood."

"You?" Erien couldn't help objecting. "Impure?"

Luthan nodded. "Nothing is simple, is it?"

"No."

She worried her lower lip a little.

"Maybe you would rather be alone." Erien felt obliged to offer again; she seemed so self-absorbed.

Luthan started, catching at his hand as if he'd begun to get up. He hadn't. She pointedly withdrew the hand. "I—want to ask you something." Her brows were drawn, making her look like a worried doll. "And I don't know how. I don't know very much about Vrellish customs. It seems to me, often, that the Vrellish simply make them up. There are so many. Or maybe none at all, not the way the Demish observe them anyhow. So I don't know what's important and what's not. Or what everyone is supposed to know but no one talks about."

"Just ask," Erien said. "I will help you if I can."

She gave him a dubious look. "I . . . don't want to offend you." She stopped a moment, gazing at him, her pupils slowly relaxing in a visual sigh, followed, when she caught herself at it, with rapid blinking and a blush. Her fingers fumbled with the pearls stiffening her waist. "For example, is it true, what the Dem'Vrel women said about Nersallians? They haven't any use for virgins? Amel's told me it is only the Demish that will pay for that—I mean in female courtesans. Oh dear, you see, he's the wrong person to ask about some things, too. Not because he doesn't know but he has an odd perspective."

"I'm afraid . . . " Erien said, "that my perspective is going to be odd as well. I can't say what's offensive to Vrellish men because I was not raised as one. I don't have anything like the same set of assumptions." He contemplated the truth of that statement for a moment. "But I do not believe Dorn will make anything difficult for you."

She wrung her hands, once, and settled them in her lap. "Thank you." She continued to stare at him, trembling a little. "Then . . . you don't think he would care, either? If I wasn't. I mean, by then."

He studied her back. Her timid exploration of the whole daunting topic of sex was backed by the same strength shown in telling Zind off, earlier. It wasn't what she'd been brought up to, but it loomed before her and she wanted, very sensibly, to know what the rules were. He felt protective. He wished he had more experience himself, just then, to help her think her way through the obstacles. He wanted very much to be useful. It was hard, in fact, not to let her stare draw him into expressing that protectiveness with actions that he could only conclude would be taking advantage of her. He didn't trust himself to do so much as take her hand, to comfort her.

"Again," he said, "I do not think Dorn is a man to espouse a double standard of sexual conduct."

Luthan wet her lips and inhaled deeply. "I know it's silly. And I wouldn't, of course, make it so public. Just something small and private that even my aunts wouldn't know about until I was out of their household. I mean, if I had my own household, within Silver Hearth," she paused to inhale again. "But I thought I might have my own, private wedding, like I did for Amy and Dorn, if I found someone . . . " her pulse was visible in the slim wrist she raised to touch a finger to her golden eyebrow, " . . . to love."

"I would be honored," said Erien, "to play for your wedding."

"Oh." She blinked at him slowly. "Thank you," she said, with a formal manner, "very much."

"Is there . . . anyone you'd like . . . to marry?" asked Erien, feeling as though this was his first fumbling essay at a foreign language. Which, upon reflection, it was.

Not looking at him, but coloring, she shook her head.

Good, said a small part of him—and the rest of him said, *What?*

But any further self-interrogation was driven out of his mind by D'Lekker's clear, taunting voice saying, "But the Monatese would know how to deal with a race that was boy-*sla*, wouldn't they, Heir Monitum?"

D'Lekker was standing in the middle of the floor, his back to Erien, feet apart, his hand on his hilt in a braggart's pose. Tatt was ten strides away, Branstatt and Deyne flanking. All three were just turning. Plainly, the errants had been walking Tatt away from D'Lekker's goading.

Around D'Lekker, faces were stiff with disbelief—and dark fascination—at the remark.

"After all," D'Lekker said, "they breed their own. We all know about Darren Monitum."

Dear Gods, Erien thought.

Darren Monitum, who had been liege before Di Mon, was Monitum's tragedy and shame. Darren had been Royalblood. When he was caught in a homosexual affair with a peasant boy, his three children—borne by contract to a Vrellish *mekan'st*—had been slain by their mother for the presumed taint in their genes. Darren Monitum had challenged, and killed, his *mekan'st*, and died fighting Nesaks within the month, leaving Monitum in the hands of Di Mon, its first merely Highlord liege.

Every Monatese knew about the scandal. Only Erien knew, through Ranar, that Darren Monitum had been Di Mon's first lover, and the tragedy explained why he had never dared to have a child. But what every Monatese knew was bad enough.

Tatt would not stomach the reference. Erien abandoned Luthan to run soundlessly out of the alcove.

D'Lekker drew another breath. Tatt started forwards, his hand on his hilt, his face bloodless. Erien thought, *No!* He threw himself across the space between them, seized D'Lekker by the right shoulder and swung D'Lekker around. He caught sight of the shock in Tatt's face and saw his hand jerk away from the hilt of his sword, honor preventing him from even thinking of drawing behind an opponent's back.

D'Lekker's face showed a moment's alarm; Erien checked Tatt with a single quick glance, standing half turned between them. *Bastard,* Erien thought, fighting the disorientation that came with his leap across this floor. *Goading Tatt here! About this.* Out of the corner of his eye he caught sight of D'Therd, aborting a move towards his own hilt. *Surprised you, did I?* he thought, giddily. *Good.* He said, tightly—and hoped the tightness sounded like the tightness of fury, not of nausea, "I am afraid that I missed the first part of this conversation, D'Lekker. But I suspect I know its tenor. If you must talk about Reetions, talk to me."

He became aware of the silence all around them. Of the watching eyes. He had stepped, he realized, very close to the edge, without thinking. In anger. Had fallen into the very trap from which he had rescued Tatt.

Tatt, he realized, with a glance at the Royalblood's blazing, iridescent eyes, did not appreciate the rescue. *Nor should he,* Erien admitted; intervention was as good as an insult.

But Gods, this would be no fair fight, on this floor, and in Tatt's state of mind. If fight there must be, it would happen tomorrow, when Tatt's head was clear, and on the plain floor of the Octagon.

D'Lekker perceived the silence, too, and measured his answer out on a sneer. "Oh." A flick of D'Lekker's hand took in Erien's braidless livery. "And who are you?" His pronoun demoted Erien to commoner. And Erien realized what had to come. It had been inevitable from the moment he set foot on Gelion.

"I," Erien said, precisely, "am the one person in this room with the experience to call your slanders what they are—lies." D'Lekker blinked. Erien stepped a little closer to him, deliberately. "I will take your apology now, in the name of the Ambassador of Rire, and the Reetion people. Or I will take it in blood, tomorrow morning."

Tatt said, "D'Lekker," his voice was shaking—as much with anger as with alarm—"the ward of Monitum—"

"Heir Monitum," Erien interjected, crisply, "at the root, this concerns Reetions and therefore this is a matter for my sword, not yours. As we discussed before—I have a latitude for action which you do not—and it might, perhaps, be appropriate at this moment to dissolve the wardship, if you feel it obliges you to support my actions when you have more pressing matters of your own."

"Like hell I will!" Tatt blazed at him. "You need a minder!" Branstatt gripped Tatt's elbow—but his right elbow, Erien noted. Tatt fought with his left hand. Tessitatt came up behind them, standing clear of any draw.

Liege Nersal spoke, silencing everyone. "Your answer?" he said to D'Lekker.

D'Lekker slowly grinned, looking at Tatt. "Sure, I'll fight him," he said, lazily. "It'll be a good warm up for the main event."

Tatt turned on his heel and, flanked by Branstatt and Deyne, strode from the hall. Tessitatt gestured to the remaining Green Hearth errants that they were to stay, and then followed her son. Her vassals fell in behind her.

Liege Nersal said to Erien, in fleet dialect, "Report. In half an hour."

Erien nodded acknowledgment, fleet-style, before he thought. Pure reflex. Liege Nersal left too, first having—with a glance—deputized Dorn to stay.

Erien heard someone say in a disparaging tone, "Vrellish squabbles." It was one of Luthan's ladies-in-waiting, chafing Luthan's hand. Luthan was on the verge of fainting. When Erien caught her eye, she bit her lip and looked deliberately away and began chattering brightly at whoever stood nearest.

The Green Hearth errants formed a loose cage around Erien. Dorn came over with two horns of wine and stood with him, within it. "Tatt will forgive you," he advised Erien mildly, "as long as it only happens once. But if you don't kill D'Lekker, he will kill you, one day."

"Tatt couldn't have fought D'Lekker, in his state of mind and on this floor," said Erien.

"No," Dorn said, somberly, "he couldn't." But his sideways glance said that he hoped Erien knew what he was doing.

They sipped wine. The reception continued its slow winding down, although the challenge seemed to have given it a perverse renewal of life. The remaining Nersallians were clearly enjoying themselves, but whether they were inflating or besmirching his reputation, Erien had no idea. He was aware of eyes and whispers. No more obscurity. Maybe, after tomorrow, no more powerlessness. He felt nauseated at the thought that this was what he had to do to be noticed.

D'Therd collected his brother and Ev'rel's remaining vassals and departed towards Demlara's Walk. The Demish party were gathering to go, forming into a strict recessional order. He glimpsed Luthan's face amongst them, looking back. Whether she saw him, he did not know.

Dorn said, "You should go now. I'll see you again at Black Hearth."

Tatt was waiting for him at the foot of Green Hearth's stair. He lunged for Erien, scattering errants, caught Erien's jacket, two fisted, and slammed him up against the stair's curve. "Are you out of your mind? Or just a presumptuous, arrogant, insolent, upstart? Who do you think you are? Horth Nersal? You haven't even got a set of house braids to call your own, and you're challenging my opponents!" Heads appeared at either end of the hall, servants' heads mainly, but some visiting vassals. Branstatt signaled errants to shoo away the former, managing as he did so to block the view of the latter. He watched, with only the occasional wince, as Tatt impugned in heated succession Erien's honor, judgment, ancestry—unknown though it was—and education. "And if D'Lekker weren't likely to kill you tomorrow," Tatt shouted, "I'd challenge you myself! And if he doesn't, I will!" He dropped Erien and half turned away to swipe his sleeve across his shining eyes, and then swung back. "Vent it, Erien! How could you be so stupid? You were out of line, you insulted me, and you're going to get yourself killed! I thought you thought you were a diplomat! I can take him!" He shouted at Erien. "That goes for all the rest of you," he said, spinning around, making all the errants start and straighten. "I can take him, and the next person who gets between me and him dies! Do you hear me? Dies!" He stalked a circuit of his errantry, glaring into faces, and circled back to Erien. "Just how good are you?"

"On a good day," Erien said, "I'd land one hit to your two."

Tatt stared into his eyes. Looking for false modesty. He found none. "Gods!" he exploded, "And you challenged D'Lekker Dem'Vrel. He will make paté of you!"

"No," Erien said, "he won't."

"Tell me why," Tatt said narrowly, "I should beat you two to one and you should beat D'Lekker, but I can't? Or is that some arcane Reetion mathematics?"

"I never said or implied that you could not beat D'Lekker. But the issue is Rire, and I am Rire's champion."

"The issue, Erien," Tatt said, "is D'Lekker and me."

"Then D'Lekker should leave Rire out of it, two days before the Swearing. He might have been trawling for you, but he got me. And with a little help from the Nersallians if they'll give it, you if they won't, I will take first blood from him tomorrow. Tatt, I have to. Nobody will listen to the first thing I say if I don't. I had no idea the situation here on Gelion was so bad. Now it is, and I have to take drastic action."

Tatt threw up his hands. "Well, hey, you butting in on my fight to challenge D'Lekker, that's drastic." He jabbed a hard finger into Erien's chest. "D'Lekker kills people! He won't spare you just because he figures out you're weak. In fact, he's liable to humiliate you, then kill you."

"I hope he tries," Erien said, "because then he'll be fighting the wrong fight entirely. I'm not out to prove I'm better than he is. I'm not out to dominate him, or to settle a grudge. I'm out to take first blood."

Tatt glowered, but on Branstatt's face was a growing look of enlightenment.

"I have seen him sparring," said Erien. "I know something of his strengths and weaknesses. Other people have seen much more. But nobody knows me, or mine. I have strengths, Ditatt, and I think they are the right ones against D'Lekker. Now, I need to go to Black Hearth. Liege Nersal wants to see me, and I need to see him. If he won't help me, then I'll need your help."

"You don't deserve it, vent you," Tatt said, bleakly.

Erien moved him gently aside with a hand on his shoulder. "Thank you, Tatt."

"Maybe I'll help you," Tatt shouted after him as he headed toward Family Hall, towards his room and the change of clothes he needed. "Maybe."

CHAPTER XI

"COME ON." CHAROUS JERKED HER CHIN to signal Amel that it was time to see Ameron.

Amel frowned. She wouldn't use that tone with any other highborn. Not even a nobleborn. She'd had him shot with a needle gun! He could demand satisfaction for that. Why not? Ameron would never condone this.

Drasous took his elbow, to steady him. Amel shook him off.

"I am fine," he said, speaking down, Pureblood to commoner. Drasous failed to take it as an insult. *Damn him.*

Amel let his anger empower him to conquer wooziness and followed Charous.

Ameron was pacing behind his desk, in the Blackwood Room. He stopped as Amel and Charous entered, his head coming up.

"Amel," Charous announced.

"Yes, thank you, Char."

The Royal *Gorarelpul* hesitated.

Dismissed again! Amel indulged in a smirk, lurking just below the level of honest expression. Charous' quickly masked pique was a sweet revenge, or would have been, if it had not looked enough like genuine hurt feelings to disturb his satisfaction.

"He spoke with the Reetion without your leave," Charous objected, speaking up with all the grace of Tatt's fiercest lunge.

"So I have been informed." Ameron's formality could lower room temperature.

Charous may not have been conscience-bonded like the other *gorarelpul*, but she was not immune. Amel watched her swallow, chastised, before taking the requisite step back to initiate her leave taking. She spun with decision, strode out, and gently closed the door.

Ameron let out the breath that he was holding. It was not relief, but barely contained anger. He did not like his dismissals resisted.

He was not happy with Amel either.

"What have you told Ranar?" Ameron demanded.

"I—" Amel floundered.

"You took advantage of your freedom here to see him!"

There was nothing friendly about Ameron's *rel*-peerage. It implied, instead, no quarter.

Amel's chest tightened. He began to answer, breathless, and had to remember to inflate his lungs. "Yes. I did. I'm sorry."

Softening rewarded his contriteness. "What did you tell him?"

"That I would take him home."

Ameron's expression clouded. "On whose authority?"

"There's been a murder! Of me, in effigy, by people painted up to look like Reetions. I can't face Ranar being caught up in that!" Amel overtook galloping emotion and reigned it back, eyes lowered. "So I told him I'd take him home. Isn't that what you want?"

Ameron wasn't placated. "There is a difference between simply going home, and an agreement to defer recognition."

"Ranar can't make Rire defer recognition!" Amel flared up.

"He could," said Ameron, "if he wanted to."

"Not without lying in his report."

"What is so wrong with that?" Ameron exploded.

"He's Reetion! Reetions have to have everything wide open! Public. Discussed. He would never be trusted again if he lied once. Ranar would not do it anyhow," Amel concluded, failing in the thought experiment of imagining Ranar being duplicitous. "It's—Reetion honor."

"*Ack!*" Ameron exclaimed, and spun away in disgust. He paced behind the desk, drawing Amel's eyes to follow one long-fingered, trailing hand as it glided over desk and chair back.

"So," Ameron summarized Amel's logic, "you would send Ranar home to tell Rire that I cannot command Sevildom. And tempt war. When you, yourself, think they're ripe for one."

"I didn't think about it like that," Amel said, humbled.

"You never do." Ameron was tart.

Amel looked down. Confusion sat on his shoulders like an ungainly weight. He couldn't shift it anywhere that made it comfortable. A clear dream exploited his confused associations. All at once he was thirteen years old, and called to an accounting before the Princess-Liege of H'Us—not Luthan but her predecessor. She was dying of regenerative cancer and looked worn, but she was fond of the pretty courtesan who read and sang to her. He was her life's last adornment. She wanted none of what her medtech laid before her now. "Mira tells me that you have been—mistreated, by Liege H'Reth of the Apron District, while attending his wife there. Is there any truth in this, *lyka*?"

"No!" Amel gasped.

"Amel?" asked Ameron.

Amel felt the Ava touch his arm. He blinked. Ameron's face fought with that of the late Liege H'Us, as if they were a single person trying to pull apart and resolve into themselves once more.

"Are you all right?" both asked.

Amel wanted to go back. He wanted to tell Liege H'Us the truth. For Mira. But he'd been afraid to die. Afraid of the conscience-bond H'Reth had forced on him.

Ameron guided him into a chair. He sat.

The past was out of reach, again. He had lied, to protect a man he hated. Mira's look of disbelief, the inverse of her former faith in his pride, burned in his memory like acid. She had not known that he was conscience-bonded, that proving her faith would have killed him. That was his excuse. But he could have backed up her brave gamble and let the bond end his shame with honor. He could have spared Mira so much, if he'd had the courage. She would never have been dismissed, and driven to the Knotted Strings where Ev'rel was in the market for skills like hers, no questions asked, no references required. She would never have been there, working for Ev'rel, when Rire disgorged him back to Sevildom.

"Amel?" Ameron sounded alarmed.

Amel focused on the Ava, feeling sheepish and at a loss to explain his lapse of concentration. "I—" he groped for an excuse, "—had to be detained, a little forcibly, by Charous."

Ameron frowned. "Do you want me to speak to her?"

Amel shook his head. Punishment, for anyone, had ceased to matter to him. "Do you remember, from my probe transcripts, the piece where Mira—my foster sister from the *gorarelpul* college—tried to expose Liege H'Reth, as a—as my *slaka'st*?"

Ameron nodded. He was crouched by the guest chair, with a lightly fisted hand on the seat by Amel's thigh, and his other hand braced on the far arm, as if to hold Amel penned should he go mad. "I did not read the transcripts," he said, "but Charous did, and summarized them. Is this relevant?" the Ava added, imperial impatience gaining ground on personal compassion.

Amel bobbed a nod. He knew it was. But he didn't know how to explain that to Ameron. The knowledge had the elusive quality of a poem, and Ameron had a Lorel mind, not a Golden Demish one.

"When I denied the truth, about H'Reth," Amel tried to say it in prose, "I couldn't accept that I did it to save myself. I thought I could make it right somehow, later. I was wrong. But I was young, and in the end, I simply did not want to die. It was ugly learning to live with that.

So though I serve you in some things, in others—in matters of conscience—I must be my own master. Not yours, and not Ev'rel's either."

Ameron's brow was furrowed. "Is this about speaking to Ranar?"

"Yes," Amel said, "it includes that."

Ameron sighed as he rose. "You are right that we must understand each other," said the Ava, "but I think, Amel, it is yourself that you do not know. You speak of conscience. What is conscience, but the arrogance of being certain that you are right, and others wrong? You have an arrogance as *rel* as mine in that regard." The Ava held out his hand, to help Amel up. "It may not be a strength that you acknowledge, but it is that arrogance I trust. As if it were my own conscience."

Amel felt upset by that, and could not put his hand in Ameron's. "I don't," he said, and cleared his throat. "I don't understand what you mean by that."

"Perhaps no more than this," said Ameron, stepping back. He walked to his desk as he spoke. "After eighteen years, I know you well enough to know that, when you thwart me, it is done in defense of someone else. So," the Ava stopped, and sat down behind his desk, "tell me who you are protecting from me now?"

"Protecting from you?" Amel was disconcerted by the fresh assault. He tightened his hands on the arms of his chair, relaxing again when his elbow panged.

"Your certainty of Rire losing patience," said Ameron, "has it something to do with your Reetion commander?"

"Ann?"

"Yes, your Reetion . . . woman," said Ameron. Like Liege Nersal, he was unsure how to name the relationship, but at least he avoided *lyka*.

Amel wet his lips. "Killing Reach couldn't stop a highborn invasion, even though half of its pilots are at least Fractional or Pettylords, with a smattering of nobleborns."

"So I have been told. Often. By Ayrium."

"Then you can understand," said Amel, "how vulnerable the Reetions of Paradise Reach must feel. All their pilots are commoner."

"Of course." Ameron experimented with patience.

"Wouldn't the Reetions be foolish, then, not to prepare somehow? To arm themselves in ways which might violate your preliminary agreements with Ranar—but buy them some measure of immediate protection?"

"Have you cause to believe they have done so?" demanded Ameron.

They both heard the door open.

"The Reetion ambassador," announced one of Ameron's errants, and ushered in Ranar.

Ameron rose.

"Leave us," Ameron ordered the errant, "but tell Charous I may want her when my guests are gone."

Amel was surprised to see Ranar. But if his otherwise unproductive visit resulted in Ameron consulting Ranar again, on Reetion matters, maybe it had been worth it. That there was distance to overcome was evident in Ameron's stiffly formal Gelack. Scholarly Monatese English was their usual shared ground for discourse.

"Amel thinks Rire is preparing for war," Ameron told Ranar, "*Okal'a'ni* war. The kind that will escalate to genocide, as it did once before."

"That is not possible," Ranar answered him, also in Gelack, but refusing to speak up like a commoner. "However, I can readily appreciate where Amel might have contracted that impression. He is *mekan'st* to Ann, the Space Service Executive of our outpost, *SkyBlue Station*." The impossible application of the Sevolite term, *mekan'st*, to a commoner, sounded right somehow coming from Ranar. "Ann did raise the issue of prepared defense," Ranar continued, "which may account for Amel's perspective. The recommendation was popular only in the Reach of Paradise, where people feel most directly threatened. Threatened people, Ava, are rarely as rational as those given the confidence that they will be heard and dealt with openly. But Reetions are nothing if not rational, and Rire understands the errors made in Killing Reach two hundred years ago. There will be no *okal'a'ni* tactics to tempt genocidal war. In broader debate, Ann's motion was soundly defeated."

Ameron frowned. "Paradise Reach could have acted alone."

"Not possible," Ranar shook his head. "Every arbiter throughout the Reetion Net shares decisions, and checks the integrity of every other arbiter's work load. The data is carried by every ship, and arbiters deprived of the traffic for too long will shut down. It is how we ensure everyone who benefits from arbiter technology adheres to our model of transparent governance. Governments cannot do things, within the Reetion Net, in secret, or in isolation. The Net itself would have to reconsider the proposal."

"Perhaps they have," conjectured Ameron. "Amel says that opinion, even on Rire, is going sour."

"People will certainly be worried," allowed Ranar, "but policy cannot have changed, substantially, or I would have been recalled. I have not," he said, and toyed, for the first time, with doubt. "Have I?"

Ameron sat, with his long fingers steepled, studying the Reetion with a frown. Amel suspected that Ameron was looking for some detail that would prove Ranar was homosexual—something he might previously have overlooked. Amel understood, because he'd done the same himself once, but being homosexual was incidental to the Reetion's character. Amel had never felt it at all, except in the tensions read, long ago, seeing Di Mon and Ranar in a room together: as if it took the light of Di Mon's terrible, stifled passion, reflecting off Ranar, to make it show. Di Mon's fatal secret was safe in the calm of Ranar's soul, because no sounding of Ranar could trace it back to him. Amel felt guilty for thinking about it, as if his thoughts could contaminate Ameron's ignorance, and wound Di Mon's fierce ghost.

"Have I been recalled by Rire?" Ranar insisted on an answer.

Ameron dropped his hands to the top of the famous Blackwood Desk. "No," he said. "Ayrium has received no such communication from *SkyBlue Station*."

"Then it is merely a matter of Amel being worried," Ranar summed up, "which is perfectly understandable. We are all concerned."

Ranar would be 'concerned', Amel thought, resentfully, *about an imminent jump collapse.*

"I am grateful for his concern," Ranar went on, "since it led to this interview with you."

Ranar was speaking English. So was Ameron. A definite improvement in relations, since in Gelack every pronoun was a battle ground for relative status. On reflection, Amel could recall the moment where they had made the transition. What he could not fathom was how the Reetion had so seamlessly accomplished it.

"There is something I wish to know myself, now, Ava," Ranar said.

"Oh?" Ameron raised an angular eyebrow.

"Did you send for Erien to come to court?"

Ameron's attention snapped to Amel, coldly furious.

"Erien is Ranar's ward." Amel defended his indiscretion.

"By Di Mon's edict, not my own," flared Ameron, "and for reasons which I have never understood, any more than I can grasp why you, Amel, continue to honor the arrangement! Surely Di Mon could not have approved of a guardian who is, by his own admission, boy-*sla*!"

Amel turned away from that argument, toward the wall. It churned him up, hard, at a wordless depth where violence and self-hatred deadlocked. He stopped when he encountered drapery, and set the fingers of his left hand on it, feeling the velvet and the hardness of the wall beyond. The velvet was lush. He stroked it, and listened to what was going on behind his back.

"Do you believe," Ranar was saying, firmly and gently, to Ameron, "that I have ever inappropriately touched your son?"

There was an awkward silence. Ameron got up, making the heavy chair of the Blackwood Desk squeak on the floor as he pushed it back. Amel mapped the rustling of clothes to Ameron pacing the length of the room behind the chair he had abandoned. Then the Ava stopped, and answered with vexation, in a rush, "Reetion, I find I have a hard time considering you a fully functioning human, in that regard, of any sort! Which is possibly as bad. The boy has ice for blood!"

"That," said Ranar with a trace of a sigh, "is Di Mon's fault. He told Erien not to risk siring a child until he knew who he was." Ranar added critically, "He did not expect you to withhold your prerogative concerning that, for quite so long."

"Di Mon," Ameron rumbled, as if he could be overheard by Di Mon's ghost, "I hope you must wait to be reborn until all your agendas are played out! Ten years dead," he addressed the living, "and I am still stumbling through the nets he cast." He paused, and said with more affection and irrepressible curiosity, "Did Di Mon know? That you . . . "

"We discussed our cultural differences, of course," Ranar answered.

Amel smiled, despite himself. *I bet they did, at that*, he thought.

"Yes, well, Di Mon could discuss anything," Ameron grumbled and dismissed the topic.

"We need to talk," Ranar pressed again, too soon, "about Erien. He is only seventeen, and has never been to Court."

"Erien is a Pureblood," said Ameron. "He'll cope."

"That's racist nonsense!" said Ranar. Such a rare show of temper turned Amel around to see what it looked like on Ranar. The Reetion seemed equally surprised himself. "With due respect, Ava," he recovered his equilibrium, "Amel was correct to inform me that Erien is here. Erien spent his formative years on Rire. Sevolite or not, he isn't prepared to make his own way in your system. He needs proper handling now. Send for him. Tell him that you are his father."

"He has declared himself for Rire," said Ameron, "and your champion. To own him could cost me the Swearing."

Amel flinched at the way that was put. Was being Ava all that mattered, here, to Ameron?

Ranar, also, fell into exploring possibilities. "Being my champion might set Erien up in opposition to Vretla Vrel, or even Horth Nersal, if the Swearing goes wrong." Ranar shook his head. "I can't have that. He is too important."

Amel wondered what Ranar meant by 'too important'. It sounded like some echo of the 'agendas' which Ameron had complained about. Erien's right to live beyond his seventeenth year seemed, to Amel, important enough. But he approved of Ranar's sentiment, whatever its motivation.

"Let me see Erien," Ranar said. "I can reason with him."

Ameron frowned. "I do not trust you not to tell him too much. Not, at least, before the Swearing."

"Erien would not act—" Ranar began.

"Erien is my son," Ameron refused the unfinished argument for nurture over nature, "and Pureblood. If he knew he was the Throne Price, he would not stay out of my business. Unless—" Ameron had an idea he liked, all of a sudden. "Unless you take him back to Rire with you, to assist you in restoring Reetion patience."

"Rire has been patient for eighteen years," said Ranar, with finality. "That is long enough."

There was a difficult silence as Sevolite and Reetion faced one another. Then Ranar let himself out. Amel was conscious of the point Ranar was making, both by having the last word, and by not waiting for an escort. There would be an errant guard waiting, of course, but the gesture was still—as Ranar might say—culturally significant. Ranar, in his own way, was very good.

Ameron turned to Amel. "We have not dealt with your misuse of my trust," the Ava said crisply. "I need to know, Amel, before you leave me now. Who do you support? Myself, or Ev'rel?"

"Are you asking for my oath?" Amel would have been frightened by that, if he had not been so certain that Ameron never would ask, for if the Ava ever asked, he did not know what he would do.

"I am asking whom you wish to be Ava," said Ameron.

"I don't care which of you is Ava, and which Avim, just so long as—" Amel let out his breath, and his anger, in a desperate sigh of frustration. The weight of impossible choices felt suffocating.

"So long as you keep us all safe?" said Ameron. "Yes, I thought as much, but if it comes to a choice, Amel, you can't go on—" Ameron's avuncular lecture was cut off by a sudden, commanding, arrival.

Liege Nersal walked in past a very nervous captain of errants, who admitted him, saying, "Highlord Horth, Liege of Nersal.

"He insisted on seeing you immediately," the errant captain added, demoting himself a rank, in his pronouns, by way of apology to Ameron.

Ameron nodded. By the laws of *Okal Rel*, the errant could have barred the Ava's champion only by opposing him with his sword. "You were right, of course, to interrupt," Ameron restored the errant's proper birth rank through his choice of 'you', in Gelack, reassuring him that the matter was not worth dying for.

The errant captain withdrew. Charous slipped in as he went out.

"I will speak with you later," Ameron dismissed her, immediately.

Amel was too distressed by Nersal's arrival to enjoy seeing Charous ejected, once more, from an audience where the Throne Price was apt to be at issue. For once he would have liked to have had her around. Ameron was not armed, which eliminated the risk of an attack, since Nersal was *Okal Rel* itself where it came to the honorable expression of aggression. But a word wrong between them could have terrible consequences, if Nersal withdrew his support.

Ameron was fearlessly confident. It was exactly how he acted when a stallion he was riding, on Monitum, acted up. Amel tended to want to get off, with an apology to the offended horse.

"Liege Nersal," Ameron opened, "I am glad to see you." He forbore to add 'at last' or to otherwise remind the taciturn admiral that all court was speculating on where, or if, Nersal would bestow his oath.

Liege Nersal said, "Erien has challenged D'Lekker Dem'Vrel."

"Lek!" Amel started, horrified. "D'Lekker has no quarrel with Erien!"

"Erien claimed a challenge meant for Heir Monitum," Liege Nersal told them both.

"Gods!" exclaimed Ameron. "Did it concern Rire?"

Nersal nodded.

Ameron said, "Ah."

"They can't duel!" Amel exclaimed, panic-stricken.

Liege Nersal looked at him as if he'd gone mad.

"One of them could be killed!" Amel tried to impress upon Ameron.

"Each risks what is his own," said Horth Nersal.

Ameron would not contradict Nersal, Amel realized. Ameron would not do anything to stop the duel, if Nersal believed that it ought to be allowed.

"When is this duel arranged for?" Ameron asked Liege Nersal.

"Tomorrow."

"Before the Swearing?" said Ameron. There was a brief pause. "What is your pleasure, Liege Nersal? I will tell Erien who he is, before, if you so desire."

"He has done this over Rire's honor," said Nersal.

"Yes?" said Ameron.

"Let him see it out as Rire's ward."

"So be it then," said Ameron. "I will tell Charous to ensure that the best possible medtech is available."

"No!" Amel came forward, feeling reckless. Ameron's cold look diverted his appeal in an unimaginable direction, toward Nersal.

"D'Lekker is dangerous," Amel pleaded, "and Erien was raised on Rire." His heart was hammering; he couldn't say any more.

"Erien," said Nersal, "has made his choice."

"*Ack Rel*, then," said Ameron; and to Amel, the phrase, which could mean anything from 'such is life' to 'let the strong survive', had never seemed so sinister.

"Win or lose," Ameron told Nersal, "I'll tell him when the duel is done. If he survives."

Nersal left.

Charous slipped in as he went out. She looked prepared to resist another dismissal. She did not have to, as it turned out. Ameron was all business.

"Charous," Ameron greeted her. "Erien, Ward of Monitum, will duel D'Lekker Dem'Vrel, tomorrow. See to it that the best medtech you can find is made available. Beyond that, let it be known that I am neutral in the quarrel. But I will want to know what is said about it by the families of Fountain Court. Now, send me a herald. I've a letter of importance to compose which must be sent, before morning, to Green Hearth."

Amel broke, and ran.

His body made the decision, rejecting the atmosphere in the room, which expelled him forth. He did not care about Charous or the errants who watched him go, uncertain of whether he should, again, be stopped. Without specific orders, his Pureblood status held sway, and they let him pass.

He went swiftly through the outer offices, and out onto Demlara's Walk, still thick with people leaving the betrothal. He heard his name spoken by someone he did not know. These people would be stragglers, enjoying the last of the wine and gossip concerning the duel. Amel dodged through them, heading for the plaza and down to Fountain Court.

As he ran, he thought, *This must not happen. I won't let it happen! There will be no duel!*

CHAPTER XII

A QUARTET OF BLACK-LIVERIED ERRANTS guarded the Fountain Court entrance to Black Hearth. Most hearths did not post guards outside, even in tense times, and mere guard duty ranked with envoy service, but Horth had made it a reward to serve in his errantry at Court. Two of the quartet watched Erien approach. The other two continued to observe Fountain Court. They had Old Swords' eyes, in faces that had seen decades of service, both to Horth and to the father Horth killed on the challenge floor nearly twenty years ago.

"Liege Nersal expects me," Erien told the senior errant.

There was no tension in them. Despite that, Erien was acutely conscious—because they were—of his left hand, and the sheathed sword hanging at his right side. The skin tingled on his fingers. *Could a hand blush?* Erien thought, absurdly.

The errant to his right shifted her eyes, just a flicker, and stepped clear to accommodate Dorn Nersal, who appeared, unheard, from one of the doors off the Entrance Hall. Dorn was still wearing his betrothal costume, though he had shed the overjacket. "Well met, Erien," he said. "Horth's just back. He said I should bring you through to the family study."

The explanation, Erien realized, was less for his benefit than the errants'. They stood aside to let him pass, informed of where both he and their liege would be if there was trouble. There was no wasted energy. No wasted attention. This was a veteran's true discipline, from within, not the strained and restive sort of Erien's fleet peers and tormentors.

Dorn led him through the public rooms of the Throat, without comment. Erien noticed, though, that Dorn walked at his sword hand, as was customary for a Vrellish host acting as a formal escort for someone treated with respect but not quite trusted. In practical terms, it meant that a draw would find no quick target, and—since they were both left-handed—Dorn's own sword hand would be free to respond.

Passing through Black Hearth's Throat made Erien recognize something that he had not expected. He had thought that Black Hearth would be like the fleet, stamped with Horth's personality. Instead, Black Hearth felt like Green Hearth. Both had a quiet order, though the order was more steely in Black Hearth: old furniture, carved of dark wood and worn by the use of generations, somber ancestral portraits on the walls, tough unpatterned carpet showing wear and frequent stretches of bare metal wall. Both had good air; the Nersallians as proud of their engineering as Monitum was of its nervecloth quasi-organics industry. But Green Hearth's air was leavened with the exhalations of living leaves, green and turquoise. In Green Hearth, life and death within the family challenge right was written in its history. In Black Hearth it was part of the present. It was not yet twenty years since the Nesaks' last attempt to annex Nersal had been settled between Horth and his father, and every few years, sometimes more than once in any single year as a new crop of the *kinf'stan* reached adulthood, Horth fought for his life to keep his title. Conspiracy was not a Nersallian vice. The deadly threat implicit in the title of Liege Nersal was an overt one. But Black Hearth itself seemed aware that even Horth's ownership was transitory.

Dorn ushered Erien through a door into the family study. This room did remind Erien of the fleet: the walls were hung not with portraits, but with nervecloth star charts, shimmering faintly with the illusion of motion. The long tables on three sides of the room held neatly stacked small equipment, Nersallian and Monatese. There was even, at the end of one of the tables, a Reetion crystronics platform, partially dismantled. There were several firm-looking chairs, with small high tables set between them.

In the center of the room stood Horth Nersal, Black Hearth's liege. He, too, still wore ceremonial attire—unlike Erien, who had changed into fleet fatigues. He was eating sliced apples imported from Demora, and had just paused to wipe his fingers on a napkin. He laid the napkin down and nodded dismissal to Dorn. Horth's son nudged Erien across the threshold and closed the door behind them.

Horth Nersal gestured toward fruit sitting in a black glass bowl on a long, narrow table pushed up against one wall. The furnishings of the room were all carved wood, without padding. The theme was dragons, either stalking deer and other Earth-life, or snarled together in ritual combat, claws splayed, tongues curling. There were no repeating patterns to torment the navigators' sense, instinctive in most Sevolites. That, too, Black Hearth shared with Green Hearth.

Erien helped himself to a handful of green grapes. His mouth was dry. Beside the fruit was a stand of decanters, and he poured himself a glass of water, bypassing Vrellish wine and Monatese Turquoise spirits. Unlike Royal receptions and several hearths, the practical Nersallians used flat-bottomed, free-standing glasses in preference to wine horns.

If Erien got what he wanted here, he would need his wits about him.

Grapes and water glass in hand, he turned to face his former admiral.

Horth considered him for a long moment. "D'Lekker," he stated, at last, "is a dangerous Sword."

"Better than I am," Erien said simply.

Horth agreed with a slight nod. He was not armed, Erien noticed. Tatt would have noticed that first. Liege Nersal had also shed his admiralty cloak with its massive dragon breast clasps. It lay draped over one of the chairs, the emerald eyes of the dragons glittering above ruby-blooded claws. The rest of his formal attire was simply cut and comfortable despite its quality: sheer black, scored with crimson insets on the left side, like the gores of mighty claws.

Erien was armed. It was expected in public, and pertinent to his petition. He knew of no obvious protocol to apply to remedy the imbalance, now, so he let Horth's own indifference guide him.

"Do you fight," Horth asked, "for Monitum, or for Rire?"

"Both," said Erien. "I was raised by the late Liege of Monitum, Di Mon, and by Ranar of Rire."

"Heir Monitum is the better match."

Tatt, Erien thought, would be delighted to know that Liege Nersal had noticed him—though being considered better than Erien was, perhaps, a meager compliment.

"Liege Nersal," Erien said, "D'Lekker slandered Rire on the way to slandering Monitum. He would have made it seem that, in fighting him, Heir Monitum was defending Rire. Rire is not Tatt's fight. It is mine."

Horth nodded.

"To have such talk in the fleet is one thing," said Erien. "To have it at court on the eve of the Swearing, is another."

Horth frowned slightly. Erien wondered at what—and then thought he knew. "I appreciate that to you it seems calculating," he said crisply, "but I will not shed blood recklessly or cheaply. You know that of me, when I served under you in Killing Reach, and nothing here on Gelion will change that." Horth was listening with his head slightly cocked, hearing the overtones. "But you also know," said Erien, "that if it is important enough to me and my cause, I will fight. And I will fight with my mind, to win."

"When you challenged, you thought?" asked Horth.

There was a silence. "No," Erien said at last, "first I reacted, then I thought."

Horth grinned, a brief flash of white.

Erien could not smile back. "I thought," he said, "that the sword would be heard where words would not. But I will not kill D'Lekker."

Horth gave him a long look, which let Erien know that the decision might not be in Erien's hands.

Erien said, stubbornly, "I do not have to be better than D'Lekker. I merely have to hit him." He set down both glass and grapes, and turned back, slapping his left palm to his right wrist. "He uses blade motion, cutovers and feints to intimidate. He exposes his arm. My defense is solid, my blade work is precise, and I believe I can last long enough to hit him. But he is strong, fast, and aggressive. I will need your help to work out the timing."

"He is right-handed," Nersal remarked.

"So are most Reetions. I am used to right-handed opponents."

Horth frowned at the suggestion that Reetion training could be adequate preparation in this, or maybe, more seriously, at the reminder that Erien defended Reetion honor.

"What D'Lekker said about Rire is untrue," Erien said. "Sex between men is accepted there, it is true—"

Horth's eyes narrowed.

"—but sex between men and boys is not." Determinedly, Erien avoided pronouns. "Sex between children and adults is not tolerated by Reetions. Rape is not. The inflicting of pain is not. The accusations D'Lekker makes are products of Gelack imagination. Reetions would be more horrified by them even than we are. This is not truth. It is propaganda—" Horth didn't know the Reetion word which Erien resorted to, so Erien defined it in Gelack, "—a way people of small courage find to feel brave, by making a false picture of an enemy whom they can then despise."

Horth looked away. He did that often when he thought. Erien had to struggle with the urge to say more. If Horth declined, and Dorn could not help him, then he would have to rely upon Tatt and Branstatt, and he doubted that either could teach him what he needed to know. But it might be enough, he fervently hoped, simply to have fought, simply to have stood up for Rire, with a sword, even if he lost.

"Rire," Horth said, after a difficult minute of silence, "is different."

It was no compliment.

Erien inhaled slowly, knowing he could not risk platitudes. "Reetions are a threat to Sevildom. I acknowledge that. They are a threat to the very basis of Sevolite society—the assumption that Sevolites should rule. Ideas have influence. It is through the spread of ideas that Rire has grown. To what extent they are a military threat—I do not know.

They are not warlike, and no Reetion pilot can best a Sevolite in space, one to one. Nevertheless, they are capable of their own kind of ruthlessness, as was demonstrated, I acknowledge, in Amel's case eighteen years ago."

"And in Killing Reach, two hundred years ago," Horth said firmly.

"Yes." Erien flexed his right hand, no happier about the habitat destruction of the Killing War which so offended *Okal Rel*, than was Horth. "They threaten, when threatened. And not in ways Sevildom can condone. But only when threatened by—"

"Us," Horth pointedly interjected a pronoun that included Erien.

Damn Gelack pronouns! Erien thought. Horth's 'us' made him realize that he'd been speaking objectively of both Rire, and Gelion, taking no side himself. Horth did not think like that. Erien swallowed, aware that he could hardly deny the pronoun, and continue to claim Sevolite rights of challenge.

"Yes," he conceded, "what House Monitum realizes is that whatever threat Rire may pose can neither be assessed nor met without understanding them better. Projecting Gelack fixations about sexual perversion prevents that.

"That, for the honor of my adopted people," Erien concluded, "and for the honor of my guardian's house, is why I challenged D'Lekker."

Horth inhaled and slowly let his breath out. He was not comfortable with Erien's oratory, or his stance. He was thinking, though. His face brooded on the thoughts, over a thin-lipped frown. Erien, waiting for the verdict, was studied like an argument, for flaws.

"I will help you," Horth said at last, "with the duel."

CHAPTER XIII

"WELL, HELLO." D'LEKKER GRINNED at Amel's intrusion. "Where have you been? You missed my finest hour."

"Liege Nersal said that you've challenged Erien!"

"Close," Lek said dryly. "But he challenged me, in fact."

"To protect Tatt?" Amel dodged through the clutter of D'Lekker's bedroom to the dressing table where his younger half-brother stood, wearing a smug look. Amel took him by both arms. "Lek, if you kill Tatt, it won't end there. You know that! D'Therd will be fighting Liege Nersal before the Swearing's done!"

D'Lekker shrugged. "That's what D'Therd wants."

Amel had to bite back the scream he felt rising. "Lek." He gripped his brother hard. "Don't fight Erien."

"Erien? He won't be any trouble."

"Don't be so sure of that!"

"You're worried about me? I'm touched." D'Lekker said it snidely, but that was defensiveness. Amel was encouraged by the evidence that what he said did matter to the younger man.

"Erien isn't the novice you might imagine." Amel lightened his grip, using his eyes to search the other's soul. "He wouldn't have challenged you if he didn't think he had a chance."

"He lost his temper," D'Lekker insisted.

"Erien? I don't believe that."

"He lost his temper," D'Lekker repeated, "the moment that I said the Monatese were naturally more apt to know what was, and wasn't, normal for the boy-*sla*." Amel's blank reaction gave D'Lekker pause. "You know," he said, "the stories about Darren Monitum?"

Amel whispered, thinly, "Oh, Gods."

"Is Erien one of them?" D'Lekker was eagerly curious. "Him and Ranar perhaps—"

"No," Amel said, distracted. "No, but—oh, Lek, you didn't! Not

Darren Monitum!"

"You know that would upset him, don't you?" D'Lekker guessed. Amel's grip on him had gone slack. He seized Amel, instead, holding his face so close that his breath touched it. "Now you're worried about Erien instead! Is he another of your precious favorites? Is that it? Like Tatt?"

D'Lekker slung Amel away from him. The lid of an opened chest caught Amel in the ribs. He stumbled, recovered, and evaded D'Lekker's grip with a one-handed deflection. D'Lekker lost his footing in a sheet that was balled up on the floor near the unmade bed.

"Lek stop it!" Amel gasped, winded.

D'Lekker slung Amel onto the bed by his weakened right arm, and pinned him beneath his weight, arms extended. Panic handicapped Amel. Gone very still, he lay looking up at D'Lekker in disbelief, aware of the other's erection between their pressed bodies and mesmerized by the intensity on D'Lekker's face.

"If you would only like me better," D'Lekker said. For a dreadful moment their breath mingled as D'Lekker lowered his face toward Amel's.

Amel refused to find out why D'Lekker was doing that. He brought a knee up between his brother's legs.

The position was awkward, but the blow didn't have to hurt much to make its point. D'Lekker came to himself and sprang off the bed.

Amel got up.

"Get out," D'Lekker ordered, shaking with ugly emotion.

Numbly, Amel obeyed him.

"I'll see you at Erien's funeral!" D'Lekker shouted at his retreating back.

Outside, in Family Hall, Amel doubled over, trying to unknot his stomach. He had to be imagining things, he decided. D'Lekker had not been about to kiss him! There were other explanations for each separate detail of the body language on the bed just now. It was the child in D'Lekker who needed his love. It was Amel's fault for turning that love off, now that D'Lekker was a man.

Clear dreams hit like slaps.

Amel dropped to one knee, his hand sliding down the wall, suffering the ghosts of childhood blows. Eyes closed, he weathered the waking nightmare with his face pressed against the wall. When it let him go, he sobbed. A servant stood watching him a few steps off, afraid to help and afraid to leave him alone. He had to get up. The fresh exposure to his memories of the UnderDocks helped him to believe that he had misconstrued D'Lekker's attack. His own sick expectations dirtied everything. That was what was wrong. But whatever had happened, he had made things worse for Erien.

Ev'rel was his only chance to stop the duel, now.

He forced himself upright and staggered the first few steps down Family Hall towards Ev'rel's room, thinking only that he could not allow Erien to die on D'Lekker's sword.

She was in her workshop.

"Ev'rel!" he cried, hand braced against the door.

A clear dream hit him as she rose.

He must have crumpled.

Sanity returned to him as he rested in her arms. She guided him into her chair, before the console which sat along the back wall of the workshop.

"Dreams?" she asked.

He nodded, relieved by her matter-of-fact acceptance. She would help him hide the clear dreams. She had, before.

"You're bloodless," she said. She stood close enough to support him against her waist, stroking his hair.

Amel put an arm around her, grateful for the reassurance of the contact. His eyes were tearing. His heart rate was out of control. "Lek," he gasped. "He's been challenged by Erien!"

"Yes," she said, in calming tones, "I heard. D'Therd is actually proud of D'Lekker. I'm not so sure, though I suppose—"

"No!" Amel wailed, and clutched at her, pressing her yielding body as he hugged her hips. A knifing sensation he could place—all too well—in his courtesan past, left his nerves raw. "No," he said again. He knew he had to be more coherent than he was. He tried to cheat stress, breathing with stage discipline, inhaling the smell of her. Monatese Turquoise and cloves. The bile of fear rose in his throat.

She drew him up, kissing him like an injured child, and saying, "Shh, shh."

He held on, but he shook. "You don't understand," he said. His eyelids fluttered as he tried to focus his dilemma in his own mind. "I've made it worse. I've made D'Lekker mad."

She stroked his cheek. He caught her hand, appealing to her with glistening, gray eyes. "He wants more than first blood now."

"Lek always wants more, of everything, and always has." Ev'rel was gentle. "It isn't your fault."

"You don't understand!" Amel drew back. As body contact between them broke, he became immediately less sure, and more vulnerable. "D'Lekker can't kill Erien. He mustn't! And Ameron won't stop him!"

"But you think I should?" Ev'rel made no attempt to draw him back to her. She was intrigued now.

Amel swayed like a drunk on a precipice. He could not make the necessary words. The obstruction was complex; strengthened by one secret ordeal and many years of frightened silence. The clear dreams clamored so that he thought he might go mad. When the words came they broke out in a flood. "You must! You've got to stop the duel. Because Erien is your son. Erien is the Throne Price that I stole from you!"

He saw, with satisfaction, how her face changed as she heard that. Ameron might sacrifice the Throne Price, but Ev'rel would not. She would do something. But the warmth she had shown him, moments earlier, was gone.

"You were right to tell me," Ev'rel said. "Albeit a somewhat belated intelligence."

Amel began shivering violently. "I . . . feel . . . "

"It's the stress," she said, and she took charge, pushing him gently but firmly back into the seat of her workstation. "The dreams always feed on stress. When it's over, you'll feel better."

A sixth sense told him something was about to go very wrong. "Ev'rel?" he said. He looked up in time to see the door slam.

Amel launched himself toward the barrier to his freedom with a cry like a wounded animal's. He stabbed at the inside controls. The door would not open. Swiftly he reviewed tricks to try against the lock— but none would affect the outside bar, which she had added while he'd been gone.

"Think, think," he urged himself, desperately. Fear ate every effort hollow. Fear too dreadful to be named, making him inhale more than he exhaled. Fear of being locked up. By Ev'rel.

"No!" He wailed in one, passionate, denial. The sound proofed room, their secret haven, absorbed the cry and did not give back even echoes.

CHAPTER XIV

ERIEN DID NOT HEAR THE HERALD DESCENDING the stairs to the Octagon. He could not afford to divide his attention. Though scrupulous about safety in the fleet, Horth Nersal disdained practice masks, and his teaching—as Erien well knew—approached what other men would call combat. Even with a practice sword, a lapse in concentration could cost Erien an eye, if not more.

Horth, however, faced the stairs. At the herald's approach he disengaged, and stepped back. Erien did not turn until Horth signaled him to do so. He knew better than to do otherwise.

"Master," the herald stood his ground, confident of his decision to intrude. "Avim Ev'rel is here. She says that she has to see Erien, Ward of Monitum."

Horth relaxed his stance, the sword in his hand no longer part of him, only an object which, lacking a sheath, he must hold. He looked at Erien, who was bending over, practice sword braced on thighs, regaining his breath.

"See her." It had the unmistakable air of a conclusion, not the beginning of an explanation.

The Nersallian herald bowed aside with the stiff-necked, minimalist acknowledgment shown by all of Horth's vassals. He led Erien silently up the spiral stairs and into Black Hearth's guest lounge.

"His Grace, Erien, Ward of Monitum," the herald announced, and withdrew.

Ev'rel was studying the portraits mounted at staggered positions along the walls. They were the room's only decorations. Over Ev'rel's shoulder stared Hangst Nersal, the father whom Horth had challenged and killed to become Liege Nersal. Hangst was an austere, Vrellish-complexioned man, whose face conveyed his hundred years with nothing but touches of the symptoms of age shown by commoners. His eyes, Erien thought, were different from Horth's, for all that they were the same Vrellish gray. Beside Hangst were Horth's dead brothers, green-eyed Zrenyl and gray-eyed Branst, each set apart in his own frame. Branst, Erien thought, looked approachable. Zrenyl looked as though he was cut from D'Therd's mold. He was powerful, certain, even a little righteous.

"I have not been in this room," Ev'rel said, peer-to-peer, "since I was younger than you are. Horth has changed nothing. It is still Hangst's."

She turned to face Erien.

Ev'rel's dress was as black as a Nersallian's uniform, with a fitted bodice and a long, sleek skirt. At her waist was a stiletto, not a sword. No one, Erien thought, would mistake Ev'rel for a Nersallian. There was something of the Demish lady about her, for all that her hair was as black and her eyes as gray as Erien's. He felt acutely aware of his sweat-stained fatigues and matted hair. She seemed not to notice. "You know, of course," she said, "that Horth slew his father to prevent him from throwing in with the Nesaks against Rire. Do you know how little that had to do with Rire, though?"

"Did you come to warn me against trusting Liege Nersal?" Erien asked, declining her flattering peer-to-peer address in favor of a less drastic compromise, which still thanked her for her condescension without proving him easily flattered. Her strategy, in speaking to him as if he was, also, a Pureblood, was baffling.

"Horth Nersal killed his father over the principle of being Vrellish, not Nesak," explained Ev'rel. "I would trust him to follow his principles again, to be sure. And to think none the less of you, dead, if you stood opposed. But enough—" She stayed his response with a raised palm. "You're quite right, this is fatuous."

She searched the ceiling with her large, dark eyes, betraying some nervousness. "There is no ideal way to have this out. I must say it, and be done."

"If this concerns my duel with—"

"Only in as much as the duel has flushed out a secret which I have long sought. Erien," she said, "you are my son. By Ameron."

Erien heard what she had said, but could not, immediately, absorb it.

"I have known only for as long as it took me to cross Fountain Court," she answered the obvious, unasked question. "Why Amel chose to tell me now, when he kept silent in the face of execution, I don't know. He is genuinely fond of children. Perhaps he still considers you one. Or Lek. He turned to me because Ameron refused to stop the duel. As to that, I do not know if I can. I will try, of course, but Lek does not do what he is told. In fact, he is increasingly out of hand."

"I am the Throne Price?" Erien found his voice. The concept felt alien. Like an ill-weighted sword thrust into his hand.

"It hadn't occurred to you?" Ev'rel wondered aloud. "Perhaps you were as cleverly deluded as the rest of us, by the very plausible notion that you were Amel's love child by a den girl, since that child was spirited offplanet by Di Mon. It accounts so well for you being a houseless highborn. But you are mine. The price Ameron paid me for the Throne."

There was a momentary silence. What she had just said invited the first question Erien wanted to ask. "Why did you settle for that? A child, for a throne?"

Ev'rel settled herself on a bench beneath the portraits. Erien did not sit, and she did not ask him to. She said, simply, "It seemed inevitable. My First Sworn, Di Mon, worshipped Ameron's memory. When Ameron reappeared, two hundred years time-slipped, it was impossible to retain Di Mon's oath. Between them they recruited the new Liege of Nersal. I had taken Demora, which offended H'Us. When Ameron took up with Amel's Purple Alliance friend, Ayrium, making out that it was a *cher'stan* romance, it bought him Amel." She shrugged one shoulder just enough to register. "Despite his life, my Amel is as quick to believe in what is larger than life as any Demish virgin." She gazed at Erien for a moment, level-eyed. "Why not let Ameron be Ava, since he wanted it so much? I had work to do. And time, I thought, would favor me."

"I needed a new generation of highborns," Ev'rel explained, "to make the Knotted Strings a greater power. You could have made that possible. Sevolite power is built upon gifts of blood, and Ameron is stingy with his rewards. It was policy with him not to child-gift, even before this fiction of Ayrium and he being *cher'stan*, which the Vrellish take as soul-business, and the Demish as a Vrellish marriage. Altogether too convenient, don't you think, for a male, disinclined to child-gift, to take refuge in a monogamous relationship? Lorel arrogance, I suppose. They were ever loath to breed, except with Monitum. He could have opted for a Demish marriage, of course, but every Vrellish house would have objected, and his *cher'st* is doubly convenient for being who she is, of course. Her Purple Alliance is a natural enemy of Dem'Vrel."

Ev'rel's matter-of-fact manner dissolved as she continued.

"Ayrium herself, and her mother, have convinced my poor Amel that they care about him. Amel needs to be liked. It makes him vulnerable. And while he is stupid about politics, he is more willful than anyone knows, once he is convinced that he acts in the service of some fairy tale principle. It is infuriating, but the Purple Alliance has convinced Amel that he must not child-gift for me, for fear of doing them harm. That is what I needed the Throne Price for. If I'd raised you, I could have got the better of Ameron, and without forcing Amel, thwart the damage which the Reetions etched into his soul with their visitor probe. He cannot help but see the good in any cause that is not his own."

The baldness of this accusation stung Erien. Beneath it smoldered signs of a banked fire of personal resentment. Ev'rel cloaked all emotion with a single inhalation.

"I need to tell you quickly," she explained her visit, "and frankness is efficient. I trust the intellect you've demonstrated. I will not claim a mother's affection on so slight an acquaintance. Birthing has been business for me, always."

Erien's heart was hammering despite his excellent self-management. His bedraggled appearance seemed suddenly much less important. "I appreciate your frankness," he said at last.

She waited a moment, watching him. He thought he should have had a dozen questions, but none came. Or questions came, but they were childish ones, demeaning to the man and the diplomat he was. He could not indulge them. Policy was what mattered. This was the Avim, the second most powerful Sevolite on Gelion, and a contender for the throne.

"Do you blame Rire?" Erien asked. "For Amel's . . . condition?"

She did not flinch, or smile, or frown, but answered him simply. "Of course." Then, upon reflection, with a sense of doubting the intelligence she had earlier claimed to approve, she added, "Do you not?"

Tension clutched at Erien's stomach. But this had to be confronted, or it would always be there, influencing things that it should not.

Ev'rel pre-empted him. She spoke with precision, but not without glimpses of those banked fires.

"Amel has cost me much," she said, "and still does. Di Mon was disgusted by him. The Purple Alliance is not above using him. D'Therd has not forgiven me for lacking the courage to execute him, when it was within our right, after he had stolen you from Lilac Hearth. Perhaps I should have. But I, too, have suffered degradation, and suffering makes its own understanding between people. Of all that befell Amel, it is the visitor probe which has left him most grievously handicapped. The Reetions used it to exploit his sympathy, to program him to save them, and it left him forced to disregard his own self-interest in favor of those who claim his protection. His loyalty is a weather-vane as a result. And yes, of course, I do blame Rire for that. How can I not?"

"Is it by the probing that you judge Rire?" Erien asked.

"It depends what you mean by that," said Ev'rel. "The probing is an event one can't discount. Others don't. I am better versed, however, than you will find Ameron, in the subsequent debate of its rights and wrongs. Rire is far more complex than most Gelacks grasp—but too ready to view us as simpletons."

"That is . . . the clearest analysis I have yet heard, from a Gelack."

"You are Gelack, Erien," she said mildly. "It is not something to be ashamed of. No more, at least, than being Reetion."

"Who else knew who I was?" he asked. "And for how long?"

"Di Mon, certainly," she told him, without mercy. "I do not know how quickly he found out, or when he told Ameron. I would like to believe it was Ameron's plot, but I truly think not. Not, at least, by any overt act. I know that Amel has been prepared to die for a kind look from Ameron, more than once."

So Di Mon had known who he was, all along! Erien's world was being turned upside down. He stuck to what was possible to talk about.

"Why did Amel take me away?" he asked Ev'rel.

She rose, in a slither of satin skirt, and touched his shoulder briefly. "Believe, because I do, that Amel thought he acted for your good, however incomprehensible you or I may find his reasons. And indeed, he may have found you a better parent, in Di Mon. I know, for Di Mon was my Vrellish guardian after my mother died. He taught me much, and since I never told him what I suffered at my father's hands I cannot fault him for not exposing that."

Ev'rel's own childhood abuse, more private than Amel's but well known with regard to the basic facts, was dismissed as merely unpleasant, and perhaps even just a bit ambiguous, by the Vrellishly-minded of Fountain Court. Di Mon, however, had regretted not knowing in time to take action on Ev'rel's behalf.

"Why didn't you tell him?" Erien felt driven to ask.

She told him, unstinting, "I believed in my father's love, unwelcome though it sometimes was. I was not so sure about Di Mon. I tripped on my own sword, and had little stomach for flying," she confessed with a smile. "Too Demish, I suppose. I wanted Di Mon to think better of me, not worse. Pride is a powerful motive for silence."

"Di Mon told me that he felt he had failed you," said Erien, "over that, and your subsequent child contract with Amel's father."

"Ah yes, Delm. Let's not omit Delm," Ev'rel said acidly, reminding Erien that the contract which produced Amel had been forced on her by a Fountain Court anxious to restock Sevildom with Purebloods.

"Di Mon should have believed me, about Delm trying to kill Amel," agreed Ev'rel. "That was hard. I loved Amel. He was the first, and the last, baby that I have loved. It was Delm who viewed Amel as a threat to his status as the last living male Pureblood of the Gelack court. But Delm was cool-headed. I was hysterical. Hysteria was hard for Di Mon to respect. Too Demish, in a woman."

She spoke of it so confidently that it was impossible to imagine her hysterical. She did not seem at all, in fact, the wild and passionate girl who featured in the stories surrounding Amel's birth and disappearance in babyhood.

"These are old wounds," Ev'rel said, and smiled soberly. "What matters, between you and I, is that I harbor no ill-feeling toward Di Mon. Until he died, I'd always hoped to find a way to spread Monatese knowledge of science and history beyond Monitum. I wanted Di Mon to take in young Dem'Vrellish errants, as pupils. And he might have. But the Monatese, as a whole, are jealous of their secrets and fearful of anti-Lorel pogroms. I could not satisfy Di Mon on either score."

She ran out of energy all at once, and looked off across the room. "Will you pour me a glass of Monatese Turquoise? Or is wine all that Nersal keeps for his guests?"

Erien agreed with a nod, grateful for a task so simple. His hands were shaking slightly as he poured.

She, too, was suffering from the intensity. She finished the strong whiskey in a few swallows and returned the glass immediately.

Avim Ev'rel sat down. After a moment, Erien did too.

"Have you considered," he carefully broached a new doubt, glad that his mind was still working, "that Amel may have told you that I was the Throne Price to manipulate you? Even if it were untrue?"

"You mean to make me stop the duel?" She followed his train of thought. "It isn't impossible. Amel seems determined to stop Lek from fighting over what was done by the Reetions. But it should be simple enough to disprove that. Ask Nersal. Ask Tessitatt. Ask Ameron. For that matter we could have a genotyping done."

"I think," Erien said, "I would like to ask Amel."

"No."

"I will not harm him." Erien promised her.

"No," she said, and gave him a moment to appreciate her finality. "I have already revealed more than I am in the habit of divulging about myself, to a stranger, and despite your Monatese upbringing, which will incline you towards Ameron. It is not something I am comfortable with. So I will say this only once, as plainly as possible: Amel is mine. To the extent that he has harmed me by his silence, he will pay my price.

But no one else's. There are matters which you and I must settle with each other, but Amel is not, and will never be, part of them. I will, if you like, question him for you. I can tell you now, though, that it will not do much good. Not if what you are after is the bald truth. He does not, exactly, lie, but he will dissemble in the direction apt to be most palatable."

Erien reviewed all she'd said on the topic. He could see that she was not wholly rational about Amel. Unease, as well as wisdom, suggested that he let the matter lie. Amel could not avoid him for the next hundred years, whatever she said. "Very well," he said, "I'll respect that. What must we settle?"

"Whom you swear to. You must, of course, survive the duel. If I cannot obtain D'Lekker's apology, I will at least impress upon him that it must go only to first blood. If he will apologize to Heir Monitum, and even Ranar, I will endorse that. Provided it is specifically with reference to the boy-*sla* slur. Anything more general would irk D'Therd, and maybe Vretla Vrel. We do not need flames fanned so near a crucial moment, over something so irrelevant. Understand that I am not convinced that acknowledging Rire will do us good. I am, however, convinced of the foolhardiness of repeating old errors. If we war on Rire again, it must be successful, and not create another Killing Reach."

"What," he asked, after a moment, "would convince you that Rire should be diplomatically acknowledged, rather than conquered?"

She frowned. "Proof it would not cost me my support."

"House Vrel, and the Dem'Vrel also, want Reetion land," said Erien. "Is there any means of convincing them, given that?"

"There is something they want more than new land," she said. "The blood to hold what they've already got. Swear to me, and child-gift for me, as I originally intended. Undo the mischief Amel wrought."

Erien felt momentarily nauseous. Breeding, again—without even the patina of religiosity that the Nesaks and many Nersallians granted it. They at least believed in the begetting of bodies to house reborn souls. The Gelack Court seemed to believe only in the begetting of bodies to house the gametes for future transactions in genetic currency. Their sexual and family lives were warped by it, and still they demanded it go on. If there were anything he admired in Amel, it had been his refusal to father children as counters in power transactions.

But had Amel ever been offered anything that mattered as much to him as Rire mattered to Erien?

Ev'rel was impressive, Erien thought. Candid, lucid and blunt about realities. She had been the first person to tell him the truth about who he was—oh, to her advantage, surely, but she had less of an advantage, now that he knew, than anyone would have had in his ignorance.

"Come to lunch, tomorrow," she said, "after you've fought. I will also invite Ranar. Between us, we can force Ameron to give his Reetion hostage up, at least for that long. Meet D'Therd properly, and Vretla. Perhaps you will have a better idea than child-gifting instead of conquest. If not—" she shrugged, "—you might consider what I've asked. I will not make quick promises for my own contribution to a pact between us, but should you be prepared to negotiate, we could make a start. You would swear to a contract laid out in advance."

And that contract would include his right to contribute to the education of his children, thought Erien. They would learn respect for Rire. He would not father another generation of conquerors, whatever Ev'rel and her vassals might want.

He caught a breath. He was thinking again. And now that he was thinking, he had one last question. "Avim," he said, "what will you change, as the Ava, should you prevail?"

"Change?" The question surprised her. She mused on it with interest, which brought out the beauty of her intelligence and quiet self control. "I would change whatever I needed to, and leave what I did not. But words are Ameron's province. Judge by Dem'Vrel. I changed that."

She was confident of his ability to value infrastructure over space melees. Her smile said that.

Ev'rel left Erien standing beneath Hangst Nersal's portrait, her whiskey glass still in his hand, a sense of ringing vacuum around him and within him. It took long seconds for him to come to himself and go to the side table to put the glass down. He laid his fingers on either side of it. They were no longer shaking, but they felt not completely connected. Not completely his. A Pureblood's hands, not the hands of Highlord Erien, Ward of Monitum, Ward of Rire. He had been aware that knowing who he was and where he fitted would alter other people's perceptions of him, would give rise to new and probably onerous assumptions and expectations. He had not anticipated that it would so shake his perceptions of himself.

Cultural conditioning, he thought. *From an objective point of view, you are merely a set of variant alleles, and probably an artificially-created one at that. Merely a bag of thinking water, like the rest of humanity. That you are socialized to think otherwise is irrelevant.*

He had never fully appreciated Ranar's Reetionness until now. Knowing he was a Pureblood Sevolite, Ranar had nevertheless treated him as a child, not quite an ordinary child. Not a Reetion child, but still a child. No Gelack commoner could have achieved that.

He heard a quiet sound behind him, a deliberate marring of a noiseless tread. He turned, to see Liege Nersal.

"You knew," Erien said, still in peerage. And then, rather than explain, repeated, "You . . ." with full differentiation, Pureblood to Highlord, "knew." Ranar had had him do it many times, role-playing all levels of Gelack society. He stammered slightly on it, now.

Horth merely watched him. No answer was needed. Of course he knew. Knew, and, like Ranar, had not let false reverence mar his perceptions of Erien's needs and limitations.

So there's no need to fear that you'll be allowed to get above yourself, Erien thought, with a flicker of fey amusement.

But he was the Throne Price. A better champion for Rire than even he thought, and Di Mon more cunning and more committed in support of Rire than anyone could have guessed. Di Mon had given him to Rire.

And it might be he who held the balance of this Swearing.

He had been fobbed off by Ameron, while Ev'rel had offered him the truth. Yet Di Mon had transferred allegiance from Ev'rel to Ameron. Tessitatt was Ameron's supporter. And Nersal was his champion.

Horth Nersal had gone unsworn for his first year as Liege Nersal. Nineteen years old, and under constant title challenge from the *kinf'stan*, he had nevertheless declined all Ev'rel's invitations, and had sworn to the pretender Ameron within minutes of their first meeting.

"Why did you swear to him?" Erien asked Nersal, graceless with intensity. "Why Ameron? Ev'rel has told me who I am, and asked me to swear to her. I don't know who else knows, whether I can defer swearing, or whether I must swear now and make the decision between two people I have hardly met. There's so much depending on the decision." He checked himself, forcibly. Talking at Horth was no way to get an answer to any question. He knew that. "Why did you swear to Ameron?" Erien repeated. "I respect your judgment. It will help me make my decision."

The silence expanded. In it, Erien's unease grew. Was Horth Nersal wavering? Was he considering changing his own allegiance? Knowing Nersal from the fleet, Erien had discounted the general gossip which fed on Liege Nersal arriving at court so late, or his not being seen much with Ameron at the betrothal reception. Horth felt no need for display before action. But others had commented, and Erien remembered those comments.

Nersal gave a minute head shake, as though in reproach to Erien's thoughts. Or, more likely, to dislodge a stubborn word. "Fight first," he said in his deep voice, "then choose."

CHAPTER XV

AMEL CAME TO LYING FACE DOWN on a padded floor. He ached. That seemed right. He did not pursue why right now.

The most frightening thing was that he wasn't exactly sure how long he had been out. His pilot's sense was dumb, as if time itself had shattered in his skull and bled white the Gap-defying powers of his soul.

He concentrated on sorting his body out.

One arm was caught under him and the other outstretched across the workshop's padded floor. Neither position was comfortable. His right elbow throbbed. His face itched where saliva and blood had dried in the corner of his mouth.

Slowly, joints complaining of abandonment in untenable positions, he gathered his wits enough to sit up on the workshop floor.

He'd been unconscious long enough for his stomach to empty and his bladder to fill up.

He wanted a bath.

His stunned brain coughed up the information that the door was locked.

The rest seeped back.

He groaned.

It was morning, his reviving brain decided. Very early though.

His strained elbow was worse for the night spent on the floor. His ribs ached where Lek had bounced him off the chest, and he must have hit his head, in a fit, to judge by the goose egg above his left ear. That seemed to be what had knocked him out. The cut had bled enough to ruin his embroidered shirt and had stiffened a swatch of hair.

He regretted the shirt, for the sake of the many skilled hours of needlework put into it by the artisan. Even small beauties deserved to be mourned.

He got to his feet to prove that he could stand.

Ev'rel's swivel chair stood empty.

Amel filled it.

He distracted himself with the console. The scene of his parting with Mira was still loaded. He viewed part of it. It was really brilliantly done, although the portrayal of his ten-year-old self was all wrong. The real child had brimmed with over-confidence, eager to hone quicksilver talents on the whetstone of Mira's greater discipline; afraid of nothing except Mira's scorn. It had taken six months in the UnderDocks to break him down. The sad-eyed, pretty creature in the remake was a baby version of the cringing sixteen-year-old made famous by Reetion exposure.

Even his boyhood was recast in the shadow of the visitor probe.

Amel turned it off.

He bowed his head over his arms on the workbench, and strove for white static thoughts, while his pilot's sense relentlessly marked time once more.

Chapter XVI

With a Sevolite's exquisite time-sense, Erien woke just before a servant pushed open the door without knocking, and placed a tray on the table just inside. The man—gray-haired, in black livery—was gone before Erien could speak or rise. On the tray was a tumbler, a plate, and several small cruets, all in the same smoked glass. On the plate were finger bread and crackers; in the cruets, small quantities of spread made of spiced protein. It came to Erien that this must be the way Black Hearth's own liege began the morning of a challenge. He lifted a slice of finger bread, dipped it in the first of the cruets and bit into it. It was surprisingly edible. He collected the tray, walked barefoot back to the bed, and sat on the edge of it, tray on his lap. He gave his attention to the food, pleased that he seemed able to stomach it, if not enjoy it. Tatt was always too nauseated to eat on the morning of a duel.

The liquid, pilot's nectar—water, glucose and electrolytes—sat less easily. He left it unfinished, put the tray back, and pulled on a fresh pair of black fleet fatigues and practice floor shoes. They were the closest thing he had to a court duelling costume. They were well-worn and familiar; their feel would not distract him. He had stripped the Nersallian insignia from his fatigues, and to the sleeve of his right shoulder he clipped a silver badge from the Reetion space service. The sword, when he buckled on the belt, sat as uneasily as the nectar, but the sword would be in his hand and the sheath left behind when he stepped onto the floor.

Another Nersallian servant met him as soon as he set foot outside the door, and, without a word, indicated that he follow. Horth and Dorn were in one of the morning rooms, formally dressed, and finishing off a breakfast as spare but interesting as Erien's. He had no sense of a conversation having been interrupted. Two pairs of gray eyes looked him over.

Dorn said, "Shall I warm you up?" Without waiting for an answer— perhaps he was unaccustomed to getting one—he stood. "It is best to have someone else do the thinking before a duel. I'm told it is also that way with weddings," he added, a little dryly.

Black Wedge was empty. Dorn noted his observation and said, "This is the way Father and I prefer it before we go on the challenge floor. We decided you were probably not experienced enough to have other preferences, and that you had enough to contend with without being asked what you wanted for the morning."

"This is what I would have wanted," Erien said. He was surprised to realize that they were the first words he had spoken. Silence was surprisingly easy here, on this morning.

"Do your usual warm-up," Dorn said, unbuckling his own sword belt. "You may feel clumsy, off-balance; don't worry about it. Your level of alertness will be higher, and your body awareness will be different. We will have time to work that out without wearing you out."

For the next hour, he kept Erien moving, progressing from a general physical warm-up to a gradually intensifying exchange of hits. Plainly, he had discussed strategy with his father, and did not insist upon any show of aggression from Erien; instead, he worked with him until Erien was moving fluidly and with all the agility developed from seven years in Rire's higher gravity and three years exercising on the launch docks. They both knew that it was that agility which represented Erien's best chance of prolonging the bout. Midway through the warm-up, Erien was aware that Horth was standing beside the stairs, watching, but when he looked again, the Highlord was gone.

A few minutes before the hour, Dorn called a halt.

"It's customary," he said, "for the challenger to arrive first. Sometimes the opponent delays his arrival: gamesmanship. I think we can rely on D'Therd's firm hand this morning. Are you ready?"

"I am ready," Erien said, lifting his sword sheath and sheathing his sword. He did not buckle it on, but held it balanced in one hand. The belt trailed against his leg, a distinctive sensation.

"Until the duel is over, let nothing distract you. Nothing." The emphasis on the word made Erien look at Dorn.

"Father told me." For the first time Dorn's differencing of pronouns gave Erien his new status. "He knew I'd be warming you up this morning; he wanted me to know what you had to contend with." He looked Erien up and down. "Ready?"

Erien nodded. Shoulder to shoulder, they walked to the tip of the wedge. Dorn opened the narrow door in the screen and stood back to let Erien through.

The crowd had already gathered: highborns, their nobleborn vassals and guests, and their errants in hearth liveries; black Vrellish heads, pale and gold Demish ones, the occasional brown-haired Lorelite throwback. The first onlookers caught sight of Erien; word spread, visibly, and the crowd drew back like the sea before a great wave. Through the long parting, he could see D'Lekker standing on the floor, sword bared.

Dorn said, quietly, "You're not late. Don't let yourself be hurried."

There was a ripple in the crowd; Tatt pushed himself to the fore and came to meet them with a quick, urgent step. He was dressed in full court regalia, brown leather and green velvet; a statement of his position. He looked pale; his nostrils flared with each breath. Dorn gave him a small head shake as he opened his mouth to speak. Tatt, blessedly, heeded both the gesture and his own experience, and fell in on Erien's far side without speaking a word.

Erien found himself listening for the sound of their feet. He had the eerie sense that he walked alone, even though he felt both the warmth and the solidity of the men beside him. And then they reached the boundary between the white tile and the Challenge Floor, and Erien walked forwards, alone. The floor yielded slightly beneath his feet, but the grip was firm underfoot. He wished he had refastened his right shoe.

D'Lekker watched him come with dangerous eyes. The first engagement of the duel had already begun. From his profound aloneness, Erien felt untouchable. Untouchable, but unable to touch. Neither to be mastered, or to master. *Early yet,* he told himself.

"Prince D'Lekker," he said. His mouth was dry. An odd bit of trivia came to him, that there had been an ancient culture on Earth which tested its criminals by offering them a bowl of rice. Those who could not eat the rice, whose mouths were dried by fear or guilt, were judged guilty. He would have to tell Tatt.

By tradition, a formal duel opened with a statement, by the challenger, of the reason for the challenge. "Prince D'Lekker," Erien said, quietly, evenly, "we meet here by my challenge. You have slandered my guardian, Ranar of Rire, and his race. Since he is not a Gelack, I will fight on his behalf. Do you accept my challenge?"

"Oh yes," D'Lekker said.

"Do you withdraw your slander?"

"What do you think . . . Erien?"

He knows who I am, Erien thought. It was just a guess; D'Lekker still spoke down to him by one step as if he was a Highlord. It was something in the way D'Lekker had said 'Erien'.

Erien drew his sword from the scabbard and turned and threw the scabbard towards the crowd, with no more care than was needed to make sure it landed clear of the floor. A lapse, but an unimportant lapse. He watched his opponent as Admiral H'Us' voice recited the cautions and admonitions to the duelists. He understood now that, though every Sevolite learned them in childhood, they were irrelevant. Something that existed only outside the floor, for the comfort of those on the other side. Inside the boundaries, there were no laws but those the opponents made for themselves.

D'Lekker started towards him, the tip of his blade whipping from side to side. Erien backed sideways and away, his own guard quite still. D'Lekker leapt forwards, feinting threat; Erien leapt back, keeping the distance. He held in his mind his place on the circular ground, knowing exactly where the boundary lay behind him. He would not let himself be harried beyond bounds to where the white tiles made bad footing.

Patience, Erien thought to himself, *patience. Make him keep coming. Make him give you the opening.*

D'Lekker attacked; blade met blade; Erien sprang back and sideways, beyond D'Lekker's reach. D'Lekker came after him, harder now, anger in his face. Erien could feel his shoulders tightening. Tension would cost him speed and fluidity, but he could not spare the concentration to loosen them. He was watching with all his will for the opening that Horth had prepared him to see. Until then, he would keep out of distance, make D'Lekker come to him. Their feet whispered on the floor, an invisible dance of life, death, and will.

There! The lift of the blade, the coup attack D'Lekker favored. But the very thought, the very recognition, took too long, and Erien's counterattack was a fraction of a second late. He converted his attack to a head parry in mid-lunge, and threw himself back as D'Lekker's blade slashed across his abdomen. He felt the tip snag fabric, and a soft sound went up from the crowd. But he felt no pain, and did not look down; D'Lekker, whose right it was to call, did not do so; his slight smile said that he could wait.

It was Admiral H'Us who called out "Halt!" and waited for the two opponents to move sufficiently apart for him to come onto the floor. With a small part of his mind, Erien felt the man's approach, yet still he started slightly as H'Us appeared before him and laid his hand over the place where D'Lekker's blade had nicked, below Erien's hard-beating heart. H'Us took his hand away bloodless, and displayed it to the four quarters of the audience, and then receded from Erien's awareness. Erien watched D'Lekker.

He was not aware of fear, though now he knew that D'Lekker would kill him if he could. A cut across the chest was a legitimate first-blood strike, a cut across the abdomen—where the internal organs were unprotected—could be lethal. D'Lekker could have had either, with Erien off-balance. He had chosen the lower. Erien acknowledged the information and set it aside. He bore down with his awareness on that hidden area on D'Lekker's left wrist. When D'Lekker moved, he responded; when D'Lekker came close, he retreated; when D'Lekker attacked, he parried, and leapt clear. The dance was becoming swift and deadly, as D'Lekker pressed him, his body and moving sword bragging his supremacy, his attacks becoming more overtly deadly, aiming not for the arm now, but for Erien's throat and heart and belly. The dance was moving too swiftly for thought, and Erien felt the first stirrings of panic. Not at the danger, but at the loss of thought, his governing principle. He could not think what next to do.

And then D'Lekker's hand lifted . . .

Erien was not aware of intention. He was hardly aware of execution. It seemed that D'Lekker's lifting hand had drawn his response out of him. He had moved and struck and slipped off-line before he understood what had happened, before hand communicated to brain the feeling of the tip biting through fabric, into flesh. Sometime later, D'Lekker's sword slashed down through the empty air where he had been, and a few drops of blood spattered the brown floor.

Erien moved away. D'Lekker stood quite still, sword raised, which meant that Erien could see the blood staining the long rent in his opponent's forearm. Erien thought, *It's done*, and D'Lekker charged him, raised blade slashing down; Erien parried, hard; a little of D'Lekker's blood splashed his face and D'Lekker's shoulder drove into his chest, throwing him back. Raw instinct brought Erien's sword up to block D'Lekker's stab at his throat; the blade went past Erien's ear. He caught D'Lekker's wrist with his right hand, forcing it up and back, using weight, leverage, and Pureblood strength. He felt D'Lekker's eyes on the side of his face, but watched not his eyes, but their hands, and D'Lekker's sword. He could feel blood warm and slick beneath his palm.

D'Therd reached from behind D'Lekker and broke his grip on his hilt. The sword dropped behind him and D'Therd kicked it aside. Erien pushed D'Lekker away from him, a short jolting distance, into the angry grip of his brother. D'Lekker struggled in a silent, murderous rage. The audience was silent.

Erien realized then that he was beginning to shake. There was a sword in one hand, and blood on the heel of the other. He looked around for the sheath, taking in the audience for the first time. He saw the shock on Tatt's face changing to delight. Dorn, beside him, looked pleased. Horth was watching, hand on hilt, as D'Therd removed D'Lekker.

Luthan, the H'Usian Demish Princess, was holding his sheath, clutching it against her body with both hands. She looked as shaken as he was. Erien wiped D'Lekker's blood from his hand as well as he could as he made his way to her. Across the boundary between floor and audience, they faced each other. "Princess," he said. "My sheath."

"Oh," she said, looking down at the object in her grip. She blushed suddenly at something he could not see, and offered it to him. He had to take it with his bloodied hand, an oddly ashamed scrabble. He tried and failed to return his sword to its sheath; the tip rattled with the tremor in his hands. Delicately, Luthan took the flat of the blade between two fingers and steadied it. He pushed the sword home. "Thank you," he said.

"Erien," she said. He looked up, into clear blue eyes. "I'm so glad—" she said, and broke off.

"So am I," he said, and smiled for the first time that morning.

A hand grabbed his shoulder and swung him around, and Tatt enfolded him, sheath and all, in an embrace of leather, cotton, scratchy braids and green velvet. "Don't you ever," Tatt rasped in his ear, "do that to me again."

"Do what?" Erien muttered, light-headed. "I had it under p-perfect control." Over Tatt's shoulder he caught sight of D'Lekker seated, his head hanging and D'Therd supporting him, or pinning him down. The UnderDocks medtech, Asher, was cutting blood-soaked fabric from D'Lekker's sleeve with one hand, the fingers of the other digging into the pressure point high in his arm. She, too, had a custodian: Charous. Erien could not see Asher's face. He could see D'Therd's, but he could not decide whether that dark loathing was for her, or his brother, or the witnesses to D'Lekker's disgraceful behavior after he had lost.

Behind him, Erien heard the Demish gathering up their wayward princess, the matrons' voices chiding, and he pulled away from Tatt to look after her. Luthan lifted a gloved hand in a very small wave.

"Cleanly done." Ev'rel's voice, by his side, surprised Erien. "But you have blood on your face." He stood still while she dabbed at the blood which had spattered Erien's cheek and brow. "I regret," she added, "my son's subsequent actions, and I hope that you do not find them cause to decline your invitation to my hearth, for lunch, with the Reetion Ambassador." She drew back her hand, taking time to tuck the corners of the stained handkerchief into themselves, smiling a small, pleased smile. Then she turned, and went back towards her wedge of the Octagon, pausing beside the medtech working over D'Lekker. "I will see that you are paid for your work here," she said.

The medtech looked up. Her face was white and set. "The account is cleared," she said in a low voice.

Charous watched with great interest. Asher returned her attention to her work. D'Lekker raised his head, and looked at Asher's face, his own changing to recognition, and a strange excitement showed as he looked from Asher to Ev'rel and back again. Ev'rel went on.

Tatt started forwards. Charous moved between them, smartly. They exchanged whispers, his harsh, hers soft. Beyond them, Asher stepped silently away from D'Lekker, sheathing her seamer in its sterilized sleeve. Before the younger man could speak, D'Therd hoisted him to a standing position, and began forcibly to march him back towards Lilac Hearth. D'Lekker broke free and walked alone, bending one dark glare back at Asher, Erien, and Tatt.

Drasous went to collect the medtech. He spoke to her; she shook her head. "I've done what you wanted," Asher said. "Just get me out of here." He escorted her back towards White Hearth's wedge. A tall woman—another of Ameron's bonded *gorarelpul*—appeared at the base of the stairs which led up to White Hearth, and stood watching Drasous as he led the medtech across the Octagon.

Ditatt threatened Charous in a fierce whisper. "If anything happens to Asher, I will hear about it."

He was flailing and the *gorarelpul*, by her bland expression, knew it. She paused a moment, watching until Drasous and the medtech had been swallowed up by White Hearth's stairs, trailed by the third *gorarelpul*. Then she said, "What could possibly happen to her, Your Highness?"

Tatt started an impulsive rejoinder, then checked himself with a sideways glance at Erien. "I'm sure," he said instead, speaking down to Charous with all the authority his rank could muster, "you know that better than I do, since you brought her here."

The Royal *gorarelpul* ran a finger beneath her scarf. "You're right," she conceded. "I brought her here for a reason. But think on this, Heir Monitum: a dead informant is no more use to me than to you." She glanced at Erien. "Well fought. Nervy. I recognize the style." She dismissed herself.

Tatt stared after Charous's departing back, his hand fisted on his sword hilt. He gestured sharply, bringing Branstatt. "We have to find Asher's clinic. There's something between her and the Dem'Vrel, something bad I am certain, although I do not know what, and now Charous is taking an interest—Asher is in trouble."

"You're assuming that Charous is going to release her," Branstatt observed.

Tatt took a deep breath. "Find her clinic. If she shows up there, send word to me, and I'll come down and offer her my protection.

If she doesn't, I'll take White Hearth and the Palace Sector apart myself until I find her. She's under my protection." He whirled, and stalked off towards Green Hearth, shouldering through the last of the spectators who had lingered in the hope of more drama.

Only then did Erien think to look for Ranar. He and Ameron were gone. Long gone, Erien thought, remembering clusters of people moving, as the audience had broken up.

Horth and Dorn were still standing on the edge of Black Wedge. Catching Erien's eye, Dorn raised a hand. Then he and his father disappeared behind their hearth's screens. Branstatt hovered, plainly torn between staying to watch over Erien, and doing Tatt's bidding. For want of any better destination, Erien started towards Green Hearth himself, and Branstatt fell into step with alacrity.

"When did Ameron go?" Erien said.

"Ameron—oh, vent it! Tatt!" Branstatt hailed his half-brother in a parade ground voice, which made Erien jump violently. "Sorry," Branstatt said, "but there was a letter for you."

Tatt ducked around the Green Hearth screens, looking equally rebellious and alarmed. Branstatt answered Erien's question quickly. "Ameron left as soon as D'Lekker was subdued. He took Ranar with him. Tatt," the errant captain broke off, as Tatt trotted up to him. "The letter."

"Oh Gods, that!" Tatt rummaged in his pockets, pulling out a folded, slightly creased sheet of vellum, sealed with a blood cipher. "It's from Ameron," he said. "It came yesterday, but you'd gone to Black Hearth, and I thought about sending it on with a messenger, but then—"

"Tatt," Erien said, "I do forgive you." And to forestall any more apologies, he pricked his finger on the seal and cracked it open.

"They've ciphered you," Tatt said, his dragonfly mind caught by this new puzzle. "When did you give them a blood sample?"

"Never, as far as I know," Erien said, unfolded and scanned the letter, and held it out to Ditatt. "As you see, it was not vital. He wants to see me, so I will go and see him now."

"But you've been blood ciphered," Ditatt persisted. "He must have been expecting you."

The great secret, Erien thought, was not going to be kept much longer. Charous' appearance saved him from further questioning. Tatt went grimly silent, as though suspicious that even thoughts were not proof against the Royal *gorarelpul*. Charous advised Erien that the Ava would see him now, if it were convenient—with a certain sarcasm on the word 'convenient'.

Tatt, ever-attentive to justice, said, "He didn't get the letter until now. I forgot."

"Ah," said Charous, and Tatt scowled.

Charous led Erien directly up the stairs into White Hearth.

Ameron received him in his guest lounge. It was a pleasantly appointed room, heavily Monatese-influenced, with painted wood paneling showing landscapes of Earth, and leather furniture. It should have felt like home to Erien, should have evoked the same familiarity as Green Hearth. But it smelled wrong. It smelled wrong, and it felt wrong, and he was angry at Ameron for having brought Ranar to the duel, for inflicting that on Ranar, and then spiriting him away without Erien and Ranar being able to exchange a word. Ranar was more father to Erien than Ameron had ever been.

Erien did not wait for Ameron to welcome him. He would perpetuate no illusions of ignorance. He stopped before a cream chair, facing Ameron over a matching couch. "I apologize, Ava, for not acknowledging your invitation yesterday. I did not receive your message until just now. I spent the night at Black Hearth." He saw the flicker in Ameron's eyes as Erien's 'I's registered, each one the 'I' not of a Highlord, but of a Pureblood peer.

In his peripheral vision, he saw Charous go as still as a hunting cat.

Ameron was angry now. His anger had a huge, open air storm quality about it. The difficulty of containing it in the confines of his parlor held the Ava silent. Erien presumed that meeting in White Hearth, rather than the Palace, was intended to set a pleasant, social tone. If so, the Ava's aspect undid that.

Charous shifted, whether out of interest or defensiveness, Erien did not know, but Ameron's head whipped round. "Out."

Her face was like carved bone. "This is the Throne Price?" she said, with an edge of disbelief. Not, Erien thought, because she doubted him, but because she doubted Ameron, or doubted her ignorance. She, at least, had not known.

"I will talk to you later, Char. Out!"

She went. Erien thought he had seen gentler eyes in Killing Reach mercenaries.

Ameron spared her not a glance. He drummed a fist on the back of the couch, a betrayal of energy impossibly bottled up.

"So," he said. "You know who you are." Ameron's grammar was textbook. The tone was coldly fearless, even dismissive, as if he was supposed to be impressed and emphatically was not.

Erien drew a steady breath, feeling at a disadvantage against the emotional pressure Ameron exerted, rather as if he were, indeed, attempting to debate with a storm.

"Ev'rel told me," he said, "last night at Black Hearth. She says that

Amel had told her only immediately before."

Ameron interrupted with a 'huh' sound that was, by itself, explanation enough for why Amel was lying low. It was useful, in that it helped Erien grasp that the Ava's anger was not reserved for him alone.

"Amel was trying to stop the duel," Erien said, in simple justice. Ameron's smoldering stare showed no appeasement. Erien abandoned the impulse.

"You, I presume," Erien continued to wield telling pronouns, "have known for much longer. Certainly since before you had me sent from Rire to the Nersallian fleet. I surmise, however, that you did not know ten years ago, when I was originally sent to Rire."

"That was not my idea," Ameron acknowledged. He couldn't have been more eloquent if he had cursed Di Mon. "As to the other, yes, I felt it was time that you learned the sword." He meant that in a broad, cultural sense, Erien knew, but it seemed an apt turn of phrase so soon after his duel.

What the act itself had meant Erien couldn't decide. It could have been anything from honest educational intent to the cynical expectation that Erien's Reetion experience would precipitate a fatal challenge. The Nersallian Fleet was not a Reetion university campus. "You seem to have impressed Liege Nersal," said Ameron, "and, apparently, Ev'rel."

It did not surprise Erien that Ameron would surmise as much, especially if Ev'rel had already requested Ranar's release, on Erien's behalf, to attend lunch at Lilac Hearth.

"She told you who you are, so she has spoken with you," deduced Ameron. "What did she want?"

"The pertinent points of my conversation with Ev'rel," Erien said, "are that she has asked me to swear to her, but recognition of Rire will only come if she is certain of keeping her support, and a condition of that is that I child-gift on her behalf."

Ameron's jaw locked.

"I am aware, I think," Erien continued, "of the dangers of doing so: higher blood would lead to higher aspirations, which would feed the greed for land that it is supposed to displace. I would have to ensure that I retained considerable influence over my children, which in turn would require," a dry smile, "an assurance of survival."

Ameron brooded on that. He gave Erien the disquieting impression of an angry adult struggling to find the patience to guide a child.

"Do you think," Ameron said, in a steady tone, "that any choice can be without risk of some sort?"

The question proved rhetorical. Ameron shook it off and made to round the couch but overshot. He was pacing. It was a trait the

Monatese viewed with familial affection, but Erien saw no more endearment in it now than one might in the frustrated stalking of a caged predator. Ameron was moving because he must. Halfway back to his starting point, he stopped and snapped his attention onto Erien with such impact that his continued silence seemed bizarre. It was two seconds before words followed.

"You are very young and new to court. The young have quick hearts. But you act within a complex web you cannot, quickly, know. Be careful how you thrash, for what may fall."

The implied accusation of clumsiness resolved itself slowly into an insult which was too novel to smart. Erien had never known rashness to be numbered among his faults.

"I do not know where to begin with you," confessed Ameron with unmistakable exasperation. "I know I must. Di Mon thought worlds of you. I will settle, for a beginning, with that." He inhaled, and concluded with some reservation. "What will serve as overture?"

"Ev'rel has asked myself and Ranar to lunch today, so that we and her supporters may take each others' measure. Will you release Ranar into my custody for that?"

Ameron frowned, clearly feeling trapped. "Done."

"Thank you," Erien said.

"Return him to White Hearth. I will have Amy provide you with an escort. I presume that is acceptable?"

"Yes."

"Later, then," Ameron dismissed him and swirled out.

He could swirl, Erien noted, even without a cloak. Air itself seemed to do.

Now what? Erien thought, as he was shown out. Another meeting, another clash. Ameron, he sensed, felt beleaguered. But the beleaguerment was his own fault. He had moved Erien like a blind pawn and had presumed that the pawn would not develop a will of its own. His mistake.

He did not dislike Ameron, he thought. There was a grandeur to him, even in his pettiness, that put him far above dislike. He would evoke large emotions, obdurate loyalty and implacable enmity. Di Mon had stayed alive for ten years for Ameron. He had been willing to die of his wounds on *SkyBlue*, except for Ranar, who had bullied him into trying the jump to Luverthan. And from that jump had come Ameron, lost for two hundred years. Di Mon had stayed alive to restore Ameron to his throne, and after, Erien realized now, to safeguard his heir. His vision blurred suddenly, and he stopped, in the middle of Fountain Court.

He wanted to swear to Ameron. For Tatt, for Ranar, who believed in him, for Horth, his champion, and for Di Mon, most of all. But there was nothing between himself and Ameron but antagonism, and between Ev'rel and himself there was the beginning of a relationship, the possibility of co-operation, the promise of a realistic approach to the recognition of Rire.

He had a day, and that was all. What was he to do? Everyone had already chosen sides, and they would be interested only in bringing him to align with them. Gelacks had no appreciation of the process of decision-making.

That was unfair, he thought, but could find no charity to argue against it.

A party of errants and women—mutually exclusive categories, amongst the Demish—came around the fountain. In the midst of white and silver clothing, and fair hair, he caught sight of hair of pure gold beneath a pearl cap.

"Princess Luthan!" He had called out before he thought, before he reckoned on his conspicuousness and her allegiances. Committed now, he took time to formulate a rationale for what he was about to do as he hurried after her—whatever her friendship with Amel, she could give him an insider's view on Ameron, Ev'rel, and the politics at court.

Luthan's party stopped. Her retinue watched him distrustfully, vexed at the impropriety of his hailing her. There was a slight perplexity in her smile, but genuine delight. She was wearing the same yellow skirts and embroidered bodice she had worn to his duel. He wondered, peripherally, why she made him so intensely aware of color.

"Princess, may I have a word with you, alone?"

She put up a hand to quell the ruffled indignation of her retinue, but her own uncertainty showed, and that illuminated better than hours of protocol instruction and pages of Ranar's briefings the constraints under which she lived. He felt embarrassed for them both. That such things need not matter to him did not mean they should not matter to her.

He said, "Princess, I realize that is a gross presumption and I would not, under any circumstances, compromise you or embarrass you, but I need to ask you something and then I want to tell you why I am asking. The questions aren't controversial in themselves, but the reason itself is . . . problematic."

She bit her lip and slanted a glance aside at her ladies, who made small and surreptitious gestures reminding her of propriety—those who were not eyeing him with bright-eyed curiosity. Then, abruptly, she shook herself free of them, dusting ladies and errants off like butterflies.

"We'll sit by the fountain," she announced, "that way everyone can see us, and nobody can hear us."

"But your uncle—" one of the ladies protested.

Luthan raised her chin. "Will you see them home, Hillian?" She addressed the captain of her personal errant bodyguard, a large, blond man, who smiled and nodded. "Come on, Erien," she said, taking him firmly by the hand, and towed him with dispatch to a bench against the fountain in the center of Fountain Court. Her retinue clattered and clucked as they were herded off. Within minutes, most of them had vanished into Silver Hearth, but the errant captain and a couple of the senior ladies remained to watch from out of ear-shot, by the hearth's entrance.

"Really," Luthan said, sitting down with a flounce on the small tiled bench, "they can be ridiculous. What do they think you're going to do to me?" This she said with an impish sparkle in her eyes, which became grave. "Now, what is it you want to ask?"

"I have to give my Oath at this Swearing, and I have to give it within Lor'Vrel or Dem'Vrel." That was truthful enough, he thought, guiltily. He hoped she would forgive him for asking her for a candid opinion first and then telling her that he would be choosing between the lieges themselves.

"Not Monitum?" she said. He relaxed a little, appreciating her quick understanding. "Then you know who you are," she decided.

"My challenging D'Lekker brought out the truth, at last. And no, I'm not Monatese."

She leaned over and touched his hand with her soft, warm fingers. The touch was brief—immediately mindful of her vigilant retinue, she snatched it back—and perplexing. Had he revealed more than he intended in those last three words? If so, it had not been in his pronouns. He continued to speak up to her, Highlord to Royalblood.

"I have hardly been here long enough to learn names," he said, "never mind if, when promises are made, they can be trusted, or whether exigency prevails over principle. I don't just carry the responsibility for my Gelack position, I carry the responsibility for Rire and the Gelack-Reetion peace, and my guardian, Ranar's, life. I need to make the right choice. I'm asking you for your opinion. Not for what you would do if you were me, but for your impressions and perceptions of the lieges of Lor'Vrel and Dem'Vrel, and the principles in their line of swearing. What you say to me, I give you my word, I will not pass on."

"Well," Luthan began slowly, "well." She appeared, for a moment, to have no more to say than that, but when Erien began to rise, to excuse himself, she clapped a hand to his forearm to keep him where he was, saying, "I hardly know where to start!"

The words, after that, came in a flood.

"D'Therd won Demora from D'Ander Dem'Dem before I was born, but my uncle says it was a fair duel. I remember an argument he had with my Aunt Latvia about Ev'rel. It was about Ev'rel putting

Sen Dem'Vrel in charge, as the regent to D'Therd's child by D'Ander's half-sister who is, still, of course, like me, the title holder—Sen is one of her Knotted String lieutenants, only Midlord, and a servant's mongrel. Not even Dem'Vrel, my uncle says, except by Ev'rel's edict—he doesn't say it nicely either. Sen's a tough woman. She wouldn't have D'Therd you know, she wanted Amel. Some people said Amel balked at child-gifting, like always, and others said he liked Sen too much, which is why Ev'rel sent her to Demora. I haven't the faintest idea myself because he'll only joke about anything really serious, but anyhow," she inhaled, a slight frown pinching her forehead at the realization that she was straying far afield in reminiscence. "Sen revoked the Banns, that's when Demorans gather to announce births, deaths, and betrothals and recite genealogies: it's very important. I don't understand what it was over. Oh! I'm sorry, this is no use is it?"

She twisted her hands in her lap, frustrated.

"What does my uncle say about Ev'rel?" She tried again, rather than let him get a word in edgewise, lifting her pretty head to stare straight ahead. Looking at him seemed to make her babble. "Ev'rel was falsely exiled over Amel's disappearance as a baby. That was her half-brother, Delm's, doing. Uncle says that Highlord Ditatt, Liege Monitum—not Tatt, his late uncle—oh, but you call him Di Mon don't you? And you'd know that he proved Ev'rel innocent by genotyping the baby Amel sired on a courtesan girl who disapp—" He could see her remember that this very child was the best candidate for accounting for himself. She bit her lip. "You know about that."

"Yes," said Erien, studiously patient.

Luthan nodded. "Uncle calls Ev'rel 'that damned woman'. Mostly when she does things for which he can't find precedent, when Demora is involved. Although, of course, the H'Usians had quarreled with the Golden Demish long before Ev'rel became involved."

Erien smiled at the way she made a centuries-old breach of the Demish lines sound current.

"But," Luthan continued, "Uncle H'Us often says that Ev'rel has more common sense than Ameron. Sometimes he's quite taken with her."

"And Ameron?" Erien prompted.

"Oh, Ameron. I've relatives, you know, who are appalled by anything to do with a Lor'Vrel. They had parents or lieges who fought the Fifth Civil War. Ameron's father, Avatlan, was Lor'Vrel and he murdered Ava Trenseel, his mother, right in front of everybody, because he knew he couldn't beat her with a sword. He said he did it to make Ameron Ava, but Ameron had him executed anyhow, which, of course, was only proper. Recently . . . "

The adjective conveyed, more forcefully than any lecture, a living sense of Demish memory, preserved in the tales of centenarian matrons, and handed down in whole cloth through the generations. She seemed like a little girl rummaging through a storehouse of adult artifacts, wondering aloud at each, in innocence. But she wondered with intelligence, for all that her understanding was that of a very naive insider.

"Everyone says Ameron gets his way indirectly, you know, through other people. But I suppose Ev'rel does as well. Avas haven't fought their own duels since before Avim Demlara—well, and I suppose, in a fashion now and then by Rene's Convention, and sometimes the Nesaks—" She stopped short and wound back the threads. "What I know, about Ameron, is that Uncle H'Us curses him as much as he does Ev'rel, but he always winds up doing what Ameron says, in the end."

She deflated and turned, her mouth petulant, to look at him, "Did I say anything useful?"

"Oh yes, thank you, Princess," he said, a little dazed, but incapable of confirming her expectation of disappointment in herself. Golden Demish memory was legendary, and in its own way as extreme as the Vrellish navigator trait. Sevolites were, he found himself thinking, a strange species. Or creation.

"Erien!" she caught his hand as he began to rise, let go at once, and stood instead herself. Her heart rate was up, inexplicably, driving a flush into her face. "I—don't know when I might see you again and I—"

"Yes?" He was prepared to be patient, whatever favor she meant to beg clearly mattering so greatly to her and being so difficult to frame.

Luthan's eyes darted everywhere as if it was painful to look at him. "I . . . wanted you to think about, that is . . . I don't mean it to be something definite because I won't know—well, that is, anything might change and of course I don't know what your own arrangements are elsewhere, but when you're here . . . "

She looked at him finally, voice falling so low that he had to strain to listen, until she cleared her throat and went on in a bolder vein. "I'd like you to call on me, when I'm a matron. M-maybe you could play the flute again?"

He was unsure what to do, or what it meant. She seemed poised, like a wild bird, ready to take fright at the least misstep and fly away.

"I would be very pleased . . . to play the flute for you again," he said, at last.

She sparkled at him, even as her face darkened with a flush.

"Luthan," he said, "which of them would you choose?"

"Me?" She paused, reviewing his expression for hitherto unsuspected teasing. Finding none, apparently, she tipped and righted her golden head.

"Oh," she said, disappointed to be back to his original theme. "You mean the Ava and the Avim?" She composed her hands, resigned to the dull business. "I asked Amel, once, which he favored. Shall I tell you what he said?"

"I'd rather know what you feel."

"It's the same answer, really."

"Then tell me."

"He said, 'It's not going to be up to me, so why worry?' I've just never thought about choosing. It's never occurred to me anyone would take into account what I felt about anything to do with politics. Not, at least, until I'm much, much older." She regarded him, suddenly, with sympathy. "But you have to decide, don't you? Does that mean you've found out—I . . . I mean if it isn't a liberty . . . does that mean that you are Amel's—"

At that moment, Tatt blew out of Green Hearth, and swooped down on them.

"I'm off to fit a glass slipper," he announced. It took Erien a moment to recall that this meant Asher. "You'll have to tell him the story," Tatt said to Luthan, then switched his brilliant gaze back to Erien. "Asher's gone back to her clinic, all right. Vish was able to tell Branstatt where it was. Branstatt—Gods, there are times he's more like a nursemaid than a captain of errants—sent word, but told me to wait until he'd checked it out and came back up to escort me himself. So," he said triumphantly, and peered at them both, "what are you two conspiring about?"

Luthan's blush refreshed itself.

"I am asking Princess Luthan's opinion, as an observer of Court, of the parties involved in this Swearing."

Tatt winced; he did not want to hear about the Swearing. "Oh, Erien, must you be so serious? Luthan, any chance you could teach him how to flirt? It would make him much more human."

Erien turned to Luthan. "I am the Throne Price." To Tatt he said, "Yes, I must be serious."

Tatt stared at him. "You? Since when have you known?"

"Since yest—"

"Yesterday!" Face shining with delight and outrage, Tatt hauled Erien bodily to his feet, his hands under Erien's arms. "And you didn't tell me?" He hefted Erien and heaved him over the shallow ledge and into the fountain.

Erien twisted, and landed sprawling, bright water and bubbles racing past his face. The water was room temperature. He pushed off the tiled bottom and righted himself, surfacing in chest deep water. Above him he saw Tatt, dusting his hands in satisfaction, and Luthan staring down at him in crimson mortification.

"And I asked you to call on me," she blurted, still using the 'you' for a Highlord.

"Him?" said Tatt, in rich incredulity, turning from Erien to her and back again. "You?" The dainty Demish princess set her hands on his back and pushed with all her strength, sending Tatt stumbling over the ledge and into the water with a yell and a resounding splash. Erien pulled Tatt upright and steadied him while he gasped and choked. "I really don't—" Tatt wheezed, "know what she can possibly see in you."

Erien looked up, but Luthan was gone. He caught the edge of the fountain and pulled himself up, to see her back disappearing among ladies and errants, into Silver Hearth.

"I'm not sure I understand," he said carefully.

"When a Demish matron invites a man to call on her it doesn't usually mean for peppermint tea," Tatt snickered. "They only have to behave until they're married and to make sure the children genotype right."

"Tatt, if you ever—" Erien searched for a threat that was dire enough. Tatt held up his hands, wordlessly protesting his innocence—which he promptly compromised by his next question. "Are you going to take her up on that offer? It's a first, you know."

"Ditatt—"

A small sound made them both turn. An errant stood there, liveried in Nersallian black. His face was seasoned and quite expressionless. No doubt he had seen stranger things than two highborns chest deep in the fountain. Tatt looked at Erien expectantly. Formal protocol demanded that the ranking Sevolite speak first. That meant Erien. Unlike Luthan, Tatt, the bane of all his protocol teachers, had just made an effortless readjustment of their relative ranks.

"You, mister," Erien said to Tatt, in Reetion, "are a fraud." Tatt looked innocent, by reflex, then perplexed, as he realized he did not know what, exactly, he was denying.

Erien shook water off his hand as best he could to receive the card the errant handed him. It was backed by a swirl of graphics, the Nersallian watermark; on the writing surface was a single *rel* symbol, drawn in black pen in Horth's draftsman's hand. Even the tiny barbs on the loops of the character were precisely rendered; *rel*, the loop of infinity, vanishing into nothingness at the barbed points of birth and death.

"From Liege Nersal?" asked Erien.

"Yes, Immortality."

It was the first time Erien had heard the title, addressed to him. He could see why it made Amel feel odd. Almost like tempting fate.

"Does he need an answer?" Erien asked, hoping not.

"No, Immortality."

Tatt peered over his shoulder, water dripping from his chin. "What's that?"

"I think," Erien said slowly, "that it may be the answer to a question I asked Horth. Thank you," he said to the errant, who nodded in minimalist Nersallian fashion, and left.

Branstatt's face appeared above them, amusement poorly hidden, and obviously very curious to know what had transpired.

"Luthan pushed me in!" Tatt complained.

"And I'm sure that you richly deserved it," his errant captain said.

"I'm going to have to get changed," Tatt said blandly, with a see-you-can-trust-me glance towards Erien.

"That's all I get?" asked Branstatt.

"If you want more, you'll have to ask Erien." Tatt dropped the subject suddenly, and grew serious. "All's clear?"

"All's clear." Branstatt sobered up instantly. "I'll wait for you." He strolled back towards Green Hearth.

Erien heaved himself out of the fountain, guarding his card. Tatt hopped up beside him. "Just as well I wasn't dressed for anything," he grumbled. They tramped towards Green Hearth, leaving a watery trail.

"Are you coming with me this time?" Tatt asked.

"I can't," said Erien. "I am going to lunch at Lilac Hearth, with Ranar."

"Well," Tatt said cheerfully, "at least I know we won't have any trouble down in the UnderDocks." At the door to his room, Erien turned to look at him. Tatt drummed hard, swordsman's fingers on Erien's chest. "Because I know exactly where the Dem'Vrel boys are going to be. Being polite and respectful to you under their mother's eye." Another thought made him brighten even further. "D'Lekker will loathe it. I hope he gets indigestion." He pushed open the door, then paused again. "Vretla too?"

"Yes," said Erien.

Tatt grinned at him. "Do try not to become the main course."

CHAPTER XVII

AMEL WAS JOLTED OUT OF A DOZE by the sound of the outside bar being lifted from his workshop prison.

He sprang up, ashamed of the joy with which he looked to greet Ev'rel, if only she had come to apologize and let him out.

The joy crashed at the sight of D'Lekker, looming in the open doorway.

"Disappointed?" D'Lekker hefted the crossbar in one hand, his other concealed beneath his cloak. "I could lock you in again if you want."

"Erien—?"

"Want to know if he's dead, don't you?"

Amel could not get air into his lungs.

"Erien does not even like you!" D'Lekker attacked. "But then you don't like people who like you back. You like Reetions. And Ev'rel."

"Lek," Amel gasped, "have you killed Erien?"

D'Lekker shook back his cloak.

His sword arm sported a nasty slash, the sleeve torn back. The wound had been expertly closed and cleared up.

"First blood," D'Lekker told him. "Nersal coached him, I'm sure of it."

"Oh, D'Lekker." Amel felt a surge of empathy for his sensitive brother.

"Ev'rel wanted me to go easy." D'Lekker would not soften. "I wouldn't. I wanted to kill him more when she told me who he was! Damn you! You told her! You told her after everything. You threw away the one thing you'd been strong about!"

D'Lekker's complaint made no sense to Amel, but he read his brother's hurt feelings well enough. "I was worried about you too, Lek," he offered. It felt hollow.

D'Lekker's eyes narrowed. "Mother has invited Erien to Lilac Hearth. She wants to make friends with him. Then she won't need you anymore. Don't think I'll side with you, if it comes to that. I can't. I won't."

Amel was distracted from the wild words by D'Lekker's body language. Lek was hurting. Stoic disregard was impossible for someone as vividly sensual and body-conscious as D'Lekker. Amel empathized because they were alike in that. D'Therd had taught Lek to be ashamed of it.

"Why did you tell her?" D'Lekker nagged. "Why did you buckle at last? That was power, knowing who the Throne Price was. That was something you knew, that she wanted. Something you held back!"

Amel just shook his head, unable to fathom why D'Lekker cared so much. That Lek was upset by the duel was obvious. Amel wanted to comfort him, but he could not ignore a new, visceral aversion rooted in that ambiguous encounter in D'Lekker's bedroom. D'Lekker's looming presence drew forth a violence that he would not own.

Amel tried to slip past him.

D'Lekker dropped the bar down into both hands, despite the pain it must have cost him, to block Amel's path. "I don't think Mother wants you out!" His pain made him cruel. He pressed closer, until they almost touched. "Maybe I should put you back in your room."

Amel put his open palm on the bar and said simply, but firmly, "Lek, I need to use the bathroom."

D'Lekker had not expected so ordinary a response. He looked confused, then moved aside with an awkward jerk.

Amel headed for the sanctuary of Ev'rel's private bathroom to clean up. He used the toilet, washed his mouth and clawed some of the dried blood out of his hair. The soiled shirt made him realize how badly he wanted a bath. He pulled it off, mindful of his bad elbow, and followed it with the rest of his clothes while he ran a hot bath. The sheer sound of the water was soothing.

He would think when he was clean again and when he had stopped aching, he promised the flutters of alarm in his gut. The pendant Mona had forced on him tapped his chest as he stood up. He took it off, and held the chain in his left hand, listening for D'Lekker beneath the sound of water pounding into his bath. He heard him approach. He was still unprepared when D'Lekker seized his shoulder and spun him around.

The pendant swung. Amel lowered his left arm, still holding the chain in a fisted hand.

The way D'Lekker looked at his nakedness seemed to accuse.

"I'm going to take a bath," Amel said, his hackles rising. Why should he have to explain taking off his clothes?

D'Lekker snatched at the pendant. Amel would not let it go. "Present from one of your Reetion whores?" D'Lekker asked.

Amel surrendered the pendant, breaking their bond. "Get out."

D'Lekker stayed where he was, too close; wheedling now for affection which Amel could not summon. "I'm trying to help you," D'Lekker said. "I let you out."

"Thanks." Amel was curt. It was all he could do not to explode with a rage which seemed to come from nowhere, like possession from the Void by one of the Lost Souls denied embodiment for their *okal'a'ni* crimes. He hated the evil emotion.

"I didn't have to let you out." D'Lekker moved within a breath of body contact.

Amel snapped. He smacked his palms into his brother's chest with a force that alarmed his bad elbow, shouting, "Back off!"

D'Lekker staggered, still clutching the pendant like a stolen token. Amel's demon fled. His brother's wounded look twisted his heart in another direction. D'Lekker was the sad, misfit child again, bullied by D'Therd, mocked by Ev'rel, and now, defeated by Erien. Amel could not bear to complete the roster with his own rejection.

"Listen, Lek," Amel struggled for patience. "Why don't you wait for me? Lie down. I'll take another look at that arm for you."

D'Lekker's expression turned spiteful. "Oh, I think the doctoring was adequate."

"What do you mean?" D'Lekker's tone made Amel's skin prickle. He knew when D'Lekker thought he had something valuable to dangle, like bait, before him.

D'Lekker stared, unabashed, at Amel's naked body.

It made Amel's skin crawl. He reached for a bathrobe.

D'Lekker caught Amel's bad arm, and twisted, just enough to force Amel to counter with his good hand. The chain of the pendant, meshed in D'Lekker's fingers, bit Amel's skin.

"D'Lekker," Amel said, between clenched teeth, "Let—me—go!"

"Weakling!" D'Lekker accused him hotly. "*Slaka!*"

Amel's anger ignited. He abandoned his weakened right arm to deliver a rabbit punch with his left.

D'Lekker expelled air, but only twisted harder.

A savage panic drove Amel to strike at Lek's wound. D'Lekker cried out. Amel hit him again, won freedom, and staggered out of the bathroom, disgusted by his own bloodied knuckles.

Ev'rel stood, waiting, in the bedroom.

Amel stopped. He straightened and composed himself, gone still as one of Ev'rel's statues.

In the bathroom behind him the bath water steamed and roared.

Ev'rel said calmly, "D'Lekker, turn off the water."

Amel noticed her hands. They were folded into the large, open sleeves of a dressing gown thrown over what remained of her formal wear. It seemed odd. Normally she did not stop in mid-change or spend much time in dressing gowns. Perhaps it was D'Lekker's presence in her bedroom. It seemed a trivial detail to unnerve him so badly. He feared his own darting emotions and tried to deny them, to stay calm.

Ev'rel's interest fastened on his throbbing elbow. He was holding it with his other hand. Her eyes made him conscious of the pain this was betraying, and he pointedly straightened the arm.

A smile gathered in the corners of Ev'rel's mouth. "I didn't think I thinned your wardrobe that much, love," she remarked on his nakedness.

"I was going to take a bath," he said. He didn't mind her looking at him as long as the pain was safely hidden, but he felt angry with her. She had locked him in. She knew he hated to be imprisoned.

Beyond her, the door to her workshop stood open.

"Erien is alive and well," she volunteered. "He is an excellent young man. You may even have been right to have fostered him with Di Mon. Brilliant choice. You were afraid of Di Mon. I never imagined that the Throne Price might have been placed with him."

D'Lekker appeared in the jamb of the bathroom door, the running water silenced.

Ev'rel's eyes shifted to D'Lekker. "I do not raise excellent young men."

"You locked me up." Amel was fed up with her attempts to distract him from his principal complaint. "You left me all night in the workshop."

"Are you angry?"

"Shouldn't I be?" Amel began to shake with fine grained tremors, hands slowly fisting despite his bad elbow.

She shrugged. "You're alive aren't you? Who knows what you might have done otherwise? Something foolish, I am sure. Something stupidly noble."

"I didn't have any definite plan for self-destructive intervention," he said as harshly as he knew how. He was sick of her opinion that the visitor probe had left him an involuntary martyr.

"You never do, but it's how you act." She drew her right hand from her sleeve and extended it to him, leaving her left arm draped in the soft, dark sleeve of the dressing gown. There was something not quite right about it.

He couldn't bring himself to take the offered hand. He left space between them.

"Ah," she said softly. "You are angry."

"I don't like being locked up." It was fundamental. It irked him that it sounded merely petulant.

"Yes, I know you don't." She might have been coaxing an animal out of its hidey hole. Or explaining life to a toddler. He felt, suddenly, stupid to be standing there, naked, blaming her for wanting to protect him from his own meddlesome compulsions. He inhaled deeply and let his breath out, hoping it might take with it his surplus emotion.

Ev'rel came to him. He held his breath, but still started when she touched the lump behind his ear, then the swelling that distorted his dancer's physique where his ribs were bruised. Frustration boiled over. He did not want to be her private statue, but he was not sure what to do or how to protest in a way which would not offend her.

"It sustains me," she murmured, "how each change only makes you more beautiful. Made over, unexplored." Her strong fingers pressed their way up his injured arm, feeling for a break. Or just to hurt him, he allowed. D'Lekker's accusations still stung. Weakling. *Slaka.*

Fine.

At least he wanted something back.

He caught her hand. "You did try to stop the duel?"

She held his eyes. "I tried."

They stood, a moment, dead-locked. Then she drew the hand holding hers to her mouth, her dry lips moving in the lubricant of her breath, over his knuckles and tendons. It sent shivers of pleasure up his arm.

"You locked me up," he said softly, unable to let it pass. The protest was feeble now.

She lowered their meshed hands. "I could never risk losing you. That's all."

Amel closed his eyes over threatened tears.

"I've had a productive talk with Erien." She moved pleasantly on to business, as if this was any other squabble they had plastered over, and not the edge of a precipice where they had not been in nearly two decades. "He will not come without us accepting Rire, but since he seems to have tamed Nersal, anything may be possible. We may yet avoid a war."

Avoiding a war with Rire mattered enough to kindle Amel's interest, but this solution chilled him with its other implications.

"If Erien can bring Nersal to you," he realized. "He'll make you Ava."

"It's only politics." She admonished him with his own attitude. "Don't you think being Avim for a while might be character-building for Ameron? His arrogance cost him Erien's good regard, even after you so carefully set things up to point Erien in that direction. Nor, I'm sure, will Ameron appreciate you telling me your precious secret in defiance of him, which is certainly ungenerous," she indulged in sarcasm, "when he's known so much longer than I have."

"It—was Di Mon who told him, not me," Amel stammered.

"But you told Di Mon. You had to, I suppose, when you decided to sequester the Throne Price on Monitum. Probably with some 'friend' to start," she hazarded, toying with jealousy.

Amel fell silent.

"I am glad," Ev'rel said, giving up the potential point of grievance, "that there are no more secrets between us."

Ev'rel's silence was expectant. Amel felt it. His mouth dried out.

"Except Mira," D'Lekker pushed forward out of the frame of the bathroom door.

Ev'rel's eyes lifted, dangerous.

D'Lekker wore his look of stubborn recklessness. "You want him to tell you he knows about her," he accused Ev'rel with energy, making her eyes widen. "You want him to prove that he's innocent, or beg for mercy if he isn't. You want to break him, and he wants to prove he won't be broken. Yes, I understand now. It isn't over." D'Lekker was actually gleeful.

Amel could not comprehend what Lek was raving about. His accelerated heart pressed darkness over his field of vision and roared in his ears. Clear dream sensations crawled in his nerves like a chronic infection.

He stayed on his feet, somehow.

Ev'rel's face, when the view cleared up, reminded him, madly, of Mira after Mona jogged her elbow in the middle of a delicate procedure.

"You have to do something about Mira, don't you Mother?" D'Lekker concluded. "Oh, yes, I know why! I know everything. You were so busy with each other, all those years ago, that no one paid me any attention. You left it to Kandral to take care of me. But I found ways to watch when Kandral was helping you, or when he went back to watch himself. I didn't understand then. I do now! I understand how Amel makes you feel. He's too perfect. He's too beautiful. And the Reetions have made it so he can't hate us. I've been trying, for years, to find a way to work it out and now I know. I want to help you, Mother. I can play now, too. I'll do whatever you want."

It was all Amel could do to keep standing. Clear dreams were not the problem though—it was blind, brutal, self-hatred.

Ev'rel was composed. "That is very interesting, D'Lekker."

"I will help!" D'Lekker's voice was thick with feeling. "I can do it. I love you more than him, Mother. I can be like you."

Amel knew he had to get out. That certainly made action possible.

"Mira is dead," Amel said, putting a dose of ill-temper into his manner and tone. He inhaled as if against the grief he knew Ev'rel would expect to surface if he really believed that. "I don't know why D'Lekker's bringing her up. I don't think I want to know. You deal with it. I want to get clean," he said, "and put some clothes on." He put ample confidence into his voice as he faced Ev'rel. If he could convince her that he thought D'Lekker was playing games to stir him up, she'd let him walk out. Where would he go without his clothes, after all, except to his own room to get some?

Ev'rel hesitated. She knew it was an act. He was sure of it in one heartbeat; the next he was planning his escape, already one step closer to the door. He'd go straight out onto Fountain Court. Freedom was that close. He could snatch a throw off a couch or an apron from a servant on the way out, but he hardly cared about that. Being naked didn't matter. He just had to get out.

Giving up sight of Ev'rel's face was agonizing. He was desperate to monitor the nuances of her expression, to see what she had figured out. Could he fight off D'Lekker? Maybe. Maybe not. Worse, there was something unnatural about the way she held her left hand, and something suggestive in the ampleness of the sleeves of her chosen dressing gown. The memory loomed large in his consciousness.

He was halfway to the door when he heard the tell-tail *pfft* of a needle gun. He threw himself left without wasting time to look back.

The needle struck him in the right flank.

He grabbed at it, falling, but his right arm didn't work properly and he needed the left to stop his fall. His fingers only brushed the shaft. It was barbed—not intended to pass through or penetrate too far. Just to deliver drugs.

His left arm buckled, dumping him on his face in Ev'rel's carpet. He recognized the effects of *klinoman*. A heavy dose. Getting onto his hands and knees was already stupidly laborious.

D'Lekker's legs appeared in front of him.

"Keep him still," Ev'rel said. "He could damage himself if he squirms around." She put a foot on the small of Amel's back and pushed, as D'Lekker slid his arms out from under him. Then Ev'rel knelt, to inspect the dully throbbing point of impact. "Only a flesh wound," she said. "Good."

He could hear her draw her stiletto.

Amel could see nothing but carpet, inhaling its clean, woolly smell with each gasp. Ev'rel, he knew, had been trained in medicine by Mira. She tugged experimentally on the needle's shaft. "Hold him steady."

D'Lekker set his feet on Amel's shoulders, and sat, holding his arm. "Ready." His precautions were unnecessary. Amel could not have resisted with much vigor.

Ev'rel extracted the needle. The *klinoman* dulled the pain but not the feeling of bodily intrusion. "It's not bad," she said. "D'Lekker, fetch a seamer. And come back alone. You understand?"

Amel could imagine D'Lekker nodding like an eager child given a grown-up role. It struck a chord of black humor. He wanted to 'play', too. The family sport.

"Can I seam it?" D'Lekker asked, excited.

Oh, Lek, Amel thought, suddenly hopeless. *What have we taught you?* He realized he'd been glad Ev'rel would, at least, contain the bleeding. Now that only made him feel as if he was playing too, by trusting her not to go too far. This was what he truly was, a *slaka*. The lassitude of *klinoman* made even anguish soggy.

"Yes," Ev'rel promised D'Lekker, "you may seam it, if you're careful. Now go on."

"But—"

"You can let him go now. He's thoroughly slack."

Amel felt D'Lekker get up, and heard the door close.

Ev'rel rolled him over and lifted his shoulders onto her lap.

"I knew you'd dodge left," she said, sorting out his hair above his glazed eyes with her clean hand. The other was vivid with his blood. "Your right arm was hurt. You protected that."

He swallowed. His senses worked, spared the analgesic effect of the *klinoman*, but his body control was as rudimentary as a new-born's. Being so helpless was terrifying: like being tied down, or locked up. He suffered a flash of the visitor probe's sterile white chamber. Immobilized. Vulnerable. The saline about to drop into his open eye.

"Breathe." She slapped him, hard.

He did, in a shallow gasp.

She turned his head back toward her, his chin held firmly in her hand.

He murmured, staring up, "You promised."

"And I did let Mira go. Once."

Her hand slid, caressing, down his throat.

"But you must understand I can't risk such exposure, here, now. I must deal with her. You will forgive me, one day, even for that."

"No. Not Mira," he promised her. "Never."

"Just pay attention to your breathing," she said, sliding him gently back down to the floor. "I've given you too much."

He didn't care if he breathed or not. He let himself drift into a stony sleep, threatened by suffocation. Ev'rel forced air into his lungs, mouth to mouth. It did not hurt, and her mouth was so familiar that the feeling bathed him with the relief of vague, sensual impressions accepted on the cusp of consciousness.

Three minutes later, the fetched seamer was inserted into his wound and turned on. Amel gasped, fully conscious all at once despite the *klinoman*. He stopped breathing again when D'Lekker's first aid job was over.

"Get him to the shower," Ev'rel ordered. Someone was annoying her. Amel wondered, abstractly, who it was, and realized in some distant faculty that he was. "Run cold, then hot, whatever it takes to keep him gasping until what I've just given him takes care of the breathing problem. Hurt him if you have to, but do no harm. I must prepare for lunch. Join me when you're sure he's going to breathe on his own. But lock him in the workshop first."

"I'll stay with him," D'Lekker offered.

"No," Lek was over-ruled by Ev'rel, "you will have to learn to get along with Erien if he gives me his oath. You will come to lunch, as soon as Amel is out of danger."

D'Lekker hauled Amel up by his arms. Amel refused to feel involved. He couldn't stop himself from reacting when D'Lekker, cursing his dead weight, was forced to blast them both with cold water, but he abandoned his body to its instincts. Let it breathe if it must. Anxiety crept back with the abatement of the *klinoman's* grip on him, trapping him between clear dreams and D'Lekker's handling in the shower. He clung to D'Lekker in the aftermath of memories worse, even, than what was happening to him now, staring over D'Lekker's arm at a diluted curl of blood swirling down the drain below him and not knowing whose it was; sane enough to know that he was going mad. One moment he was being drugged and beaten in a dingy den, the next he was revived in a hot shower with D'Lekker shaking him, or forcing air into his lungs, his body pinned between Lek and the shower wall.

D'Lekker acted like someone trying to resuscitate a loved one: fretting, cursing fear itself, and his own injured arm. It was too bizarre. Amel felt a distant sympathy that mocked him for its very existence. He couldn't hate. He didn't seem to know how. A lifetime of denial couldn't change the facts. He had done this to himself, somehow. He must have. Mira knew that, when she pitied him instead of doing what he asked. She knew, and her loyalty would kill her now.

Self-hatred was a relief, of sorts.

Somewhere, in the regime of D'Lekker's slippery handling in the pounding water, and the battering of his burned-in past, Amel managed to lose consciousness.

Chapter XVIII

RANAR AND HIS ESCORT, LED BY AMY, were waiting for Erien in the entrance hall to White Hearth. There were curiosity seekers from every occupied hearth, out to get a glimpse of Ranar while pretending to be lounging by their doors or resting on the seat around the fountain. Amy and Ranar were talking horse pedigrees, apparently nonchalant. Or rather, Amy was enthusing about a bloodline that Ameron was maintaining on Monitum, and Ranar was listening with every symptom of enthralled attention. Not, Erien suspected, for what Amy said so much as the phenomenon of Amy herself: the Ava's love child, and heir to the Purple Alliance in Killing Reach through her mother, Ayrium.

Amy was his half-sister, Erien realized.

He could not see how to employ that information.

Amy's expression became neutral as she broke off to watch Erien approach. He suspected she did not approve of him pressuring Ameron to release Ranar to this luncheon at Lilac Hearth. She was, herself, solidly pro-Ameron. She stood with her left thumb hooked over the hilt of her sword, waiting for him to speak first, with strict formality that reminded him he was now her superior by birth rank, and less an intimate than he had been as Tatt's friend and Luthan's visitor.

"Royalblood Amy," he acknowledged her, hoping that was adequate. She nodded. "Pureblood Erien."

Ranar was dressed in an open-necked yellow shirt, meticulously eschewing any house associations. Around his neck he wore a pair of Reetion chains—one plain gold, one strung with small topazes. Erien recognized them as a gift from Ranar's Reetion partner, Evert, and had to remind himself no one else would make such an association. Ranar looked himself, but moved to Erien's side with an eagerness that betrayed he had not thrived in ostracized confinement. It was not like him to let his scholarly enthusiasm for field work show through the diplomat's sober facade. Ranar noted the lapse also; he was beginning to take formal leave of Amy when she cut him off—looking much like her father—with a wave of her hand.

"Enjoy your sightseeing," she told them both, speaking in English, like a Monatese, to avoid Gelack pronouns, "and tell me about it when you're done. I've never been in Lilac Hearth."

The hand of errants Ameron had provided deployed themselves around Ranar and Erien, leaving them side by side as they crossed Fountain Court. Erien felt Ranar looking him over a little anxiously. "Di Mon," Ranar said softly, in Reetion, "did not want me to tell you until Ameron decided to do so. I hoped—I hope—you can forgive us."

Erien answered with silence. At least now, he thought, he understood why he had sometimes sensed a constraint in Ranar's affections. He had thought it was because he was a Gelack on Rire, and had doubled his efforts to assimilate. But it had been because Ranar knew who he had in his charge, all along, and its implications.

He said, after a few steps, speaking Gelack, "I do." It was the one and only time, he resolved, he would use the full seven-step differencing between himself and his foster father. "Ev'rel told me," he added, in Reetion. "Not Ameron."

The Reetion diplomat measured the distance they had to go. It wasn't far enough. "Erien," he said, "you worry Ameron. Do you realize that?"

"He wants my oath but not my Reetion sympathies."

Ranar shook his head slightly. "He needs your oath, but he needs Liege Nersal's more. Nersal wants you acknowledged; he has made that plain. If Ameron does not acknowledge you, he may lose Nersal. If he acknowledges Rire, as things stand, he loses Nersal. If he does not acknowledge Rire, he loses you—as you have made plain—and he may thereby also lose Nersal."

It was Erien's turn to shake his head. "Horth doesn't follow me. If he did, it would simplify a great deal. I could tell him, myself, to accept Rire's independence."

"'Horth'," Ranar prodded him, mildly, "is not plain 'Horth' to many people. Nor does he coach any highborn who asks, before a duel. But I take your point. Liege Nersal follows only *Okal Rel*—his own personal interpretation, I would say, although I doubt that he sees it that way. I have known the man ever since he saved *SkyBlue Station* from the Nesaks eighteen years ago, and I have never had any doubt that he acted entirely out of his own convictions. We were incidental." He paused as their escort slowed, approaching the open doors of Lilac Hearth. "Horth Nersal could demand that you be recognized, and still oppose you with his own sword if he thought that it was right to do so."

"If there is one person I don't need you to explain to me," Erien said, irked despite himself, "it is Horth Nersal."

"Then you understand him better than Ameron does." Ranar got the last word in.

They were passed through by the Lilac Hearth guard. Erien dismissed their own escort—whether they liked it or not, it would have given insult to have retained them inside another's hearth when they came as guests. A Lilac Hearth herald greeted them and led them through the entrance hall, visiting lounge, and a gallery of weapons which was obviously D'Therd's, into the dining hall, which bridged the outer public rooms and increasingly private regions of the Hearth. It was large enough to accommodate, as a centerpiece, the base of the spiral staircase leading up to the plaza.

"The Demish influence shows," Ranar remarked, with a nod in the direction of the room's white draperies and the figurines made of marble, set on pedestals. He was not given to idle observation. Erien wondered if it was a sign of nervousness.

"Do you welcome this?" Erien asked the Reetion, suddenly uncertain. He had presumed Ranar would want the opportunity to represent himself to his opposition. There had been no chance to discuss it—true, but he had not thought to insist on checking with Ranar regarding his wishes. Was that a Sevolite presumption, or merely a thoughtless one?

Ranar smiled at him. "It promises to be interesting."

They were not alone in the dining hall. There were servants, standing waiting. Ev'rel had been waiting herself, but stayed apart to give them privacy for a moment, idling beneath a long, ethereal landscape done in white and pearly colors. It portrayed Waiting Souls partaking in a stately meal by a misty lake side. Maybe it was meant to be Earth. There was probably a Demish story attached to it. She turned her head when the murmur of their voices fell, but waited for them to approach her. She was wearing a high-necked, deep blue gown with house braid worked in silver and blue thread. Erien stopped before her and bowed. Ranar bowed, more deeply, and having done so took one step back. She raised an eyebrow at him, interested, before shifting her attention to Erien.

"I have told all my guests who you are," she warned Erien. "It prevents misunderstandings and resentments about withheld information. And, perhaps, ill-advised spontaneous reactions."

"I have already been thrown in the fountain once today," said Erien, "so I'm sure that is wise."

"Ah, so that was why Heir Monitum did it," she said, with a slight smile. The smile assumed a touch of mischief at his surprise that she knew what he referred to. "Well, Erien, it is a rather public place, the fountain. I gather he got his comeuppance immediately thereafter, at the hands of Princess Luthan. She is not without spirit, that one. She'll need it, going into a political marriage." A slight shadow crossed her face and with an irritable flick of her hand she gestured a servant over. "Would you care for something to drink while we are waiting? And you?" she asked Ranar, discriminating between them with all the deftness of her years of experience at court, such that even her steep differencing of pronouns did not seem to insult Ranar due to the uniform politeness, in every other detail, with which she addressed both Ranar and Erien.

Erien had wine, preferring not to risk strong spirits. Ranar had fruit juice, but he hardly sipped it, standing back to watch them together. Ev'rel said, "I have invited Vretla Vrel of Red Hearth, and my sons, of course. Prince H'Us will definitely come. Princess Chandra, my house guest from Demora, has been asked, and will boycott to express her abhorrence of anything so newfangled as Reetions or as irregular as a long lost Throne Price." She drank from her own drink and held the horn decorously, at her waist, in both hands. She had beautiful hands, much like Amel's.

The table was set for seven. Her tally suggested eight would attend. Who else was she not expecting to make it?

"I trust," Erien said, making an intelligent guess, "D'Lekker is recovering well from the cut he took?"

"Oh, yes," Ev'rel assured him, "and he'll be here. I'll be very interested, in fact, to see if he conducts himself with wisdom." Her smile, as she raised her glass, assured him D'Lekker would not fly out of control under her supervision.

Perhaps it was Amel she did not expect, thought Erien, since she had declared her opposition to him being questioned.

The door opened. D'Therd and H'Us came in together. Steel blue and smoky blue eyes glanced off Ranar and came to rest on Erien. D'Therd did not trouble to conceal his distaste. H'Us did. The H'Usian Admiral bowed to Ev'rel with the crispness of decades of inculcation in Demish ceremony, but he did not convey the impression of a man who kissed female hands, and she did not convey the impression of a woman who expected it.

D'Therd placed himself at Ev'rel's shoulder and scowled past Ranar's left ear.

Ev'rel said, "Thank you for coming, Prince H'Us. May I introduce my other guests," a small pause, "Pureblood Erien Dem'Vrel Lor'Vrel—" deftly, and in defiance of Demish custom, she placed the matronymic first. The Vrellish, if they strung names together, made the surname that of the most Sevolite parent, or the house to which the child was gifted. Often they simply picked what they wanted and forgot what they didn't, which the Demish complained was confusing and insulting to the dropped line of ancestors, dead as well as living. "And the Ambassador sent to us from Rire," Ev'rel concluded. "Citizen Ranar."

H'Us ignored Ranar to concentrate on Erien. "So," H'Us said, and paused, holding the floor. Erien had the distinct sense that if he himself had any decency at all he would disappear. When he didn't, H'Us—reluctantly—went on with ponderous good manners. "You will be giving your oath this Swearing, will you lad?"

Erien forgave him the 'lad'. H'Us was, after all, more than a century his senior in age, and had known more Purebloods on a personal basis than there were Purebloods left alive, now. H'Us did speak up the one level required.

"It seems so," said Erien.

"And you served with the Nersallian fleet?"

"Three years."

"It is too bad they are tied up in Killing Reach," H'Us said, with a sharp glance towards Ranar. "It's a waste. Nersallians policing commoners."

"That may be," said Erien, "but it was a strategic decision on Liege Nersal's part."

"You approve?" D'Therd spoke up.

"Yes," Erien said, turning. "Not of the blockade as such—but if *SkyBlue* is to be blockaded, then I would rather it be by the Nersallian fleet than by anyone else—forgive me if I offend by that," he told them both.

"I would not be blockading if I was there," D'Therd confirmed. "Only conquering Rire will end this plague of *okal'a'ni* foulness. The Reetions have more than they deserve, and they're no threat to us."

"But Nersal," H'Us objected, "believes that *SkyBlue* ought to be blockaded. To keep them out. He's not invading. I can't imagine he would bother with the blockade if the Reetions were no threat to anyone."

D'Therd gave a snort.

"That the Liege of Nersal sees Rire as a military threat, I can confirm," Erien said. He could feel Ranar's steady eyes on the side of his face, willing him to play this card with great care. Ev'rel lowered the glass she was raising towards her mouth, without drinking from it. "But I must disagree with D'Therd's remedy," said Erien. "We have no right to Reetion territory, and too many Gelacks seem to underestimate both the capacity and the will of the Reetions to defend themselves."

"Exactly," H'Us agreed with vigor. "Rire can and will use *okal'a'ni* weapons. It has before. Weapons of mass destruction turned on space habitats and even against life-supporting planets! Your soul must be as young as your body, Erien, if you'd praise them for it!"

"Ranar does not represent the regime which Ameron's mother, Ava Trenseel, fought in the Killing Wars, two hundred years ago," insisted Erien. "Our impressions of each other are out of date."

"But Erien," Ev'rel warned gently, "the Reetions of *SkyBlue Station* do belong to the current regime. And destroying their own station was their second choice, if Amel had failed to rid them of Liege H'Reth under the visitor probe's influence."

"Aye," said H'Us. "One choice as bad as the other. Now I'm not proud, myself, of the part played by H'Reth in that business. He was Demish even if he wasn't a H'Usian. But *Okal Rel* takes care of such people. There is no longer a House H'Reth. The Reetions have not even executed their *sla*-medtech, Lurol, for what she did to Pureblood Amel."

Ranar's mouth inclined down at this reference. He stayed Erien with a Monatese hand gesture of his fingers at waist level. Ranar wanted to respond himself.

"Lurol," Ranar began, "is not a medtech. She is a psychiatric researcher. Her profession has a stringent code of ethics which was brought to bear when her behavior on *SkyBlue* was examined by inquest." Ranar moved from court Gelack into Golden Age Demish dialect, which H'Us, at least, still followed. "Lurol was vindicated. I appreciate that this verdict does not satisfy you, Admiral H'Us. Reciprocally, I am disturbed by the admission that you had no objection to the razing of House H'Reth for the sake of its liege's dishonor. I had heard that you were, personally, upset by the slaughter of H'Reth's pregnant wife, for instance. Was I in error?"

H'Us reacted as if stung in the ankle by something on the floor beneath his notice. Quite apart from what he said, Ranar had dealt an insult in his grammar, if not an obvious one even to most Gelacks. His pronouns were differenced accurately for a commoner speaking to a Royalblood. But Demoran dialect allowed for spiking verbs with literary allusions to a classical canon which enriched conversation with a whole, second layer of significance. Ranar had, subtly, called H'Us a bungling hypocrite.

Erien saw D'Therd following the body language, not the words, much as Horth would.

H'Us, on the other hand, reacted as if a verbal sword had been drawn.

"I took no hand in Lady H'Reth's murder, and would have protected the unborn child of course," H'Us insisted to Ev'rel, "if I had known that it was more likely to be Amel's than H'Reth's."

"I have no doubt of that," Ev'rel assured him, as accomplished as Ranar in Golden Demish nuances.

"Solutions to such things can be imperfect," Ranar offered reconciliation. "Yours, as much as ours."

"Both the visitor probe and Liege H'Reth are, I think, aberrations," Ev'rel made Ranar's point for him, and turned to Erien. "I would like to hear you answer the charge concerning habitat. Rire was prepared—in resisting H'Reth—to destroy *SkyBlue Station*. Surely that is *okal'a'ni*."

A servant came by, offering wine in tapering horns without bases. Ev'rel took one. D'Therd passed. H'Us knocked his back and returned it immediately, empty, refusing a refill.

"A *rel*-ship contains breathable air," Erien pitched his explanation at H'Us, as he believed Ev'rel wanted. "It has a limited recycling system which relies on living organisms. It is a micro-habitat. But in shake-ups, *rel*-ships are destroyed quite purposefully. They are regarded as expendable when sacrificed to a greater need. The Reetions regarded *SkyBlue Station* as expendable, in defense of the habitable worlds beyond. Where is the boundary?"

H'Us wore a frown that deepened as Erien talked. He accepted the premise of the argument, but had to sift through a century's experience to reach his own conclusion.

"You would agree," H'Us set some more parameters, "that damaging a habitable planet is anathema."

Ranar looked inclined to quibble but Ev'rel said, firmly, "Yes. Let's start with that."

"Then the trouble, lad," H'Us told Erien with an air more of explanation than true debate, "is lack of protocol. *Okal Rel* has protocol for resolving disputes. Strictly speaking, the shake-ups you cite are failures of contract and sword, which is why you quite correctly criticize them, but at least in space there are no ecologies to threaten. The Reetion conceit I'll never tolerate is that they," he shot a glare at Ranar, "in this life, individually think that they matter more than the stage on which the next round of lives is to have its chance. That is *okal'a'ni*—anti-life—acting outside honor. It is the worst form of greed and selfishness."

"If you believe in reincarnation," said Erien.

"Belief is irrelevant." H'Us shrugged. "Only fools think their opinions influence the truth. Commoners are reborn just as we are. The Reetions shouldn't be upset by Nesak nonsense about them being soulless vermin. But the thing is, you can't trust them not to think that, and I can see, of course, why believing you are nothing more than the flesh you stand in is an acid thought, and poisons the honorable acceptance of defeat if you lose a fight. The Reetions suffer from the Lorel disease," he concluded grimly. "The need to win at any cost."

Action near the doors drew attention. Vretla Vrel stood there, tossing a flame red traveling cloak to a servant. Making it red defeated the usual purpose of wearing one, which was for anonymity, but this cloak was not only red but slippery satin and lavishly embroidered in crossed swords— the emblem of House Vrel. She laughed when Ev'rel's servant dropped it. "Ev'rel!" she cried. "Picked this one for his hard calves, did you?"

Ev'rel inhaled carefully beneath a quaver of annoyance at the petty vulgarity.

Vretla strode in. She had a swagger the Nersallians called 'space legs', that would do for a range of variations in ambient gravity—provided all hovered near or above one g—and an energy that was vigorously sexual. The first look she gave Erien was as frank as any Tatt might cast toward a courtesan, but no more offensive either. All the same Erien resented the sense of being something nice disguised in dull paper asking to be unwrapped.

H'Us ignored Vretla's arrival.

"So you see," H'Us continued to lecture, "the problem is a lack of protocol. That is why Ameron was negotiating possibilities with him—" he contrived not to look at Ranar, and spoke down to him firmly in court Gelack, "—but I think this Rose Garden affair yesterday proves the futility of all of that. We cannot interact wholesomely with Reetions. All contact should, as Ameron originally realized, be cut off."

"Like sealing up a plague in the UnderDocks," Vretla waded in, wine in hand, "eh, H'Us?"

"If you like," H'Us granted her peerage with a scowl.

"And if necessary, sterilize the lot!" Vretla swigged from her wine horn and put the unfinished drink down, any old way, on a passing tray which she didn't have to look at to accurately make the deposit. It spilled—but that was a servant's problem. "Commoners, brown or not, are too valuable for those tactics," said Vretla. She gave Ranar a thoughtful look which ended in a sly smile, as unperturbed by his supposed depravity as H'Us was clearly homophobic. "I don't think there's anything wrong with them that can't be cured."

Ranar could not repress his irritation. Erien knew he hated being pestered even by Reetion would-be reformers. Ranar was very clear, and exclusive, about his sexual preference, although he was far from demonstrative about it, even at home on Rire.

"I think the entire Reetion Net might prove too much for even your appetites, Liege Vrel," Ev'rel told her most trying vassal. "There are, I understand, millions of males with Citizen Ranar's opinion, that a *mekan'st* of the same gender is preferable." She pointedly chose *mekan'st*, not one of the less-respected terms for lover. "As well, I understand, as women."

"Huh," Vretla told her. "Women are never really girl-*sla*. It's something Demish matrons do when Demish men get too impossible."

Erien watched Ranar bite his tongue again. H'Us wouldn't dignify the insult with a response. Vretla clearly disconcerted him, as if he didn't know quite what to do about her. She was no Demish princess, but there was no denying she was female.

Unlike Ev'rel, whose clothes played her figure down, Vretla wore flexible leather trousers and a clinging bodice. The neckline exposed slices of her compact breasts and her hard nipples stood out unabashed against the elastic material. Her vest was a large, loose accessory worn to display house braid, not to conceal her figure. She was taller than Ev'rel and as strong as any male of her size and birth rank. She was Vrellishly lean, but within the physical bounds set by that, her bare left arm showed the same sort of muscular emphasis from sword play as D'Therd's right. Erien knew, from Tatt, that she was not in D'Therd's class but those who were could be counted on the fingers of one hand. She belonged, like Tatt, in the second rank of Sevildom's master duelists.

"How people have sex and with whom doesn't bother me," Vretla said, and grinned, chin tipped rakishly, "so long as they do it with somebody. It is Rire's thinking machines that are *okal'a'ni*. When we've destroyed those, the Reetions will behave like human beings. It was a machine, after all, which decided that Amel was not human."

"That has been corrected," said Erien, too quickly. He saw Ranar react to Vretla's prescription for conquest and shared the chill. Reetion governance was predicated on arbiters, and their use penetrated every aspect of ordinary life.

"Corrected?" Vretla drilled Erien with the word, then laughed hotly. "You must be Ameron's!" She set a hand on her sword hilt, turning to Ev'rel. "Didn't you contribute anything of Vrel to him?"

"One need not be Vrellish to agree with you, Liege Vrel," H'Us told her stiffly. "It was not Pureblood Amel but his Sevolite nature which the machine considered inhuman when it judged him ineligible for the legal protections Reetion law would otherwise have granted. We've had that explained to us," he deferred—once again with minimal eye contact—to Ranar, "but can you 'correct' a thing like that? To consider it a mere error is, itself, preposterous."

"Not a mere error. An error can be very serious," Erien countered. He realized he had expected the same sort of ignorance here that he'd encountered at the Rose Garden. It made him impatient with himself.

This was not Rire, where information was a communal trust aggressively kept public and homogeneously distributed. It was natural that the elite would know more than the commoners. He filtered the impatience out of his voice, to answer H'Us more thoroughly. "The *SkyBlue* arbiter had never experienced a Sevolite and found Amel sufficiently different from the human norm that it failed to classify him as human, automatically. As a consequence it never stopped Lurol when—ordinarily—it would have. She expected it would—if it became aware that Amel was experiencing the sort of distress he did, apparently. No Reetion consciously decided not to grant Amel human rights. The arbiter cannot be blamed, merely because while intelligent, it isn't sentient. No computer can be better than its programming."

Vretla's fists locked in Erien's shirt so fast it surprised even his reflexes. Everyone else caught their breath.

"Are you trying to tell me," she snarled in his face, "this Lurol was so stupid she could not tell she was torturing Amel?"

Erien snapped his arms up inside hers, hard, breaking her grip. Three years in the Nersallian fleet had taught him the consequences of allowing someone to manhandle him. He sprang back, hands coming up instinctively into fighting stance. He heard, like a gust of wind, the slide of sword from sheath, and her blade was between his wrists, pointed at his sternum.

"Erien! Vretla!" Ranar and Ev'rel rapped out in unison. A surge of adrenaline constricted his chest; he drew breath involuntarily, his muscles locking against further rashness. This was not the Nersallian fleet. If they fought, there would be consequences greater than the injuries they inflicted on each other. All that was left for him to do was to meet her hot, intimidating gaze without flinching. They stared each other down a moment. Then, with a grunt of irritation, she stepped back. Ranar and Ev'rel exchanged a glance in fleeting recognition of shared purpose. Ranar looked like he'd just run a block. He'd been frightened. Ev'rel immediately reverted to the gracious host.

"Perhaps we should eat now," she suggested, before Erien caught his breath to continue the discussion.

Sitting down to the table was a tacit assumption of equality, under the circumstances. Erien had the sinking feeling that none of the Sevolites would commit themselves, regardless of what Ev'rel expected; or worse yet, would rise and leave if she forced Ranar upon them.

"Vretla," Ev'rel said, as if the failure of anyone to sit was wholly natural, "Amel is late. Would you see if he is dawdling in his room? D'Therd, please see if you can find D'Lekker. It really is insupportable that two of my own sons should be late when we have guests

to entertain. Oh, Vretla—why don't you take Erien? I'd like him to
see more of Lilac Hearth. Admiral H'Us, perhaps you'd give me
your opinion on the centerpieces while we are waiting for them.
I've designed two and can't chose between them."

"I did wonder why you had two on the table," H'Us commented.

Ev'rel brushed past Erien as she went to join the H'Usian Admiral. She
smelled of something familiar; he identified it a moment later as the resin
used to flavor Monatese Turquoise. Integrated with her body scent it
was quite distinct, but not unpleasant. "You are Dem'Vrel and Lor'Vrel,
not just Vrel," she instructed *sotto voce*. "Remember it. You need to
understand the Vrellish point of view. To do that, you must listen."

The emphasis she put on 'understand' reminded Erien of Ranar.
Erien had always had difficulty starting with things the way that they
were now, instead of immediately pressing for reform. Changing
Vretla's mind was not at issue, yet. Not until he knew a lot more.

He joined Vretla, but withheld his defense of Lurol, and waited for
her to speak.

"Seventeen, aren't you?" Vretla said as they started down the Throat.

Her braid made explicit the ancestry she shared with Ev'rel. Noticing
it, Erien was conscious of himself and Ev'rel, as Dem'Vrellish hybrids,
between the poles personified by H'Us and Vretla.

"Yes," he acknowledged.

They went around the stairs that twined up to the plaza floor, and
passed into a library. It was another chimera, this time of Monatese
scholarship and Demish love of literary arts. The nervecloth portraits
here and there were blank. A scattering of painted cameos on one
wall portrayed a host of ancient babies in Demish nursery clothes.

"So that's fourteen to seventeen as a Nersallian," Vretla remarked.
"How many years on Rire?"

"Seven."

"And before that Monitum." She paused to usher them through
another room. "No wonder you are confused. So—I'll forgive you
a few mistakes. But I make no apology for who I am."

"Understood," said Erien.

She gave him an answering grunt which made him wonder if he'd
already had to be forgiven once.

"You're cold as a dead moon." She explained what she disliked.

"You do not know me," he pointed out.

She looked sideways at him. "I've seen you fight."

She cruised on through a gallery of painted portraits and a glorious
collection of white marble statues of human—all male—figures.
There were too many, even for the spacious room. Vretla trailed a

hand over the waist of a marble courtesan frozen in his execution of a sword dance, but didn't slow down.

"Delm had a mixed male and female collection," said Vretla. "Ev'rel's got the female ones stored." She glanced around, like a sightseer mildly bemused by another civilization's aesthetic excesses. "Vent me if I can see what use any of them are in stone."

She lost interest and picked up the pace, walking with her spacer's gait just a half a step ahead of Erien. It took him the length of a private reception room to figure out that her tendency to speed up if he walked abreast was utterly unconscious. Where Vretla did not lead, she could not walk. Divorced from the social threat of fending off unwanted advances, Erien could not help but appreciate the female heat and cat-sleek physical confidence she gave off. For the first time he personally felt a glimmer of the over-stimulation the Vrellish of both genders inflicted, constantly, on one another. It was distracting. She had strong features, focused forward in a pantherish composition and polished up by Vrellish sharpness in the chin and cheek bones. She wore her hair short. Her eyes were her best feature. They were large, wide-set almonds of a gray that was almost black. Like Ev'rel's.

"You have objected to everything I've said," Erien prompted the Royalblood Liege of Red Vrel. "What do you make of Rire, yourself?"

"I've spent time in Killing Reach," she said. "It's a mess."

"Do you mean the Purple Alliance?"

"No."

Erien reminded himself to think of Horth, and let her get her ideas nailed onto words and out of her mouth before he dove in too fast. She was derailed now, considering what he'd asked.

"Not always, anyhow." Vretla qualified her 'no', and carried on. "But there can't be any more Killing Reaches. We're poison to each other, us and Rire. I believe that."

"Then why not, as H'Us wants, leave Rire alone?"

She gave him a sharp look and stopped. Her eyes narrowed. "You need to know? Or are you trying to find out if I do?"

Erien swallowed. Horth would not react like that. Vretla was just that much more verbally dexterous that his attempts to lead the conversation were doomed to backfire. "I need to know what you think."

"I don't think," Vretla told him with emphasis. "H'Us thinks. I know." They emerged out of the end of the Throat into Family Hall.

Vretla snagged a servant. "Is Amel in his room?"

The young boy began, and aborted, a bow. Erien guessed Vretla was a frequent guest, and didn't appreciate Demish-style flourishes. The trouble for the servant was remembering who did and who did not.

"I do not know, Your Highness," he told her. "The room's locked. He locks himself in sometimes."

"Huh," Vretla grunted, and scowled. "If it's locked there's no point trying to get in," she told Erien, and once more raised her voice to command the servant. "Go bang on the door and tell him to get his pretty butt into the dining room. Right now."

"Yes, Your Highness!"

"Tell him I said so!" she called after the boy, and waved Erien back up the Throat, looking sour. "He's probably in there dancing," she muttered, like someone walking on the Flashing Floor and trying not to think about resolving navigational problems.

Erien was confused and a little irritated. He had thought they had been talking about serious political matters, not Amel.

"He does that when he's upset," she said, "and for Ev'rel. Just for Ev'rel," she added, and transmuted her frustration to aggression. "If Heir Monitum doesn't kill someone over that Rose Garden obscenity I will!"

"Tatt will deal with it," Erien said quietly. Vretla's need was more for blood than justice. Was this how she felt about Rire, also? A lust that could turn easily to violence? A lust—in this case—for land and people.

Walking cooled her off. She resumed their conversation spontaneously in the midst of Ev'rel's forest of half-naked male statues.

"D'Therd talks conquest, like a Nesak," she tossed off. "It's a big word. Me, if I'm pushed, I push back. If I want something," she looked at Erien, considering, maybe, whether he might one day qualify, "I take it."

Just before the dining room she stopped and turned, blocking his path with her body. "I'm not so different from a Reetion, really. I will fight to be what I am. To the death. And forever. Look closely. You'll see they are as eager to turn us into Reetions as I am to make them my vassals. *Okal Rel* of a sort, after all, in a larger arena. H'Us's mistake is believing that we must repeat all our errors when we fight them—or that either side will ever leave the other alone again. Does that answer the intelligence test you set me earlier, Lorel? You asked why I don't think like H'Us. That's why." She smiled. "But I believe in clean fights. And I will treat them accordingly, so long as they do likewise."

Erien watched her pivot and plunge back into Ev'rel's dinner party with the sinking feeling that he might as well try explaining vegetarianism to a panther. If panthers still existed, and were not as vanished as the Earth they came from.

"What?" Vretla exclaimed, in outraged horror.

Erien's nerves jumped. She sounded truly furious. He pushed through the doors to discover long looks and shocked expressions. Ev'rel, herself, stood with her right hand on her throat, chest rising and falling with deep inhalations, eyes widened.

Vretla was already on her way out.

Her departure revealed D'Lekker, standing in the midst of the effect he had, somehow, created. When he saw Erien he smiled, clearly enjoying the vengeance value in what he had to say. "Heir Monitum has finally put his foot in a live snake pit," D'Lekker told Erien triumphantly. "He was ambushed in the UnderDocks. Rather more than first blood, this time. There was lots of blood. Lots and lots and lots of it!" D'Lekker's voice soared in sing-song triumph.

Ranar caught Erien's left hand as it closed on his hilt. The soft hand and hard grip jarred him out of a step he had been unaware he had taken. "He's not dead, Erien," Ranar hissed. In his expression, Erien saw what he had almost done. Sanity returned. If D'Lekker were involved, then time would show.

D'Lekker's stare welcomed the hope of a rematch.

Ranar let go of Erien. Erien took his hand away from his hilt, shaken by his own reaction. "My apologies, D'Lekker, for blaming the messenger for the news." He was not nearly as fluent in Golden Demish dialect as Ranar—and he had no idea whether D'Lekker had been educated in it—but he inflected his verbs to convey lack of faith in the other's trustworthiness as a messenger.

D'Lekker looked uneasy, not understanding. H'Us blinked. Ev'rel was not listening. She said, "He must die though, surely, mustn't he? Wounded in the heart? Didn't you say," she asked D'Lekker, "that he was wounded in the heart?"

"That's what the rumor is." D'Lekker kept a sly eye on Erien as he answered her.

Erien was stunned by the thought.

"How terrible!" Ev'rel was trembling.

Prince H'Us responded to her distress as he would to a Demish princess's, taking her elbow to steady her. "Maybe it isn't as bad as all that. Young D'Lekker, you know, he likes to dramatize."

D'Lekker scowled at H'Us, turned on his heel and stalked down into the Throat.

Ev'rel collected herself forcibly. "Erien," she said, "I am sure your natural impulse is to return to Green Hearth. Do, please. We can continue this—" she smiled a little tensely, "—occasion at some other time."

Gratefully, Erien collected Ranar and hurried after Vretla out of the dining hall, past flustered servants trying to give them their cloaks, which he ignored, and out onto Fountain Court.

Amy shouldered through the errants and house staff who had preceded Erien out of Lilac Hearth to learn more. She had with her some of Ameron's palace guard. "I don't know any more than you've probably heard," she told Erien. "Keep Ranar out of sight in the middle, and come on. I'll get you to Green Hearth."

Green Hearth was under siege by news-seekers. Erien bore straight through them, Ranar almost jogging to match his stride, Amy and their escort eliminating the risk of someone starting trouble.

He found Green Hearth's entry hall almost as crowded. Most were Monatese, either Sevolite family retainers or, surprisingly, commoner civil servants or foremen in Monatese livery. That a mixed cross-section of Gelack society loved Tatt, Erien knew; that Tessitatt would respect that love at such a time left him more surprised. A leavening of Vretla's vassals peppered the hall, mixed with messengers and errantry of all houses. Erien instinctively spotted the Black Hearth herald, already leaving under errant escort.

"Where is Ameron?" Ranar fretted, irritated by the chaos.

Wordless, Erien led him down Green Hearth's Throat. Amy and their escort let them go. A handful of family friends and vassals rose in expectation as they passed, but none intruded on the feeling Erien expressed in his very walk. The dining hall was cluttered with servants holding an impromptu tea on hastily assembled tables, serving commoner and petty Sevolite friends and retainers.

Erien and Ranar passed swiftly through the other rooms into Family Hall.

Here, they found Tessitatt. She stood with a hand on the library door, at one end of the wide corridor decorated tastefully in Earth green and Monatese turquoise. There was no sense of having disturbed her in the act of opening the door, but rather in a state of paralysis in which the act of beginning to open it had seemed too irrelevant to finish.

Ranar peeled off, with a touch of Erien's elbow, and went to comfort Di Mon's niece. Tessitatt let him touch her, raising no objection even to the gross familiarity of his shepherding her through the door with a hand across her back and at one elbow. It was as if Di Mon's aura endorsed Ranar with its trust although Tessitatt had not been told the nature of the love which had sat so uneasily with Di Mon. It caused Erien a pang to see how surely Green Hearth was still Di Mon's.

Tatt's door was further down. Branstatt stood guard, looking unkempt, unhappy and misplaced in a blood-stained tech's uniform suitable for the UnderDocks.

"What happened?" Erien had to know.

The green-eyed errant inhaled with an effort. "We walked into something bigger than we were," he said flatly.

Erien waited, hardly breathing.

"You know that I found Asher?" Branstatt continued. "She wanted to see Tatt. I went ahead to scout, to make sure there was nothing . . . waiting for us. Gods," Branstatt leaned his head back against the wood paneled walls. "If I'd just brought Asher upstairs then . . . but he was determined to offer her protection in person, so we went back down. She was packing to clear out—she didn't say why, but I know a frightened woman when I see one. The door was locked, and a venting good lock it was, too, but they sprung it with no warning. There were four of them," he said, in answer to Erien's questioning look. "Tatt's an Octagon trained duelist, not a street fighter," Branstatt said, in anguish. "He knows nothing about fighting gangs."

Erien said, feeling cold, "Go on."

"I didn't do so well either. We'd all be dead, but Charous and Drasous came through that door like they'd been launched off a spinning hub, and they were armed with needle guns. Tatt killed one, they killed two and the other one got away."

"Tatt?"

"We didn't know he'd been hit until he folded up. He'd been stabbed in the heart. We thought we'd lost him, but Asher made us get him upstairs into these hidden labs and started pushing instruments into his chest. That woman has hullsteel for nerves. But she called it right, because he's still alive. Not good—she couldn't get at all the damage—but he's alive. Green Hearth has been like a kicked-over anthill since we brought him back."

Not dead, Erien thought. *Not dead.* He could breathe again. He could think again. "How did Ameron's *gorarelpul* come to be down there? Was Asher under suspicion of something? Or were they following you?"

"What?" Branstatt said distractedly. "No, not us, I'm nearly sure. Tatt was adamant that we not bring trouble down on—Erien! I don't know what I need, or want, of you but—this is Tatt!" Branstatt's eyes filled up with an excess of emotion.

I am frightening him, Erien realized, *by not being more demonstrative. Creating distrust even?* But he was as inhibited in his emotional vocabulary as Horth could be with words. The more he felt, the harder it was to let it out.

"Is Asher with him now?" he said instead.

Branstatt shook his head, sharply, as though to clear it. "She's in custody, here, in Green Hearth, on Tatt's authority. That was the best I could think—"

There was a sudden upswell of noise from the direction of the private parlor, where the Throat opened into Family Hall.

Tessitatt came out of the library.

"What's that?" Ranar asked, standing beside her.

Her face lightened of its grief as she said, "Ameron."

The tall Ava came through the door, shedding followers. Only Charous stayed with him. He went straight to Tessitatt, who offered him her sword hand which he clasped in a firm acceptance, their arms laid elbow to elbow: a spontaneous reaffirmation of allegiance. And comfort, Erien saw.

"Drasous is with him?" asked Ameron.

"Yes!"

"He will live," Ameron assured Tatt's mother. "He will live if only to tell me, without rancor, that this is all my fault. You've seen us argue. His soul would not pass up the chance."

The appeal to *Okal Rel* raised a quiver on her lips: not out of literal belief—Monitum was proud in its skepticism—but for the sense Ameron conveyed of putting the decision back in Tatt's hands.

It struck Erien, bizarrely, that the two discussed their son. The relationship between them was utterly vassal to Ava.

"I will not let Tatt down again," promised Ameron.

"He understood why you held back, my liege," said Tessitatt. "It was prudent, under the circumstances."

"Heir Monitum's assault by criminals in the UnderDocks can hardly be construed as your fault," Ranar agreed in his own fashion.

"Prudence be damned!" Ameron flared with contempt for excuses. "He'd be dead now, if not for Charous." He shed this gratitude on her through the conduit of a hand, lighting briefly but solidly on one slight shoulder. "My thanks to you, also," he carried his thanks in swift strides to Branstatt, laying his hand on the errant captain's arm, "Though I know you would shield him with your body, for your own love."

"If he'd but let me, Ava." Branstatt rallied at this brave exchange of sentiment.

Ameron smiled.

Erien began to move aside and was surprised by Ameron's other hand falling on his nearer arm. From Ameron's side Charous counseled Erien with her eyes to tolerate the physical detention. She looked, herself, he thought, a touch uncomfortable. If there were more behind this than unhappy chance, she well deserved to.

Still holding Branstatt's arm, Ameron looked at Erien. Then, with the confidence of monarchs, he let both go.

That was all. He pursued no claim beyond this physical inclusion in a family grief.

Commiseration over, Ameron was all action.

"Ranar," declared the Ava, "I will acknowledge Rire, in you, tomorrow. Enough is enough."

Tessitatt shoved forward. "You could end tomorrow liege of nothing more than Monitum!"

"Then it will be honestly!" Ameron fired back at her.

"It's reckless!" Tessitatt stood her ground.

Ameron cocked an eyebrow at her. "You mean, Di Mon would not approve. What about you, Regent Monitum?"

She frowned. "You are right; I give voice to my uncle's point of view. Your security came before anything else, with him. But I speak for myself, too. I do not approve of you taking a risk like this, now, for this reason. You are overreacting, because of Tatt."

"Am I?" said Ameron. He consulted the grief around the room, including, inexorably, Erien's. "No," said the Ava, "reacting too late, perhaps."

The Ava spoke next with finality. "I know what I am doing, Tessitatt. I have not, for some time, and put caution before acting out of my convictions. Look what it has brought about. I am Ava. I will not have my Justice Minister," he promoted Ditatt to his coveted post, over-ruling the unvoiced protest in Tessitatt's opened mouth, "ambushed in the UnderDocks without consequences. This happened because I feared, publicly, to defend slander aimed at Rire. Others have been nobler." He flicked a glance at Erien. Then he confronted Ranar with, "Tomorrow I will recognize Rire."

Ranar received the Ava's stare with quiet satisfaction.

Tessitatt protested. "But—"

"Enough!" Ameron would not entertain further protest. Tessitatt fell silent.

"What do you expect will be the outcome?" Ranar asked, soberly, in English. The ancient Earth language was used among the educated Monatese as a refuge from status laden Gelack.

Ameron noted the move into English with a slight frown, but accepted it as an insider Monatese choice, not a challenge—this time—to his Sevolite superiority.

"That will depend on many things," Charous answered for Ameron, which appeared to be normal. "Including Pureblood Erien," she said, and asked Ameron, "Will you acknowledge him?"

Ameron snapped, "Of course."

He had no choice in that, thought Erien. The word was out and would be spreading fast.

Ameron looked prickly. Charous had no qualms, despite that, about giving him a verbal nudge. "Erien appears to have some influence with Liege Nersal, and, apparently, the Princess Luthan Dem H'Us."

She had made up for lost time concerning him, Erien noted with involuntary admiration, and despite an instinctive resentment at this proof that he had been subject to her professional attention.

"Be that as it may, or not," said Ameron, turning to Erien, "it is up to Liege Nersal and Admiral H'Us where they bestow their Oaths. What of your own, son of Dem'Vrel and of Lor'Vrel? Which will claim you?" Ameron met Erien's eyes, proudly, just for a moment. "Choose now."

It seemed, all at once, that there were none but the two of them in the room. The regal weight of a dismissal, bordering on exile from his Gelack roots in Monitum, hung over the words and the Ava's grave study of Erien, as he waited for his son's response.

Ranar began to say, "Of course he—"

Ameron silenced the Reetion with a raised palm.

For Erien, the Ava was prepared to wait, Vrellish gray eyes sustaining contact with Lorel patience.

Erien felt calm. "I will swear to you, tomorrow, Ava. As I was always meant to."

Ameron only nodded. "You must tell Ev'rel. She is waiting for more than the public news of Tatt, in the Azure Lounge. Convey my respects. Whoever is Ava tomorrow, we will still have work to do and I believe you have noticed that she can be reasonable."

"First," Erien had to ask, "may I see Ditatt?"

Ameron nodded. "Tell Drasous, who attends him, that I will want his report when he deems it safe to leave his patient's bedside."

Erien took his leave. Ameron called after him down Family Hall, in Gelack *rel*-peerage. "You will find us in the Breakfast Room when you are done!"

"What is for lunch?" Ameron immediately asked Tessitatt.

Behind him, Erien heard Tessitatt answer, incredulously, "We're going to eat? Now?"

Erien left them to look in on Tatt and to convey Ameron's orders to Drasous, the medtech-trained *gorarelpul* who was attending him. A moment was all he could cope with for now. Tatt, in any case, was unconscious.

In the Azure lounge, Ev'rel was standing with her back to the door, undefended, studying a portrait of Di Mon, the late Liege Monitum. Beneath the dark purple of her cloak her shoulders stiffened slightly, but she let a moment elapse before turning. Composing her face, Erien thought. As he himself would have.

All the likeness he had resisted seeing in Amel, or could not find in Ameron, he saw in her. It made what he had to do hard.

"Ah, Erien," she said. He wondered whom she might have been expecting, or bracing herself against. "How is Heir Monitum?"

He started to give the prepared, factual response: As well as could be expected: badly wounded, but likely to live. Instead he said, "Very . . . still." For Tatt's composed stillness had been truly shocking. Tatt was seldom still, and never still and composed. Erien remembered him sprawled across his bed in unruly possession, the puzzle or toy or wooden sword—never book—he had been clutching still gripped in one or both little hands, a drift of other playthings spilled across pillows and sheets and floor. Laid out straight under the neat covers, Tatt looked lifeless, even though his chest rose with each breath.

She looked away. "He will live," she said, after a moment. She returned steady, dark eyes to his. "He was fortunate to have had such good medical treatment."

Erien remembered Amel tricking information about Asher out of Tatt, and Asher's face at the duel when Ev'rel stopped to talk. Charous must have forced Asher to attend. And she must have been watching Asher's clinic, afterwards. Erien could not put all the pieces together, but decided not to speak of Asher now, with Ev'rel.

"Yes," was all he said. "It was very fortunate that Charous and Drasous were so close at hand."

"Was anyone else injured? Or killed?"

"Three of the assailants, according to Branstatt. There were at least four."

"An unfortunate coincidence," she said, with a quick frown, "that Heir Monitum should be at such a place, at such a time. The assailants were, I suppose, after drugs?"

Erien did not offer information.

"You think it was more than that?" Ev'rel remarked. "What a dangerous thing for a Royalblood to be doing, investigating kill-shows in the UnderDocks. I suppose, after this, he will be forced to stop."

"I do not think anything short of death will stop him," Erien said, "and even death will find it difficult."

Ev'rel caught her breath at Erien's vehemence, then smiled.

"You are very fond of Heir Monitum," she observed, "even though you have not met for years." She sighed. "When all this is over, we shall have to talk about your time on Rire. Your insights will be useful."

"Avim," Erien said, "Ameron has decided to acknowledge Rire tomorrow. I have therefore promised him my Oath."

She went very still, again, her expression held calm against all observation. Only a slight quickness in her breathing betrayed agitation.

What was she thinking? he wondered. She had seemed prepared not to presume upon their relationship to conduct business; was she equally capable of accepting a relationship if his Oath went to Ameron?

It was harder keeping silent in the face of her silence than keeping silent in the face of Horth's. But he waited.

"That is," she said at last, "a pity. Still, we shall see what transpires tomorrow. At any other Swearing, your Oath would have given Ameron all he needed. But packaged with the acceptance of Rire, the outcome may be different. Horth Nersal, for one, will not follow him so readily. Watching them all weigh the balance will be interesting." She gave him a dry smile, her version, perhaps, of the duelist's defiance, but too cool and aware and devoid of recklessness. "Another day, perhaps, Erien. But remember, you are still my son."

"I am well aware of that," he said, with quiet honesty.

He saw her to the hearth entrance, and watched her cross Fountain Court towards Lilac Hearth in the company of the hand of Dem'Vrellish errants she had brought. He was just about to re-enter Green Hearth when Amy and another woman came out of White Hearth. The second woman was Highlord Ayrium, of the Purple Alliance, the woman said to be Ameron's *cher'st* and acknowledged as Amy's mother. Even without the clues of Ayrium's braid and Purple Alliance badge, he could have guessed who she was. She had a dose of Golden beauty, from her hybrid Demoran father, robustly expressed in a Vrellish style despite her blue eyes, and was reputed to be court-class with her sword. Amy and her mother were headed for Green Hearth's door, where Erien waited.

Ayrium greeted him with a nod, and a brilliant sparkle in her extremely blue eyes.

Amy said, "Erien, come with us."

He followed the two women deeper into the Throat, to the door of the Breakfast Hall, and was just in time to catch the uncommon sight of Ameron losing track of his own words at the sight of Ayrium. Golden hair, cropped short enough to wave; worn, white flight-leathers with purple piping and a small crest showing a silhouette of purple hills; white gloves. A slight swagger to a confidently female walk. Ayrium, like Ameron, imparted energy to a room, but whereas Ameron's energies were force and charge, she brought brightness with her. Her smile was luminous. "Hello, lover," she greeted the Ava, in Killing Reach patois.

"Welcome to court, Highlord Ayrium," Ameron said, somewhat frostily, but their gazes held and promised, while everyone around the couple studiously rearranged their eyes.

Ayrium ran her hand over her hair, and broke the spell. "I heard about Tatt at the docks. How is he?"

"Uncertain, but hopeful," said Ameron, getting over his pique at her mildly rude greeting.

"You tell him from me that before he goes down to the UnderDocks again, he's taking lessons from my mother and Vrenn. What she doesn't know, that pirate does."

Ameron did not approve of her bluff humor, and frowned to let her know.

"I hate to make your day worse," Ayrium said, "but I didn't come just for the Swearing. The Reetions are, uh, well—upset."

"Upset?" Ranar stood up.

Everyone abandoned their chairs to rearrange themselves, Ameron and Ranar standing closest to Ayrium.

"For one thing," Ayrium said, "Rire is demanding the extradition of Amel on some charge to do with Ann and arbiters. We have that solely on rumor. The Nersallian blockade has effectively shut down the usual leaks between *SkyBlue* and *BlindEye Station*. But the Nersallians let one of my pilots go out to meet the Reetion envoy sent to deliver this, to you, Ranar." She hooked open a flap on her jacket with a thumb and extracted an envelope bearing a Reetion motto. "I don't read other people's mail," she said, "but given the tone of the rumors, I guess I don't have to. I bet it is a diplomatic recall."

Ameron plucked it smoothly out of the air as it passed from Ayrium's hand to Ranar's. Watched by them all, he scanned it. Then he looked at Ranar.

"Messages," he said, "can go missing." He looked at his *cher'st* to see if she would challenge that assumption.

"We live to serve," Ayrium said, "and to take the blame."

Ameron made to hand the message to Ranar. "No," Ranar said sharply, and raised both hands, palm outwards. "If I am not to have seen it, I do not want to see it."

"Hah," said the Ava, in good humor. "I shall make a Lorel of you yet, Reetion."

With a flick of his wrist he dropped the dispatch into Erien's hands.

It was, as they all guessed, a recall. Reading it, Erien appreciated Ameron's wisdom in giving it into the hands of the only person, beside Ranar, who would be able to read not only the words, but the tone.

"They are upset," he said. "This is very strongly worded."

Ranar twitched, his hand coming halfway out, but he mastered his urge to read the message.

Bluntly, Erien asked Ameron, "Do you know what it was that Amel did?"

Ameron bridled at the tone of accusation. His narrow nostrils flared as he inhaled. "I asked him to gauge Rire's temper," he said curtly.

"And he will have done it in his own inimitable fashion," Ayrium murmured. She added to Ranar, "Amel messed with your arbiters."

"That is not possible," Ranar insisted.

"Perhaps it is something else," said Ameron. "You said the rumors mentioned Ann, of *SkyBlue Station*. Find Amel," he ordered Charous. He looked back at Erien, his eyes hot with muted temper. "When this is done, if I am Ava still, then the Reetions are your problem."

It took a moment for Erien to realize what Ameron meant, in this new context of himself as the Ava's Pureblood son. Ameron was still not taking the Reetions seriously. He considered them a burden, or a nuisance. Erien drew breath to stress what the tone of the letter implied, and how seriously the Reetions would view arbiter manipulation. Ameron's eyes were glittering; he would not listen to explanations. "I do not have," Erien resorted to, instead, "the experience for a major diplomatic role."

"Perhaps," his father said, "but I would spare anyone else your admonitions." He gestured to an empty chair with the flick of one long hand. "Sit. Eat. And after—find something fit to wear for tomorrow."

Chapter XIX

Amel's sleep left a sense of time passing without defined content to fill it up. In it, nebulous handling resolved to stillness then slowly to quiet awareness.

He hurt, but it was nothing that he couldn't handle. He opened his eyes.

Above him was the ceiling of the workshop. The room was quiet. He felt fragile, lying on his back with his limbs extended, the rubberized floor firm beneath him and the air in the room slightly cool on his bare skin. He was naked.

Ev'rel sat beside him on the floor, refilling a tumbler from a thermos. The hot drink spiked the air with the smell of cloves and Monatese Turquoise whiskey. She was wearing a dressing gown. Her expression, in profile, was as distant as the stars.

When she looked like that, he knew, she ached inside; her soul stretched as thin as the great, hungry void of his poem.

"Ev'rel . . . ?" He tried to move. He was bound at ankles and wrists by cords. "Ev—" Her name broke up into a breathy fear-sound in his mouth.

She turned around. Her hand reached for her medical bag to drag it close. His heart rate took a sudden bound as panic overwhelmed him. He tugged. His limbs confirmed they could not move. A feeling of exposure fluttered over his naked skin, making hot nodes about points of vulnerability: groin, throat, his throbbing arm—and he was entombed within a white chamber, utterly immobilized.

He came to himself with a voiced gasp.

"Bad dreams?" Ev'rel remarked.

His heart hammered as if against eight skim'facs of thrust. This could not be happening! Not again! They had come so far! He could make it stop, he told himself, if only he could give her nothing, if he could make himself invulnerable. His faith in the possibility was as bright as life, and fragile as blown glass.

"Let's have a look at that elbow." She probed the swollen flesh to test the integrity of bones and tendons while he schooled himself not to reward her too much.

"Only a torn muscle," she decided, "maybe a stretched tendon."

Recent pain and fear of pain lay on his nerves like a map. He watched her face. It was hauntingly beautiful. Sad. He could not accept that they were here again, after eighteen years, with him helpless and her toying with her desolation like a torn cuticle. He decided she was only trying to frighten him. She'd let him up.

"I am going to self-destruct," she said. "Is that how the poem ends? Is space destroyed for mastering the pilot's soul?" She drank from her tumbler glass and set it down, drawing her knees to her chest. Her hair was a raven mass framing eyes that were eerily dull. "It is always about dominance. Even with you and I and Mira. Your approach is subtle. Hers was to deny me my own strengths and the powers of my station, as those with less power always must—by claiming the moral high ground."

"M-Mira?" he stuttered. Could Ev'rel have Mira?

Her expression warmed with broken trust. "I know you have been keeping her in the UnderDocks, and running her errands I suppose. Did you find her down there when you went looking? Or was it something that you organized, together, from the day she left us?"

His throat constricted.

"Answer me!" She struck his face on impulse, then waited for him to recover as she retreated into coldness once more. "I want to know. I want to know how great a fool I have been to trust a *slaka* whore."

He struggled with the animal urge to pit his strength against bonds that he knew would hold. He dared not become frantic. "Mira is no threat to you," he promised, pleased to hear his own voice sound so calm.

"Maybe she was not," Ev'rel allowed, "but she is now. Whether Heir Monitum dies or not."

"Tatt?" Amel clutched at slipping self-control.

"I did not know about Mira, of course," Ev'rel reduced their agony to business with a conversational tone. She despised any need that was personal. It was why she hated where she loved. He had lived in the fault zone of that love for his entire life as a Sevolite, by the terms of a promise made when Erien was an infant. It was territory he knew. Reminding himself of that, he began to relax as she talked.

"I did not know about Mira," said Ev'rel, "that is, until Charous dredged her up. Mira said, 'The account is cleared.' " Ev'rel drank from her tumbler and put it down. "It is not, of course."

"I did not conspire with Mira," Amel told her.

She cast him a look of skeptical admonishment for presuming her credulous.

"I did keep her, as you say, in the UnderDocks," Amel quickly followed up. He realized with a belated shock that she had been talking down to him as if he was a commoner and he had unconsciously granted her the right in his own pronouns. Instead of challenging her grammar in Gelack, he slipped into English now. She had learned it in Green Hearth in her youth.

"She—Mira was working with the real Asher," Amel told her, "the medtech whose clinic she took over."

Ev'rel's eyes narrowed at his linguistic evasion, but he was afraid to take the English back now and went on. "Asher hired Mira, when she'd run out of other work, freelance. They were partners by the time he died, trying to implement her plan to save plague victims. He was trapped in the plague zone when it was sterilized. The clinic was trashed, too, in a backlash. Mira took Asher's name, to disguise herself, and tried to start over, but she'd lost a lot. Too much."

He remembered Mira then, depressed, a two-year-old waif—Mona—clinging to her arm. If he could just explain it properly, maybe Ev'rel would understand. Mira had been her friend once. The only friend she had ever had. "Mira didn't want my help," Amel remembered that, also, and hoped that it might ring true. "She hated me! But she needed—"

"To use you," Ev'rel snorted. Her mocking tone stuck a place where he was vulnerable. "You fool! Mira does not need anyone but her lab. What do you do for her? Let her conduct experiments on you?"

"No!" Anger taunted his helplessness.

"I suppose," she drawled, dangling the tumbler over her knees in one hand, "you kept her filled in on my progress with—what was her English for it? Sadism."

"No," he said. "I have never told anyone anything that is private between us. That was my promise. I've kept it."

"You are wondering if I'll keep mine," her eyes tracked across his prone body to her medical bag. It was leather. The same bag that Mira had taught her how to use before Amel came to live with them, wracked by the visitor probe's aftermath.

He felt sick to his stomach but there was nothing in his digestive tract for nausea to work on.

"What fail-safes have you set up to destroy me, now that I've discovered Mira?" Ev'rel asked.

She startled him with the cold question. He stuttered, "N-none."

"You may be that stupid; Mira is not."

"Sh-she was living—as an UnderDocks medtech. What could she have—"

"Heir Monitum was poking around the UnderDocks! She's told him! About us."

"No! If she was helping Tatt, it wasn't—"

Her hand dropped into his groin. Pureblood fingers dug into his scrotum. "Go on," she said, "explain it to me. Convince me she would never do me harm."

"I can't—if you don't want to—listen!"

She hurt him so much he had to stop, shoulders pressed back into the floor, breath held and eyes half-closed, helpless to prevent himself from pulling at his bonds.

When she'd had enough of watching that, she stopped squeezing and began, gently, to massage his groin.

"Ev'rel . . . " He shuddered, searching for her through his fear and her anger, breathing back under his control. "What has gone wrong?"

"My life?" she suggested in aloof amusement. "Yours. We can never fit back in, you know. Not once our illusions are shattered and we recognize life's bone-deep truths. We survive as we are, or we're doomed."

He stifled a fresh surge of questions, needing to rest, and to listen. There had to be a way out. There was so much more between them, now, than when he had come to her, sick with clear dreams, eighteen years ago.

"I do not shrink from what I am," she said. He heard limbs sliding against the floor as she rearranged herself, not touching him anymore, a voice in the darkness that was closing around them both. "That is honor, of a sort."

He heard the tiny, distinctive release of a latch on a case of needles that he thought she did not have anymore. He closed his eyes rather than watch her draw the dose, concentrating on her words alone.

"The *pol* things which the Reetions maimed you to believe in," Ev'rel lectured, pointedly returning now to Gelack, "they are just a trap. Comforting lies, like *Okal Rel* and every other system of morals. We are utterly alone and locked in competition for what we want. Few can win. So many must be reconciled to loss. That is what *pol* feelings are for. That, and to attempt to hold the *rel* back with phantom threats of punishment and reward. We are respected according to the power which we hold over others. Only the powerful need not bow. For me to have my will, someone else must yield theirs up. Including you," she paused, looking down, the Rush needle drawn. "The rest, dear fool, is just negotiations. You did well in the last round. So well, in fact, I see no way out for either of us now. I should have made you child-gift all those years ago."

A desolation welled up from his buried storm of foulness. So much of his experience confirmed her point of view, but did he have to accept it for so meaningless a reason as it happening to be true? It negated all the treasures of his soul. On the heels of rejection came the suspicion that he believed because he was too weak to win; too maimed to take what he desired. She was not. And she would.

He did not care what she did to him anymore. He closed his eyes, willing himself erased from the scene by any means available. There were none.

She kissed his parted lips. His eyes sprang open, catching hers by surprise with their sudden life.

"You are," she said, "beautiful. For your very wounds." She anointed his temple with a gentle touch. He shuddered, responding to her like the strings of a tri-lyre being tuned by an expert hand. Every detail about her compelled his attention now. She was both looser and more sudden in her movements than usual. Relaxed. She straddled his naked waist, showing flashes of thigh and stomach. Her dressing gown bunched under her. She straightened it out; her buttocks on his abdomen felt firm and warm. The contact reassured him somehow.

"Where is Mira?" he found the strength to ask.

"Mira," she said, "is in Green Hearth, where she will gain a hearing I can ill-afford—she saved Heir Monitum. I didn't mean to get him, of course. Much too dangerous. I meant to get her. He was there, that's all." She leaned forward, spreading her hands over his chest, across and down. The confusing sensations of her weight and strong, caressing hands perturbed his expression. She was drunk on anticipation of what she meant to do. He couldn't stop feeling the sexual resonance despite the pain he knew it would involve. In the grip of Rush, the two would become one, and identity itself was squeezed out.

"She was trying to use Heir Monitum to destroy me." Ev'rel put the loaded needle down on his chest, to reach for her tumbler on the floor. When she had drunk the last swallow she set the tumbler's warm base on his stomach, below the case of needles. "Now Erien has rejected me and Mira is with him in Green Hearth. He might listen to her. Ameron would not, although Charous might, perhaps. It doesn't matter!" She shoved away her empty tumbler. It rolled in an arc, wider at the rim than the base, and came to rest on the workshop's rubberized dance floor. Ev'rel shook her hair back. "D'Lekker knows. Mira is alive." She laughed, then her face convulsed in mortal terror and she pinched the bridge of her nose.

Understanding what she feared revived his hope. "Ev'rel—it doesn't have to happen. No one has to find out. Let me help you!"

"It is too late for that," she told him bleakly. She drew her shoulders back. Her breasts swayed inside her robe. "You forgave. Mira will not. Now she is in Green Hearth where she'll do me harm. She is there.

I made sure. I could not tell from Erien. Very closed-mouth about it, he was, when he ever so honorably turned my offer down. Perhaps he's already been told. And that would be it, wouldn't it? She will expose me as a *slaka'st*." She picked the needle up. "And you know, love, what that makes you. Two cc's at five percent to start?"

Staged doses, Amel thought, and forced himself past the fact. "Mira won't tell Erien," he insisted. "Who would believe her? She doesn't trust any Sevolite!"

"Trust?" Ev'rel raised an eyebrow, the needle still held steady in her hand. "It is not about trust," she said, and lowered her hands to rest on the bare skin of his torso, "but since you bring it up—you do not trust me and you never have. That is how you have kept your side of our precious bargain! You have kept me dangling for eighteen years in the hope that you would trust me enough to child-gift as I need you to. But you never will. Forgive me, yes. But that is only thanks to what the Reetions did to you."

"No."

"You would forgive anyone anything."

"No!" He felt stronger the more drastic her claims grew.

She set the needle point against the skin below his navel.

"I don't trust you," he gulped. "All right. Should I have?"

She smiled very slightly. "No."

"Ev'rel," he said, reasonably, "let me up. We can work this through."

She put the needle down, and touched his left wrist where the cord held it. His fingers remained, carefully, relaxed. But her touch floated back down his body to the waiting needle.

"No," she said. "You will want to save Mira. Mira's kept you from me, all these years, not your Purple Alliance friends and your Reetion *mekan'st*." Her Gelack pronouns raised Mira to an equal, in hatred. "Mira uses you as easily as I do. She, too, knows where you're flawed. But she does it better. I owe her for that. I owe her and she'll know—" she stroked the undamaged musculature of his torso from throat to stomach, where the needle waited, "—she'll know I'll take it out on you. She never could stand that."

"Ev'rel!" he cried, and watched, helpless, as she shifted to administer the needle. "Don't!"

Clear dreams clutched at his attention but did not displace the rising sensitivity already spreading where the needle had entered. This was stage one. It was painless, except for inflaming the discomfort of his existing hurts. Sexually, it made him feel as if he'd been petting for too long.

She turned on music, dimmed the lights, and set his image dancing on the walls. He waited with eyes closed, mind darting, too finely balanced between reality and clear dreams to find words to talk. She announced her return by dropping the silk scarf which they used to bind his hands in their surrogate ritual. It wafted across his closed eyes.

"Need a blindfold?" she mocked.

He shook the scarf off.

"Ev'rel," he said, helped by a faint ghost of anger. "You're drunk. Think this through when you're sober. You know you should."

"I'm not that drunk."

He wet his lips and pleaded, "Don't."

"I really should kill you," she confessed. "That would be best for both of us."

He rolled his eyes to find the needle case. It was there. Open, on the floor.

Staged doses, he thought. *You could do so much more, so much longer, with a* slaka *whom you knew was a highborn.* Before she was done, it would be agony just to be touched, but he felt neither hatred nor courage, both good, *rel* emotions. All he felt was a bleakness in his soul, like rot.

"Ev'rel," he said, blinking at the tears that filled his eyes, "I can't cope."

"I don't want you to cope," she explained, staring down, sympathetic but aloof. "You really don't understand, do you?" She picked up the second needle, dose already drawn. "It's essential. That you hate it. Do you understand now? I have wanted to do this so often, when you have meddled with my methods. On Demora. With D'Lekker. And every time I wondered when you would desert me for some *mekan'st.* I will win this round."

"No." He shook his head in rejection. "Winning and losing isn't all it is about. You love me!" His voice dropped to a whisper. "You resent it. But I know you do."

"Perhaps I do," she said. "Perhaps you'd call it love. I just don't know. But I must eliminate Mira. And I must figure out what to do about D'Lekker, too." She was talking to herself now. He listened with shame, devastated to the bedrock of his own love.

"If—you have to kill me," he watched her face, trying to appeal to the woman with whom he had shared so much, "please, do not do it with Rush. Even if you have to do it slowly—not with Rush."

She blinked, and focused on him once more, with a look which was as tender as leaves falling on his heart. "I won't kill you, Amel. Don't be absurd!" Her voice rose at an affront which he lacked the strength to fathom any more, and fell again with love. "You are my own."

He did not try to talk to her after that.

WHEN HE WOKE, Amel knew that he had passed the night all but comatose. Thirst woke him. Thirst was simple. He drank. The drink offered was a warm, sweetened broth, with a protein-rich aroma which he recognized as a concoction the Monatese gave over-exposed pilots and sick children. A spasm hiccuped the liquid up.

"Careful!" D'Lekker admonished, and took away the cup, laying him back down. Amel's weakness was that of exhaustion, with a veneer of *klinoman*, wearing off. He felt like a beanbag doll. Post-Rush sensitivity rose through the dispersing wisps of sedative, promising a bodyscape of muscles wadded into knots. He did not dare to move.

They were still in the workshop.

D'Lekker hovered at the side of a narrow cot taken from a servant's room. Crisp sheets held Amel in, with a quilt of Ev'rel's to stave his coldness off. His pillow was one of hers. Soft.

"Okay now?" D'Lekker asked.

Amel found the question hard to grasp. He realized, with a burden of sick disappointment, that he had not imagined it would be possible to wake up. He was hungry. That also seemed ludicrous.

His skin was sensitive. Even the touch of the bed clothes was becoming intolerable, particularly between his knees and waist where the post-cramp knots were worst.

"Wh—" Amel swallowed over what felt like gravel in his throat. He had been screaming, he recalled. He was hoarse. "Where is . . . "

"I'll get you more *klinoman*," D'Lekker began to get up.

"No!" Amel called him back. His voice sounded sloppy, burred and sluggish. It was his only weapon. Wearily he smoothed it out. "I've got to get up, Lek." Just saying it made him feel faint.

"Not likely! Not in that condition." D'Lekker sounded impressed. Amel did not want his admiration. Not for enduring this! Anger gave him strength he didn't think he had.

"D'Lekker . . . " Amel pushed himself over on an elbow, and had to pause. The position relieved the discomfort of the bed clothes against his groin, but his muscles shuddered at being asked to work. "You've got to help me," Amel gasped, "and Ev'rel. You've got to get me to Green Hearth—no," he realized. "No—I can't be seen like this. But I need your help!"

D'Lekker listened with an anxious look.

"I thought I told you not to let him talk," Ev'rel said coolly from beyond them both.

D'Lekker sprang up. "I wasn't going to!" he cried, indignant.

Amel let his left elbow collapse beneath his quaking body. The pillow was soft against his face. It was clean. So was he. He was pathetically grateful to Ev'rel for that.

Ev'rel's skirt swished into his field of vision, all solid velvet belled out by petticoats. She moved a chair to the bedside and sat down. Her hair was done up in a style which, like her dress, expressed more than her usual concession to Demish fashion. She looked intelligent and well-mannered, an arch statesman and a vulnerable Demish woman. Amel felt a bewildered touch of awe, unable to associate this vision with the torture he had endured the night before, as if all the ugliness adhered to him, leaving her unmarred.

"You have plans," he realized.

She arranged his black hair on his white brow. "Nothing you'll approve of."

"Mira?"

"I'm sorry," she said it without malice, merely matter-of-fact.

Her quiet, objective finality denuded him of hope. He closed his eyes. She took his hand.

"The solution came to me while I watched you sleep," she told him. "Something you said last night put me on the track. Who will believe Mira? Who can she trust? It is not her knowledge but her credibility which I must attack. I spent the early hours finding out enough to damn her thoroughly with H'Us. He'll get her out of Green Hearth for me, and see her executed for what she has in her back rooms." Slowly, she relinquished his limp hand. "I know you'll hate me for it now. But you don't hate very well, or very long."

He opened his eyes again. "Don't hurt Mira."

She stood up. "It is a relief, you know, getting back to the point where you balk. You won't forgive me for silencing Mira? I believe you! The Reetions made you incapable of hating for your own sake but—" she smiled, "—you are my son. Your will is quite formidable when you are able to apply it in another's cause. I will break you in the end, though. What did it take in the UnderDocks? Six months? You will child-gift for me yet, and be glad of it, Amel."

"We could make the Reetions cure him," D'Lekker interjected from the sidelines. Amel watched Ev'rel's warm expression cool as she turned with thin patience to her other son.

"Yes," she said, slowly. "Perhaps we could."

"We are going to conquer Rire?" D'Lekker asked.

Amel thought about Ann, and the defense he had helped her prepare against just such an invasion. At the time it had felt hypothetical. It felt horribly real now. Could he keep that from Ev'rel? For how long? For that matter, how could he bear not to volunteer the truth, knowing what Vretla Vrel and D'Therd might be heading into if they tried to take *SkyBlue*? But if they knew, they would only be more determined to destroy Ann, and more likely to succeed for being forewarned. It seemed cruel that he should still know secrets so large. He felt very weak and small.

"Whether or not we invade Rire hinges on today's Swearings," Ev'rel informed D'Lekker. "There is the open question of Liege Nersal, though if he even abstains—yes, perhaps. I will agree to conquest if it makes me Ava. First though, there is something very important which I need you to do. Something, D'Lekker, I will always be grateful to you for."

Amel opened his eyes in time to see D'Lekker nod. He looked proud, Amel thought. A child pleasing his mother.

"Let Amel rest a while now," Ev'rel instructed. "Then, when we are all at the Swearing, I want you to take him to the UnderDocks. Kandral can help you get him there privately. Take him to the Rose Garden; no one is watching or using it anymore. I am leaving you a good supply of *klinoman*. Keep him asleep with that. Use the needles in the case which are already drawn before you start the new vial. Kandral will bring you supplies. We need to hide Amel until he's fit to travel to FarHome—a day or two, no more. I will send Kandral to you when it is time to go. In the meantime I trust you to look after Amel." She handed over a needle case. "Watch his breathing. And remember, do not let him talk. Do this properly, and I will be in your debt for the service." She paused to hold D'Lekker's eyes. "I am counting on you."

"You will not be disappointed," D'Lekker promised.

"He is precious to me," Ev'rel warned.

D'Lekker nodded gravely. "I know."

Ev'rel rewarded him with a smile. She knelt, then, by Amel's side, and covered his mouth and nose, depriving him of oxygen.

"Goodbye love," she murmured, "until later. When we have more time."

Lying on his good arm, Amel tried to raise his badly swollen right one to resist her. She forced it down.

"Remember," he heard her telling D'Lekker as he blacked out. "Don't let him talk."

AMEL CAME TO BEING HAULED UP. It was nearly an hour later. His body had greedily slept without regard for circumstances. Being lifted woke him with a body-wide slap of shock.

"Lek!" he gasped.

D'Lekker laid him down again on the cot. He had stripped off the covers. Over the shock of pain, Amel felt the coolness of his nakedness studded with stiffening bruises and the aftermath of Rush-cramps.

He could not cope until D'Lekker opened Ev'rel's case and gave him a small dose of *klinoman*. Slowly the pain became bearable, at the expense of the control he had softening under the influence of the drug.

D'Lekker reached to block his mouth and nose as Ev'rel had.

"No!" Amel gasped. His half-brother paused.

"I've got to do this to you," D'Lekker warned.

Amel nodded, groping for a way to slow him down. "I'm afraid."

D'Lekker found that reasonable enough. He cleared his throat. "Ev'rel said not to let you talk."

"Please? Just—until I can cope."

D'Lekker frowned. "You don't care about me. You pretend, but you don't. I know that now."

"I did," Amel said, in all honesty, "when you were little. I cared a lot."

D'Lekker's mouth turned down, hard, in a spasm and relaxed. He blinked, twice, rapidly. "So I wasn't supposed to grow up?"

Amel shook his head. "I don't know, Lek. I—just don't know. You were badly treated." He hesitated. "You still are."

D'Lekker cascaded into an outburst of emotional confession. "Yesterday—in the bedroom?—I don't know why I—it just seemed that was how it had to be, I mean, with you—I'm not a Reetion!"

"No," Amel said softly. "It is possible not to be a . . . Reetion . . . but to get confused."

"It is confusing," D'Lekker latched onto the excuse. His agitation showed in his posture now, the earlier bravado winding down. "I love Mother. I've always loved her, but you're the only one she loves and she does things like this to you." He paused, chewing on a lip as he tried to work it out. "You were nice to me, when I was little. She never was." He shook it off. "But she cares about me now. She never used to, but she does. Because I can help her, with you."

"Do you think," Amel ventured, frightened, onto treacherous ground, "she will trust you with what you know?"

D'Lekker twitched. "She told me not to let you talk."

"Why, do you suppose?" Amel cursed his voice for its clumsiness, mourning his refined control. He cleared his throat. "Maybe because I do care about you. Think, D'Lekker. Why the Rose Garden in the Underdocks?"

"Because it's empty."

Amel shook his head ever so little. "No. She has to package something more with Mira, to satisfy Tatt and to vindicate the Reetions for Erien. She needs a scapegoat. And she has to get rid of you because you know too much. Even if you get a chance to accuse her, it would only seem a desperate—"

"Shut up!" D'Lekker struck him. Amel's warding arm was flung across his own face by the impact. D'Lekker hauled him off the bed and shook him like a rat. "Shut up! Shut up!"

Amel's head jerked back and forth. He held on to D'Lekker's arms, his right hand feeling as useless as a rubber glove. D'Lekker was weakened in his wounded left arm. *A dance of cripples*, Amel thought.

D'Lekker hurled Amel clear. He sprawled across the bed and rolled off with an ungainly clunk. The floor hurt. Amel lay, winded, listening to D'Lekker crashing around and making terrible, stifled, sobbing sounds.

I must get up, Amel thought.

It seemed impossible.

He got one knee under him. That held. His left arm shook as it pushed against the floor.

D'Lekker seized him under the arms, from behind, and lugged him up onto the bed again. "What's she going to do?" he demanded. "How is she going to set me up?"

Amel squinted through a delirium of pain, struggling to hold himself together. "I think—" he said, "you'll be blamed—for my condition."

D'Lekker gave an anguished howl.

He believed Amel. That much was good.

Amel was certain that D'Lekker should. Ev'rel would get sympathy for casting D'Lekker as Mira's accomplice. It was the last piece of a tidy package. The contraband in Mira's clinic would be proof enough to damn Mira with H'Us, Tatt would get D'Lekker, and D'Therd would be only too glad to see Amel removed from court to recover in seclusion on FarHome. How D'Lekker was to die was all that Amel wasn't sure about. Did Ev'rel have the nerve to wait for others to act as the executioners? Or would Kandral ambush D'Lekker with a Dem'Vrellish 'rescue' of Amel, and let the Monatese help find the evidence? If he didn't do something now, Amel knew he would not find out until he was allowed to regain consciousness, on FarHome.

He could not black out!

D'Lekker appeared, brandishing the needle case at Amel. "*Klinoman*, she said," he shook the case, nostrils flaring and pinching with each breath. "I bet the extra vial is really full of Rush. They'll find me, with you like that, and Rush." His hand was white on the case. "She thinks—" he gulped. "She thinks she is so much more venting ruthless than I am! Well, she is not!"

D'Lekker's hands were clumsy with rage as he fumbled open the case and took a needle out, spurting the *klinoman* into the air to empty it.

"We'll see," said D'Lekker, "we'll see if it's Rush or not."

Amel watched in horror as D'Lekker prepared a new dose from the unused vial. Horror turned to uncomprehending pity as D'Lekker gave it to himself, not to Amel.

"Lek," he breathed, helplessly bewildered.

D'Lekker left him.

Amel managed to roll off the bed into the tangle of bed clothes on the floor. The impact made him gray out, but he did not entirely lose consciousness. Teeth gritted, he began to get up on his knees again, listening to D'Lekker struggling with Ev'rel's console.

Suddenly the lights dimmed and Amel's dancing image sprang to life upon the walls around them.

The leg Amel had under him collapsed in spasms. He fell against the bed, anchoring himself on it with his left arm, but at least he could see what was going on. D'Lekker was rummaging through Ev'rel's collection of recordings, playing a series of apparently random selections.

"Lek!" Amel called over tri-lyre music played five times too loud. The bed slipped as Amel tried for leverage to push himself up. The tri-lyre recording was replaced by a snatch of Demoran choir.

Amel lost seconds waiting for a cramp to stop, tears of pain making his dancing image shimmer as it fled, too fast, about the walls.

D'Lekker found one of Amel's arrangements of Dem'Vrellish folk music performed by a quartet of West Alcove courtesans.

The trouble with crawling, Amel discovered, was his right hand. Maybe he could drag himself somehow. He called again and was ignored.

Had D'Lekker gone mad? If he believed what Amel had said, why wouldn't he come back and talk with him? Help Amel figure something out? They had no time for tantrums!

A march played by a Reetion band came on so loud that the brass and percussion parts challenged the soundproofing of the walls.

Amel sensed, more than heard, D'Lekker approach. He looked up. D'Lekker loomed over him, flushed, his face set in bitter, blind anger and hopelessness.

Lek hauled Amel up, bracing Amel's back with his wounded arm, and pulled Amel's head back by his hair.

"I am going to kill you," D'Lekker ground out into Amel's ear, as Amel ineffectually tried to tear free of him. D'Lekker yanked Amel's body against him with a jerk of his encircling arm, making Amel gasp.

"That will hurt Mother more than anything else ever could. To do exactly what she is going to accuse me of!" D'Lekker's breath on the side of Amel's face was hot. "I'm going to kill you, but not before I show her how it's done!"

Amel barely grasped what was said, the music was so loud. He tried to respond, but D'Lekker destroyed his rationality with sheer pain by dragging him across the floor. Amel cried out. He could not even hear himself. The band's vibrations saturated air, flesh and bone.

D'Lekker fastened Amel's wrists into Ev'rel's manacles on the floor. The cords settled into the white gauze bandages wound around the rawness which the cords had made the night before.

Amel gathered all his will to draw back one leg. His muscles raged at demands which cost him agony, but he made them move. Amel's kick made D'Lekker howl. Provoked, D'Lekker shook his sword loose, which was all, Amel realized belatedly, he could really hope for now—but D'Lekker did not dispatch him where he lay, bound, on the floor. D'Lekker dropped the sword, and used his sheath to lash Amel across his chest and waist and thighs, leaving him pain-stunned.

D'Lekker shucked off his pants. Then he straddled Amel, pulling a long knife from his boot. Amel felt the weight. It was harder to isolate the pain of the boot knife as it slid into the muscle layer of his abdomen, but he sensed the foreign object's presence and his body froze in sheer suspense. D'Lekker's eyes were wild in the eerie shadows. Amel held D'Lekker's stare, willing him, please, to get it over with and drive the knife down.

D'Lekker drew the blade out straight. Amel gasped. D'Lekker cast the blade away and reached for the new wound to finds its edges. Amel dissolved into pulpy limpness, breathing in thin shudders. He felt D'Lekker's rape as a great pressure where none should be. The silly music was appropriate. This death was farce.

Amel did not notice, at first, when D'Lekker stopped. His consciousness skittered nervously over the body to which it belonged. The belonging was so very inextricable; his pilot's grip saw to that. He resented that just now. He wanted to feel distant and aloof. He wanted to be gone. At least the warm trickle down his sides promised that would not take long.

D'Lekker sunk on his knees beside him with a heart-breaking sob. *Someone should help Lek,* Amel thought. He wasn't sure why or how. It was hard work fighting his pilot's instinct to stay alert in crisis for as long as Pureblood adrenaline could inspire, but it was all that his will was fixed on, and all for which he had the courage left to hope.

CHAPTER XX

So THIS, ERIEN THOUGHT, WAS WHAT HE WAS. Across the room, from the mirror, someone looked back at him that he did not recognize. A Pureblood of Sevildom. The leather panels of his overjacket were held together by intricate braided knots which proclaimed his ancestry in as much exhaustive detail as any Demish genealogical recitation. The front fastening had taken the braid-weaver nearly an hour, and much lacing and unlacing, to accomplish; plainly, he had given little prior thought to how one should combine Lor'Vrel and Dem'Vrel. But then, Erien observed to himself a little bitterly, nobody had given much thought to accommodating the Throne Price.

Well, he was braided now, braided and dressed and decorated, his parentage proclaimed in the threaded colors of two hearths, the red and blue of Dem'Vrel and the white of Lor'Vrel. The sleeves of the jacket were a dense plaid of the three colors, and though the front leather was red, there were flashes of blue at the sides and the back was white. He felt like a placard. Beneath the jacket he wore a plain white shirt, tucked into blue trousers with narrow stripes of braid marking the side-seams. It had only been with difficulty—and some quickly regretted sarcasm—that he had stopped Ameron's valets replacing his plain sword sheath with something more elaborate.

Then there was the cape, which if anything was worse than the overjacket. It would have been attractive enough if it were worn by somebody else, Tatt, for instance; and if the red, blue and white, were merely colors, and their combination merely a pleasing design and not a measured political statement. He felt like the patchwork man. Its weight dragged his shoulders.

To be so conspicuously defined oppressed him.

Erien brushed a fingertip across the paired heavy grips which held his cloak to his jacket: another bone of contention between himself and the dressers sent from White Hearth. The clasps had arrived from

Lilac Hearth this morning, matching gold double hooks, ornamented with polished jet. The intended grips—enameled red, blue and white, of course—lay on his bedside table. Let them lie. He owed Ev'rel recognition of her gift, even to the extent of allowing her to make her mark on him.

The Sevolite in the mirror was gripping his sword belt. Only when he saw that did Erien feel the clench in his left hand. He hated this! Ill-prepared, ill-advised, thrown from one to the other and made to choose far sooner than he wanted to—he had no idea whether what he was about to do was right. Or not.

He shook out his left hand with a snap, irritated with himself now. Brooding served no purpose. If he could derive no entertainment from this harlequin costume, let him display it to someone who could.

TATT'S ROOM WAS IN SEMI-DARKNESS. Vish was sitting on a plush chair in the far corner of the room, playing quietly on her tri-lyre, to an audience of Drasous and a drowsing Tatt. The titian-haired courtesan and UnderDocks informer looked subdued. She broke off and started to rise when Erien came in. Erien said, "No, don't. I won't be long."

He crossed to the bed. The ghastly stillness had gone; Tatt lay a little obliquely, left arm on his stomach, right flung out, palm uppermost. His covers were starting to rumple and his pillows had been pushed askew. His face turned towards Erien before his eyelids lifted, weightily. His eyes were dark against his pallor.

Erien went down on one knee, leaning on the edge of the heavy, dark green quilt. "You said," he told his half-brother, "that I couldn't be trusted to dress myself for formal occasions. So here I am for your approval." Tatt moved his head: a weak, imperious jerk of the chin. Erien stood up, turned slowly, heard a rustle behind him and looked back to find Tatt struggling to turn on his side and reach for the bedside lamp. Erien eased him back and switched on the light himself.

"So much *klinoman* . . . " Tatt whispered, " . . . just a puddle . . . can't see . . . how people like this . . ." He squinted at Erien's braided chest and understanding suddenly, urgently, came. He fumbled Erien's hands into his. "Who?" he said, on a painful gasp.

"Ameron."

Tatt breathed out a fragile sigh. " . . . so afraid . . . "

Erien said, "Tatt, I still am." He heard Drasous shift slightly on his chair in the shadows, and did not look in that direction. "I'm afraid I'm doing the wrong thing. I'm afraid that I might be going with Ameron because he hasn't asked me for anything in return, except my Oath, and he hasn't weighed the costs, and he doesn't understand Rire as well as Ev'rel does."

Ditatt frowned, cloudy-eyed. "You're . . . strange, Erien," he said, and nothing more. He seemed to have drifted off to sleep, but when Erien started to ease his hands from Tatt's loosening grip, he roused. " . . . way it should be."

"How so, Tatt?" Erien said softly, leaning close.

"No conditions. Just because . . . you think it should be . . . " His consciousness wavered again. When it refocused he whispered, "Erien . . . did I die?"

"Tatt, you're here. You're alive. You're going to get better," Erien smiled, gently, to make his words teasing ones. The smile felt too stiff. "Far sooner than you ought to."

Tatt's weak grip tightened. "I heard . . . my heart stopped."

"It did. But Asher repaired and restarted it before your brain suffered any damage."

"Erien, I saw . . . I knew . . . things. I can't remember, but I know . . ."

"A bright light," Erien said, "a sense of presence."

"Yes . . . " Tatt breathed.

"You are not the first, Tatt," Erien said, settling himself on one hip on the floor with a creak of new leathers, "when you are better, you can read what other people have written about near-death experiences. I read about them when I was on Rire, after Di Mon died. I was trying to understand death, trying, I think, to find some loophole."

"Only you . . . could research . . . " Tatt drowsed; Erien sat on the floor, waiting for him to come back. Which he did, once again in the middle of the conversation. " . . . be all right."

"I hope so," Erien said. "At least I finally understand this." He took the card, which Liege Nersal had sent him, out of a pocket in his cloak, and held it up so that Tatt could see the *rel* symbol inscribed on it. "I asked Horth why he swore to Ameron. This card was his answer. I did not understand what he meant by it at the time, but I think I do now. *Rel* means many things to Gelacks. It means strength, and honesty, and just about everything which isn't *pol*, its opposite. But to Horth I think it means acting boldly, out of deep, and positive, emotion. I saw that yesterday, after you were hurt, when Ameron decided to go whole-heartedly with what he wished to do. Ameron loves you very much, Tatt, but then, you probably know that." Erien's throat was tight, saying the words. Tatt's eyes had closed, but his face was not lax; he was listening. "In a way, it's contrary to everything I am, doing this," continued Erien. "Nothing's been thought through. It's just been a decision to go and be damned; risk everything if need be."

" . . . *rel* . . . " whispered Tatt.

"Yes. I never thought I was that Gelack," said Erien.

Tatt smiled slightly.

"But that is what troubles me," said Erien. "Ameron has given me what I want, without conditions. Ev'rel was probably more realistic, when she made it clear that there would be a cost. Am I going with Ameron simply because I want to get out of paying the price which I was told about?"

Tatt opened his dark eyes. "Are you?" he asked, with some effort at clarity.

"Truly," Erien said, "I don't know. It's just that he is willing to do what he believes despite the risk. She is . . . not."

"That's it . . . then," Tatt said. He freed his hand from Erien's, and gestured with a flicker of fingers. " . . . Up . . . " he said. "Let me . . . see."

Obediently, Erien stood and turned. Tatt watched him, smiling.

" . . . 't'll do," was Tatt's opinion. "You'll . . . need better to call on . . . Luthan." He was tiring, the words were beginning to slur.

"Tatt, I am not—"

"Oh yes . . . you are . . . "

"Pureblood Erien," said Drasous. Unnoticed, he had risen and moved to the other side of the bed. "Heir Monitum has to rest."

Tatt smirked, his claim on the last word secured. Erien leaned over, with a protest from his leathers, and kissed him on the forehead. Let them make whatever they would of that. Before straightening, he tucked Liege Nersal's card under Tatt's limp hand. "You look after that for me," Erien told Tatt. "You should know, as well, that Horth also thought I was presumptuous to have pre-empted your challenge. 'Heir Monitum is the better match,' is what he said."

"When I'm better . . . " Tatt breathed.

"When you're better, and Gelion's first Justice Minister," Erien said, sternly, "you'll have more important things to do than indulge your own grudge matches."

Tatt whispered something. Erien did not catch the words but the tone was enough. He leaned close to murmur, "The Reetions outlawed that a long time ago as hazardous to the human person."

Outside in the corridor, he simply stood a moment, cherishing the sense that something very precious had been carried out of danger. He fingered the blue-red-and-white knots of his new jacket, reflecting that he could be glad of their brotherhood, if nothing else. He was Gelack enough, he thought, in that. Blood mattered.

Of course, he thought wryly, he was equally related to D'Lekker and D'Therd Dem'Vrel. And Amel.

The pleasant feeling soured. Damn Amel, Erien thought, where was he? The Reetions' recall message for Ranar had accused Amel of 'arbiter manipulation'. That was less than explicit; Erien had no clear idea what it was that Amel had done, and whether it was for Ann or in the service of Ameron's request to assess public opinion on Rire about Gelion. What was Amel capable of, and what would it take to get the truth out of him?

Of this he was certain—he was not going blind into dealing with the Reetions on Amel's account.

He was suddenly aware of activity in the Throat, and could see through the doorway a stir of Monatese green and H'Usian blue-and-silver with splashes of bright color like a tropical aviary. As he started down the corridor, Luthan burst through, pulling the little girl Amel had delivered with her. The Monatese errant in pursuit caught sight of Erien, and decided to leave the Princess to the Pureblood. Luthan and Erien met each other at a half-run.

"Erien," she gasped out, "you have to stop him. He promised me they were innocent." Erien sorted pronouns—a Pureblood 'you' in Vrellish common gender, a masculine form of 'he' in *rel*-peerage, a male Pureblood 'he', and a commoner 'they'. In order: himself, a Demish Prince, a Pureblood with at least some Demish qualities—probably Amel—and . . .

"Who is innocent?" asked Erien.

"My mama," said the little girl. "Where's my mama? Where's Amel?"

Luthan glanced at her, a little helpless before such imperiousness. "My uncle has a warrant for her arrest—"

"Whose?" repeated Erien.

Luthan caught a quick breath at his sharp tone and looked into his eyes, questioningly. She seemed to be reassured by what she saw. She was dressed for the Swearing, but since she was not expected to participate, she had not been confined to hearth colors, and was wearing a full dress of warm rose, embroidered with gold. Her curls had been wound with rose and gold threads.

"Asher's," she said.

"Mira," said the child stubbornly. "That's her proper name."

"Uncle H'Us wouldn't let me see the warrant; he says she's done terrible things, *sla* things, only Amel said before he brought Mona to me that the people he wanted me to protect were innocent. He didn't tell me any names, but Mona says that Asher is Mira, her mother, and I'm sure that she has to be the one who would be in danger if Amel disappeared, only the warrant . . . " Luthan trailed off and said in a small voice, "I know I don't know what Amel would think is innocent."

The churning in the Throat, which had stopped while errants and ladies watched them, suddenly started again. "Oh, no," Luthan breathed.

Branstatt nudged his way through the people clogging the Throat, his expression grim.

"H'Us?" Erien said.

"H'Us."

"With a warrant for Asher," Erien said for him. Branstatt's eyes flicked from Erien to Luthan, tallying his knowledge and her presence. Erien could see the sudden relief on Branstatt's face as he realized his opportunity for upward delegation.

"I'll go," Erien said.

The Royalblood Admiral of H'Us was standing in the center of the atrium, in a phalanx of errants. The Monatese guard had refused him the entry they had allowed Luthan and her party. Hands hovered near swords. The Demish Prince frowned at his niece and future Princess-liege as she emerged from the Throat half a step behind Erien. Mona had been left behind inside Green Hearth.

"I have come for the woman, Asher," Prince H'Us said, bluntly, and thrust out a piece of paper, backed with blue marbling and folded in three. "I'll not soil my mouth by repeating the charges; read them if you will."

Erien took the paper, unfolded it and started to read. He heard H'Us say, "Luthan," in a commanding, parental tone.

At his side, the Princess said, not entirely steadily, "Amel asked me to protect these people." She leaned close to Erien, reading over his shoulder. He could feel her breath on his wrist.

The warrant was, for a Demish document, brief and to the point; prepared in haste, although the fine script did not show it. In it, Asher was accused of illegal genetic manipulations with contraband Luverthanian stocks and equipment; and of importing, copying and distributing visitor probe pornography using illegal Reetion equipment.

"How," Erien said, looking up, "would a commoner medtech get access to this kind of equipment and supplies?"

H'Us looked as though he'd bitten into rotten fruit. "She had help."

"From whom?"

"None of your concern," H'Us said brusquely, though his pronouns were respectful. He was as close to distraught as such a phlegmatic man could come.

"Who laid these charges?" Erien said. "Was it you?"

H'Us scowled. "Princess Ev'rel," he said, shortly, "and she has exposed her own son, D'Lekker, as the medtech's accomplice. Ev'rel says to tell you that we have done your Reetions a great wrong in accusing them of what, as you have said yourself, is a Sevolite vice." The message sat ill with H'Us' prejudiced, honorable soul, but he gave it, resolutely.

Good news at last, Erien thought, looking down at the paper. And now, of all times, just before the Swearing, this came as a gift. He said, "Prince H'Us, it will do the Reetions no good if this is hidden behind hearth doors. We must—"

"No, Erien!" Luthan burst out. "Amel wouldn't say she was innocent if she had done those things. This is wrong," she told Erien, "and you're going to let it happen because it takes blame away from the Reetions. Oh Erien!" she caught his hands in both of hers, crumpling the paper slightly, "I know why you want to believe it, but it's wrong. Tatt would be angry with you. Amel would be angry with you. And I . . . I'll be disappointed in you," she finished, a little lamely, going scarlet as she realized she was clutching his hands. She pushed away from him. Erien felt the jolt in his center. She had not meant it as the rejection it felt like, he told himself, she was only embarrassed.

For a moment longer he thought about it. Justice need be deferred only a few hours, until Rire was recognized and the Swearing was over. But this was Gelion, and for a commoner such as Asher, a few hours in H'Usian hands, with these charges against her, could be hours too long. He could not, in good conscience, risk that if she were, as Luthan believed, truly innocent.

"I appreciate the gravity of these charges," he said, slowly. "Nevertheless, I must assert Monitum's prior claim to the prisoner. The responsibility she bears for the grievous wounding of my brother, Ditatt Monitum, is as yet unclear. If she had a part in that, then she will face Monatese capital justice. If not, and these charges are substantiated, she will be released to you." His claim for Monitum was tenuous, given that he stood there in red, blue and white, but after a long, hard look, H'Us simply grunted.

"I'll grant Green Hearth that," H'Us said, and ordered, "Come, Luthan."

Luthan raised her chin. "I wish to talk to Pureblood Erien a moment, then I will come."

H'Us, to his credit, never entertained the idea of taking her by force. He scowled, dauntingly, and Luthan bit her lip, the habit of obedience to her uncle being as deeply ingrained as any fleet discipline. But she stood fast, her back very straight. H'Us growled, "The sooner you're married, my girl, the better," and to Erien, "See that it's done." He spoke, obviously, of applying Monatese justice to Asher/Mira, but the juxtaposition gave Erien an absurd start. H'Us and the blue-and-silver clad errants filed out, leaving Luthan and her personal guard. She looked up at Erien, her blue eyes very grave. "Thank you," she said. "You did the right thing."

"I'm not sure," Erien said, starkly. "Given what D'Lekker made of Monitum's friendship towards Rire, Tessitatt may not thank me for what I've just done. Before I go up to the Swearing, I want to know whether there is any truth in these accusations."

"Then I'm going with you," Luthan said. "I'm responsible for these people."

"But Highness—" one of her ladies protested, "the Swearing—"

"Oh hush," Luthan told her irritably. "It hasn't started yet, I don't have anything to do except look well-bred, and Erien's the one who has the important bit. I can't be late until he is, and he shouldn't be late at all. So if you just let us get on with it—" and she pushed her way through them, making them fold aside from her.

Erien followed Luthan back down Green Hearth's Throat, to where they'd left Mona.

"I want to see my mama," Mona insisted, thrashing aside a cluster of embroidered skirts.

Erien looked down at the small, set face, remembering her as Amel had left her in Luthan's parlor. "We should at least confirm that the child is right, and that Mira and Asher are the same woman."

Luthan studied him briefly. "And we ought to let her see her mother," she said firmly.

In the small, sparely furnished room of her captivity, Mira was seated in an armchair, reading. She seemed at ease, but she lifted her head and brought her attention to bear on them as sharply as any Sevolite. She looked as though she had not slept. Mona said, "Mama!" and broke away from Luthan's side. Mira laid down the book and rose to receive her daughter. She put one arm around the little girl's shoulders as Mona pressed herself against her side.

"Amel?" Mira said, to them both.

"We don't know where he is," Luthan told her.

Mira nodded, once. What she felt, her face did not show.

"How is Heir Monitum?" she demanded, while they hesitated.

"I've just spoken to him," said Erien. "He's very weak, but sounds like his usual self."

"What are they using as an anti-hypertensive?" Mira asked, sharply. "They have to minimize the load on the right side of his heart until the septal defect reduces. Oh, don't tell me . . . *klinoman*." She twisted away from her daughter, still holding her, pulled pen and notepad from her pocket and, leaning on the back of the armchair, scrawled three lines, ripped the paper off, one handed, dropping the pad, and held the paper out to Erien. "Tell them to use these. They're Luverthanian, but the Monatese will have them in stock. He'll be at less risk of hypoperfusing other organs. And tell them to watch his urine output. Sevolite volumetric status is difficult enough to monitor without *klinoman* complicating the picture. It's not the best thing to give after blood loss."

"I will tell them," Erien said. "Mira—that is your name, is it? Not Asher." Mira pursed her lips.

Erien continued without being answered. "Prince H'Us was here with a demand for your arrest. I have forestalled it for the time being, by asserting Monitum's prior claim, but I may not be able to do so indefinitely."

Mira's eyes were on the paper in Luthan's hand. She said, "May I?"

Luthan stepped forward, a little uncertainly. Mira took the paper, but kept her eyes on Luthan's face, their grimness softening. "Princess Luthan Dem H'Us, am I right? Amel spoke fondly of you. Thank you for sheltering my daughter."

Luthan nodded. Mira, Erien saw, daunted her.

"Yes," Mira answered Erien, belatedly, "I am Mira. That will be the name, of course, that I am accused under."

"Mama, you didn't do anything *sla*," Mona insisted.

"That may be irrelevant," Mira said, remotely. With a snap of her wrist, she opened the document and scanned it. Her lips set, thinly. She turned, one-handed, to the next page, looked it over, and then handed it back, to Luthan.

"D'Lekker is also accused as your accomplice," Erien said.

"D'Lekker. Poor fool. He'd do anything for his mother's love, you know." She shook herself, more an involuntary shudder than deliberate motion. "Please," she said, "get my daughter off Gelion. You—and Amel—are the only people who know she is mine. She's only eight years old. Anything I did, she had no part of. Take her to the Purple Alliance. Amel has friends there. Or to Rire. Anywhere where the education I've given her and the intelligence she has won't damn her."

As mine has damned me, Erien heard, quite clearly. And only then realized that behind her calm and authoritative face was utter despair.

Luthan had realized it long before. Her face and eyes were full of uncertain compassion. "Shouldn't . . . shouldn't we wait for Amel?" asked Luthan.

"Amel won't be coming back," said Mira.

Erien gestured towards the letter Luthan held. "What of it is true?" he asked quietly.

Mira gave him a look which said she would have expected no better, from him. "That's the beauty of it. That's the beauty of all her work. I am a genetic researcher. I study Sevolites. I have a laboratory behind my clinic filled with Reetion and Luverthanian contraband equipment. I couldn't have operated on Heir Monitum without it." Her mouth twisted with brief, bitter amusement at what had come of that good deed. "But she'd have known to look. She has her own secret rooms."

"Ev'rel?" Erien confirmed, though there could have been no other given the pronouns.

"This is her work," said Mira. "And if she wants me dead, then she no longer cares what Amel thinks, or does. So Amel is dead, or as good as. Or worse." For the first time, her coldly level voice wavered, and tears shimmered in her eyes. Mona tightened her arms around her mother's waist, eyes huge. Mira stroked her head.

"But for Mona's sake," she said with a downward glance, "I want you to know this: I am a medical scientist, not a sadist or a pornographer. Amel brought me that equipment for my work, not D'Lekker. If D'Lekker was responsible for any of the other, which may or may not be true, I had no part of it. I do not pretend to have the interest of Sevolites front and foremost—I and mine have suffered too much at their hands for that, and I know too much about what highborns are, and why—but I would never have done anything to harm Amel Dem'Vrel. We were raised as brother and sister."

"I know," Erien said.

"Ah yes, the visitor probe records," she said, and fell briefly silent, then gently began to detach her daughter's arms. "Go with Princess Luthan, Mona."

"No, Mama! You haven't done anything bad!"

"Maybe not in your eyes, or in mine, but this is Gelion, and what I am they are afraid of."

"Amel said he'd take us away!"

Mira went down on one knee. It was a stiff movement, suggesting old injury. "I do not think we will be seeing Amel again, Mona," she said, with a stark gentleness. "If he could have come to us, he would have by now."

"Then we go get him!" Mona said, and grabbed Mira's wrist in both small hands, bracketing a silvery band which looked to have a wide nervecloth panel. "See!" She jabbed a clear stud and a bright point lit on the cloth. "He's there!"

"Mona," Mira said, her voice shaking, "that's you I'm sensing."

"No it's not!" The child pulled open the tie on her shirt triumphantly, to bare her chest. "I gave it to Amel."

Mira stared at her a moment, then got swiftly to her feet and swept her wrist through two arcs, high to low, left to right. "It's a strong signal," she murmured. She keyed the stud. Reetion characters shimmered on the nervecloth. "And it's untransformed—no hullsteel between him and us." She keyed the stud again. "And it's reading body heat."

Mira's head came up; her arm snapped out. "What's in that direction? Inside the Citadel."

"Lilac Hearth." Erien's answer came before he understood the implications.

"But Ev'rel said—" Luthan began.

"Ev'rel was lying," Mira interrupted her, harshly. "I should have known." To Erien, she said, "Get over there. Now. You were there yesterday; you have hearth right of entry. You're the only one."

"I have a Swearing to attend," Erien said, angered by her manner towards Luthan. "I will go afterwards."

"You must go now. Gods know what she's done to him."

"I will go later," Erien said, for the first time using fully differentiated *rel*-to-*pol* address to her.

Mira caught a desperate breath, made to say something and then got control of herself. Her eyes glittered. "Mona," she said, "go outside. This is not for you to hear."

"But Mama!"

"Mona, go!" Mira softened her voice with her will. "It may still be all right. We may still be able to save Amel. Just don't make me waste any more time!"

Luthan, with a glance at Erien, reached out and took the hesitant child's hand, and drew her round and out the door. She was back a moment later, her chin high, her pretty, not-yet-mature face set and protective. Mira took her measure with a look—which Luthan returned—and turned to Erien.

"I know Ev'rel," Mira said, "better than anyone else. Perhaps even better than Amel. I was her medtech for years. I was her friend and teacher. She is herself, a more than competent medtech. But in the end, I became her collaborator."

"I was the instrument of your existence," Mira told Erien. "I made it possible for her to conceive a male child. It was a technical challenge for me, to see if I could ensure a sex-selective conception when manipulation of the sperm sample was out of the question. She would have aborted a female; she has before.

"She was determined, after you were born, not to become attached to you. She would resist your need. She would keep you in need of her. My part was to monitor you, to prevent you suffering too great a physical and developmental delay. It was only your emotions she wanted to deform.

"When you were four months old, Amel came. He heard you crying, and he asked her to feed you. She refused. She said, 'This child will learn to need me.' He was distressed. And then she asked him what he would be willing to do for her if she were to feed you.

"She meant Rush," Mira said, dryly didactic. "She is incapable of sexual arousal except as a *slaka'st*. She was seduced by her father and raped by Amel's father—her half-brother, Ava Delm. That is one part of it—that she cannot attain sexual release unless the male is powerless and preferably unwilling to oblige her. The other part of it is Amel. Amel has not had much to be proud of in his life. But he is proud of his sexual skill. When she takes that from him, makes it sordid, she takes part of his soul. Had Ameron had to watch her misuse you—and he would have, as he was willing to watch you fight D'Lekker, for the greater good—she would have taken part of Ameron's soul. She would have found a way to take yours.

"If you are in any doubt as to what you would have become," Mira said, "consider D'Lekker. He is Ev'rel's creation."

"Why," said Erien, "didn't you tell anyone any of this before?"

She looked at him with cold, dark eyes, utterly undeceived by his efforts to mask his revulsion. "You see how we would have been believed. Amel has lived with the Reetions' blabbering his shame for twenty years. I am a commoner, and a geneticist. I could kick away the foundations of your race's godhood," she said with a flash of arrogance, "but I'd only be flogged to death for it. Besides," she told him bitterly, "I tried to expose H'Reth, once. It did not work. I do not think there is any hope for me. Ev'rel wants me dead, and she'll have me dead. I have nothing to hide and nothing to lose. But by all the Gods, you owe Amel, Throne Price, and I will collect on that debt if it is the last thing I do. She would have made you as twisted as D'Lekker; that was her purpose. Amel saved you."

"Amel," Erien said, "acted for his own reasons, and Ameron's."

"Reasons!" She stepped forwards, so she was standing face to face with him, a thin commoner woman a head smaller than himself, her hair coarse and raggedly cut, and beginning to gray. He could feel the force of her authority and her determination like heat on his face. "Reasons are for Reetions," she said with contempt. "Never mind his reasons. He came back to her, fool that he was. He's her fool, you understand; if anyone fails to see it, she readily marks it out for them. Gods," she said bitterly. "I was angry with him. She wanted your whereabouts, and she set out to get it from him. She'd always been interested in my work—and the Gods knew I was starved for colleagues who weren't bound up in the repugnant prejudices of *Okal Rel*—I'd talk to her and answer her questions. So I taught her—and she tortured him. Each day inflicting a little more pain, a little more damage. Then she'd bring me in, to check her work. And I would check her work, her seaming, her bandaging. And then she went a little further than she'd intended, and alarmed herself, and brought me in to stabilize him. And I did. And so it went on. Each time she damaged him a little more, and each time I used my skills to reverse what she had done. And each time he refused to tell her what he had done with you. And I thought if he was such a damned fool, then he should suffer. He should suffer until he told her, and he should suffer until he knew her for what she was. Until he could see, as I did, that his pain was as arousing to her as Rush is. 'You suffer beautifully,' I heard her tell him. We were caught in a grisly dance of suffering, she and Amel and I, and I started to think he was better off dead than willing to submit to that. But I kept repairing him. I was dead to myself. I was only a commoner, only an instrument. I knew what I had become. All I wanted was to see them know what they had become."

She stopped, expecting some kind of reaction from Erien, who had long ago found the place inside himself where emotion could be stored. It had nothing to do with him; he was merely a trophy, an emblem, an excuse by which their grisly dance could be set in motion.

"One day, I do not know after how long, Amel asked me to stop. She did something—did too much—ordered me to help him, and I refused. I would not take her orders. She begged him, in the end, not to die. She said she needed him. She promised him that she would never again use Rush. She promised him that I would not be harmed. So he gave me his word. And I did what she asked. And I knew I never wanted to see either of them again. I left the Dem'Vrel soon after that. I fell as hard and as fast as I could contrive, all the way into the UnderDocks, until I found Asher, Mona's father. And when Asher died, I took his identity, and I died.

"Only Amel found me again," she said, with a bitter twist to her lips. "And the Gods know, if there was ever a worse time for him to find me, if ever I needed him more, I do not know it. I had lost my clinic because I fought against the mass murder of commoners to contain a plague outbreak—I'd developed an immunoglobulin, vent their superstitious horrors. Four hundred people died needlessly. I'd injuries that weren't healing and a two-year-old child dependent on me. And so Amel got to re-enact his rescue fantasy. If only he was as willing to rescue himself. He was still her lover, still swearing that the promise was holding. He set himself up as my provider, and the Gods forgive me, I took what he could give because after ten years of sinking lower and lower, my skills and my knowledge were rotting away and I knew I wasn't worthy of this brand on my arm that I'd damned near sold my soul to earn. So there we were, he being ever so careful not to let me know what was happening upstairs. He used to object to my keeping Mona in the clinic and lab—likening it to the way we grew up, he and I—but I think he liked us there, the way we used to be." She spoke with a bitter love. "And I could see she was eating him away inside. Nibble by nibble. And then suddenly there was all this muck of the Reetions—and he wouldn't fight, again he wouldn't fight, and I was angry, I was furious, because he was back in my life, and we were getting caught up in the same dance as before. Only this time I was not going to let it happen. I was going to stop it." She stopped, as though becoming aware of where she was, and what had become of her. And she smiled at him, a terrible smile. "And I've failed. You're right. You don't owe Amel anything. He rescued you because he likes to rescue people, especially innocents. No, he has to. He keeps going back to those hours and days and years when nobody rescued him." She stopped again. "Get out of my sight," she said, in a harsh whisper. "You've all had your sport of us. Why should you be any different, after all."

Erien got out; he did not know how. He leaned against the door, shaking. He could not imagine that Mira would have lied, not about this. Her account contained the truth Ev'rel's had not; she made her own sins part of it, along with everyone else's. He felt befouled. He had had no illusions about the relations between the Purebloods who had begotten him—he was merely a transaction. But he had never imagined this. He understood with horror something of what Di Mon must have felt, the need to rip his fouled self utterly out of creation, the wish not merely not to know, but not to be. He wished he had never been born.

"Erien—" Luthan stood, white-faced, at his elbow. Her hand hovered near his arm, shaking slightly. He pulled away out of pure reflex; he could not bear the thought of touch. She started to cry, then controlled herself, glancing towards the errants standing at the end of the hall. Erien said, "I'll have to do . . . what she wants." *If I do,* he thought, *I might feel clean again.* "I'll take Branstatt. Say I forgot something during lunch yesterday."

"Oh, Erien," she blurted, wavering, "that was awful."

"Don't think about it."

She nodded, swallowing words. "Take my errants."

"No," he said, but had to think a moment why not, beside not wanting people near him. "Political repercussions."

Her mouth set. "Then if you're not out in seven minutes we're coming to get you. And I can count."

"Luthan—" he said, but was rendered wordless. He brushed her embroidered shoulder with his fingertips, the skin wanting to remember warmth, cleanliness, beauty and goodness. "Thank you."

Chapter XXI

"Tomorrow," Branstatt said, in the tone of a man taking an oath, "I'm going to request a nice, quiet tour in the Home Guard, on Monitum, where nothing ever happens, and none of you people who like to woo trouble ever bother coming." Erien only half-heard him. His attention was focused on Lilac Hearth. If Ev'rel were still there, or D'Lekker, or D'Therd, this visit would be brief indeed. Mira's presence committed them, and Mira, once she knew he was going in, would neither surrender the locator, nor be left behind. She had pulled on the over-tunic of a Monatese *gorarelpul*, and she looked as grim and dangerous as any of the breed.

"Good day," Erien greeted the door guards. "Has Avim Ev'rel already gone to the Palace?"

"Avim Ev'rel has already left for the Swearing, Immortality," the senior of the three errants said, his eyes drifting from Erien to Mira and Branstatt.

"Forgive me," Erien said, a little ruefully, "but after what happened to Heir Monitum, they are not letting me out of their sight. Is there any member of the family at home?"

"No, Immortality."

"Ah," Erien threw a vexed look at Branstatt who played his part with a disappointed look and matching shrug.

"Can we be of any help?" the errant asked.

"Maybe," said Erien. "There was a piece of Reetion equipment, very small, that I brought with me to show at lunch yesterday, and I think I left it behind. Liege Vrel wanted to look at it again, in the reception after the Swearing. Might we—as I say, they won't let me out of my sight—go into the dining room and check? I'm not sure any of the house staff would recognize it."

Without a word, the errant stood aside, his face impassive.

"Nicely done," Branstatt muttered.

The dining room was empty. Mira pushed back her sleeve, exposing the locator. She turned in a half circle. "That way. I'll wager he's in her bedroom."

"Or it is," Branstatt said.

"Or it is," Mira returned.

"Hush," said Erien, ear to the door, eyes half-closed, forming a mental picture of the spaces beyond and their occupants. He could hear nothing from the Throat. He said, "Let's go."

He led them into the Throat, and towards the family rooms, through the corridors, rooms and ornaments he and Vretla had passed by the day before. Branstatt forgot himself so much as to pause and stare at the room full of statues. Mira said, "Come on!" Erien found himself wondering at the similarity of layout between the three hearths he had so far seen, given Gelack paranoia; why offer a blueprint to invaders? The constraints on design imposed by the impenetrable hullsteel framework of the Citadel did not affect internal hearth layout. When he reached the point where he and Vretla had encountered the servant— the limit of his familiarity—Mira stepped into the lead. She wheeled them, now almost at a run, into a corridor which Erien recognized as the equivalent of the family rooms in Green Hearth, where Tatt now slept, unknowing. He should have left Tatt a note, Erien's mind ran on, in case . . . But why drag him into the mire? Luthan, he thought, with pain, Luthan . . .

He heard a whisper behind them, a man servant, whispering urgent instructions to a page. Ev'rel seemed to have no female servants. Mira said, "Left, ahead," and he pushed open a door and found himself in a bedroom. Behind him, Branstatt said, "Shit." He took a stride into the hall, without drawing, and planted a booted foot in the stomach of a very young man in errant's uniform. The youth sprawled backwards, hand flying out from his half-drawn sword. Branstatt grabbed Mira, and half-flung her though the door. He closed the door as the young errant, still retching, scrabbled to rise. Mira's hand slapped a flat plate above the ornate handle and a heavy bolt slammed home within the frame. Branstatt looked at her. "She was once married to Ava Delm," Mira remarked on the bolt, her gaze clashing with Erien's.

"I hope you have a plan for getting us out of this," Branstatt said to Erien.

Across the room, two servants stood frozen in the act of spreading a sheet on the bed. Erien said quietly, "Go into the bathroom, please, and stay there." He pointed towards the door that stood open.

They went quietly.

There was another door, a plain, white door, barred with a single heavy strip of metal. Mira was standing in front of it. She had not spoken. Erien joined her, and Branstatt took up a position at the foot of the bed, midway between the bathroom and the main door into the family hall.

Mira was staring in loathing at the blank door.

"Mira—" began Erien.

She said something in a whisper, and then stepped forwards and set her shoulder beneath the bar. She seemed to have forgotten that Erien was here; she seemed not to notice that it was he who lifted the bar from her and set it aside. Her fingers fumbled on the handle. Erien stepped back.

The door swung outwards. Music assaulted them from within, a pounding in the bones. Naked figures cavorted on the walls, overlaid on each other and run double speed, so that they spun and leapt and twisted in a frenzied chorea. In the dim center of the room their light splashed upon two other figures, still figures, whom Erien could not see until one of them raised his head. Could not see, or did not wish to see, for when he looked at them, there was an abundance of light for horror. Amel lay on his back on the floor, his wrists tethered. Across his abdomen was a shallow, torn-looking wound. Blood had run from it, pooling around his body and smeared on the floor.

He looked as dead as the courtesan in the Rose Garden.

Mira had been right, but they were too late.

Beside Amel huddled D'Lekker, naked, blood-smeared and as still as Amel until he raised his head. In his face was madness and utter desolation, and on his chest hung a chunky pendant. Mira made an inarticulate sound. The pendant, Erien thought. The pendant whose signal they had been following. Then the body heat and pulse . . . was D'Lekker's.

D'Lekker and Erien looked at each other for a suspended moment, and then Mira cried out a hoarse warning, even as D'Lekker's expression transmuted into pure fury, and he came up from the floor in a lunge straight for Erien's throat. Erien felt more than saw the knife in D'Lekker's hand, and struck it sideways, feeling it score his left forearm, and then bite, deep into his shoulder. D'Lekker dropped, slamming into Erien's knees, dragging the knife down through muscle. Erien threw himself away, fell, and rolled to his feet. D'Lekker waited for him, on his knees.

"First blood," Lek whispered, slowly rising to circle Erien.

In the better light of the main bedroom, Erien could see that stimulants or arousal had swollen both of Lek's pupils black. Erien held his arm, hugging himself, and blood oozed through his fingers. Past D'Lekker, he glimpsed Branstatt starting forwards, his face shocked and his hand seeking his blade.

Through the open door to the workshop there came an explosion, and an eruption of white sparks. Erien could hear a woman's harsh sobbing, broken with exertion.

D'Lekker raged, "Mine!" And flung himself back towards the door. Erien slammed into him with his left shoulder, his right hand grappling for control of D'Lekker's blade. D'Lekker's mad gaze looked past him as Lek swung them both, with stimulant-enhanced strength, throwing Erien back against the wall beside the door. He pinned Erien, grinding his pelvis against Erien's, in a wordless, animal display of dominance, the knife falling forgotten beside him. With failing strength, Erien pushed him away. D'Lekker reached across Erien's body, his fingers grabbing at, gouging into, the open wound. Erien screamed.

To the end of his life he would never remember what he did to stop the agony. To the end of his life he would deny remembering anything. That would be a lie. He would remember the black ferocity which burned up, through and out of him. A black ferocity which had nothing to do with fear, hatred or even anger. It was not even an emotion; it was pure energy. He never wanted to learn its name.

The energy poured up his spine and through his right hand. He felt his fist strike, heard the muted crunch of breaking cartilage. Released, Erien slid against the bloody wall, and went down on one knee. He found himself looking up at D'Lekker, with Branstatt just behind Lek, frozen in the poise of an executioner, sword held two handed, upraised—but unbloodied. D'Lekker was still upright, staggering, the whites of his eyes showing around the irises. His lips moved; only a croaking sound emerged. He took a step towards Erien, and went down on one knee. As Erien watched, D'Lekker fell forwards on his face. He writhed, and heaved himself onto his back. His skin was darkening even as Erien watched. He reached for Erien with a clawed hand.

Branstatt slammed his sword into his sheath with an oath and dropped to his knees beside Erien, ripping apart Erien's sleeve with his dagger. "Shit," he said. He gripped Erien's arm brutally with his left hand, his thumb digging into Erien's armpit, and turned his dagger on his own sleeve, shredding it to ribbons.

Behind them, D'Lekker's heels beat against the floor, a counterpoint to the pounding from outside the bedroom door.

Erien said, "Help him."

By way of answer Branstatt seized Erien's right hand and jammed it into place on Erien's left arm.

"Squeeze," he ordered. "You'll bleed to death, you fool."

Erien thought about dying. He thought about his right hand. Presently, it answered him, closing on his own flesh. D'Lekker's back arched in a terminal convulsion. Erien moved, and Branstatt grabbed Erien's good shoulder and slammed him back against the wall. He growled into Erien's face, "If you hadn't finished him, I would have."

And there was silence. Erien felt himself beginning to shake. His vision was graying out. With the deftness of one experienced in such things, Branstatt packed a solid pressure bandage of torn toweling over Erien's wound and grimly bound it down with strips of torn sheet and sleeve. The pain, like the arm, seemed like someone else's. Erien could smell a blend of sweet scents, orange, sandalwood, cloves, and over them, a sharp reek of electrical burning. Over the shouts of the people pounding at the door, a siren yelped. He discovered that he was sobbing, and he covered his face with his bloody, killer's hand.

CHAPTER XXII

AMEL WAS MAKING PROGRESS IN WOOING OBLIVION before things changed. There were new noises. Voices. The music stopped and room light blotted out the flutter of his dancing image that had penetrated his closed eyelids.

The smell of burning penetrated. Fire was deadly in UnderGelion, choking its enclosed spaces and consuming life-sustaining oxygen. Fire in Lilac Hearth was more important than anything happening to him.

He opened his eyes, blinking at the sting of smoke.

A woman was attacking Ev'rel's console.

Inhaling to call out made Amel cough.

The mad woman spun around, to stare.

"M-Mira?" Amel wasn't sure. He had never seen Mira look quite like that. But it was! He recognized her at once in the competence with which she snatched up a dropped bag and skidded to her knees on the floor, through his pooling blood.

An upwelling gratitude cleared pain from his face with surreal beatitude. He opened his eyes wide despite the smoke, inhaled to speak and didn't cough although the smoke burned in his throat and lungs. "Mira! She said—but you're not."

He was feeling no pain. It was wonderful!

The slap registered only because it was Mira's hand. It smashed his hard won detachment. He began to cough. She sprung the cords holding his wrists and grabbed him by the legs to drag him out.

Pain savaged reason.

She was retching on inhaled smoke when he became aware of her again, seconds later. They were in Ev'rel's bedroom where the smoke coated only the ceiling. He tried to crawl to her, to help, but post-Rush sensitivity amplified his pain beyond endurance and she recovered before he got anywhere. She pried his arm clear of his rape wound and plastered the torn slit with an oozy mass. It smelled and stung like medicine. He clutched at the strange, cold feeling. She pushed back his interfering hand. "Stop that!"

"Hurts," he moaned, and lost control, trying to curl up.

She gave him a shot in the flank. It wasn't *klinoman*, because it didn't slacken his muscles, but whatever it was took the edge off. He mastered the remaining pain to the sound of her tearing a sheet up. Amel's teeth began chattering as she bound his damaged arm. Mira cursed and shot him up with more drugs.

A riot of drugs and shock competing for him, Amel listened to what else was going on.

He heard Erien plead, "Help him."

Branstatt answered "Squeeze. You'll bleed to death, you fool."

They spoke over the sound of someone's death throes.

"Lek?" Amel tried to sit up. Neither his arms nor his abdominal muscles co-operated. "D'Lekker!" He cried louder, alarmed.

"Damn you," Mira muttered. She helped him prop himself against the far side of Ev'rel's vanity and shoved a wad of cloth between the rape wound and his left arm. "Hold that!"

"I c-c-can't s-s-see what's going on," Amel chattered.

"Stay put." Mira was brusque.

Amel listened in an agony of helplessness. Bodies moved. Branstatt shouted at Erien. Ev'rel's fire alarms cut in over the pounding on the door and a man's sobs. *Erien?* Mira left Amel to attend to something else and at first he was frightened to be alone, but he was tired. He was fading out when a prickly feeling made him look up to find Branstatt frowning down.

Mira was holding a dressing gown. It was one which Ev'rel had given him, patterned with colored sea shells on a sea-blue background. She must have found it in Ev'rel's wardrobe.

Mira said, "Lift him up."

Amel thought, *Please, no.*

Branstatt looked as if he'd rather touch a rotting carcass, but he reached down and hauled.

It wasn't as bad as Amel had dreaded. Mira, of course, would have given him some very effective and specific drugs. It frightened him, feeling dysfunction where there was no pain to explain it, but the trade was worth the disorientation. He helped Branstatt as much as he could and somehow they got the robe on. Branstatt got a firm grip on Amel with an arm across his back. Amel whimpered from simple aversion to touch, but held on to Branstatt's uniform.

Branstatt asked, "Can you walk?"

Amel was nearly undone by the errant captain's *rel*-peerage, which was less than his due, but more respect than he'd expected under the circumstances. He wanted to deserve it, badly.

Amel tested and found that his legs would move. He nodded.

Erien was waiting by the door. He looked awful. People were pounding to get in from Family Hall. Amel recognized individual voices. Erien inhaled bravely and threw the lock, saying, "Now."

There was pandemonium in Family Hall. Servants were rushing around, out of control, with errants trained in Ev'rel's drill trying to organize them. A handful of commoners were massed behind the senior staff who had been pounding on the door. Seeing people coming out, they moved to help rather than to attack.

"Immortality?" The herald got Erien's new status right despite the crisis. "What is going—"

"Pureblood Amel!" Ev'rel's steward would have taken Amel over if Branstatt had let him.

"Look, the workshop!" The herald began a small rush around Erien's party, raising his sleeve to ward off the smoke.

Erien stopped the herald. "D'Lekker is inside. Get him a medtech."

The commoner nodded and darted off.

"He's dead," Branstatt snapped with curt impatience, speaking down in brutal tones which doubly damned the dead man.

Erien stumbled. Mira held him up.

It was only then, in a time slice between concern for the fire, and knowing that Branstatt would be correct about D'Lekker, that Amel realized Erien was badly hurt, and that they all had to get out.

"Mira!" Amel called, and coughed, reaching towards her. "Fall back." He hitched himself up against Branstatt. "Take me forward."

Branstatt hesitated.

"This is Lilac Hearth," Amel tried to explain.

Erien seemed to grasp his logic, and Branstatt complied when he saw that. Amel took the lead with the Monatese errant's support.

"Prince Amel!" They were hailed by the first errant they encountered. The errant pushed aside commoners to whom he had been handing out breathing masks, his hand dropping to his sword at the sight of Branstatt and Erien.

"No, Lerl!" Amel raised his club-like right arm.

"You're hurt, Immortality!" The errant, Lerl, was young and not long out of the Knotted Strings. He looked frightened. "Where have you been? What is—"

"Lerl," Amel said with genuine urgency. "There is a fire in the Avim's workshop. The people fighting it will need masks."

The errant nodded, but he clearly realized that something strange was going on. The gauze ringing Amel's wrist showed at the end of his robe's sleeves, marked with fresh blood.

"Maybe . . . " Lerl was disconcerted, "I should take care of you, Prince Amel?"

"I'll get your prince out," promised Erien, with authority.

Lerl looked at Erien, hovering between respect and distrust. He accepted the reassurance with a slow nod, still staring at Erien with that unsettled look.

Another errant pushed through a couple of frightened commoners, his hand immediately flying to his sword at the sight of Amel in an intruders' grasp.

"It's all right!" Lerl pre-empted further action, breaking eye contact with Erien at last. "They are taking Amel out. Evacuate the untrained staff. Amel wants me to help with the fire."

They drew no more attention passing up the Throat to the entrance hall. D'Therd's favorite errants were missing. Good swordsmen all, they would be serving him and Ev'rel today as escorts.

The entrance hall door guards had kept their posts.

Amel knew all three: reliable men, without particular ambitions, but an earnest sense of house which, more often than not, he offended. The watch captain, D'Tan, put his hand to his hilt at once.

"Is that your missing Reetion toy," he questioned Erien, nodding toward Amel as he slowly drew his sword.

Amel knew he had to stand alone to prove that he was not under any duress from Branstatt. He did it by shifting most of his weight to his better leg, but he swayed against a side table, knocking a china lady to the floor. "There was—an explosion," he improvised, "in Ev'rel's workshop. They got me out."

D'Tan eyed Amel's unsteady pose. "One they set, perhaps?" His 'they' lacked the respect it should.

"No. They got me out," Amel corrected on all counts. "Go help Lerl with the fire."

Fast! Amel thought desperately, feeling his will start to lose the battle with a threatening thigh cramp.

The junior errants obeyed at once, reacting as much to the word 'fire' as to Amel's command. D'Tan's reaction was less prompt. He slowed as he passed between Amel and Branstatt, casting the former a look that was openly contemptuous.

Amel's leg gave out. Branstatt caught him as he buckled, and Amel clung to him, struggling to stay conscious.

Erien looked white with stress and blood loss.

But Fountain Court lay before them. They were nearly out.

Mira ran ahead to open the doors.

Then Krandal appeared from a side passage.

Ev'rel's captain of errants already had his sword drawn. With one glance, he knew that he was not facing three hale opponents, and his thin mouth smiled. The odds improved even more as first two, then a third errant of Kandral's command issued from the barracks door behind.

Krandal singled out his enemy with stone hard eyes. "Hello, Mira."

Mira stood, frozen, a step from the door. "You'll have to kill that one," she told Erien and Branstatt.

Amel released Branstatt, and buckled in a heap to the floor.

As he did, he watched Branstatt intercept a lunge which the wounded Erien could not have countered in time. Erien fell back, trying to draw his sword right-handed as he was engaged by a second errant. Amel felt a surge of alarm. Then he lost sight of the action as one of Kandral's henchmen grabbed him by the lapels of his robe. He tried to block. His left arm succeeded but his right disabled him with pain by trying to help. He got a knee in the chest for his trouble. Breath left his lungs. The floor flew up and struck him.

A boom, the sound of running bodies and Hillian's shouted orders, came between Amel and the next blow.

He rolled on his side, half-curled up, and forced himself off the floor with his left elbow. He couldn't inhale, but he saw clearly enough.

Hillian, Luthan's captain of errants, stood between a gasping Erien and the remaining Dem'Vrellish errants of Kandral's command. Immediately in front of Amel lay Erien's erstwhile assailant, twitching over spilled intestines on the floor. The dying man's name, Amel recalled, was Kanp: the third son of an undistinguished house, who had joined Ev'rel's errantry two years before. The worst Amel knew of Kanp was that he followed Kandral, and did what he was told. As Amel watched, Branstatt killed Kandral. Amel could summon no regret for that. One of the H'Usians was fainting from a ten centimeter gash on his arm.

Mira had let in Princess Luthan's bodyguard. Now she appeared beside Amel demanding, "Are you all right?"

Amel squinted at her, nodded, still unable to inhale, and passed out.

In the gray period that followed, Amel was carried between two strong men. His lungs recovered from their winding and remembered how to take in air. It felt good being able to breathe again.

They were near the fountain, rounding it on the way across the court from Lilac Hearth to Green Hearth. The sounds of watching people pressed through the soothing water noise: their breathing, their movements, opening and closing doors, and swords being slowly drawn or tested in their sheaths and put back.

Amel dragged his head up.

His first sight was of Monatese retainers running towards them out of Green Hearth. Black Hearth, counter clockwise from Green, and ahead on Amel's left, remained closed. So did Red Hearth. Behind him, Demish whispering told Amel that people were still issuing from the H'Usian holding of Silver Hearth, adjacent to Lilac. Amel's view back was blocked by Hillian's bulk. The H'Usian errant had joined Branstatt in supporting him. Their shifting grip told him they knew he was conscious, and he tried to help them all he could.

Mira walked ahead, safe, beside Erien.

Amel began to wonder, with awe, if his ordeal might be over. The possibility felt too large to manage, bringing with it floods of joy, and burdens, hand in hand.

Their party slowed, and then stopped. The reason was Hillian. He was responding to the approach of people in marching order, sent from Silver Hearth. Fear swarmed over Amel's back; he had to turn, to look, his skin convinced that injury was imminent if he did not. But he could not stand on his own. Branstatt had to take over as Hillian let him go. Fresh fear and Branstatt's strong hold collided in panic that made Amel unmanageable. He had to turn around! He slewed himself and Branstatt—who was trying not to hurt him—halfway around, and saw that Erien had turned as well, to watch Hillian returning to the H'Usian fold as Admiral H'Us overtook them from behind, with a six-guard. H'Us looked grim and cross.

Monatese errants and house guests fell in behind Erien and Branstatt, facing out to all quarters.

In the same breath, Red Hearth opened. A burst of sleek movement in his peripheral vision became Vretla's Vrellish deploying themselves around Ev'rel. The Avim was resplendent in her Vrellish adaptation of formal Demish dress for a Princess: a full skirt without petticoats, pale blue to make the braid-threads prominent, slit to mid-thigh on one side; a tight bodice with a short, open jacket; leather belt bearing her stiletto; her hair severe, widow's peak, sensuous features and faint olive skin tone as haunting as a portrait by a master. This was her public face, submerging woman and statesman in the unstable amalgam which Amel thought he had taught her to integrate. To him, she looked frightened.

Amel knew he was. Adrenaline strained his constitution, demanding he remain alert beyond his strength.

"You!" Branstatt cursed, the 'you' commoner. He let Amel go to grab Mira, who had tried to snatch the knife from his boot to attack Ev'rel.

Erien moved in, behind. Amel managed, somehow, to stand alone. He knew he had to keep standing or he would be touched, again, by someone.

Branstatt held Mira's arms pinned, the hatred in the stare she fixed on Ev'rel so stark that Amel hardly recognized her.

"That is the *sla* medtech," Ev'rel said, looking more confident as her fear transformed to hatred as pure as Mira's was. Their hatred hurt Amel to the heart with blind, wounded love. He was afraid even of Erien, standing behind him in case he fell, and he too could hate Ev'rel for that. He felt sick on force-fed hate—even the hatred he bore himself for continuing to love them both—the only family he could ever have; the only people who shared the Gap he navigated, inextricably bonded to him. His vision swam with tears. He blinked, beginning to tremble so violently he did not have to blink again to make tears start to run. The warm flow ran down his face in counterpoint to sudden dryness in his mouth.

"Pureblood Erien wouldn't give the woman up." H'Us was explaining his failure to confiscate Mira to Ev'rel, sounding awkwardly apologetic and displeased by the need for that. "He claimed prior right of trial for his adopted house of Monitum. There is, you see, the matter of her guilt concerning Prince Ditatt."

Ev'rel was so cool it was hard to believe that she, herself, knew Tatt's wounding was on her hands. "We'll discuss that," she promised H'Us. "Amel is injured. By D'Lekker?" This latter was addressed to Branstatt.

The Monatese errant captain answered with a nod.

"Injured how?" Vretla demanded, narrow-eyed and instantly suspicious.

H'Us glared his disapproval of the very question, "Must we inquire?"

D'Therd snapped, "No!"

Vretla silenced a general surge of comments when she drew her sword, along with her own conclusions. "D'Lekker will answer for it, to me. Now."

"He's dead," Branstatt rapped back. She fixed him with her unblinking Vrellish stare, as if he was a puzzle to be solved—at the point of a sword, if other resources failed her. Tessitatt's hand went to her own hilt, pulse jumping at her throat in restrained alarm. She was even less Vretla's match than Branstattt was. But Branstatt was her love child and the man he shielded was her liege's heir-son.

Vretla looked past Branstatt to Erien, cued by the Monatese errant's body language. "Convenient, Lor'Vrel," she said with the weight of ancient prejudice.

"Vretla," Ev'rel ordered, "collect Amel." The words penetrated Amel's nerves one by one, eliciting a tiny, quantum gasp with each syllable.

Thought and action were one thing to Vretla. She began to move at once, flanked by Red Hearth vassals quite willing to test swords with Green Hearth.

Amel was numb with shock. Mira was in Monatese hands. If they took her back to Green Hearth there was still hope. He could not quite bind the hope to one or the other of them: Mira, himself, Ev'rel. It was enough that there was hope, of some sort, for someone. And yet he stepped back. Retreated. His shaking was terrible. Even on his feet, still, he was blacking out.

When Amel bumped into something, behind him, he didn't know that it was Erien.

There was roaring in Amel's ears. Vrellish and Monatese faces and bodies slewed across his vision. Erien caught him one-handed, staggering a little, and eased him down to the floor. Vretla hesitated, not sure what was wrong. Ev'rel forced her way through the press and the murmur. Amel saw her vividly despite his weakness. She smelled of cloves and Monatese Turquoise resins.

She reached for Amel, saying firmly, "Give him to me."

Amel heard Branstatt order, "Take this medtech to Green Hearth!" and knew that Mira was getting out of hand, but he was confident that the Monatese would not let her come to harm.

Ev'rel looked so intense it hurt, but Amel's body revolted, nerve by nerve and muscle by muscle. He whispered, pleading, "Don't touch me. Don't touch me. Please! No more."

She said, "Shh," with sweet compassion and he cursed himself for failing to die before now.

Erien said harshly. "Leave him alone." His sound hand gripped Amel's shoulder.

Ev'rel sounded bewildered. "Pardon?"

"He does not want to go with you," Erien explained to her.

Ev'rel was not daunted. "Amel is hurt," she said. "Upset. Possibly clear dreaming. He could as easily mean you."

Amel could not defend himself. He couldn't think at all. He wouldn't meet Ev'rel's eyes. He looked up at Erien, whose white face seemed very sane and competent. He wanted to believe it was. "Kill me or take me to Green Hearth!" he implored, and lost control in shameful sobs.

Chapter XXIII

"THAT," SAID ERIEN, GETTING TO HIS FEET with an effort he tried not to show, "seems clear enough." *Or would be,* he thought with frustration, *if it had carried any distance in the press of bodies.* It was possible that no one but himself and Ev'rel had heard Amel at all.

Facing Ev'rel over Amel's huddled form, Erien felt as cold as space. It was unimaginable, comparing her cool demeanor with the man cringing at her feet, that Amel might be the saner one. But a moment ago, Erien had seen her fear.

And he had seen something worse. There was a deadness in her eyes which came alive when she looked at the prostrate and shivering Amel. A sort of hunger.

Mira had told the truth.

Erien would not have yielded up Amel if Amel had been his worst enemy, and not someone to whom, no matter how little he might like or understand him, he owed his life, his mind, and his integrity.

Ev'rel knew it, too. She looked pointedly at Vretla, reminding her of the order she had given. Vretla started forwards. Erien said, forcibly, "Stop," reaching for the voice Tatt had likened to Ameron's. At least that was strong. "There are things you do not know," he warned Vretla. To Ev'rel he said crisply, "Do you want them known?"

The corner of Ev'rel's mouth twitched. Then her eyes shifted sideways, to the Monatese. She numbered them and let him see her numbering, and then she ran her eye over the blue and red Dem'Vrellish, the red Vrellish and the blue and silver H'Usians.

"I do not know what you have heard, Erien," she said, with every sign of patience, "but be aware of this: Mira is an old retainer of mine who bears a fierce grudge. And she is a proven dabbler in *okal'a'ni* science." She collected a nod from H'Us. "Who knows what she and D'Lekker have done to Amel? He could believe anything. His mind has always been pliable since the Reetion probing."

"So pliable you couldn't break him, under torture," Erien said. He scored, to judge by Ev'rel's sharp intake of breath.

D'Therd drew his sword. Vretla laid her hand to her hilt, shock giving way to rejection.

Ev'rel stayed her champions with a raised hand.

"I am sure Mira has told him that, and other things," she said, mildly. Then, in earnest, "Think, Erien. If you oppose me, you stand almost alone. The H'Usians have the wisdom of all Demish, to witness where they need not be involved. Vrel and Dem'Vrel stand with me." Her glance slid past a very tense Tessitatt to Black Hearth's entrance, where Horth Nersal stood, alone. "Nersal doesn't look inclined to dirty his hands." Her attention snapped back to Erien. "This is a Dem'Vrellish matter. Amel and D'Lekker are of my hearth. Mira was my medtech. Is it really worth risking the Monatese? And for what? You don't care about Amel. I do."

Erien had a sense of unreality. He had never thought he would come to a place where he could not simply speak the truth. But to accuse D'Lekker of abusing Amel would be to risk true innocents, D'Lekker's children, gifted to a Dem'Vrellish *mekan'st*, and he could not do that. He would not let them suffer the fate of Darren Monitum's children. And to accuse Ev'rel, on the word of a commoner, and one so deftly discredited, was futile. There had to be another way. If he could only think it through. But he did not have the time for that.

"I won't—ask Monitum for anything more than they have already done," Erien said. "This is my debt. I owe Amel . . . something. And the bar . . . the bar was on the outside of your workshop door. Amel was a prisoner."

"Aw, hell," Branstatt said, in English.

Vretla Vrel shifted subtly as the half-Nersallian errant stepped up to Erien's left shoulder, his expression ironic. "You might not ask," he remarked to Erien, in Gelack, "but he'd never let me hear the end of it." The 'he' being Tatt. He faced Ev'rel. "Like Pureblood Erien says, the door was barred on the outside, Avim."

And with a soft whisper of rose and gold, Luthan Dem H'Us came to stand beside Erien, her skirts brushing against Amel's huddled figure. She was white as mist, and trembling, and her eyes shimmered with tears. She looked at Ev'rel in disbelief and with a kind of apology, and said, "I care . . . about Amel."

"You care!" Vretla Vrel exploded, eyes firing at the implied insult.

"Luthan!" cried Admiral H'Us. Luthan flinched but she didn't move. Hillian and her personal guard began gathering to cover their exposed Princess as Dem'Vrellish re-enforcements appeared in the mouth of Lilac Hearth.

"It is simple enough!" Ameron's voice cut through the tense silence. Heads turned as he made his way through their forming ranks, flanked by his swordswoman *cher'st*, Ayrium. Ayrium stopped just behind him, her right hand on her hilt, Ameron's implied champion. Horth Nersal made no move to displace her, but shifted to ensure a clear view.

Ameron himself wore a duelling sword, hastily strapped on over his formal Lorel-crested whites.

"Amel will tell us what to do," said Ameron.

Vretla Vrel, at least, gave him a grudging nod, but a couple of Vrellish nobleborns spread out, blocking Ameron from Black Hearth, and raising the tension of the Monatese a notch.

Ameron knelt—Ayrium glaring over his head at D'Therd—and carefully turned Amel over under Vretla Vrel's scrutiny. "Do you know who I am, Amel?" He asked in *rel*-peerage.

Amel gripped Ameron's sleeve with his left hand, leaving bloody traces. "A-Ameron," he said, shivering. His face was as white as Ameron's clothes.

"You are ill," Ameron told Amel. "Where do you wish to be tended? Lilac Hearth, Red Hearth and Green Hearth have all offered."

Ev'rel held her breath.

Amel stammered, "Di—Di Mon?"

"Is dead," Ameron said gently. "Lilac, Red or Green. Choose now."

Amel quivered, and blinked once, spasmodically. "I t-told Di Mon I'd—I would never—endanger—" He came to himself with a catch of breath, focusing on Ameron. "Green H-hearth. Take me to G-green Hearth."He swallowed, and implored Ameron with a stare that seemed to beg forgiveness for having no more strength to offer. "I'm s-so tired."

Ameron said firmly, "That is all right."

He got up then, Amel in his arms, and handed him off to a Monatese errant, saying, "Take Erien in as well."

D'Therd stepped clear of Ev'rel. "Can you use that, Lor'Vrel?" He baited Ameron, referring to his sword, and pointedly ignoring Ayrium who wordlessly kept herself between them.

"I can, but I don't think," said Ameron, "you would find me much of a challenge."

A Monatese errant—Ketatt—nudged Erien and hissed, "Come clear." He ignored her. She gave up with a soft curse, preoccupied with Amel's care.

"I could settle any offense, if you'd like, with your liege, Ev'rel," said Ameron, looking at the other Pureblood while Ayrium kept her eyes on D'Therd.

Ev'rel gave Ameron a narrow smile, and said, "Wouldn't that be interesting?"

"Or," the Ava suggested, "you can wait for Heir Monitum's verdict on the guilt of the medtech, and for Amel to walk back across Fountain Court, when he is better. Which he will, of course, be free to do if he desires."

Vretla relaxed a bit, although she concentrated on Ameron with a frown which seemed intent on deducing treacherous duplicity in every reassuring word.

"All right," Ev'rel agreed, "take Amel to Green Hearth. But I want the medtech, Mira. You keep Amel, I'll keep her, until Heir Monitum is well enough to deal with my accusations."

Ameron seemed inclined to agree to that.

"No!" said Erien, on gut impulse, and explained with a coldness matching Ev'rel's, "Mira is not to be given up."

Ameron's sideways glance condemned this latest stubbornness, but he did not contradict Erien openly, merely looked back at Ev'rel and D'Therd.

"You will answer for this insult by the sword!" D'Therd told Ameron and Erien. "D'Lekker's shame will not sully the honor of Dem'Vrel. We can see to our own!"

"I am not casting doubt on Dem'Vrel's honor," Ameron told D'Therd, with unshakable composure. "I am simply asserting that while I am Ava, I will be Ava. This is Heir Monitum's affair, in as much as it touches his Justice Ministry investigations. And that is a Throne affair."

"All the more reason, then," said Ev'rel, "that you should no longer be Ava."

Horth Nersal, finally, moved out of his hearth's entrance. He was still alone, but he did not need to be backed up by a dozen errants to make an impression.

Erien heard Tessitatt breathe, "Thank you, my ancestors."

Vretla scowled, and even Admiral H'Us stood down his guards to an at ease position, acknowledging the implied clash of titans.

Horth met D'Therd's stare across Fountain Court, and nodded once, in acceptance. Then he went back into Black Hearth.

Ameron said to Ev'rel, "Let's say, tomorrow."

Ev'rel's mouth had fallen into a soft frown which was more the absence of expression than something in particular. She answered him huskily, "Tomorrow."

"I suppose," Ameron said, almost as if to cheer her up, "it was inevitable. Good day, Avim."

"And you, Ava. Tomorrow it may be the other way around, and you'll not take my Throne again so easily as you did the first time." She said this with a parting glare at Erien.

A stern-faced Hillian claimed Luthan from Erien's side, steadying her as he walked her back towards her uncle. "Thank you," Erien whispered after her—after them both—but he could not be sure that she had heard.

Then Ameron descended, Tessitatt and her errants closing like a cloak around them, and swept Erien towards Green Hearth. "Why did you stay when I ordered you to fall back?" the Ava upbraided him.

"You would have let her have Mira," Erien said, keyed up and light-headed.

"You'd have been a liability in a melee. We had not the numbers to spare a sword to defend you."

Erien had to admit that, with silence.

"Trust me to make the decisions," Ameron concluded the lecture, and sped up to capture the lead.

"Liege Nersal didn't stand with us until the last," Tessitatt said anxiously, as they moved off Fountain Court into Green Hearth's entrance hall. "Do you think he is wavering?"

"And Admiral H'Us did not stand with us at all," Branstatt answered his mother with a frown. "He was angry with Luthan." Branstatt stayed close enough to stop Erien falling if he passed out: a precaution Erien appreciated. He was avoiding looking at his left arm.

Ava Ameron turned, with uncanny precision, at the moment that the last of his entourage was off the court. On his first syllable, the hearth sealed with the controlled *thrum* of heavy doors.

"Charous—Amel and Erien are injured, have Dras—"

"Mira!" Amel's panic spiked through Ameron's tone of command as Mira was detached from him by a couple of Monatese errants.

"Leave him the woman!" Ameron interrupted with a flare of bad temper. "If he trusts her, so be it. Let her treat him. But see that she touches neither Erien nor Tatt until she is cleared of Ev'rel's charges." He defined Mira curtly with his pronouns. She looked, once, to Erien, thanking him, perhaps, he thought. Erien watched her take possession of her charge, very glad when the sound and sight of Amel were gone.

Ameron seemed to be glad to see the last of Amel as well. He inhaled with a flare of thin-walled nostrils and shook his head back, like a stallion about to bolt. "We have until morning to prepare for the worst outcome, though we may still hope for the best. Ayrium, you will leave before Lights Up. Take Ranar to Killing Reach. He will have to make Amel's excuses to Rire on the matter of their summons if I lose my throne tomorrow, for I doubt Ev'rel will let him go."

"I'll take Amel too!" said Ayrium.

"Impossible," Ameron countered. "Amel and this cursed medtech are the stake which drew the challenge. It could provoke escalation, to melee or space war, if they are not present."

Ranar passed a couple of Monatese errants to reach Ameron. "I will not return to Rire unable to declare that you have recognized us. You have promised, that at this Swearing, finally—"

"Not if I lose my throne tomorrow!" Ameron cut him short, and mitigated the reprimand with a hand on the Reetion's shoulder. "If I emerge Ava, consider it done, Reetion."

He broke off, displeased by Erien's condition. "Have his arm seen to," he ordered Branstatt, who was, by now, discretely holding Erien up by his sound elbow. "I will be in the Breakfast Room if there are questions he must ask." He met Ayrium's eyes with a promise. "I will be unavailable after that."

The intense stare between the *cher'stan* was remarkable for the complete stillness it imposed upon the almost hyperactive Ava, even though it lasted only seconds.

The next moment Ameron was crackling with action and orders again, calling for Tessitatt, Charous, Ranar and Ayrium to attend him, praising this or that errant, and calling for attention from the kitchens. The sound of their voices, feet, and laughter passed into the Throat through Azure Lounge.

"Come on," said Branstatt to Erien, sounding noticeably restored. "You need a drink to replace all that blood. Maybe a stiff one." Drasous appeared, silent footed, from the direction of Tatt's room. "And I need Drasous to critique my work on your arm," Branstatt concluded.

In Erien's bedroom, they sat him down. Drasous cut away Erien's sleeve at the shoulder and between them he and Branstatt eased Erien out of the remainder of his overjacket and shirt. Erien was shivering fitfully, and while Drasous began the task of working free the clotted bandage, Branstatt pulled the quilt from the bed and threw it over him. Then Branstatt disappeared momentarily, returning with decanters of water and Monatese Turquoise whiskey, and a pair of glasses. Drasous broke off his work briefly to doctor Erien's water glass. When it was held in front of him, Erien shook his head.

"It's glucose, salts, and some protein," Drasous said, "*rel*-fighter's nectar, they call it in the fleet. You need fluid."

Erien shook his head again. "I'll not hold it down," he said, through a tight jaw. "Branstatt . . . in my kit, a medical supplies box . . . " He pointed. When Branstatt gave it him, Erien rummaged, one handed, until he found the anti-nausea patches which Lurol had prescribed for him to use in the low-gravity environment of Reetion docks. Branstatt had to tear the package open for him, then, recognizing the Reetion writing, would not touch the contents. Erien worked the patch out and pressed it on the nearest clean, bare skin that he could reach on his upper chest.

Drasous said, "If you've got a painkiller in there, I suggest you apply it. You may not be feeling much now, but you will. I'll do a local nerve block before I seam, but I can't give you *klinoman*, not after that much blood loss."

That reminded Erien of Mira's instructions. He yanked his discarded jacket towards him and scrabbled in it, looking for the scrap of paper she had given him, found it, and pushed it towards Drasous. "Mira said you should use these on Tatt."

Drasous scanned the paper, folded it neatly with one hand and tucked it into his own pocket. "We're watching," he said, "but I'll see what Charous knows of these. Luverthanian, I expect." He glanced up at Erien. "The Luverthanians won't train *gorarelpul*. I suspect because— due to the conscience-bond—we would not be able to keep their secrets."

The analgesic blunted the worst of Drasous' probing. "There's been some nerve damage. These muscles—" Drasous tapped Erien's upper arm, "will be weak until the nerves regenerate. You'll notice altered skin sensation, too." He then proceeded to compound this effect with the nerve block, turning Erien's arm to insensate stone. Erien turned his head away as Drasous positioned the seamer, nausea threatening. He hated the sound and stench of seaming flesh.

Branstatt, seated with his feet up on Erien's dresser, was draining the last of a healthy draught of Monatese Turquoise whiskey. If unwatered, it would have been enough to slow even Branstatt's highborn reflexes, but Erien doubted it was. The errant's green eyes were still focused and clear. They looked at each other, neither wanting to think of what they had left behind in Lilac Hearth.

"Thank you," Erien said, at last.

The errant shrugged.

"Still going to apply for a stint with the home guard?" Erien asked.

"More than ever," Branstatt said, and paused. "Day after tomorrow," he added, with very Gelack relish. It took a moment for Erien to remember: the duel.

Erien's anger rose. "There isn't going to be a duel."

Branstatt blinked.

"Horth's life should not be risked over this."

The errant raised both eyebrows. "You'd bet on D'Therd? You'll be popular in Black Hearth."

"This is not about bravado!"

"I know that," Branstatt snapped back. "Everyone knows D'Therd and Horth Nersal have to have it out—the same way Tatt and D'Lekker

. . . " he stumbled briefly, thinking about Tatt, and let that example drop. "Ev'rel and Ameron have headed for a clash ever since Amel stole the Throne Price—" Branstatt paused, again, and said in the right grammar, "You. Ev'rel could have forced it, then. She let it go. But it was just the first postponement. It's been 'nearly' half a dozen times since. That they had to clash over—" He passed over reference to the scene in Lilac Hearth. "Well, it's not the stake I'd pick, either, for Liege Nersal. Or D'Therd, for that matter."

"And what about Dorn Nersal?" Erien said. "If Horth dies, Dorn will be fighting the *kinf'stan* to hold his inheritance, until either he dies or they give in. What do you rate his chances of survival?"

"You can't go through life avoiding all risk. That's Reetion!"

"And throwing lives away on any absurd pretext is Gelack," Erien said grimly. "Not this time."

"What do the reasons matter?" Branstatt said. "What will be remembered is the duel!"

"Which pretty much sums up . . . aah!"

Drasous said, quietly, without raising his eyes from his work, "Please keep still, Immortality."

Erien was certain that he hadn't moved. On reflection, he was just as sure that what he had been about to say would have been intemperate and unwise. He took himself in hand, and tried again.

"Ev'rel is guilty of attempted murder in the assault on Mira, which Ditatt interrupted—" began Erien.

"How do we prove that?" Branstatt objected. "Besides, she's a commoner."

"—and of negligence in what happened to Amel, if nothing worse," persisted Erien. "That won't be settled with a duel. It should be dealt with openly, with testimony and evidence—"

"Delm's way," Branstatt referred, contemptuously, to historical precedent. Ev'rel's Demish half-brother, Delm, had got her falsely blamed, with words and 'evidence', for Amel's original disappearance. An injustice which cost her exile to the outback of the Knotted Strings.

"Yes," Erien allowed. "And Di Mon's way, when he proved her innocent."

Branstatt bridled at what, to him, was an insult. "Di Mon was prepared to fight H'Us to be heard, and he would have, if H'Us had not preferred to talk!"

Erien ignored the typically Vrellish implication that all Demish Sevolites were wind bags. "Good!" he said, instead. "There's precedent. Liege Nersal is prepared to fight D'Therd. Let's convince D'Therd, instead, that his mother is a criminal."

"The Avim?" Branstatt scowled at Erien. "You can't hold her responsible for what D'Lekker—"

"Ev'rel tortured Amel to learn my whereabouts," Erien told Branstatt, "using his foster sister, Mira, to keep him alive. Amel stole me, at the start, because Ev'rel planned to use my infant helplessness as a handle on both Amel and Ameron. Beginning with demands that Amel submit to Rush."

Branstatt's face looked as if Erien was rubbing his nose in something he expected the servants to clean up. "Says who?" Branstatt accused. "This Mira? What if Ev'rel's right about her supplying D'Lekker? I'd as soon find her truthful as believe Amel could hold out under torture! You heard him just now! You saw him in Lilac Hearth!"

That was so utterly irrational Erien was briefly confounded.

Erien said narrowly, "Mira is commoner and Ev'rel is Pureblood. Is that the problem? Branstatt, you are Tatt's first lieutenant. You have to be prepared to listen beyond the pronouns. Tatt would!"

The errant put down his empty glass, his green eyes dangerous, got to his feet and slammed out of the room.

Drasous set aside his seamer. "Perhaps Your Immortality forgets," he said quietly, "that you are debating a thousand years of deeply rooted hierarchy."

"Then it should be changed," Erien said blackly.

"You will get no argument from me," said the gorarelpul, placing the slightest stress on the pronouns which bracketed the extremes of that very hierarchy. Drasous pulled a pad from his kit and taped it over Erien's ugly, seamed, and weeping wound. "Even if Liege Nersal loses tomorrow," he continued, "his soul will be reborn into a world already changing. If we are all patient and subtle in our work."

"Horth should not be expendable," Erien responded spontaneously, and then set himself to wait for the gorarelpul to go on, perplexed by what Drasous implied but had not said.

To consciously act against Ameron's wishes would be fatal to Drasous. Did that mean that Ameron had his own plans for the transformation of Sevildom?

But Drasous did not volunteer any more, except to say, "You will find the Ava in the Breakfast Room, eating."

Erien did have to see Ameron. Urgently.

In the Breakfast Room, the Ava had transmuted bad nerves into a lively, family meal. Even Tessitatt was eating, and giving Ameron back as good as she got, though from the snatch of banter Erien caught as he pushed open the door they were talking about nothing much.

At the sight of Erien, in a black shirt, arm sling, and wearing a grim expression, Ayrium rose swiftly from her seat by Ameron's side.

Her right hand went to her sword hilt. Ameron got up more slowly, stroking her arm as if to gentle her. His hand strayed briefly around her waist as he moved past, coming toward Erien.

"Come with me," Ameron invited Erien, firmly. "You will ruin all our appetites with that face."

To Erien's surprise, Ameron took him into the kitchens through the service door at the back of the Breakfast Room. Only Charous followed.

The kitchen staff were even more surprised than Erien. They stared a moment, not quite believing their eyes, then a middle-aged man in a cook's apron gestured to the others, and they laid knives down beside half-chopped vegetables, moved pots from burners, and filed silently out. Here, Erien realized, he could damage no morale.

Ameron browsed the kitchen's long central worktable, brushing his fingers lightly over the hilt of a knife and the stem of a mushroom. Behind him, Erien could hear the clicks from the long range as it slowly cooled. Pots murmured and burped to silence. There was a pleasant scent of herbs in the steam, though he could not identify which ones.

"What troubles you?" asked Ameron.

Erien spared Charous a glance, preferring that the interview be private. But Ameron seemed to treat her like his shadow, expecting her to be there.

"This duel," said Erien. "If Horth Nersal dies, the *kinf'stan* will slaughter each other until one person makes enough kills, in succession, to hold Black Hearth, and the first person in their sights will be Dorn Nersal. The Dem'Vrellish may do likewise, if Ev'rel loses her champion."

"Ah, but that is *Okal Rel*," said Ameron. "You must accept that."

"Why?" Erien said flatly.

Ameron flicked over a mushroom slice. "It is a good question. Not an easy one to answer in words." He looked up. "Ask it again in twenty years. For now, accept the wisdom of the thousand that have gone before." Erien's face did not satisfy the Ava. His expression shifted towards impatience but ended up expressing an unwilling sympathy. "Erien," he said, "beware your Lorel soul. The urge to force our will on Vrel and Dem has ever been our hubris, and our hazard." The Ava's sympathy deteriorated with a scowl as he became aware, himself, of his unguarded lapse into archaic Gelack. The change reminded Erien that Ameron was two hundred years time-slipped from his period of origin, the period in which Sevildom and Rire created Killing Reach between them in the wake of their first contact. Could that explain why he could not grasp what seemed to Erien to be so plainly wrong?

Erien inhaled deeply, determined and truth-bound to make him understand. "There is something you must know."

Charous raised an eyebrow fractionally. Ameron's mildly surprised and expectant look reflected her expression. Or perhaps it was the other way around.

"When Amel returned to Ev'rel after taking me, seventeen years ago," Erien said, "Ev'rel tortured him to try and learn my whereabouts."

Ameron looked skeptical, but said nothing. Charous merely relaxed her cocked eyebrow.

Quickly, Erien gave them both as dispassionate a report as he could. Ameron winced once. That was all that distinguished his listening from the impassive gorarelpul's. When Erien was done, the Ava resumed his contemplation of the objects between them on the cutting table. Erien willed him to respond, breathing hard and shakily.

An abandoned cake caught Ameron's eye and without seeming the least less kingly for it, he casually scooped off a fingertip's worth of icing to sample.

"Suppose," he allowed, at last, "Ev'rel did try to force Amel to tell her what he had done with her infant son." He lifted and idly laid down a carving knife, and glanced up at Erien. "She was within her rights. Amel's life was forfeit to her for violating the trust of her hearth. I myself told him to return the—to return you."

"But you never asked him why he took me in the first place! Or why he would not yield me up."

"The Ava asked Amel to explain himself," Charous said, speaking for the first time. "Amel refused."

Erien ignored her, focusing on Ameron. "Ev'rel used Rush on Amel. And she would have used me to ensure his submission. I would have been a pawn in their games."

"Enough!" Ameron said, hand upraised. "There is a Demish notion that the telling of a thing gives it life, true or not." His demeanor softened with a sigh. "Think what harm Amel's shame has done. And Darren Monitum's. If you accuse Ev'rel of this, the ugliness of it could taint even you, as her son. The *sla* use of Rush is as vile a thing in a woman as boy-rape is in a man."

"I had . . . thought of that." Erien swallowed, his mouth dry with bloodloss. "I will risk it. For justice."

"Indeed," Ameron said, dryly. "Perhaps you would." He barbed the remark with a nursery-grammar 'you'.

"And if you would not," Erien said, ignoring the goad, "then arrange an in-camera session. Settle this privately. Use what you know to back her down from the challenge. It would ruin her more surely than it would ruin me."

"And how, pray, would I induce Ev'rel to sit through your private session?" inquired Ameron. "She would gain nothing by it."

He dropped a hand onto the countertop, restless fingers finding a spoon to toy with. "I have long suspected that Ev'rel too much appreciates Amel's courtesan past. She is too cold in the bedroom for her Vrellish blood. But may the Gods forgive me, Erien, I have made use of that, and not asked how Amel applies the influence he has. If she has pleasure of him, by his will, I'll not begrudge them." He grew disturbed by his thoughts and frowned. "They are both adults. This Mira may be jealous. I've seen Amel stir women up, even ones who would sooner die than confess it." He rapped the spoon on the countertop and set it down with finality. "What's done is done. It will play itself out by *Okal Rel.* We owe our champions no less."

"What you may not understand," Charous said, "is that the declared cause of this duel is not the whole cause. Ev'rel is no longer content to be Avim, and D'Therd wishes to prove himself against Leige Nersal. Sooner or later, over something, this was going to come."

"This is about which Pureblood will be Ava," Ameron confirmed, "and that must be settled by *Okal Rel* because it is the one law of Sevildom without which there can be no honor, only war. For me to evade it by smearing my opponent's character would appear dishonorable." He scowled. "Besides, the facts are unlikely to prove as decisive as you seem to think. Amel lived as a member of Ev'rel's household for years after this supposed torture. Does that make sense to you? It is hard to believe a bitter woman known to deal in contraband."

"Then what about Tatt?" Erien demanded. "He fell protecting Mira—only hours after she had been paraded before Ev'rel. Do you think that was just coincidence?" Charous went very still. Erien said directly to her, "You don't. You brought her to the Octagon."

Ameron turned on Charous. "What do you know of this?" Her hesitation was fleeting; he lanced it with his voice. "Tell me!"

Charous took an involuntary step back. "I knew," she said tautly, "there were times that Amel went somewhere other than to you or Ev'rel on his return from space. With this Swearing so closely contended we had to know who was loyal and who was not. I was having him followed. When he came back this last time we traced him to a medtech's clinic in the UnderDocks. His usual decoy routines broke down; I don't know why. We identified the medtech as Mira, Amel's foster sister and Ev'rel's former medtech. Mira was in Ev'rel's employ when Amel was returned after the Reetions captured him and when you," to Erien, "were born, but left shortly after he," to Ameron, "was stolen. She was supposed to have died in a disease outbreak." She took a deep breath. "I found it extremely suspicious that Amel's foster sister and a Luverthanian-trained medic would be living under an assumed name in the UnderDocks. So when you asked me to find a good medic to attend the duel between Erien and D'Lekker, I had her brought to the Octagon."

"Ditatt and I knew her as Asher," said Erien. "She was one of Tatt's informants concerning the murder in the Rose Garden. She was terrified of being seen by the Dem'Vrel, but we did not know it was anything other than their reputation."

Ameron's expression accused no one. He said, very faintly, "Gods." Then he turned his head towards the door, and the ordinary sounds of the meal in the Breakfast room. "Is it possible?"

"Where are you going?" Charous said, before Ameron had even moved. When he turned, she shifted as though to intercept him. He did not even look at her as he strode past her, close enough for their clothing to brush.

The Royal *Gorarelpul* turned visciously to Erien. "What have you done?" she accused and pushed ahead of him out the door.

Ayrium sprang up, hand on sword, as they passed. She had been seated at the table talking to Ranar, who stood as well, but with merely human dispatch.

"Come," Ameron told them both, "but cross me at your peril."

Erien had time to think about the connotations of Ameron's grammar as he hurried after the gathering party down Family Hall. The Ava had elevated Ranar to Highlord status in answer to the problem of addressing him and Ayrium with a single, plural form of 'your'. And his slide toward archaic usage, Erien was learning, betrayed strong emotion.

What had he done? Erien wondered.

Ameron was building up power like a forming thundercloud.

The fear that he might have begun something that he could not stand by and watch raised fine hairs at the base of Erien's neck. He did not know if he could withstand having more terrible deeds and decisions forced upon him.

Chapter XXIV

"THAT'S ENOUGH!" AMEL BLURTED, pushing Mira's hand from his abdomen with clumsy strength as she returned to her work, armed with a new instrument.

Mira was tart. "Amel, stop that!"

"We have to talk!"

"That wound is filthy!"

He flinched at her choice of words.

"I—didn't mean—"

"I know," he swallowed thickly. He was restless, his body sense alarmed by the numbing which spared him intolerable discomfort. And he was ashamed. Ashamed of each new detail her attention to his wounds discovered. He averted his eyes, but she had already read that in them.

"All right!" She yielded. He looked back to see her use her wrist to push stray hair from her eyes. "I've dealt with the worst of it. I'm not satisfied but I could close now. Any infection's on your own head."

He nodded, grateful, knowing Mira was probably right and would treat him, whatever she threatened, as professionally as if he had complied with her every wish. Even if she had meant it though, he could not stand to be an object to be worked on any longer. Not even by Mira. Maybe even especially not by Mira, he had to admit. It stirred up memories he'd rather keep buried. Very deep.

The seaming was swiftly accomplished. It did not hurt, but the oddness strained his self-control. The wound became a stiffness bound into flesh where it did not belong.

"Mira," he caught her hand as she put down the seamer, "tell me what happened on Fountain Court! I—didn't quite follow it all."

She sat beside him on the bed, holding his hand. She looked tired. But he had to know.

"Erien," she said, "blocked Ev'rel from claiming you. Ameron prevented a bloodletting over it. He asked you where you wanted to go. You chose Green Hearth."

Amel winced.

"You took your time about it," Mira said harshly. "You were blathering about Di Mon."

"I remember thinking I had let Di Mon down," Amel explained. "I promised I would watch out for Erien and there I was letting him defend me. And Ameron. Oh, Mira, I've failed!"

"You succeeded," Mira disagreed acidly, "long enough for Erien to grow up and make his own choices." Her mouth turned down once more, lines coming into relief at the corners. "I was proud of Erien today. I have no right to be; I would have left him in her care. It was you who kept him from her. From all of them. That young man, little brother, is no failure."

Amel absorbed the words slowly, with relish. Then he smiled at her. "Thanks for putting it like that."

"It is true," she said gruffly, "but we still have a problem. Ameron drew Ev'rel's challenge. And we're the stake."

Amel's eyes grew wide, his heart hammering. "A duel?"

"Tomorrow."

He began to hyperventilate. "I should have chosen Lilac Hearth! I should have gone back to her!"

"No!" She took his head between her hands and held him steady. "No. You should have walked out sooner."

"She never broke her promise!" he protested. "Never. Until—" His mouth went dry. With his ingrained elegance of understatement, he broke down in a sob.

"Don't you dare grieve for her," Mira told him sternly, gathering him into her arms. "Or her sick whelp."

"Mira!" He pushed her away. "Mira—if D'Therd wins—if Ev'rel—you have to get off Gelion!"

"It is too late for that," she said, and touched his face. "Amel, I'm a prisoner here."

Ameron came through the door, followed closely by Ayrium.

Mira backed away as Ayrium displaced her at Amel's side. Amel sat up, seeing Iarous—one of Charous' *gorarelpul*—come in next, followed by Ranar, Charous and Erien. The room felt, suddenly, too close.

Amel's adrenaline surge made him swoon a little. Ayrium supported him while the *gorarelpul*, Iarous, plumped his pillows, then Ayrium laid him gently back down. Mira had helped him dress in a pair of Tatt's lounging pants. Amel drew the waistband over his rape wound with an expertly casual tug and left his arm to screen the rest of the angry flesh above. He could do nothing about D'Lekker's sheath welts on his naked torso, nor the red-in-white bracelets of Ev'rel's gauze bandages about his wrists. Ameron did not seem to notice any of it, though.

The Ava was in an impassioned mood. When he spoke, his voice reverberated in Amel's chest. "Was it Ev'rel, seeking the medtech's death, who nearly cost Tatt his life?"

Amel blinked up at the towering Ava. "I don't . . . "

"D'Lekker is dead," Ameron rained down facts like bolts, "and I do not care what you and Ev'rel might willingly share in the bedroom." The dismissive disgust in that stripped Amel raw. "But would she, to quench this woman," Ameron flicked a gesture at Mira without looking at her, "be content to murder my son, Ditatt Monitum?"

Amel swallowed in his constricted throat.

"Yes," Ameron's voice cracked with authority, "or no."

Amel nodded, once. His heart sank. No matter what Ev'rel had done, it was betrayal, and it hurt him.

Ameron turned his interrogating stare on Charous.

"I did not know that," she gave him back, bravely game despite the uncharacteristic quiver of emotion betrayed by her voice. "I told you—I tracked Amel to Mira's clinic only two days ago. I wanted to flush out the connection by bringing Mira to attend Erien and D'Lekker's duel. That was all."

"And the feint meant for Amel drew Ev'rel's lunge," Ameron thought aloud.

The next instant his attention was back on Amel. "I know Ev'rel had the right to kill you eighteen years ago for kidnapping your half-brother. But did she carry that into torture? And your reasons for stealing the Throne Price, were they as Mira has related them to Erien? Is Ev'rel a *slaka'st*?"

Amel could not reduce so much to so little. Was he, really, just Ev'rel's *slaka*? As surely as he had been Liege H'Reth's so long ago. The thought made him sick beyond cure.

"Yes!" Mira cried, goaded, moving toward Amel once more. "But why must you make him tell you! It's his own pride that you're fighting now, trying to break!" She came close to tears of rage. "Does that astonish you? That he could still be proud? You didn't know him when he was ten!"

Charous made a move towards Mira, threatened and offended by her tone. The medtech jerked back, seamer raised.

Amel lurched off the bed strongly enough to force Ameron's interception. "Leave her alone!" he shouted at Charous, past Ameron. "Don't touch her!"

"Gently!" Ayrium took Amel from Ameron and helped to ease him back down onto the bed while Ameron called Charous off with a hand gesture. Mira lowered the seamer, shaken, her chest heaving.

"Yes, it's true!" Amel panted in the grip of his passion. "What she's told you. About me. About Ev'rel." He flashed hurt gray eyes up at Ameron. "All of it."

Ayrium, who thought that she knew him, who Amel had counted among his best friends for many years, drew back.

"Why?" Ameron exclaimed in disbelief. "Why didn't you reveal it then?"

Amel turned away, into the pillows, feeling like something vile caught by sudden sunlight through an opened window.

"What would you have done?" Charous spoke up, pushing as though to square off against Ameron when even Mira no longer dared. The Ava turned to greet her question. "What are you going to do, now that you know?"

Ameron's expression darkened. "I will do," he told Charous, "what I must!"

"Which is why he didn't tell you before! It would have put you in a position your Sevolite honor wouldn't brook—I know you can be driven by your Vrellish blood! I'm afraid of it, now." Charous was almost begging. "Amel did it to protect you, then and now. I could almost thank him for it, if he'd followed up with a knife through Ev'rel's heart!"

"That's enough, Charous!" Ameron commanded.

"No!" the *gorarelpul* protested. "Don't you realize what will happen if you confront her with this? Who will listen to you? You are Lorel. In alliance with Reetions! You've had Amel here for hours. No one but us even inspected his wounds. What she can't blame on D'Lekker she can blame on you. Amel is no credible witness! She has seen to that. You'll just be accused of trying to sully her, like Delm did, to keep her out of power. Vretla will be down your throat. Ev'rel will buy H'Us by handing Ranar over and accepting his 'no contact' agenda until it suits her to please D'Therd more. And Nersal will no longer want to be associated with your cause. You saw him walk off Fountain Court back into Black Hearth without a second look at you! He is teetering, even now. How much more of Amel's muck do you think he will stomach?"

Ameron absorbed Charous' verbal assault without response.

"Nersal is not his only champion!" Ayrium's aggression drove like a spike through the powerful silence. She blazed. It was frightening. This, too, Amel had feared, ever since D'Therd had defeated Ayrium's father to gain Demora for Ev'rel. But her fury also warmed him, for he felt in it not only the old blood feud with Dem'Vrel, but proof that his Purple Alliance friend's affection for him had survived knowing the worst. Ayrium came back again to his side, dropping a hand to his shoulder in a gesture which gave him strength.

Ameron went white about the mouth. "Indeed," he acknowledged Ayrium's offer and *rel* reputation, "but it will not come to that." The volatile Ava flowered into robust cheerfulness. "Liege Nersal is not much for long arguments, particularly ugly ones," he agreed with Charous, "but I know what he will respect. Erien! We've a visit to pay."

"I'll come with—" Ayrium began to move.

"No," Ameron insisted, as only he could. "I will be back," he promised her. "We will make a good night of it then, be sure. Charous, you will meet me, with Ranar, in the library prior to—"

"Ameron!" Amel pushed himself up on an elbow.

The Ava went still, and turned to him.

"I want Mira gone," Amel said, "before the duel. Even Liege Nersal can lose. Ev'rel must not have her."

Ameron looked from Amel to the *gorarelpul*. "Char?" he asked. "What do you think?"

"I believe," she said, "that Heir Monitum would expect no less." She gave Amel a hard look which startled him for its new lack of brooding suspicion. "And it may behoove us to have Pureblood Amel in our debt, if you find yourself Avim with reduced support."

"The Purple Alliance will shelter Mira," promised Ayrium. Amel thanked her with his eyes.

Ameron looked at Erien, who said, "I will not accept giving the medtech up to Ev'rel."

"So be it!" Ameron bowed to consensus; then grumbled, "One more thing we'll have to make them swallow on the challenge floor tomorrow."

Ayrium folded her arms. "Do 'em good."

"I want to see Mona, to say goodbye," Amel told Charous, speaking down to her a little shakily.

Charous dispatched Iarous with a curt hand gesture.

Amel expected everyone to leave then, but they all waited. He was uncomfortable about it until he grasped that it was not for his sake, but because of Ameron. The Ava showed no signs of leaving. Instead, Ameron was being more than usually demonstrative, in public, with Ayrium. Knowing Ayrium as well as he did, Amel was quite sure that the content of the *cherst'an's* conversation was meaningless. Ayrium knew more about smuggling fugitives off Gelion than any court highborn, especially Ameron. Ayrium was listening to Ameron's advice about it anyway, conspiring with him in this excuse for semi-privacy. Ameron spoke in a low murmur, touching her frequently. Amel decided that the Ava was mustering courage. But what for? Ayrium sensed something was odd and was trying to fathom Ameron's intentions without risking dismissal by asking him, outright, what it was. Charous was studying Erien and Ranar suspiciously, as if they might be privy to the Ava's plans. Amel did not think so, somehow.

Erien looked terrible. He was white-faced and dry-lipped, with an unhealthy energy smoldering in his eyes. Amel watched him with sympathy, grateful that Ranar tried, at least, to make him sit and rest. Amel appreciated why Erien would not. He knew what it felt like to be wound up inside, like a spring about to tear through your own skin if you didn't do something. It was a highborn liability, and Erien was not only as Sevolite as himself, but considerably more Vrellish.

Mira came to sit by Amel's side, her movements leaden with weariness.

"You'll go?" he asked.

"Yes," she said and squeezed his hand. "You looked a lot like a Sevolite just now, you know."

"Sorry."

"Don't make a habit of it."

He smiled, and squeezed back. "I won't give you any more orders than you give me, how's that? And thank you. For getting me out of there. It was—bad."

She inhaled with what he knew was a brave attempt to cheer them both up. "Don't thank me," she said, "thank Mona."

Chapter XXV

"ERIEN, YOU ARE WOUNDED," Ranar pointed out. "You only feel energetic because you are highborn. It's a typical stress response."

"I am aware of that," Erien told his anxious foster parent.

He was still a child to Ranar. He knew that. He loved the Reetion for his concern. But Ranar did not know what it felt like to be in the grip of a 'typical stress response'. Sitting down was the last thing he wanted right now and relaxing was utterly impossible. Everything around him seemed to have sharp dazzling edges and threatening points. He could not concentrate. Urgent as he knew it to be, he could not bring his mind to settle on the problem of what Ameron was intending to do, or what held him back from doing it and doing it now. It seemed unlikely that the Ava was delaying their departure solely to intrude on Amel's reunion with Mira's daughter. So what was it?

Iarous came in, shepherding Mona.

"Amel!" The child struggled to escape the tall, willowy *gorarelpul* woman.

Amel smiled with that familiar uncanny control which Erien now recognized as false. "You were right," he told Mona, and signaled Iarous it would be all right to let her come forward. "I did need the pendant more than you."

Released, Mona rushed past his offered hand to hug him with simple passion. Amel didn't heed the wounds he wasn't feeling thanks to painkillers, but Mira disapproved and eased Mona off.

"Mama said we'd never see you again!" the child told Amel.

Amel caressed her forehead with his good hand. "It does her good to be proved wrong, now and then." He noticed Erien watching them with ill-concealed impatience. It disturbed his sweet humor; he drew back his hand. "You have to go with Ayrium now."

"And you? And Mama?"

"Mama too."

"You'll come when you can?"

"Of course." Amel said it so lightly the child sensed no lie. It hardened Erien. It was wrong to so glibly deny the child the warning that much could still go wrong. Erien felt he had no right to intervene, but the protective dismissal struck an unwelcome chord.

"I'll take good care of them, Amel," Ayrium promised, abandoning Ameron's side with a final touch. Ameron stared after her a moment too long for it to go unnoticed.

"Thank you," Amel said to Ayrium, with warmth.

Mira took charge of Mona and herded her out without looking back. The child waved over her shoulder. Amel's smile turned off the moment the door was closed.

"D'Therd," Ameron asked Amel slowly, somber as well now, "wants this duel?"

Amel's expression stirred. He seemed reluctant to answer without knowing why the Ava asked, but the pressure of Ameron's stare was too much. "Yes," Amel confirmed, "he has for some time, in fact."

"If Ev'rel wanted to," Ameron asked, "could she force D'Therd to back down?"

"I don't know. I don't think so," Amel said in worried innocence. "Why, Ava?"

Ameron shook off his spooky mood with a sudden, strong smile. "It is not your *rel* anymore," he told Amel. "Sleep now."

He turned to Erien. "Come."

Erien detached himself from Ranar, whose attention was claimed by Charous. She was especially curt and unhappy. "We will wait in the library," she told Ameron, taking Ranar's arm.

"But—"

The door closed on Ranar's protest.

With Erien a stride behind him, Ameron headed down Family Hall for the T-junction it made with Green Hearth's Throat. He paused there, waiting for Erien to catch up.

"Do you remember Ava Rene Lorel from your Monatese history?" Ameron asked abruptly, as they headed up the Throat to Fountain Court.

"Yes," said Erien, "of course."

"My father's house, Lor'Vrel, preserved some of Rene's journals," said Ameron, "until they were destroyed in the Fifth Civil War." He frowned at the vandalism implied, still fresh to the time-displaced son of its victims after more than two hundred years. "Tell me what you know of Rene Lorel," he ordered.

Where was Ameron going with this? wondered Erien as they passed out of Green Hearth onto Fountain Court, alone. Their problems were of the moment, not the past.

He said, "Rene was the Pureblood Lorel who re-established duelling as a means of title challenge by staking his own life with his champion's. He ruled during a period of disorder eight hundred years ago, in which, for various reasons depending on your source, the *Okal Rel* system was breaking down. Rene was partnered to a Pureblood Vrellish woman, Esrilat, who fought as his champion. He ultimately lost the throne to the Demish. And his life—since under Rene's Convention he himself—"

"Indeed," said Ameron, "but the Demish Golden Age began and ended on Rene's terms. With *Okal Rel* intact."

"What is your point?" Erien said, with a sense of rising panic at his inability to make the connection. "I don't under—"

Ameron's patience was thinner than Erien's. "There are times when one can lead Sevildom, son, only with a bared soul. Remember that. All the more so because you are, now, also my heir."

"Ameron, what—"

"Later. We are here now." They stood before the guarded doors of Black Hearth. "Behave as Di Mon would expect of you," said Ameron. It was a low blow, but solid; it silenced Erien.

The Black Hearth herald let them in, wordlessly.

Horth Nersal received them in his entrance hall, armed, and flanked by seconds: Dorn on his left and, on his right, a niece of similar age and experience, named Sant. His thin lips were relaxed in a shallow frown. It was the way he looked before a duel, or getting into a *rel* ship before combat. His eyes studied them in gestalt, with a wordless intelligence. He noted Erien's sling and the strain on his face, without emotion.

Dorn spoke first. "How is Heir Monitum?"

"Well enough." Ameron flicked his eyes that way, unafraid of Horth's imposing silence. "Or as well as can be hoped. Drasous has done all he can."

Erien could see Dorn's jaw lock. The Nersallian heir's right hand tightened on the hilt of his sword. It was non-threatening, although to the untutored eye his tension might seem more so than Horth's inhuman watchfulness and Sant's holstered needle gun.

The gun startled Erien—for all that he was as acquainted with Horth's practicality, as he was with his commitment to honorable conduct. His sense of Sevildom's potential threat to Rire edged up a notch, as did his awareness of the long history between the hearths. There was bad blood between House Nersal and House Lorel.

Ameron seemed to have a fine appreciation of that, and of Horth's limited receptivity to argument in the absence of complete trust. He was uncharacteristically simple in his diction.

"I have learned things which make it impossible for me to accept Ev'rel as Ava, now or at any time," the Ava told his champion. "Nor, in fact, to share Fountain Court with her any longer."

Horth Nersal gave no visible response.

Ameron continued. "This matter is quite separate from that of Rire. It concerns Heir Monitum, Erien," he hesitated only briefly, "and Amel."

Horth glanced at Dorn.

"Tatt was investigating the snuff killing, in effigy, of—" Heir Nersal stopped his explanation when his father raised a palm.

Horth's slate gray eyes panned from Dorn, across Ameron, to Erien.

"Erien is the Throne Price," said Ameron.

"We heard." Sant's alto voice was pleasant. She looked Erien up and down, taking his measure.

"Tomorrow I will name him as my heir," said Ameron. "Heir Lor'Vrel, and Heir Gelion."

"And Rire?" Horth spoke for the first, and last time, in the interview.

Ameron floundered on that. In the seconds it took him to react, Erien found himself driven to an offering of honesty, on his own behalf.

"If you fight," he told Liege Nersal, "it will be, in some measure, in recognition of Rire's right to independence. Only that. Independence. As freely self-governing commoners. Beyond that you yourself can, and must, judge when you know more. But knowing more won't be possible, sanely, if we start with war."

Ameron cued Erien to say no more with a light touch on his nearer arm. He, too, must have noticed how Horth deflected his gaze right while he thought, after hearing or reading something he considered important. Any attempt to move or speak again before what had already been said was digested, could sever the fragile trust.

Ameron waited until Horth's eyes returned to him. When he was certain he had his champion's attention, Ameron announced, "I see no gain in spreading shame further than it has already gone, but as to Ev'rel, I, myself am sure enough of her dishonor that I offer you this bond: I will stand with you, as Ava Rene stood with Esrilat."

Horth's nostrils flared slightly.

Erien felt the blood drain from his face.

Rene's Convention.

Ameron meant to place his life beside Horth's, thereby forcing Ev'rel to do the likewise for her champion—as Rene Lorel had staked his life, over and over again, until he had lost it.

Dear Gods, Erien thought, in blind shock.

Horth's easy alertness stiffened up into a slow grin.

Erien stared at Horth, then at Ameron. "You can't!"

"I have more Vrellish than Lorel blood," Ameron said proudly. He looked as pleased with himself as Horth. The solving of the knot left his mind free to race once more. Mental energy all but sparkled around the Lor'Vrellish Ava.

"When will you test the Avim's will to accept Rene's Convention?" Sant asked. She, too, seemed more relaxed: arms folded across her fleet jacket, the needle gun forgotten.

"Tomorrow, on the floor," said Ameron. "But I do not think D'Therd will let her back down. If he does—" Ameron shrugged. "Sooner or later, I'll have this done."

Ameron had them, Erien thought, he had them in the palm of his hand. He could see it as clearly as if it was a Reetion anthropology documentary pointing out body language and lines drawn by eye contact. History and ancient distrust was swept away by their common intoxication with the duel, the great risk, the *rel*. He had never felt so alien, here at the heart of his own culture and heritage.

"Sleep well, Liege Nersal," said Ameron. "Ayrium is waiting for me in Green Hearth, so I know that I shall."

Horth appreciated that.

Their parting was abrupt; Horth simply turned away, giving Erien a nod as their eyes glanced off each other. What it meant—approval, dismissal, caution—Erien had no idea.

"Give Tatt my best wishes," said Dorn quickly.

There was no time for any more. Dorn was gone, after his liege-father and cousin.

Erien stood a moment longer, feeling them all move away from him, feeling the lines of connection draw thinner and thinner. Except for the errants standing in the doorway, somber and stark and emblematic of the Nersallian *kinf'stan*. Which of them would challenge Dorn if Horth fell? Which of them would kill, or be killed by him?

Ameron's voice commanded. "Erien."

He started walking towards it. He knew he could not faint, could not show public weakness. He felt, more than saw, Ameron; felt Ameron touch his shoulder. "No," Erien said. "You can't."

"Wait," Ameron advised delay, his voice absolute. He did not touch Erien or support him again, but matched his step with Erien's across the endless expanses of Fountain Court.

Branstatt met them as the doors of Green Hearth closed behind them once again. "What's happened?" he asked.

"Ameron intends to invoke Rene's Convention," Erien said with hollow anger, before Ameron could speak.

"That does not go beyond these walls," Ameron said curtly.

"Why not?" Erien swung on him. "What's the point of it, other than to display that you have no more reason than the rest of them, since it seems to be intellect they distrust, and posture and manipulation they hold faith in!"

He saw Ameron's face with sudden clarity, sharp with startlement, anger and concern. Then it cleared, and softened. The Ava's voice was almost gentle.

"Erien," he said, "there are no perfect actions. Did you foresee Rene's Convention when you forced me to see rot?"

The reflection of responsibility felt like a blunt blow to his chest.

Ameron said kindly, "I thought not." He inhaled, energized again. "Come. Ranar and Charous will be waiting."

He was gone, then, down the Throat. Erien followed, carried by his unquenched anger. They went into the library at the end of Family Hall.

It was a uniquely Monatese room, lined in bookshelves from floor to ceiling on the inner three walls, with wood paneling on the fourth, through which they had entered. Charous turned from where she was standing, frowning at the leather-covered volumes on the bookshelves. The majority would be historical works, chronicles of Monitum's thousand-odd year history, transcribed by hand as a conscious act of reverence, as their originals—or copies of them—deteriorated. The floor of the library was wood inlay, tiled in dark and pale pieces which hinted at—rather than trumpeted—patterns. A heavy rug formed an island of green for the reading chairs and lamps. Ranar rose from a leather-backed chair which had been Di Mon's. He had a book in his hand, but he had not been reading. He set it down.

"Ava Ameron?" the Reetion asked, sounding unnerved for the first time.

Charous took a couple of quick steps toward Ameron and halted with her hand upon the chair, holding her breath.

"Horth Nersal will stand with me," Ameron told them both with a brooding scowl, "because I stand with him if he should fall."

Ranar exclaimed, "Rene's Convention!" with a snatched breath and a look of horror.

The silence that followed was profound. Ameron didn't like it.

"Sit down!" he told Ranar, and swirled toward Erien, stabbing at a second reading chair with a commanding gesture. "And you." Erien sat. He found he needed to. Ameron made sure of Charous with his eyes alone, and launched into his theme with force. "Liege Nersal does not lose duels. But you must know my mind, all of you." He locked, and willed loose, his jaw, making a Gelack truism potent when he spoke. "Anything can happen on the challenge floor."

"You, Reetion," Ameron told Ranar, "are going home. Rire baits us by summoning Amel to answer its charges. Deal with that." He rounded the back of Ranar's chair to stop before Erien. "I know something of you," he said. "Enough to fear your idealism and the arrogance of Vrellish youth. This is a crucial hour for Sevildom. Accept what I say, for if you do not, you may carry the burden of a new dark age into death with you. And waste my sacrifice."

Ameron used the time this earned him to inhale slowly. "If Ev'rel cannot make D'Therd back down from Rene's Convention, then she cannot hold him back from Rire even should she so desire. He will invade Rire with Vretla's Vrellish at his back."

Erien snatched a breath to object. Ameron flashed into temper. "If you throw the Monatese upon Vrellish swords, may you be the first to fall!" The force and the sentiment made Erien flinch despite himself. Ameron saw. He swept away in a turn, and pivoted back to face Erien from a few paces away.

Crisply, he continued. "D'Therd will be eager for conquest. He will pass through the Nersallians in Killing Reach. In the wake of Horth's death, some may break ranks to follow. Ayrium and the Purple Alliance might resist the Dem'Vrel, but not the Vrellish. Even Nersallians back down when Vrellish blood is fired. I want the Purple Alliance safely out of it until the worst is over, then they may make a great difference, for D'Therd will not find Rire an easy conquest any more than my Vrellish mother did two hundred years ago. That error," he said, with an unreadable flash of gray eyes, "both my parents died for. Rire will not be taken without another Killing War. They have no *Okal Rel*." He said it with such contempt it took an effort to remember that Ameron was the Ava who had halted a vengeful genocide by the costly evacuation of Reetion survivors from Killing Reach. It took an effort for Ameron, also, to get past the long shadow which Killing Reach cast.

The Ava resumed with now-familiar force. "When the invasion forces begin to retreat, Ayrium will challenge. In space or with a sword. I doubt," he said, with an awkward mix of resentment and pride, "I could do anything to prevent her doing that, even if I asked. If she can kill D'Therd it may be over, at least for now. Ev'rel is less interested in war than reliable access to food stuffs, which means safe shipping between her Knotted Strings and Demora. Unfortunately the Purple Alliance has an interest in Demora, and Ayrium is D'Ander of Demora's daughter. That interest may entice them to push too far. Dem'Vrel will fight to retain its hold on the groceries needed to sustain its burgeoning population, which is thriving under Ev'rel's governance, no matter who is Liege of Lilac Hearth when all is done."

Ameron paused to regroup his thoughts.

Erien looked across at Ranar, in disbelief that the Reetion Ambassador could listen to this cold blooded, bigoted disposal of Reetion lives, as pawns in a strategy. Ranar returned a calm look and a small shake of his head that Erien could not interpret. Very well, Erien thought, if Ranar would not put an end to this, he would.

Erien got to his feet and faced his father, catching him about to take his first stride of another bout of pacing. Ameron stopped, grasping something was wrong even before Erien spoke.

"No."

The timbre of Erien's own voice startled him. He had to remember that he was a civilized man who had spent a lifetime learning self-control and the art of argument.

"You presume," Erien accused, "that Rire would see a generation of its pilots slaughtered and count itself lucky to be spared worse. Let me put it to you that the Reetion Net collapses and with it the Reetion Administration which has never gone to war, and what rises from the ashes is hostile. Hostile enough to look into history, and its science, to find solutions equally devastating to Sevildom. Attacks on planetary holdings, or use of biological weapons, might be *okal'a'ni* war, but it would not be a war that Rire started. It would have started when Sevolites entered Reetion space and killed Reetions.

"You give me orders in utter disregard of who and what I am! Why should I not realize your nightmare, as you seem prepared to realize mine? The Gelack lust for blood must be slaked? Fine. Then let it be slaked here!" he jabbed downwards with his right hand. "In a blood bath on Fountain Court. And that, Ava, will not be done out of idealistic arrogance or the stupidity of youth but out of the certainty that Sevildom is a malignant creation, something neither allowed nor tested by evolution. We have done our utmost to do each other to death through the scant thousand years of our span, with the virtual elimination of Purebloods and most of the high Vrellish, not to mention large parts of our cultural and technological heritage, and now it seems we wish to extend our killing range to include everything human. But it will take only a small cut to start the blood flowing—right here, with swords—perhaps even so little as inciting the Monatese not to let you be killed by Rene's Convention. You know that, don't you? That is the nightmare you know it is within my power, as your heir, to bring about!"

Ameron had never looked so Vrellish—and so Lorel—both at once. He looked dangerous.

Quietly, Ranar got up. "Erien," he said, very calmly, "you would not do that."

Erien shot him a look which made even the Reetion anthropologist blink in startlement. Then Ranar's eyes flickered from Erien to a point behind his left shoulder—Charous. Erien could sense her behind him now, as if Ranar's face was a mirror. Was she waiting for some signal from Ameron? That made unwelcome sense. An Ava who could glibly sacrifice unknown numbers of innocent Reetions would not hesitate to eliminate an unruly son. Erien locked stares with his father, holding onto his resolution. Ameron would never see him waver. To do so would mean that he could be intimidated. If it was Ameron's way or none, he would rather be dead.

"You are both proving, I think," Ranar observed as though nothing else was happening in the room, "your Vrellish blood. But I promise you," he told Ameron, "that Erien would never squander lives, whether Reetion or Sevolite. As for the rest, it is not up to either of you to decide how Rire will respond." He looked from one Pureblood to the other, calm as a cat in the sun. "You sent Amel to find out how Rire would receive another postponement of our recognition," Ranar reminded Ameron. "Did he tell you what we have decided to do if, instead of diplomatic progress, we should be invaded?"

"Do?" Ameron was nonplussed. But he gestured Charous to stand down with a Monatese hand signal.

"You did not even ask," guessed Ranar. "You paid attention to Ann's defeated defense plans, because you understand the threat posed, but our—naturally—public debate of how we should instead respond made no impact on you. And clearly never featured in Nersallian intelligence either," he glanced at Erien.

"I do understand," Ranar assured them. "The language the debate was couched in would have seemed opaque and alien, the solution chosen only one of many floated, and the final resolution left the details to Foreign and Alien Council. Naturally you focused on the military proposal. But Ava, you are wrong. And you, too, Erien. Rire does respect *Okal Rel*. We have learned how to be conquered. I have advised Foreign and Alien Council to surrender outlying space stations, immediately, if threatened. But only to the Vrellish."

Ameron blinked at him. "The Vrellish?"

Ranar nodded.

"Not the Dem'Vrel?" Ameron hazarded.

"No," Ranar said, firmly.

Ameron was silent for a terrible moment in which his eyes swung right then left in rapid thought above an undecided mouth. He puffed air in an involuntarily spasm which burst out of bounds into a laugh.

Charous spoke for him, as if their two minds had processed the same thoughts. "The Vrellish are the fiercest fighters. But it is the better organized Dem'Vrel to whom Rire cannot afford to lose. The Dem'Vrel are land hungry while the Vrellish prefer to live in artificial environments and have an established tradition of conceding mundane matters to near-commoners. You'll co-opt them to defend you."

Ranar disliked her choice of words. "We will give them whatever they desire, in all honesty," he said.

"I shall be very sorry to miss that, if it comes to pass," exclaimed Ameron, though his amusement had a grim edge. "But I very much doubt that you will find the Vrellish as predictable as you imagine, Liege Rire."

"I am not a liege," Ranar said patiently. "Rire has no lieges. I am a Research Exempt advising anthropologist, to Foreign and Alien Council."

Ameron scowled. "Have your Reetions ever weathered a Vrellish occupation, Ranar?"

"Paradise Reach space stations are manned solely by volunteers briefed by resident anthropologists," Ranar assured him. "No one will do anything rash."

"This plan of yours balances on a sword edge!" cried Erien. Ranar's eyebrow quirked slightly at the very Gelack metaphor and then settled when he saw Erien was in no mood for humor. "All it takes is one atrocity—one Reetion being killed whose friends do not accept this as a necessary sacrifice—one act of retaliation by *okal'a'ni* means— and then you have your Killing War in Paradise Reach."

"It will not happen," Ranar said, stubbornly.

"It may already have." Ameron had lost all signs, now, of humor.

"If you mean Amel's veiled warnings," Ranar said sharply, "I told him that Ann could not possibly have prepared a space defense because it would require—" he stopped dead, suddenly uncomfortable, "—secret communication with the Megan government. Over the Net. Through the arbiters."

"And Amel," observed Charous, "is wanted by Rire for arbiter manipulation."

Ameron sighed. It was a peaceful sound, but heavy-hearted. "We are fools, all three of us, to think we can predict so much, for so many, as if they had no right to their own choices. To act out of one's own convictions, that is *Okal Rel*. And those who make the choices bear the consequences."

"You must ask Amel!" Ranar said, agitated.

"I doubt that he knows, himself, what Ann has actually prepared," Ameron demurred. "It would be like Amel to make mounting a defense possible, but not want to know exactly what it was. Ann may be Reetion but she has the soul of an admiral. She will not have volunteered the information. But suppose Amel could tell us more than we have guessed?

It is burden enough for me to suspect, and do nothing to warn those who may be flying into an *okal'a'ni* death. That, Erien," he told his son, "is a Lorel burden. One which cannot be worn without galling lest it turn evil. Beware. For it can. It should gall." He was silent a moment, then, brooding.

"Erien will decide," Ameron said, "about whether to warn the Vrellish and D'Therd, and how best to deal with Ev'rel herself. He will be Liege Lor'Vrel, if nothing else, and will have the loyalty of Monitum. By then I will have tried my way, and failed."

Ameron looked sympathetically at Erien. "This has been a poor beginning for you, all around. That is my fault. I should have brought you, long ago, to court. I am no good with family." Ameron, weary, was an odd phenomenon, a bit like the sky drooping.

Just then Ayrium entered the library. She was tense, and it showed; she had to catch the door before it slammed against the wall from her over-forceful thrust and jarred the portraits from their hangings.

Ameron's gloom became day again. "Ah," he said. "Prepared?"

"I leave in three hours." She strode over to Erien and flipped a card at him without taking her eyes from Ameron. "Message for you." Unprepared, Erien missed the catch and the card fell face down on the floor. The pattern on the back of it was Nersallian, like the card he had tucked under Tatt's hand when he left the sick room. Erien did not bend down to pick it up, but watched Ameron and Ayrium.

Ayrium, tall but still inches shy of Ameron's height, rose on her toes to confront him. "Tell me what the hell's going on! Branstatt just scuttled out of my sight like he had a guilty conscience!"

Ameron nodded, calmly. "I will tell you, but not here." He turned to Erien, and Ayrium's gaze followed his, resting on Erien with impatient intensity. Ameron said, "One thing more—my bonded *gorarelpul* I will devolve on Charous, not yourself. Consider it a personal matter owed to them all. They will serve you no less well for it."

"Ameron!" Ayrium's voice had a rising edge to it.

"Contingency plans, no more," he said, collecting her arm as he swept past, turning her and bearing her towards the door.

"I am not going to like this," she said, her voice low and potent.

The library door closed on his answer, leaving Erien alone with Ranar and Charous. The Royal *Gorarelpul* had not recovered from Ameron's final remark, giving her personal command of his bonded *gorarelpul* if he died tomorrow. Erien could almost feel sorry for her. She was moved, and would doubtless not have chosen an audience of any kind to witness that. To give her a moment, he went carefully down on one knee and picked up the fallen card. When he stood up, she was watching him with an expression he could not interpret.

If she could not forgive him for his part in bringing Rene's Convention about, Erien thought, it would be best to know now. "I will," he offered her simply, "accept your service if you and the others give it."

She shot him an explosive look, then took possession of herself and nodded with dignity. She was a professional, whatever the intensity of her feeling. And then the professional mask was dashed aside. "But he will not die tomorrow!" she snapped, and made to leave.

Duty halted her midway. "Heir Gelion," she said to Erien without turning.

It took only a heartbeat for him to recognize himself now, in the title. "Yes, Charous?"

She looked back at him. "You must stay on the best terms that you can with Ev'rel, if D'Therd wins tomorrow. Do you understand?"

Erien could not find breath to answer, remembering the bar on the room in Ev'rel's bedroom.

"She is correct," Ranar said, deeply troubled.

Ranar was seated once more, and had lowered his eyes to the book he had been holding when they first entered, turning it over to expose the title "Ameron Biography" across the front. It was Di Mon's favorite copy of a Monatese classic, written after Ameron's initial loss to time-slip, two hundred years ago. "Until and unless we can unseat her—" Ranar made himself look up, but hesitated at the sight of Erien's expression.

"What," Erien said, hoarsely, "would you need me to do for you?"

"Negotiate with Ev'rel. Reinforce her support so that she can stand up to D'Therd and prevent him from mounting an invasion. The Vrellish lack the organizational skills to make a permanent impression on Rire as conquerors, but the Dem'Vrel are a different matter. So are the Nersallians. Either could mount and maintain a permanent occupation. I would much rather that they did not get the chance."

Erien swallowed. "Child-gift for her?" he asked his foster father bluntly. "That's what she said it would take."

"If you don't," Charous said from the door, mercilessly, "she could be prepared, now, to simply force Amel. He has many friends, a lot of them within her jurisdiction. She could make him cooperate by threatening them. But using you would probably be safer for her. And it would give you access to her inner circles."

A small muscle twitched once at the corner of Ranar's mouth. "I am sorry, Erien," was all the comfort he could muster.

"And would that," Erien said, "be sufficient?"

"It might," the Royal 'Relpul said. "Depending upon how you manage the rest of it." She nodded to him, dismissing herself, or him, and went out the door, leaving Erien alone with his foster father.

Exhaustion came over him in a slow wave. He endured it, waiting for it to ebb. Or for himself to grow accustomed to it, as to cold water. The closed door offered nothing, and slowly his gaze shifted to the smaller of the two portraits hanging on the wall. The larger was of Ameron. The smaller one was Di Mon.

It was strange to realize that he had not seen Di Mon's face since he left Monitum. If Ranar kept a picture, Erien had never seen it. Ranar might not, since a need for images was inherent neither to his culture nor his personal nature. Erien wondered how old Di Mon had been when this portrait was painted: younger than the man he had known, for there was a suggestion of fire in the gray eyes, of temper in the set of the lips, of pride and formidable intellect in the fine Vrellish features. There was, he thought, something eerily familiar about that face, as though he had seen it recently. Di Mon was wearing heavy, formal clothing, a cloak with jade clasps in the shape of leaves, and the green and black braids of his station. His hand was posed, uneasily, on the hilt of a sword laid before him. The painter had had difficulty with that hand. Di Mon could sit as still as a huntsman in a hide, but for his restive fingers. Erien had forgotten the sound of them tap-tap-tapping as Di Mon read or listened to long arguments or simply stared out the window, thinking. The pulse of his fingers was the pulse of his thoughts.

"That was painted," Ranar said, coming quietly to his side, "the second time he gave his Oath as Liege Monitum. He was not yet thirty." He looked from the portrait to Erien and back, his brow creased slightly, almost in pain. "The resemblance is quite remarkable."

Erien swayed slightly. Ranar put out a hand, by reflex, and stopped himself before he touched Erien, who was not a child anymore, even to Ranar.

Erien said, "I may have killed his Ava. Or Ev'rel. Di Mon loved her, also."

"Not as he loved you," Ranar said, simply. "And he would have understood. You can't stop Ameron, not any more than Di Mon could have. Ameron is Ameron."

"I shouldn't . . . "

"Shouldn't what?" said the Reetion, with some academic asperity. "Shouldn't have told Ameron all that you knew about Amel and Ev'rel? Surely I taught you better than to prefer lies to the truth."

"Ameron warned me that I didn't understand. I thought . . . I thought he was saying that only to deter me from taking any action."

"He was," Ranar said bluntly. "But that does not make this your fault."

Erien pressed the fingers of his right hand to his forehead. A sharp edge scratched his brow. Taking his hand away he found the Nersallian message card, forgotten in his palm. He turned it over.

The handwriting was, he presumed, Dorn's. At least it was not Horth's, though the message was brief enough for that.

"Horth wants me to stand as his second tomorrow," Erien reported to Ranar.

Thoughts flickered behind Ranar's eyes as the Reetion sorted implications, far more deftly than Erien could have, even hale and well rested. Ranar said, "It's an honor, Erien. Though I'm not sure whether Ameron would approve. There is risk."

Erien drew a shuddering breath. A breath, he realized, of surrender. He thought of that odious tricolor cloak and of his distaste for it, which now seemed such a petty thing. The truly dreadful obligations, the truly crushing burdens, were the unseen ones. A cloak could be shed—in truth he could not recall where exactly he had left that one—but this, never. To do whatever he had to, to ensure that Gelion, Rire and as many of his kin—of blood as well as mind—survived. Di Mon would have. That young man with the fire, temper, pride and intellect had served weak, degenerate Avas whose value as Purebloods had exempted them from all risks, even under *Okal Rel*. And Di Mon had served with only a memory, written up in the 'Ameron Biography', to inspire him. Hope of more would have been a madman's illusion.

Di Mon had had much more, in the end. Nine years of his Ava, and the care and shaping of that Ava's heir. Ranar was no doubt right about the stamp of Di Mon's character on Erien's face. May that character see him through this *rel*.

Erien said, "That, too, will be my decision."

CHAPTER XXVI

DORN WAS WAITING FOR ERIEN in the entrance hall of Black Hearth. He smiled gravely at the sight of Erien. "Thank you for coming, Heir Gelion. I hope this is not too early for you. How do you feel?"

"I have been better," Erien admitted.

Dorn nodded. "The question wasn't just polite," he said, leading Erien into the Throat towards the stairs that led down to the Octagon. "Horth may want to use you this morning. You have a decent right-handed form." That was being charitable. But Erien was far closer to ambidextrous than any Nersallian he had ever encountered; they tended toward Vrellish left-handed dominance. "Could you give him ten minutes?" Dorn asked.

"I will give him whatever I have," said Erien.

Dorn nodded and moved on to his next concern. "I don't know whether you've ever seen him before a duel, but if you haven't, don't try to talk to him." He glanced at Erien, assessed his understanding and compliance, and seemed satisfied to move on. "How is Tatt?" Dorn's tone warmed.

"Drasous is still keeping constant watch. He is worried about fluid in the lungs, but he says Tatt is stronger. He won't let me see him."

"I am not surprised," said Dorn. "You look like you've been through a shakeup without a ship yourself." He paused at the top of the spiral stair. "Erien, this was inevitable. Horth and D'Therd would have had to meet this way, now, or the next time."

Erien drew a deep breath. "I wish," he confessed, "I had had no part in it."

Dorn put a hand lightly on his back, behind his injured shoulder. "You're not the kind of person who takes no part in things, Erien. Just like your half-brother, Tatt." Then his gaze shifted past Erien; his face changed and he pushed slightly at Erien, moving them both back from the top of the stairs. Erien turned, knowing who he would see.

And found a stranger.

The stranger had Horth's crisp features and purposeful economy of movement. It was the eyes, Erien realized. An intelligence too great to be animal, but perhaps not quite human.

In a single glance, Horth read Erien's body, its hurts and its strengths, in his posture. Horth read his spirit, its grudges and wounds, in the set of his face. Horth read his fighting skill in the way he held his sword and balanced his body. Horth recognized him; knew who he was. But this Horth, the stranger, did not know his name. Perhaps he did not even know his own name.

Horth passed them without a nod and descended the stairs. Erien did not know he was gripping the banister until he felt the throb of Horth's step, like a pulse in the metal.

Dorn gestured Erien to follow Horth down the stairs, which Erien did, after that soundless pulse had faded.

Horth had already started a circuit of Black Hearth's practice area, which filled most of the wedge. Dorn laid the braided jacket he was carrying on a bench. Erien shrugged out of his. A White Hearth valet had been supervising tailors and tying knots most of the night to salvage the bloody ruin he had made of it, and it was now sleeveless. Under the jacket he, like Dorn and Horth, wore fleet fatigues.

"Run one circuit," Dorn suggested, "then stretch. You need to loosen up but not to wear yourself out." He started after his father, leaving Erien to choose his own pace. Which was slow, because every step jarred his arm, sling or no sling. After a quarter circuit Erien shed the sling and let his injured arm take its own weight. Dorn ran a second circuit, took a moment to give Erien some brief advice about working around an injury—something which the son of Horth Nersal would have had to do more than once—collected a sword from the racks and laid it beside himself, in easy reach, as he started an intense warm-up. At no point, Erien saw, did Dorn's awareness shift from his father, so that when Horth suddenly veered towards the racked practice swords and drew one, Dorn was ready to snatch his own up. He had to be.

Erien stood blinking, his eyes trying to adjust to the uncanny speed of Horth's attacks. He could not even see what Horth was doing; it looked like a single attack, as though Horth's point skimmed rather than traveled through space from start point to target. *Gods*, Erien thought. He saw the thin line of Dorn's lips and the sweat on his face, through the flickering facets and shadows of their moving blades. All he could hear was the click and snap of metal, and the scuff of their feet and their breathing.

I cannot do this, Erien thought.

The physical demands were the least of it. Horth needed from Erien what Dorn was giving him, the resistance, the struggle, the *rel*, so that

that wordless, nameless power inhabiting Horth Nersal's skin would be roused to its true purpose. To kill. And to win.

I can't do this. I haven't got it in me.

A day ago, that would have been the truth. But Erien knew what he had in him, now. He had used it to kill D'Lekker Dem'Vrel; that force which had leapt out of his right hand to shatter his half-brother's windpipe. He looked at his right hand. It was trembling.

I can't.

He wanted to be the civilized man he had believed himself to be. He wanted to be the innocent with bloodless hands who had arrived on Gelion four days ago. He wanted to be Highlord Erien, Ward of Monitum and of Rire, not Pureblood Erien, heir of Lor'Vrel and fratricide. But it was not Erien, Ward of Monitum, whom Horth needed now. It was the Throne Price, conceived for political ends, dragged into the depraved sexual game between mother and brother, stolen, kept ignorant, and moved like a blind pawn by father and brother—he pulled himself forcibly back from sick remorse at what his ignorance had wrought. Horth needed the darkness. He needed the anger. It was the only strength Erien had to give him.

Shaking slightly, Erien pictured himself in a locked room feeling along the walls, looking for a weakness he could break though to let whatever was in that room . . . out. The irony of it was that he had built the wall himself. But here on bloody Gelion, all that the civilized constraints did was lead him to be despised as weak, mocked as a Reetion, moved as a blind pawn.

"Erien," Dorn's voice said softly, "he's ready for you now."

Erien opened his eyes. He looked past Dorn at Horth and met the wordless intelligence in those eyes. Liege Nersal, *kinf'stan*, patricide, Highlord Admiral, and would-be conqueror of Rire. He set aside his knowledge of the man's honor, courage and quirky humanity. He put them inside that locked room in his mind. Dorn pressed a hilt into his right hand and he went to face his nemesis.

Horth left him on his knees, two minutes, ten minutes, an hour, fifty hours later. He did not know how long he had withstood the barrage, or how many times Horth had hit him, or whether he had hit Horth at all. He let himself down to lie, stomach down, face turned to one side on the cold floor, unable to turn his mind from breathing long enough to throw up. By the time he had got his breath back, his nausea had abated to the dull unease he had wakened with that morning. He hadn't eaten. He had nothing to lose. His arm, he thought, actually hurt less. Endorphins. Or maybe nervous systems, like nervecloth, could overload.

Dorn crouched beside him, looking worried. "Erien, are you all right?"

No, he thought. But what hurt most was not physical. He hadn't thought much about belief past the age of seven or eight as he grew into reason, but perhaps that seven-year-old had been right and there were such things as souls. How could a mythical construct hurt so much? From further away he could hear the eerie whisper of feet, shuffle-stalking; that, rather than Dorn, drew his head up. Not twenty feet away, Horth was fighting alone against an opponent he saw only in his mind, an opponent stronger, faster and more powerful than either of the ones he had already defeated.

Erien pushed himself up to a sitting position. *Sevolite stamina,* he thought bitterly. Dorn checked Erien's shoulder where a small patch of fresh blood was already congealing, and retied his sling and then settled cross-legged on the floor beside him to watch Horth. As his breathing settled, Erien could hear sounds from the direction of the Octagon. Voices. People moving. Sounds he had not heard before his own duel. Dorn sensed him tense up, and leaned as close as he could without jarring Erien's arm. "He'll know when it's time."

Moments later, Horth stepped back, disengaged, turned, looked at Dorn, nodded once, sheathed his sword and walked over to the bench, where he collected a towel and dried his face—almost the first ordinary movement of the day. Dorn got smoothly to his feet and offered Erien his hand. Erien let himself be pulled up. He felt light-headed, but not unpleasantly so. Dorn studied him with a quizzical, slightly uneasy look, interrupted by the sound of Horth drawing his sword, a sound that made the little hairs rise on the back of Erien's neck.

The Ava's champion laid down his sheath and belt, leaving his sword naked in his hand, and started for the door to the Octagon. Dorn ducked over to snatch up their jackets and a sword belt for Erien. He pulled his jacket on and got Erien into his, which was easier now that it was sleeveless. They had no time for anything else. Erien had to carry his sheathed sword in his hand. Dorn whispered that they'd deal with it outside. They caught up with Horth and fell in on either side, just before he stepped out onto the Octagon.

WAITING WAS MISERABLE for Amel.

He was escorted out through Green Hearth only minutes prior to the duel, flanked by Branstatt and Ketatt. He did not know if he felt himself protected, or a prisoner. That was equally unclear, he feared, to Vretla Vrel, Zind D'Therd, and the other retainers of Red and Lilac Hearths, ranged about Ev'rel across the Challenge Floor.

He touched Ketatt's hand where it rested on her belt, and said, "Let me stand by myself."

The Monatese errant let him move off.

His movement, though he only went six paces, fetched a hundred pairs of eyes. The attention made him walk better, stubbornly denying his hurts, because to be a dancer in his every step was to be whole. He saw Ev'rel smile, guessing that. He could almost have smiled back.

She was Ev'rel, after all. His lover. Liege of Dem'Vrel. His patron and coach. Of course she knew him inside out. Just as he felt he could almost read her thoughts.

The desolation, in Ev'rel, which had tossed him on its horns, had spent itself in the act. She was her old, public self. Composed. She would be Ava soon, or she would be rid of a rival, for that was what D'Therd had become. She was thinking, also, that she would have Amel back. That, as she had said, he did not hate well or for too long. She looked at him with a possessive confidence, holding his eyes for a heartbeat with the promise in hers of deep, obsessive love.

But he knew how the poem ended now. The pain they shared was not as vast as space but just the darkness of that pit into which he was so loath to look. He'd discovered a bottom to it after all, and ordinary love could fill it up.

A peace broke over him, of certitude, and he relaxed.

She read him, heart and soul. He saw the tiny muscles of her brow contract. And he was as sorry for her as he would have been for himself if the darkness inside had indeed proved cold and infinite.

The arrival of Horth Nersal and D'Therd Dem'Vrel commanded attention like a spike of ice lancing up his back.

D'Therd was large and proud. He had attained his goal. Somehow, he managed to bask in the attention of the assembled Court without showing an interest in anything but Horth Nersal. No lover could have paid more attention to his object of desire. D'Therd gave off an aura like a *rel*-ship in a shakeup, prepared to force an enemy ship out of existence with the tearing power of his wake.

Horth Nersal's leanness was that of a razor's edge. Amel had the eerie sense of the Nersallian's sword extending through the hilt into his left arm, as much a part of him as bone.

He shuddered. They were incomprehensible to him, bent with relish on proving their supremacy against the other's life. The emotion struck no resonance. He was unable to feel concern for either man.

Prince H'Us forced words upon the silence. "Where is the *okal'a'ni* medtech?"

His demand stirred up the Demish outside Silver Hearth, the ladies bunching together as their men screened them by drawing to the front. Luthan stood against the tide. She stabbed a glance at him, then at

Erien, before Hillian took charge. The ladies were being withdrawn. The ladies were being withdrawn, as were other non-combatants. Ameron gestured to Charous to clear out his *gorarelpul*. With trust atremble, he could not afford to have the possibility of a loaded needle gun at his back, negating his claim to honorable conduct.

Amel felt, acutely, his lack of a duelling sword. But it would have alarmed him more to be encumbered by one. His personal awareness extended to cover all the living, breathing bodies on the Octagon: a space which could be filled, as swift as thought, with naked swords. The heart rates and deepened breathing around him set the rhythm of his own.

Ameron answered Prince H'Us's demand to produce Mira. "Would you muddy a great moment over one commoner? The medtech is Heir Monitum's concern."

"At my request!" Amel felt the declaration pulled from his lungs by the sharpening attitudes of the Avim's Oath retainers. He drew Vretla's attention at once, her whole body focusing on where he stood. Her face gave up its dawning scowl. Zind Dem'Vrel's eyes narrowed. A nobleborn relative, at her back, let his poised hand relax. Amel found himself as surprised at this proof of his influence as Ev'rel's face declared her, his heart hammering in his throat.

"The medtech is absent by my desire," Amel told H'Us, holding Demish attention with words, and Vrellish with body language, for he felt very strongly what he spoke. "I claim that right," he said Pureblood to Royalblood. "It is I that she is said to have injured."

That did not cover the whole truth, but it proved poetically true enough, at least as corollary to Ameron's statement.

H'Us scowled, and let it drop with a nod.

Ev'rel swallowed.

Amel saw that Ev'rel was frightened by him! To feel fear was her greatest horror and the last thing he wanted to inspire in her. He felt a stab of guilty panic.

"This challenge," said Ameron, "is about who shall be Ava."

Something terrible was going to happen. It was in Ameron's ringing tone.

"I am prepared to stand with my champion today," he fixed his stare on Ev'rel. "Are you?"

Ev'rel was unprepared. She went as white as the marble of Fountain Court.

Please, Gods, Amel thought, *Let her back down! And this could be over now*! He wanted to shout it, and could not get breath into his lungs.

Ev'rel took no comfort in how she saw him react. It only convinced her that Ameron was serious. She looked to Vretla Vrel, and her other alert, wary vassals. She looked to the family of Zind D'Therd Dem'Vrel. She looked to the Prince-Admiral of H'Us.

"You do not have to, Avim," Prince H'Us spoke in the voice he used with Demish women. It earned him a rude sneer from one of Liege Vrel's male retainers, Vretla herself oblivious to the gender dynamics that Amel knew she simply did not fathom. But Ev'rel had been raised by Demish rules. She understood the refuge, in dependency, which Prince H'Us offered. It must have been tempting for her. Amel held his breath, waiting, not sure what he hoped for.

It felt right when Ev'rel rejected Prince H'Us's overture. His protection would cost her her hard-earned power. Power, Amel knew, was life to her.

But neither was she prepared to roll dice on the Challenge Floor with Ameron.

"A very pretty gesture, Lor'Vrel," she answered, stressing the 'Lor'. "And thank you, Prince H'Us, but no—you may not have Demora."

A titter rippled through the Vrellish and Dem'Vrellish ranks. Even the Nersallians smiled. It was well known that the H'Usians considered Demora a strayed trust, as the vestige of Golden Demish power, which ought to be theirs to benignly administer. The H'Usian Demish looked sour.

"Are you willing to continue by Rene's Convention?" Ameron usurped the stage once more. "Or will you end this, here and now, by backing down?"

"She accepts!" D'Therd boomed, without turning around to met his mother's eyes.

It was a challenge. If she contradicted him, she would lose her champion and gain a rival.

Ev'rel's nostrils flared.

Muscle locked in tension in Amel's back.

Ev'rel's Vrellish blood rose. Her face flushed. Her eyes shone. She breathed through parted lips, fast, her chest shaking with each inhalation.

Amel's heart pounded too hard. Wetness fled his mouth. A shivering red veil of blood vessels wavered before his open eyes.

Ev'rel's voice struck like a gong.

"I will," she said, strong with anger, "have back my Throne."

"No," Amel tried to scream. The sound was the faintest gasp. And he flashed back to a helpless youth.

Ev'rel did not react to Amel half-collapsing in a faint. She hurled the word 'Throne' at Erien, dismissing him as a defective pawn. Amel understood, of course. Everything hinged on D'Therd now, and she had eyes only for her champion. Amel himself was fully occupied with his past, bowed on one knee on Fountain Court. Erien moved toward him to forestall anyone else intervening, and stopped as Amel came to himself, and struggled, silently, back up, feet shifted wider apart.

Then the Octagon sucked sound to silence and complete stillness made space for sudden death.

It should *not last long*, Erien thought. And then, surely, he would be able to draw another breath. Dorn, on his left hand side, was very still. Amel, on his right, trembled finely.

H'Us did not insist upon Demish ceremony. What needed to be said had been said. No one else had a right to a place on the killing ground.

The champions closed on each other very slowly, moving sideways step by step across the rough brown floor, postures mirroring each other, Horth left-handed, D'Therd right, Horth in black, D'Therd in a blood red vest with blue mesh on the shoulders. Erien felt Dorn tense. Neither combatant had moved into the other's range. The edges of their blades burned like diamond under the lights. D'Therd's blade inscribed tiny blazing circles in the air, point held low and threatening. Horth's did not move. The onlookers on the far side of the circle eased back as the swordsmen neared the edge. A white mist gathered before Erien's eyes. He thought, *I am* not *going to faint.*

Horth lunged. D'Therd surged forwards to meet him. Light flashed along their blades; there was a rasp of metal on metal. The swordsmen jarred against each others' hilts, and stood hand to hand, thrusting against each other. A needle of brilliant metal jutted past the backs of each.

The difference of color was subtle. Had Erien not had the blue-white of the length on Horth's side for comparison, he might not have perceived the blush, the thinnest lacquering of red, on D'Therd's side. Certainly the swordsman's face, in profile, hardly changed. D'Therd jammed his hilt against Horth's, his blade carving the empty air past Horth's shoulder, and pushed with all the power of his right arm. Horth sprang back—and Erien, who had not yet taken in the meaning of that faint red wash, felt a sudden pulse of alarm as Horth did not raise his hilt to block D'Therd's lifting sword, but gave, instead, an odd little twist of his wrist. Erien saw, then, the tip tearing free of D'Therd's chest, and the ripple of the fabric with the first pulse of blood. With that last small twist, Horth had severed the heart wall or the great vessels. A puzzled expression crossed D'Therd's face, as though he had forgotten his immediate intention, finding himself suddenly faint. Without looking down, without taking his eyes from his opponent,

D'Therd brought his left hand up to the wound, cupped, as though to catch the blood. Erien saw the moment in which he understood. And a heartbeat later, perhaps, the moment in which he died, still standing, sword still raised for a stroke that would not fall.

Time stood still for Erien. As it did, he remembered another death, years ago, on Monitum. The memory was like a chord, plucked by the sight of Horth's blood-filmed sword, and in it, Erien was a child.

A door opened into a sunlit study. The child Erien saw a man's foot, in a plain shoe. A bar of sunlight tracked in from the window. In it he saw Di Mon's bloody hands, wrapped in a strip of green leather, still gripping the blade which protruded from beneath his sternum. Di Mon had been wearing black, and the blood was merely a darkness on his shirt. He had rolled back the rug which lay beneath his desk. He had tried to make the leaving of his life as orderly as the living of it. He had almost succeeded.

In all the years since, Erien had never let himself remember Di Mon's face. He saw it now, and it was terrible. Terrible not in its pain, but in its peace. A peace which flowed, somehow, from *Okal Rel*.

Ev'rel's cry pierced Erien's reverie.

She wailed, "Amel!"

Erien shuddered. Brown, white, and color rushed in on him. He was back on the Octagon. It was not over yet.

AMEL WATCHED D'THERD DIE. His eyes burned. His stomach forced bile into his throat. It felt impossible. In his life, D'Therd was a constant, like a mountain he struggled to move, rock by rock.

He stared, compelled to assimilate the new fact.

And heard Horth Nersal move.

His brother's slayer walked toward Ev'rel, as inexorable as a comet in its track.

On the first step, the Dem'Vrel drew back. The Vrellish took stock of the Nersallian numbers on Fountain Court. H'Us saw it, and looked shocked. Ameron's jaw locked. A melee was not yet ruled out.

On the second step, Ev'rel caught up with the audience, grasping her own peril. Amel watched her raise her hand to her throat, a familiar and vulnerable gesture. Her lips moved. He saw his name on them, but she produced no sound.

On Horth's third step, Ev'rel backed away from him.

Vretla Vrel drew her sword. Those few who misread her action gasped. Amel saw what the Vrellish liege meant to do: press her weapon's hilt into Ev'rel's hand. He could imagine her saying, bewildered, "Fight, woman!" For Vretla, at the very least, it would be preferable to die fighting.

Ev'rel would not take the sword Vretla offered. She blinked at the swordswoman blankly.

Then she wailed, aloud, "Amel!"

It was simple. She wanted protection.

Amel felt calm. Like a mote in the eye of a storm. He had eternity to decide how he would respond. He did not have to go to her. He could stand and watch her die, alone, empowered by the memory of her inflicting on him what she knew he could not endure. It was his choice, whether to hate or not. If he closed his eyes, he believed that he could. Her terror undid his resolve. Terror made her as vulnerable, to him, as Erien's infant cry, long ago: an anguish he could not ignore. He had no defense against his own compassion. No idea, either, what he meant to do.

Erien's hand gripped his upper arm, stopping him before he started forward.

It was only then that he realized his crossing to Ev'rel could have sparked mayhem. He murmured to Erien, feeling foolish, "I am sorry," unsure himself what he meant by it. He felt ethereal.

A clash of swords snatched him back to the challenge floor.

Vretla had engaged Horth—not in combat, although she took the risk of inviting it—but simply to get his attention. Her Vrellish and his Nersallians bristled.

"Give her death choice!" Vretla demanded, through her teeth, over their crossed swords. In her eyes, and the arm holding her sword steady against Horth Nersal's, was neither truth nor complaint, just Vrellish fire.

Horth stared back. The words penetrated.

They disengaged with a long, spine-grating slither. Horth relaxed. To Vretla, once, he nodded. The Nersallians on the floor stood down. The Vrellish still buzzed with energy which focused now, on Amel.

Amel knew what death choice meant; the right to pick one's executioner. He could not conceive what that had to do with him, except that Vretla had misunderstood Ev'rel calling his name aloud.

Erien said, very low, "They expect you to kill her."

Amel looked at him, stricken. His half-brother's face was pale, but composed. Amel's eyes raked it for proof of kindred feeling and found only cool Reetion reason. If he did not kill Ev'rel, someone else would, and the odds of losing other lives was greater. Amel swallowed. The sober man who held his duty before him, so strong but so unmoved, was the very incarnation of Di Mon's soul. It gave him a spooky turn. He blinked, and moved away.

Ev'rel waited.

She had figured out, before him, what was going on, and seemed oddly calm. He could not believe that she accepted this death, at his hands or anyone else's.

He did not know if he could kill her. But he crossed the floor.

Vretla offered him her sword as he drew abreast, but Ev'rel drew her stiletto from her belt and held it instead, hilt first, toward him. Vretla drew back.

He began to smell Ev'rel's cloves and Turquoise. To feel her. Woman's passion and human love smothered forever inside her space cold cocoon. And he understood at last, that she had to want the path out of darkness which he had chosen, for him to ever have walked with her, side by side. He had failed, but it was not a failure any greater effort on his part could cure.

He was so lost in his revelation, that he did not see her turn the stiletto now that his body screened her from all but a few of the Dem'Vrel. It was one of them, sucking in breath, which alerted him. Then he felt the touch of the stiletto's point against his light jacket, between his ribs.

"You are such a fool," she whispered, in fond triumph, looking into his eyes.

Mira, he thought, would be very disappointed in him.

He found himself speaking from the heart even as he planned how to resist. If he could even deflect the puncture, he might last long enough to be helped.

"Let me live," he said simply, "to remember."

A Demish sentiment, he thought, bemused, as he watched her weigh up the odds with Vrellish wits. Behind her, those Dem'Vrel with the best view grew restive, and a quiver went through the ranks of those close enough to overhear what they were whispering to each other.

It was Vretla taking an interest which decided Ev'rel.

"Finish the poem," she said.

He resisted jerkily as her hands closed on his, coming up to defend himself. But she had turned the stiletto back again. Two handed she dragged it and his hands to her heart, from his. He helped, at the end, when her will faltered.

Then they were sinking together, to the floor, and he was free just to hold her. She held his hand in her grip, face turned in against his waist. No last words. Death could only be endured.

No one spoke for what seemed a long time after she was dead.

He was wet. Her blood, warm still, was soaking them.

He bowed over her, and caring nothing for the audience, he wept.

ERIEN FLINCHED AT THE BELATED AWARENESS of an unperceived approach. It was Amy, coming up to Dorn. Had the tableau been less tense, or the audience more sympathetic, he was certain she would have flung herself on her beloved, snatched from the swords of the *kinf'stan* by his father's triumph. It was all there in the look they gave each other as they settled for a touch of hands, both breathing through parted lips in the stale air, still heavy with the burden of what might have happened. Then she broke away, going quickly to her father, her mother's representative after all, in that.

Ameron had likewise attracted Branstatt and Tessitatt. The rest of the room still watched Amel and Ev'rel.

Except for Horth.

The dead did not interest Horth. Only the living, moving and pressing. He still existed in combat's *rel* world, alert to threat and threatened, dangerous, his dark eyes flicking from form to form, distrustful of stirrings of movement as the spell cast by death began to release the crowd. Vretla Vrel turned her head and met his gaze; two predators who needed no reasons for challenge save the other's existence.

"I'd better go to him," said Dorn. He took a step towards Horth and then swung back, and a smile burst across his face. With that startling Vrellish swiftness Erien was coming to know, Dorn reached across to grip Erien's sound arm in a hard grasp. "Just do one thing for me, Erien," Heir Nersal said happily. "Don't ever teach Tatt that move."

Erien's lips shaped the word, "Teach?" but Dorn was already gone, trotting lightfootedly through the uneasy grouping around Horth. Horth stared as Dorn approached, his sword held, point down, in his hand. Then darted a look past Dorn, at Erien.

To Erien's mind came, unbidden, the image of Horth's lunge, and D'Therd's counterattack, of their blades twining around each other . . . no, of Horth's blade twining around D'Therd's—binding it and trapping it—the point levered high and clear of Horth's left shoulder as Horth's point drove on to D'Therd's heart. He blinked at what he saw in his mind's eye, and then went back, and *looked* at it again, the images coming more reluctantly than the memory of how it felt to execute that particular attack. He knew the sense of impregnability when it worked, as he rode in along his opponent's steel—and the chagrin as it failed, when he missed the taking of the blade and neatly impaled himself on a waiting point. A blunt point, always. It was a sportsman's attack, learned on Rire, tried on occasion in the Nersallian fleet, usually with humiliating results. Horth had hardly been impressed. He had picked up Erien's timing without effort and driven home his own attack.

Gods, Erien thought. He would never have imagined anyone would use it in a challenge with live blades. It was chancy as the favor of Earth's homeless, quarreling Gods.

Horth seemed to read Erien's thoughts in his dawning dismay and awe, and answered it with a sudden white flash of teeth. The expression was so much like Dorn's that Erien suffered a moment of involuntary belief in the soul's blood connections—which rebounded on him with the knowledge that his own half-brother and mother lay dead on the Challenge Floor.

New movement from the Dem'Vrel quenched Horth's grin. He sobered, lifted his sword as Dorn stood beside him, and acknowledged the approach of D'Therd's family with a salute of respect for a fallen foe.

Zind D'Therd Dem'Vrel saluted back. It would have been Dorn saluting D'Therd, if it had been Horth who had fallen on the Challenge Floor. Erien had the uncanny sense a mere blink might still make it so.

Then Erien was caught up on the crest of a mighty sound, as twenty Nersallians drew and saluted the Vrellish of the Avim's Oath, and as many Vrellish and higher Dem'Vrellish cleared swords in a metallic rush to answer back. Some of the lesser Dem'Vrellish looked bewildered or alarmed, moving closer to where Amel, oblivious, still held Ev'rel's body on the floor. The H'Usians watched, struck by the moment's power, too late to have taken part and too moved to be petty about it.

Okal Rel reigned undisputed on the Challenge Floor.

Then the glory was past, and the bodies still waited to be cleaned up.

Erien watched as the Dem'Vrel collected their fallen champion from the rough, brown floor. D'Therd's size and dead laxness made him a difficult burden, and they managed him clumsily at first, without dignity; his head slid back and his limbs sprawled. Erien bit his lip against ordering them to do better. D'Therd did not deserve that. But they laid him down again and organized themselves, and when they lifted him anew, it was carefully.

Amel paid no attention to the people who expected something of him. He still knelt with Ev'rel against him, her face turned against his shoulder, his eyes closed and the tears moving in a steady flow down his matchless face. Erien started moving before he thought, and kept moving—kept moving because people were looking at him, and because—because ten years ago he had been kneeling beside the body of someone he loved. And Amel had been there.

It had not been Erien who had drawn the sword from Di Mon's body, but Amel. It had not been Erien who composed Di Mon's body to match his face, before they called the Monatese, but Amel. Amel had done the needful things and had freed Erien to begin grieving.

He went down on one knee in front of Amel. "Amel?"

Amel shook his head, a gentle swaying from side to side.

Erien cleared his throat. "Amel, you should take her in now." He remembered Amel's injuries. "If you can. If not, I will help you."

Amel opened his clear gray eyes and gazed at Erien, as if from a great distance. Erien endured the gaze. Then, without the least change of expression, Amel gathered his will and began to lift himself and Ev'rel, still holding her close. Erien made a move to slip his right hand under Ev'rel's body, but stopped at a flare of rejection in Amel's possessive glance. He did no more than brush her skirts with his fingertips as he watched Amel struggle to his feet beneath his burden. But though rising was an effort, Amel held her so carefully that her head did not loll or her hands trail. She might have been asleep in his arms.

Willing hands pushed aside the Lilac Hearth screens, so that Amel need not shoulder through a narrow door. Then the Dem'Vrel closed the screens behind him, claiming Amel for their own.

"*Okal Rel*," declared Ameron, "has been satisfied in blood. It is finished. Let heirs and victors thrive and bear no grudge."

Erien felt Ameron's presence behind him in more than the words— like a change in the charge of the air—and turned, too quickly, catching himself as he lost his balance.

A transient whitening of his vision gave his father's form an otherworldly luster. Or maybe his loss of balance was inflicted by Ameron. All the lines of force in the room seemed to converge on the one tall man in Lor'Vrellish white. Life seemed to have redoubled in him, in his untidy brown hair, the sharp, mobile features, the intense, iridescent gray eyes. Ameron was a force. Erien could not, in his presence, know what he thought of him any more than one could see clearly looking into the sun.

"Rire," the Ava said, speaking to Erien, but in a voice clear and firm enough to fill the room, "shall fall within the protection of the Throne, in as much as any house would which is Ava-sworn. They shall have representation at court, through my heir and son." Ameron's look schooled Erien not to dispute the terms until he was done. Erien could not have. He could not speak to claim this triumph. Nor, he knew with shame and self-loathing, could he refute it. He had done what he had come to do: secured Ameron's recognition for Rire. But he had never imagined the cost.

"No one shall invade or threaten Rire without as great a provocation, or as great a consequence, as any other house of man," concluded Ameron.

There was a disturbed rustle among the Demish at his use of the English word for humanity, where Gelack custom would have favored 'Sevildom'.

Vretla Vrel developed a crease between her dark eyebrows. "What does that mean?" she fired across the Challenge Floor at Tessitatt Monitum. "What is 'man'?"

"The Reetions are human, of course," said H'Us, coming forward with the Demish, halfway across the floor. "But do you mean to consider them Sevolite? Impossible!"

"If they are Sevolite," said Vretla, content, "they can be challenged."

"Discuss it," ordered Ameron, "with Erien. Tomorrow." He dropped his voice. "We will do no more business over fresh blood. Clear the Octagon. Palace staff are prepared to Feast the Dead on Demlara's Walk beginning in half an hour. Every house of both Oaths is invited." He set his arms akimbo, spreading out his white cloak. "It could have been my wake. I've seen to it that it will be worth attending."

"Tomorrow," Vretla told Erien with a narrow look. She swirled into her own ranks and withdrew.

"Yes, good," said H'Us, looking confident all at once as he turned from Ava and heir to reassure his following of uneasy princes. "We will work something out that sees to it that we have nothing to do with them, just as I've always known we should." H'Us was met, immediately, with arguments, but the Demish did, at least, retreat toward Silver Hearth.

"Take the Monatese off the Octagon, too," Ameron ordered Tessitatt.

She frowned. "I want no trade in Reetion goods that threatens Monatese monopolies!" she told her Ava, firmly, before she obeyed the order. "Remember that."

Ameron nodded, and said cheerfully, "Take it up with Erien."

Finally they were alone.

Ameron surveyed the room, cavernous now that the two hundred-odd bodies of his assembled Court were gone. He owned it. And them. He had seen them through his way, and won. He revealed it in a slow, slyly Lorel smile. Then he turned with irrepressible joy in his triumph to his weary son.

"I would get some sleep," he advised with the satisfaction of someone contemplating for himself nourishing food and wholesome exercise. "We have just begun."

GLOSSARY

ACK REL:

A Gelack expression implying that, struggle though we may, things will fall out as luck and skill dictate. It is often taken to mean "let swords decide" but can be offered in sympathy as well, in the sense of "tough luck".

ARBITER, ARBITER NET:

An artificial intelligence designed for law and administration on Rire and its associated worlds of the arbiter net. Connections between arbiters on different planets are maintained by reality skimming pilots, who carry crucial data with them.

AVA, AVA'S OATH:

The Pureblood Sevolite with the most Fountain Court vassals is called Ava. The Ava's vassals constitute the Ava's Oath.

AVIM, AVIM'S OATH:

The Pureblood Sevolite second in power only to the Ava is the Avim. The Avim's Fountain Court vassals constitute the Avim's Oath, and if enough vassals change allegiance, the Avim and Ava switch roles.

BIRTH RANK:

Gelacks belong to one of eight birth ranks depending on Sevolite genetic inheritance. *Purebloods* are 100% Sevolite and *commoners* are natural humans with no Sevolite traits. The birth ranks in between, in descending order, are: *Royalblood, Highlord, Seniorlord, Midlord, Pettylord* and *Fractional*.

CHALLENGE CLASS:

Sevolite birth ranks are grouped into challenge classes bounded by ability. On the low end, *petty Sevolites* (Fractionals and Pettylords) are not much tougher than commoners. *Nobleborns* (Midlords and Seniorlords) can fly harder and live longer than ordinary humans but lack the regenerative capabilities and top-notch reality skimming prowess of *highborns* (Highlords, Royalbloods and Purebloods).

CHER, CHER'ST, CHER'STAN:

The *pol, rel* and plural forms of the Gelack naming word for lovers joined for all time through multiple reincarnations, by a soul bond. Considered rare but treated with reverence if a claim is believed.

DEMISH:

The racial line of Sevolites typified by blue eyes, blonde hair and a view of women as the gentle, or *pol*, sex, protected by men, who possess *rel* virtues. Demish look back with reverence to a legendary Golden Age when the Ava was a Pureblood from the Golden Demish homeworld called Demora.

GELION, GELACK:

People native to the planet Gelion, whether Sevolite or commoner, are called Gelacks. Those governed by the Gelack Empire may also be referred to collectively as Gelacks. The common language of the empire, spoken on Gelion, is Gelack.

GORARELPUL:

A well-educated commoner bound to his or her Sevolite master by a conscience bond. This invasive mental conditioning operates at a subconscious level and enforces loyalty on pain of death.

HAND OF ERRANTS:

A detachment of five house guardsmen, known as errants. Sevolites spontaneously organize themselves in 'hands' of four followers under a hand-leader after fleet usage.

KINF'STAN:

The collective body of highborn Nersallians entitled to challenge for the title of Liege Nersal. Due to House Nersal's simple, unfettered policies for determining entitlement, there are a lot of them. *Kinf'stan* have a fierce reputation not only as duelists but for prowess in space and uncompromising honor.

KLINOMAN, KLIN (slang):

A drug of Luverthanian manufacture that relieves the symptoms of exposure to reality skimming. House Monitum imports it and other drugs designed specifically for Sevolites.

LYKA, LYKA'ST, LYKA'STAN:

The *pol, rel* and plural forms of the Gelack naming word for participants in a sexual relationship between a Sevolite protector (*lyka'st*) and his or her commoner lover (*lyka*). Vrellish in origin, favoring status distinctions (*pol, rel*) over those based on gender.

LUVERTHAN, LOREL:

The almost extinct and notorious House of Lorel is said to have survived on the half-legendary world of Luverthan, which interacts with court only through the exchange of Sevolite-specific medical supplies mediated by House Monitum. Any Luverthanian material entering the empire by other means is contraband.

MEKAN, MEKAN'ST, MEKAN'STAN:

The *pol, rel* and plural forms of the Gelack naming word for participants in a long-term sexual relationship founded on mutual friendship. *Mekan'stan* are nearly always Vrellish and the relationship is not exclusive. In fact it is more common to have two or three *mekan'stan*.

MONITUM, MONATESE:

House Monitum is one of the eight great families of Fountain Court. Members of the family, and those ruled by them, are called Monatese. Monitum is also the name of the planet ruled from Green Hearth. The Monatese have a reputation for being scholarly and keep English alive as a private language spoken by their elite.

NERVECLOTH:

A quasi-organic information technology developed for use in *rel*-ships, and now used for a diverse range of computational purposes. Monitum has a monopoly on nervecloth programming and manufacture.

OKAL REL, OKAL'A'NI:

Okal Rel is the "way of moral conflict", which is tolerant of lethal force in conflicts so long as the carrying capacity of the environment is held sacred. The *okal'a'ni*—those who place themselves outside *Okal Rel*—forfeit the right to reincarnation.

POL:

The opposite of *rel*, most commonly equated with the inferior, weak, indecisive or passive. *Pol* case, in grammar, denotes the inferior Sevolite in a comparison.

POL-TO-REL ADDRESS:

Pol-to-*rel* address is used in Gelack when an inferior speaks to a superior. Status is a function of birth rank. The inflections are applied to pronouns.

REALITY SKIMMING:

The faster-than-light method of space travel, in which *rel*-ships flicker in and out of ordinary existence while maintaining a subjective acceleration proportional to their net displacement. Reality skimming is both physiologically and psychologically harmful, but requires the guidance of a self-aware and willful pilot to work. Sevolites, by their very natures, are good pilots.

REL:

The opposite of *pol*, most commonly equated with being superior or assertive in pursuit of one's desires. Being *rel*, in Gelack terms, is usually good. "Possessing the traits of a good pilot" was the earliest definition.

REL-FIGHTER:

A personal, spherical reality skimming ship made of hullsteel and lined in nervecloth, which is specialized for small-scale warfare in space at reality skimming displacements against other *rel*-fighters. The pilot operates the fighter from a gyroscopic cage at its center.

REL-SHIP:

Any reality skimming vessel smaller than a battlewheel or space station.

REL-TO-POL ADDRESS:

Rel-to-*pol* address is used in Gelack when a superior speaks to an inferior. Status is a function of birth rank. The inflections are applied to pronouns.

RIRE, REETIONS:

Rire refers collectively to the six planets governed by the Reetion arbiter administration, and individually to its central and most influential member, the planet Rire. Citizens of either are known as Reetions.

SEVOLITE:

An individual who is, in varying degrees, tolerant of reality skimming, long-lived, physically regenerative, and possessed of an exceptional memory (Demish) or exceptional spatial sense (Vrellish). Sevolites have varying explanations for their origins, ranging from the mythic to the scientific, while Reetions suspect Sevolites of being bioengineered for piloting. There are three founding Sevolite lines, with distinct characteristics: the Vrellish, Demish, and Lorel.

SHIMMER, SHIMMER DAMAGE:

An aspect of reality skimming. Shimmer damage causes cumulative wear and tear on non-regenerative physiologies. Highborn Sevolites, and nervecloth, are designed to be self-repairing within limits.

SKIM'FAC, SKIM FACTOR:

A measure of net displacement while reality skimming. How high a skim'fac a pilot can sustain, and for how long, depends on how Sevolite the pilot is.

SLA:

Gelack adjective suggesting something perverted or disgusting, and certainly dishonorable, but not necessarily a sin against *Okal Rel.*

SLAKA, SLAKA'ST, SLAKA'STAN:

The *pol, rel* and plural forms of the Gelack naming word for participants in a deviant relationship. *Slaka* is the *pol* (inferior) form, designating the victim. *Slaka'st* is the *rel* (superior) form, designating the abuser.

SLOW REBIRTH:

Less-worthy souls must compete more fiercely for access to suitable infants in the struggle for rebirth, than must those who impress the Watching Dead with their honor and excellence.

SWEARING:

A ceremony held at variable intervals, at which the leiges of Fountain Court formally offer their oaths of loyalty to the Pureblood candidates for Ava, thereby selecting or reconfirming their choice for Ava and Avim.

VISITOR PROBE:

A Reetion technology developed for retrieving pilots over-exposed to reality skimming from gap-induced coma.

VRELLISH:

The racial line of Sevolites typified by gray eyes, black hair, hot tempers and a unisex attitude to everything except one's choice of sex partner. Red Vrel is the most purely Vrellish house of Fountain Court, but hybrid lines such as Monitum and Nersal also consider themselves Vrellish.

Printed in Canada